THE INTERTWINED SOULS SERIES

MARY D. BROOKS

AWAKENINGS

INTERTWINED SOULS SERIES, BOOK 4

Nuance

Bedazzled Ink Publishing Company • Fairfield, California

978-1-939562-48-7 paperback
978-1-939562-49-4 ebook

Cover Art
by
Lucia Nobrega

Cover Design
by
Jasmina Trafikowska

Nuance Books
a division of
Bedazzled Ink Publishing Company
Fairfield, California
http://www.bedazzledink.com

To my dear friend Rosa Alonso
Every writer needs a Rosa in their corner

ACKNOWLEDGEMENTS

Awakenings has taken a great deal of time to see the light of day and there have been a few people who have made it possible.

My dear friend Rosa Alonso. Any writer who has you in their corner is one of the most fortunate of souls. I love you even though you have Tim Tam addiction. Maybe we should acknowledge Arnotts for their Tim Tams in powering you through this novel. Awakenings has been a real pleasure to write with your collaboration. Couldn't have done it without you.

Lucia Nobrega. Thank you my dear friend for your time and huge talent in creating the Eva and Zoe art for the book. Your artwork is inspiring!

Jasmina Trafikowska. Thank you Jazzy for the incredible book cover. Your talent is just extraordinary as is your friendship..

Manfred Reichardt you were an invaluable help! Your memories and knowledge of the Berlin borough of Zehlendorf, Berlin during the war and beyond was incredible. Researching this novel was made so much easier with your help.

Ms Leila Brum for her help and support; always a pleasure Leila!

Bedazzled Ink. Thanks for the extra polish!

GROWTH
by Unknown Author

For every hill I've had to climb,
For every stone that bruised my feet,
For all the blood and sweat and grime,
For blinding storms and burning heat,
My heart sings but a grateful song—
These were the things that made me strong!
For all the heartaches and the tears,
For all the anguish and the pain,
For gloomy days and fruitless years,
And for the hopes that lived in vain,
I do give thanks, for now I know
These were the things that helped me grow!
Tis not the softer things of life
Which stimulate man's will to strive,
But bleak adversity and strife
Do most to keep man's will alive.
O'er rose-strewn paths the weaklings creep,
But brave hearts dare to climb the steep.

PROLOGUE

QUESTIONS. QUESTIONS AND more questions circulated like an out of control carousel in Eva Haralambos' mind. She blinked in the semi-darkness of the bedroom. She was trying to get to sleep, but the turmoil in her mind prevented her from attaining that elusive goal.

Her back. The pain from her back intensified the longer she stayed in bed. No matter which position she tried, she was unable to achieve any respite. The legacy of her father's brutal beating and mistreatment was a constant reminder of what she had been through. The nightmares had increased, and her dislike for painkillers or drugs of any kind only made the situation worse. There was no relief.

Eva turned to glance at Zoe, sleeping beside her. Eva had met Zoe Lambros in 1942 in Larissa, Greece, and Zoe had saved her life two years later. Zoe, the redheaded whirlwind, whose childhood had been ripped away from her when the Germans invaded her sleepy town, was the love of her life. Zoe had become a courageous member of the Resistance and together they worked against the Germans to aid the Jews. That was the start of their story, a story that had taken them to Australia to build a new life for themselves.

They were back where it all began for her and Zoe, back in the village that she despised, and back in the place that almost killed her.

Larissa had changed Eva's life in 1944, and now, six years later, once again revealed one unexpected piece of a puzzle that she was not even aware was missing.

Theresa Rosa. Her aunt Tessa. The woman that her family thought had perished in a fire before Eva was born, was alive. This revelation led to more astonishing news. Her aunt was gifted in a way Eva would never have anticipated or thought possible if she hadn't seen the evidence. Tessa's gifts were a blessing or a curse depending on how one interpreted them. Being able to see into the future with such clarity was disturbing and frightening.

How did Tessa cope with knowing the pain and anguish of what was to come for someone who wasn't even born?

Was God playing some sort of bitter and twisted game?

Was Eva cursed as well with these gifts?

Eva's life had been one of privilege until the Night of Broken Glass, and then fate threw her into a world where revulsion and torture became her reality. To her horror, she ended up in war-torn little Greek village that became her hell on earth—she was despised by her step-father and villagers alike.

Eva sighed.

With a grunt, she threw the blanket off her legs and quietly got out of bed. The bed squeaked but the noise didn't wake Zoe. She put on her robe and stood at the foot of the bed, watching Zoe sleep for a moment before she turned and slipped out of the room.

Fate was laughing at her again and she was powerless to stop whatever was heading her way.

If only she knew what the fates had in store for her.

CHAPTER 1

STELLA WAS TIRED, but she couldn't sleep. It had been a very emotional day, meeting up with Zoe Lambros, her niece, and her new adopted niece, Eva Haralambos. She glanced at Tessa, her partner, who was lying on her back, sound asleep, oblivious to the rattling windows and the storm brewing outside. A gentle thump in the hallway made Stella look at the closed bedroom door. Then she heard another quieter thump.

Stella pulled back the covers and got out of bed. She found her robe and put on her slippers. Just as quietly, she opened the door and slipped outside.

Further down the corridor was an unmistakable tall figure, although at the moment she appeared to be just a little bit shorter. Eva was leaning against the wall with her knees slightly bent. Stella knew that stance intimately, since Tessa often sat like that to ease the pain in her back.

Stella padded quietly to Eva's side.

"You know, I think this part of the building won't fall down," Stella whispered, earning her a brief smile. "How much pain are you in? Ten being the world is coming to an end and one being you're just too relaxed."

"Nine." Eva's voice sounded as pained as her back looked.

"I've been studying a new technique—"

"No."

"You haven't heard it yet."

"I don't like doctors. Is it the Salvatore Technique?"

"The Salvatore Technique . . . I've never heard of that." Stella mimicked Eva's stance on the wall.

Eva glared at Stella. "Are you making fun of me?"

"Of course I'm not. I'm not just a doctor. I'm your aunt. I know you haven't had an aunt before, but now you have two. I'm just keeping you company, since Tessa is asleep and I'm guessing Zoe is as well."

Eva glanced at Stella before she looked away.

For a few minutes Stella kept silent but she wasn't very good at staying that way. "Do you want some painkillers?"

"No. I don't like taking any drugs."

"Hmm," Stella mused. "You are just being asinine."

Outraged blue eyes glared back at her.

"Not taking medication when you need it is foolish."

"I don't take drugs."

"So you keep saying. I know you don't like doctors, but did you at least speak to one about pain relief?"

Eva sighed. "I saw one during my physical examination for our visa for Australia. Told me I won't ever be free of pain and it would get worse. Gave me painkillers. Didn't take them." She stuck her hand inside her robe pocket and took out her cigarette case and a box of matches. She rolled a cigarette between her fingers as she thought.

Eva intrigued Stella. *Goddess, Zoe must be extremely patient with this one.* Eva lit the cigarette and took a drag.

"You don't make it easy for people to get to know you. Actually, you make it very difficult." Stella didn't miss the half smile that creased Eva's face. "I'd say you rather enjoy people not knowing you."

"I don't know you at all."

Stella smiled. "I like you. You are trying to make me walk away from you. You want me to think you are too much hard work and that I should leave you alone."

Eva brought the cigarette to her mouth and took another drag.

"It's not going to work. Tessa did the same thing when we first met. I know all about the Mitsos technique. I'm not sure if it's the same as the Salvatore Technique, but I can tell you that it didn't work for Tessa and it certainly won't work for you."

"Why are you interested in me?"

"You are married to my niece and I'm married to your aunt. That makes us family."

Eva glanced at Stella. "You are very direct."

"Yes, I am. So tell me something about yourself that I don't know."

"How do I know you don't know it?"

Stella smiled. *Progress, slow, slow progress.*

"Have you heard of AEMullerStahl?" Eva asked.

"Yes, very large German steel manufacturers."

"That's an odd thing to know."

"Is it? I tend to remember things I read. It's called a photo—"

"Photographic memory. Zoe has one."

"Yes. Her father also had that ability."

Eva watched the smoke rise from her cigarette. "AEMullerStahl was run by my grandfather. When he passed away, my grandmother, Beatriz Muller, ran the company with the help of her sons Wilbur, Hans, and Dieter. My stepfather, Hans, was an officer in the army and my uncle Dieter ran a clinic-spa in Aiden."

Wow, Stella thought as she watched Eva find a position against the wall that she liked. She had not anticipated that revelation so soon. "You are one of those Mullers."

Eva smiled. "Yes, one of those Mullers, but you already knew that."

"Did you say your uncle ran a clinic? In Aiden?"

"A hospital, clinic, and spa. I was taken there not to embarrass the family name. We wouldn't want the Muller name scandalized," Eva bitterly replied. "I spent a few weeks there recovering from the beating my stepfather gave me. I was then moved to another part of the hospital where I was . . ." She took a deep breath and released it. "You saw what happened."

"Without a proper examination I can only guess here, but I would say the attack damaged your spine, and the after-effects of the shocks caused convulsions which fractured the already injured areas."

"They broke my back?"

"Yes, you can say that. Repeated treatments would have caused more damage. That's what the aim of the shocks was—they cause the brain to spasm and produce convulsions. These are very severe, and your spine bore the brunt. What is astonishing to me is that they would do this while knowing how damaged your back was already."

"I don't know." Eva took a drag of her cigarette. "In 1941 I went with my stepfather to Paris. He wanted me to be with him so he could keep an eye on me. I got caught up in a bomb explosion."

"The Resistance bombed the house where you were staying?"

"Hmm. The ceiling fell on top of me, and my back was injured. I wasn't able to walk for a long time and by the time we went to Larissa, I was just barely back on my feet."

"In addition to your damaged spine, you also sustained damage during the bombing. That is quite an ordeal."

"Yes. I was an emotional and physical cripple in the middle of a war-zone."

"You have been through a lot. For now, I can show you and Zoe how to temporarily relieve the pain. It won't make it go away but it can help."

Eva closed her eyes and nodded. "Zoe has wanted to take me to chiropractors, but most of them just haven't got any idea. She was shown a technique on the ship by a Dr. Salvatore. I think he took a liking to her and he gave her lessons."

"Chiropractors don't know how to treat someone like you. The other thing you can do is to strengthen your back, legs, and stomach muscles. Do you do any exercise?"

Eva's head dropped. "No."

"In the morning I'm going to go through the exercises you need to do. As your doctor—"

"Who said you're my doctor?" Eva asked.

"I just appointed myself," Stella replied. "Bend your knees more, like you are sitting on a chair."

Eva hesitated for a moment before she lowered herself down.

Stella nodded. "This will strengthen your back, your bottom, thighs, and your stomach muscles." She lightly patted Eva's middle. "You need to build strength so your spine will be supported more easily."

"No one told me that before."

"Stand," Stella instructed. "Now wait a moment before doing that again. No one told you about that because they don't think. In addition to this exercise I will show you some more tomorrow. Alright?"

Eva nodded and stood up to her full height again.

"Come with me." Stella took Eva's hand and waited till she pushed herself from the wall. She led her to an empty bedroom.

"Can you take off your robe, please, while I go and get some oil?"

Eva blinked in the lamplight and hesitated before Stella turned her back and left.

Stella entered her bedroom and very quietly went to her dressing table and opened the drawer.

"Angel, you are making a racket," Tessa mumbled.

"Did I wake you, my love?" Stella sat on the bed.

"No." Tessa turned to her side to face Stella. "I woke up after hearing voices. It's three in the morning."

"Did you think you were having a vision?"

Tessa smiled. "Your voice, angel. You were trying to whisper but I could hear you, and that robe . . . I need sunglasses this early in the morning."

"Ha Ha. At least you won't ever lose me in the dark."

"Heavens, we wouldn't want that." Tessa chuckled.

"I think I made some progress, but baby steps. I finally got her talking about Beatriz and Aiden."

Tessa yawned. "Beatriz Muller, one of the most powerful women in Europe. Well, she used to be before the war. Did she ask you how you knew about shock therapy?"

"Not yet."

"She will. What are you doing now?"

"Giving her a massage."

Tessa grinned. "Oh, I like those."

"Not that kind of massage, my love." Stella chuckled and tenderly kissed Tessa on the lips. "Go back to sleep."

Stella retrieved the oil and stopped in the doorway of the spare bedroom.

Eva was facing the door and Zoe was resting on her haunches. Zoe tweaked Eva's chin and Eva smiled.

Stella cleared her throat and walked into the room. "It seems we woke up our girls."

"Is Tessa awake?" Zoe asked as she turned and gracefully sat down on the floor with her back against the base of the bed.

Eva rested her hand on Zoe's shoulder.

Stella smiled at Eva's action. "She was, but I told her to go back to sleep. You should do the same."

"I sleep better with Eva beside me," Zoe said. "She has been telling me about the exercises."

"Yes, later in the morning I'm going to show her how to strengthen her back."

"How do you know so much about what those shocks do to the spine?" Eva asked as she rested her head on her arms.

And there it is, Stella thought as she poured a little of the oil in her hands to warm it up.

She very gently massaged Eva's shoulders. "Before I met Tessa I was a young intern in Athens. I was assigned to a Dr. Kannadas—a horrible man at the hospital who thought women should be at home. He always called me Miss Andronikakis, never Doctor Andronikakis. I was married then to my Timothy. He disliked me so much that I was given the jobs no one wanted to do."

"Charming man," Eva mumbled.

"Yes. In the spring of 1916, Saint Gregori Lunatic Asylum was short of doctors for some reason I can't remember now. Dr. Kannadas thought I would be perfect for the job, so he sent me there to help and to learn."

"You had no training in that area?"

"No, I hadn't done my internship in psychiatry yet. I mentioned this to him but that fell on his two very large deaf ears. Dr. Frankoulis ran the asylum and was a gentle man. He truly cared for his patients." Stella continued to lightly massage Eva's back.

Eva groaned a little as Stella probed the unscarred areas.

"It was a small asylum with fifteen residents."

"Prisoners," Eva said, and caught her breath as Stella pressed down on the scarred flesh.

"No, they were not prisoners, Eva. They were there because their families wanted them to get better," Stella gently corrected. "The doctors thought they were doing good by trying to cure them of their illness."

"What did you do there?"

"At first pretty much nothing, but I observed and wrote notes on the various illnesses," Stella said as she felt an adhesion under her fingertips on Eva's lower back and applied pressure.

Eva groaned and exhaled.

"It's going to hurt a bit here because you have a band of rigid tissue."

"Uh huh." Eva's voice was strained.

Zoe took her hand. "Why is that hurting so much?"

"Adhesions can block circulation and cause pain. Eva's back is very tight." Stella concentrated on the rigid tissue under her fingers. "Where was I? Oh yes, I was sent to Saint Gregori and out of Dr. Kannadas' hair, the little that he had. That's where I learnt about electroshock therapy and the use of drugs to treat mental illnesses."

"It sounds like torture," Zoe said as she glanced at Eva, who had her eyes closed.

"Well, sometimes the medicine appears to be harsh, but it does work." Stella finished the massage and stepped away from Eva. "It's a long story and I want the two of you to go to sleep."

Eva responded with a relieved grunt, which earned her a kiss from Zoe.

"Are we going back to our room?" Zoe asked.

Eva shook her head. "I don't want to move."

"We are sleeping here." Zoe chuckled. She got up from the floor and gave Stella a kiss goodnight before closing the door.

Stella stood in the hallway for a moment. *Goddess, we have a lot of work to do with this child.*

She entered her bedroom to find Tessa sitting on the edge of the bed.

"Angel, we need to get the girls to come here," Tessa said.

"Where?"

"Here, the farm, until they leave for Germany."

"Why?" Stella sat on the bed and blinked at Tessa and tried to focus. She looked into her eyes and knew instantly what Tessa was saying.

"They need to move."

"I know, but can it wait till the morning?"

"No, we need to go to the cabin, collect their belongings, and bring them here."

"Zoe and I will go. Eva's in no condition at the moment to go anywhere, and we won't talk about your knee."

"Angel, make it quick." The urgency in Tessa's voice made Stella dress quickly and leave the room.

ZOE HEARD A knock on the door and looked up. The opened and Stella stepped in.

"What's wrong?" Zoe whispered.

Stella approached the bed and sat at the end of it. "You and I need to go up to the cabin and pick up your belongings."

"Why?"

"Tessa's had a vision. She said we need to get your belongings and for you to stay at the farm until you leave."

"Oh." Zoe looked down at Eva.

"Leave her here . . ."

"I'm not staying," Eva mumbled. She opened her eyes and looked at Stella. "Wherever Zoe goes, I'm going."

"What did you hear?" Zoe asked. "Because I know you were asleep."

"Um . . . leave her here." Eva yawned.

"Thought as much. Aunty Stella says that Tessa had a vision. We need to go to the cabin and get our belongings."

"Alright." Eva threw back the covers.

Stella threw them right back. "Where do you think you are going?"

"I'm going with you and Zoe."

"No. I just gave you a massage and you had a level nine backache. Do I need to remind you of that?"

"Level nine?" Zoe asked. She looked at Eva, who was being unusually passive.

"I asked my patient what level her back pain was and she told me it was a level nine," Stella said.

"Are you her doctor now?"

"Yes."

"Did a miracle occur while I was asleep?" Zoe gently teased. Eva gave her a wry smile.

"Now, getting back to why I'm here. Zoe, get dressed. We are going to the cabin. I'll get Hercules hitched up to the cart—"

"Hercules?" Eva asked.

"My horse."

"Of course." Eva chuckled. "You're a Lambros, so you name everything."

"You, smarty pants, are going to stay here with Tessa. I don't want her outside."

"Does something happen to her with the visions and she can't go outside?" Zoe asked.

Stella shook her head. "No, the silly woman didn't listen to her doctor when I told her to rest. Selective deafness must run in the Mitsos family." She gave Eva a mock glare and left the room.

Eva watched as Zoe got up. "Bossy women run in the Lambros family," she said in a raised voice.

"I heard that," Stella shouted from somewhere.

"I sure hope so," Eva mumbled. She pulled the covers over her.

Zoe chuckled. "I'll be back soon." She bent down to kiss Eva lightly on the lips. "Was your back a nine?"

"No." Eva shook her head. "Ten. I think I did something to it when I helped Mr. Kostas with his car."

"Hmm. I knew something was wrong." Zoe shook her head. "Stay here."

"Yes, mutti." Eva grinned as Zoe left the room.

CHAPTER 2

EVA GOT UP. She was wide-awake and staring into space. She was
worried about this vision, worried about what it meant to them, and
worried about Zoe going into windy weather without her. She walked into
the kitchen and filled a glass with water. She took a sip while standing in
front of the kitchen window. A lit cigarette was in the ashtray on the kitchen
counter. Outside the howling wind caused the trees to viciously twist.

"Here." Tessa came up behind Eva and placed a small plate with two
tablets in front of her. "Please, take these."

Eva turned and looked into Tessa's eyes and the protest died on her
lips. One eye was dark blue and the other a lighter shade of blue. Whilst
she stared transfixed, the dark blue eye changed to match the lighter blue
shade.

"Your eyes."

"Hmm, yes. I'll talk about my eyes as soon as you take those
painkillers."

Eva looked down at the pills and back to her aunt. She took a sip of
the water and swallowed the pills. Then she took the cigarette from the
ashtray, tapped the ash, and brought it to her lips.

Tessa eased herself onto the bench and faced Eva. Her cane was hooked
onto the chair nearby. "Now, that wasn't so hard, was it?"

"I don't like taking any drugs." Eva took a drag of the cigarette.

"What do you do when the pain becomes unbearable?"

"I'm not completely silly," Eva said a little defensively.

"No one said you were, sweetheart." Tessa took Eva's hand and held it
tenderly. "What do you use?"

"Devil's Claw," Eva responded. "We get it in a powder and then mix it
with water. We found out about it after Zoe read a book on herbs and how
to use them for medicinal purposes."

Tessa smiled. "She's quite resourceful, that young woman."

"I think if they came to Zoe to solve the world's problems, she would find
a way or start banging heads together when she lost patience." Eva lightly
laughed. She stared at Tessa in amazement. "Your eyes are getting lighter."

"Yes. The color changes when I have a vision. They go black, then
blue, then a lighter shade of blue and then gray."

"Wow," Eva exclaimed as she gazed into Tessa's eyes.

"Stella has a fondness for the gray." Tessa smiled.

"Zoe keeps saying she loves my blue eyes. Must be a Lambros trait."

"They do seem to share some idiosyncratic traits."

"If your eyes change color when you have a vision, how did you convince them that you were cured?"

"I didn't. I couldn't. My eyes would betray me."

"Wow. When did all of this start for you?"

"I first noticed the change when I was eight years old. I had my first vision and I thought I was dreaming, but it happened in the middle of the day." Tessa slightly twisted and took a piece of bread and some olive oil from the table. She dribbled the oil on the bread and spread it. She offered some to Eva, who shook her head. "I looked in the mirror and my gray eyes were dark brown." She took a bite of the bread.

"Not black?"

"No, dark chocolate brown. The older I got the darker they became. Now when they change, they're the same color as Stella's."

"Did it scare you?"

"It terrified me. I kept it a secret from my parents for a few months, thinking it might be like a cold and it would go away. I didn't know that a cold doesn't change the color of your eyes. I reasoned it away. Not a good way to deal with problems."

"How often did it happen?"

"At first once every two to three months. I could get away with it because it would happen at night, and by the time I got up, my eyes would be fine. I convinced myself that I was dreaming."

"What is it like? Is it really like a dream?"

"No, it's not like a dream. I feel like I'm there, wherever it is, interacting with whatever is going on but not being able to influence events. Very scary."

"How did you convince yourself you were dreaming and stopped worrying about the eyes?"

Tessa smiled. "Our minds are very powerful, Eva. You can fool yourself very easily and believe very easily what you are telling yourself."

"To the point that you forget your eyes are changing color?"

"Yes."

"Until?"

"Until it happened during class." Tessa took a bite of her bread and chewed. "My teacher was talking about the Ancient Greeks one minute and the next I was watching a car plough into a tree. When the daydream stopped and I returned to my class, my teacher came to scold me and then she saw my eyes."

"What happened after that?"

Tessa smiled. "Why don't we wait for Zoe to return and I'll tell you both? She won't forgive me if I don't include her. I've known her for a little while through my visions, but after meeting her, I do not want to upset her." She chuckled.

"You've seen her in your visions?"

"Yes." Tessa nodded. "I don't want to talk about Zoe now, I want to talk about you." She kept her voice light. "You might want to grab one of those cushions Stella has in abundance. They seem to multiply at a fast rate."

Eva went into the living room and picked up a bright orange cushion. She looked at it and smiled. "She does like bright colors," she said as she came back into the kitchen.

"The brighter the better is her motto."

Eva placed the cushion on the chair to brace her back and sat down.

Tessa put the bread down and eased herself off the counter. She pulled up a chair, sat down in front of Eva, and took her hands. "I'm so very proud of you."

"I haven't done anything."

"That's where you are wrong. You listened when I told you to make them believe, you listened when Sister Irene came to visit."

"Irene." Eva's mouth dropped at the name she hadn't thought about since 1939. "She was real?"

Tessa smiled. "She was real."

Eva closed her eyes and rested her head on the chair's back. *Sister Irene. My god. The pain was never ending and she felt she couldn't take anymore. There had to be an end, even if she had to make that happen herself.*

"I wanted it to all end," Eva said so softly. "I thought Sister Irene was just someone I made up. Her voice was so soothing."

"She told you not to give up, right?"

"How did you know?"

"I will tell you that soon. You believed Sister Irene and you didn't give up."

"She wasn't real. She was a dream, but she had such a soothing way about her that it eased my mind."

"Irene is very much alive and she is close to you. She is family, Eva. She's your great aunt. I don't have enough power to do what she does so I asked her to do this for me. Irene's gift is stronger than mine."

"She's a real human being?"

"Yes, darling, she's real. She lives in Germany and she's expecting you and Zoe."

"She's real?" Eva repeated, not quite fully grasping the implication of this news. "I can meet her?"

"Yes."

"You were in Germany?" Eva felt like a child asking questions. She couldn't focus and her mind was swirling into a thousand fragments.

"No, there are devices called telephones. They were invented by a fellow named Alexander Graham Bell. Very useful. Even people with special gifts use them."

Eva smiled. "Yes, I would like to meet her."

"Good. You were never far from my thoughts from the moment you were born. My sister, your mother, loved you so much, and she loved me too. Giving you my name as your second name . . . That just made me cry."

"Where were you?"

"I lived in Thessaloniki with Stella."

"Oh."

"I think that story needs to be told with Stella and Zoe in the room."

Eva looked at the rain now lashing the window and hitting the glass sideways. "Zoe and Stella are out there."

"They will be fine, but poor Hercules may hate them after this is over."

"I listened to you and to Irene. I made them believe," Eva said in a childlike voice. "I didn't know how."

"But you did. You found a way."

Eva wiped her eyes with the back of her hand. "I overhead some nurses talking about a man who had an accident and he couldn't remember it."

"You know what I find amazing? Despite you being in such a weakened state, you still managed to use your brain."

"Even if it was being jolted," Eva said and realized it was the first time she had joked about her time in Aiden.

"Even with overcooked brains, you still found a way to convince them you couldn't remember your name."

"That was partly right. After each treatment I couldn't remember my name for a while, but after a few hours it all came back to me."

"Until you overheard the nurses."

"Yes."

"So you had to wait until your next treatment?"

"Yes. That was the last one, although Papa never believed me."

"I know." Tessa nodded. "How were you able to fall in love with Zoe without their conditioning making you physically ill?"

Eva looked down at the darkened floor and thought back to the first time she had kissed Zoe. The pain that shot through her body on touching her was so intense she had collapsed. "First time I kissed Zoe, my legs just couldn't hold me up and I collapsed in a heap."

"The aversion therapy works. It produces such a powerful reaction that you are not going to want to do the very thing you want to do."

"It worked. I was ill just thinking about kissing Zoe before I even kissed her."

Tessa placed a reassuring hand on Eva's knee. "No one can change who you are, Eva. No amount of aversion conditioning can change you."

"It does change you. It does. I didn't want to fall in love with a woman ever again and I married a man I didn't love to avoid that pain."

"Erik Hoffman." Tessa nodded. Eva was surprised her aunt knew about Erik. She had fooled the man into thinking she had loved him when she didn't.

"Is there anything you don't know about me?"

"Yes, quite a lot, but I know more about you than most people. This gift I have is a curse and a blessing."

"Sounds like a curse to me."

"Well," Tessa said and patted Eva's knee. "That's a talk for another day. How did you manage to break those mental bonds?"

"I had help. I couldn't do it on my own no matter how hard I tried."

"Zoe?"

"No. When we were in Egypt waiting for our turn to be assigned a ship to Australia, Zoe overheard some refugees talking about a psychiatrist who was helping them," Eva explained. "I couldn't hold Zoe or do anything at that stage. It was too much. Zoe was patient with the emotional cripple."

"Eva!"

"That's what I was. Zoe was patient with me and when you get to know Zoe, you'll see that patience is not one of her virtues."

Tessa smiled. "I'm sure she isn't, but when it came to you, she found patience."

"She did. She found this doctor and she talked to her and then convinced me to get help."

"What was the doctor's name?"

Eva gave Tessa a quizzical look. "Doctor—"

"Dr. Hannah Koch." Tessa smiled at Eva's shocked expression.

"You were never alone, Evy. Dr. Hannah was sent to help you. There is always someone looking out for you, even if you are not aware of them."

"Did you maneuver Zoe into my life?"

Tessa shook her head. "No, I had nothing to do with that. God is to blame for that." Tessa smiled at Eva's exaggerated eye roll. "Everything that you have done since Aiden, you did on your own. You chose to fight, you chose to fall in love with Zoe, and you chose to beat their conditioning. You had help to achieve all of it but without you wanting to do it, no amount of help would have achieved what you have done."

Eva took a deep breath and released it slowly. "I don't know what to say."

"Now comes the next step."

"What next step?" Eva stood and stubbed out her cigarette in the ashtray. She gazed outside at the rain.

Tessa wrapped her arms around Eva waist. "Time to leave Aiden," she whispered in her ear. "Time to walk out."

"I have walked out."

"No, you are still there, up here." Tessa gently tapped Eva's temple. Eva turned around and gazed into Tessa's gray eyes. "In your mind and in your heart, you are still there."

"I don't know how."

"Forgive yourself, darling. It wasn't your fault your mother died. It wasn't your fault about your stepfather."

"If I had been there with mutti . . ."

"What do you think would have happened? You would have been killed."

"You don't know that."

"They killed her. Do you think they wouldn't have killed you? They were animals on a rampage."

"If I had listened."

"You would be dead," Tessa reasoned. "What do you think a seventeen-year-old child can do?"

"Nothing, but if I hadn't gone with Greta . . ."

Tessa made a growling noise which surprised Eva. "Greta."

"You know about Greta?"

"I know about this woman, yes. I know you loved her, but she wasn't worth it, Eva."

"I know."

"You don't forget your first love." Tessa tenderly cupped Eva's cheek. "I understand that, but Greta was the offspring of vipers and she was disloyal."

"How so?"

Tessa took Eva's hand and led her to the living room, where they sat down. "Greta was the one that told your father you were a lesbian."

Eva blinked. Her hand flew to her mouth. "She couldn't have. She was with the rest of our friends. Are you sure?"

"Yes, I'm sure. How much did she love you?"

"She said she did and we were going to run off together. That sounds so stupid now, but I believed her."

"The heart wants what the heart wants."

"What does that mean?"

"The heart will believe even though the mind may disagree. She was not the woman for you, she was everything Zoe isn't."

"Oh, I know that. Greta is nothing compared to Zoe."

"Zoe isn't interested in money or property either."

"No, but what does that have to do with it?" Tessa rose and stood beside the fireplace. "Are you having a vision?"

"No. I'm trying to think of a way to tell you without hurting you."

Eva sighed and let her head fall back against the headrest. "Wasn't the news that she betrayed me to my stepfather enough?"

"The betrayal goes deeper. Much deeper. Your grandmother paid her to stop seeing you."

Eva raised her head and stared at Tessa. "My grandmother paid her? This all sounds like a bad serial drama."

Tessa held up her hand and left the room. She came back a few minutes later with her drawings.

"Oh god, not those things again," Eva exclaimed and turned her back to Tessa.

"My art is pretty good, thank you, missy." Tessa sat down next to Eva and put her arm around her shoulders. She flipped through some innocuous-looking drawings, and then picked one and handed it to Eva. "The one is not about you. It's alright to look."

Eva reluctantly took the drawing. It depicted her grandmother and Greta sitting opposite each other in her grandmother's library. "I don't understand."

"Your grandmother offered Greta money, or in this case property in Bonn."

Eva stared at the drawing and then looked up at Tessa in shock. "I . . . I don't know what to say."

"There isn't much you can say."

"My grandmother knew?"

"Knew what? That you were a lesbian?"

"Yes."

"Yes, she knew."

"Did my mother?" Eva asked, her voice breaking. "Did she know?"

"Yes. What mother doesn't know her child? Yes, she would have known."

"Oh. Do you think she would have hated me?"

"Heavens, no. Your mother could never hate you. She doesn't hate you. Banish that from your mind. Your mother loved you so very much. Goodness, she accepted me when she thought I was possessed and insane."

"That's why she gave me your name."

"That's right. If she had hated me for who she thought I was, she wouldn't have given you my name. You're lucky, you know."

"How so?"

"You could have been called Kaliope instead—that was one of the aunts and they all had horrible names." Tessa smiled. "Darling, you need to forgive yourself. Only then will you be able to leave Aiden in your mind and in your heart."

"I will try."

"You have to. You have to because those babies of yours . . ." Tessa put her hand over her mouth. "Forget I said that last bit."

Eva grinned. "Babies? More than one baby? You said babies."

"I don't know what you are talking about." Tessa's face creased into a huge smile. "I know absolutely nothing."

"More than one baby." Eva giggled.

"They are going to need you whole, up here." Tessa touched the side of Eva's head. "And here." She touched Eva's heart. "You have walked through the valley of shadow of death and you have made it out. You must never fear what man could do. They have done it, but you are still here."

"I will."

"I have a feeling our girls are back." Tessa got up.

Eva carefully stood.

"How's your back?"

"Just a dull ache."

"Amazing what those drugs can do." Tessa chuckled as she threaded her arm into the crook of Eva's elbow. "Let's go see how cold those girls are."

CHAPTER 3

EVA LEANED AGAINST the doorjamb of the kitchen and gazed outside at the rain as Stella brought Hercules to a standstill. She was surprised to see Theo car's following the wagon. The wagon was covered to prevent the contents from getting wet. Sitting in the wagon was Zoe. She shook her head at Zoe who drenched from head to foot.

Zoe met her gaze and gave her a cheeky grin before she removed the covering. Theo stopped the car and quickly got out. He took the larger bag and one of the smaller bags. Zoe picked up another small bag and followed her brother inside.

"Theo! You were out in this weather?" Tessa asked.

"I was heading to the farm when I ran into Aunty Stella and Zoe. Good thing I did because the wagon got bogged down."

"Good thing you were there," Tessa replied and followed a very wet Stella inside the kitchen.

"You're so wet," Eva said to Zoe as she came inside.

"Yes." Zoe giggled. "I love a good summer shower but this one had a light show."

"You won't love it so much if you catch pneumonia." Eva took the towel that Tessa had given her and tried to dry Zoe's hair. "We have got to get you out of these clothes."

Eva ushered Zoe into their bedroom and placed her on the bed as if she were a child. She removed Zoe's socks and tossed them aside. "That's some drenching, Zoe. I hope you don't catch a cold." She unbuttoned Zoe's skirt and it fell around her bare feet. "I don't want you getting sick."

Zoe tried to unbutton her blouse, but Eva pushed her hand away. "We can't have you catching a cold after . . ." She looked up. Zoe grinned at her like a maniac. "Uh, what?" She stepped to the side and retrieved a blanket.

"Does this remind you of anything?" Zoe laughed. She tossed her blouse to the floor, followed by her very wet brassiere and panties.

Eva was a little confused and then she realized what Zoe was talking about. They had uttered those same words five years before, the night they had stopped lying to themselves about their feelings for each other. She looked around the room, at the very wet clothes and at Zoe's wet limp hair, and laughed. She laughed so much her head ached and she fell backwards onto the bed.

"You're not a boy," Zoe quipped before joining her on the bed. She rested her weight on her elbow and grinned at Eva. "You are definitely not a boy."

"I can't say that I am." Eva repeated the words she had uttered five years previously in a room similar to the one they were in and on an equally stormy day.

"That's good because," Zoe gazed into Eva's eyes, "I don't like boys."

"Come here." Eva cupped Zoe's face in her hands and pressed her lips to hers. The kiss deepened until she felt the excited response from Zoe and sought to quench her desire.

"Oh, boy!" Zoe whispered as they parted.

"Good or bad?" Eva grinned at the look on Zoe's face.

"Oh, good. Better than good," Zoe exclaimed.

They shared another kiss and dissolved into giggles on the bed.

"Michael and his three stages of love: Like, Heavy Like and Deep Love?" Zoe teased. "What stage are you in?"

"I'm in the deepest love of love you can imagine and then triple that. There is no cure, and I don't want to be cured."

"I don't think Michael had a triple deep love stage."

"Michael doesn't, but Eva does." Eva smiled and softly kissed Zoe again.

"Girls . . ." Stella came into the room, did an about face, and left the room.

Eva and Zoe laughed hysterically.

"Oh, my god." Zoe sat up and looked down at her naked self. "My aunty saw me like this."

Eva rolled onto her back and giggled. "Stella is a doctor, Zo. I think she's seen more than one naked woman."

"Eva!"

"Yes, love?" Eva lifted her head and lovingly gazed at Zoe, who was standing naked before her, her damp hair hanging limp, her green eyes directed at her.

Eva swallowed the lump in her throat. She felt tears in her eyes.

"My god, you are the most beautiful woman I have ever seen," she said in awe as she pushed herself into a sitting position and took Zoe into her arms. "We have been truly blessed. We are going to have the most beautiful babies."

"Jump off the cliff and enjoy the ride." Zoe's voice broke on the words she had told Eva so many years ago.

"Let's jump off another cliff together. I sure wish kissing would make you pregnant." Eva looked down at her own body. "Well, I'm not a boy but right now I wish I were."

"Maybe we can ask Aunty Stella how to do it."

Eva couldn't help but smirk. "Oh, I think Stella has a good idea that we know what we are doing."

Zoe shook her head. "Your jokes are getting worse than Earl's."

"No, mine are better."

"Do you think we can? She can tell us, can't she?" Zoe asked seriously. Eva nodded.

She smiled broadly, tilted her head a little, and regarded Eva. "Did something happen while I was gone? How's your back?"

"Tessa gave me some painkillers," Eva admitted, and smiled at the look of shock on Zoe's face.

"Real painkillers?"

"Devil's Claw is real, love. Yes, they were proper round white pills."

"Did they work?"

"Yes, they did." Eva hadn't felt this relaxed since they had started their journey. "Tessa also told me about some other things. We need to talk about it later."

EVA ARRANGED THEIR suitcases and took out a few clothes to put in the wardrobe while Zoe got dressed. When they were both presentable they left the room and went into the living room, where Stella was reading and Tessa was sitting near the open door, painting the storm.

"I'll iron those black pants for you for the wedding. You're coming with me to the wedding, right?" Zoe asked Eva.

"No."

Zoe leaned against Eva as she intertwined their fingers. "They did invite you."

"Because they had to, love."

"You are going." Tessa looked up from her painting.

"No, I'm not." Eva shook her head.

"Oh yes you are," Tessa replied in a singsong voice. "Everyone in the village is going to the wedding except me."

"Who said you won't be going?" Stella asked as she joined them at the door.

"Demon possessed, quite dead former lunatic. Remember?"

"It's been thirty years. No one remembers the lunatic. You're going." Stella patted Tessa on the backside, and Eva snickered.

"This is like listening to the comedy serial on the wireless." Zoe giggled.

"I'm not going," Eva persisted, and turned away from the door to be met by Stella, who was staring up at her, daring her to get past her. "Yes?"

"If Eva is not going, I'm not either," Tessa announced.

"It is important you both go."

"Why?" Eva and Tessa said in unison.

"You need to be there because you are a friend of the groom." Stella pointed to Eva. "You need to be there because . . ."

"Because?" Tessa grinned.

"Because you need to be there. It's the first time you've been back to Larissa, and I want them to see what a strong woman you are." Stella leaned against the table and smiled.

"If no one remembers the lunatic, what good would it do if I'm there?"

Eva thought that was a very clever response. She and Tessa grinned at each other.

"There are some that still remember the lunatic, and you are going."

"Hmm. Wow, she's got you there," Zoe said.

Tessa smiled. "I don't have anything to wear."

Stella smiled sweetly. "Yes, you do. I packed your blue suit."

Eva put her hand over her mouth and giggled. "Is she like this all the time?"

"Yes." Tessa took two steps towards Stella and put her arms around her. "Yes, she is like this all the time."

"The things I put up with." Stella laughed and patted Tessa's cheek. "Zoe, darling."

"Yes?"

"Did you find your missing clothes?" Stella asked as she went back to her book. Eva tried to suppress the snicker. She definitely liked Stella.

"Angel, leave Zoe alone. You know how hard it is to keep your clothes on when you're wet," Tessa said from the doorway and chuckled.

Eva suppressed the urge to tease Zoe, who was taking the ribbing in her stride. She walked to the window and watched the raging storm outside. Something was going to happen. She didn't know what, but she was getting an uneasy feeling.

CHAPTER 4

ZOE STIRRED AND opened her eyes to find Eva was not in bed. Eva had been tossing and turning for most of the night because of her back despite Stella's massage. Zoe was not surprised to find the bed empty. Eva had probably got up to make herself a cup of tea and left the door open.

Zoe threw back the blankets and sat on the edge of the bed, willing her body to move. She heard a yelp that was quickly followed by glass crashing to a stone floor. She bolted for the door just as she heard a thump.

Zoe ran down the corridor into the living room. Her heart was in her mouth when she saw Eva lying on the kitchen floor. A man's silhouette was in the semi darkness. She grabbed a vase from the living room and brought it up just as the man touched Eva's face.

Zoe swung the vase and smashed it against the man's shoulder, sending him sprawling on top of Eva. Water and flowers exploded all over the man, Eva, and the kitchen as the vase sent shards of ceramic everywhere.

"Theo!" Zoe screamed as she launched herself onto the man, who screamed and tried to fend himself against her.

Zoe heard Theo's footfalls and was grabbed by the waist and pulled off the man. Stella and Tessa rushed into the kitchen.

"Oh, dear Goddess," Stella muttered as she dropped to her knees beside Eva.

"Theo, let me go!" Zoe screamed as the man crawled away and collapsed onto the stone floor.

"Stop!" Theo yelled and held tight.

Zoe struggled to free herself from his powerful hold.

"Stop screaming, I know the idiot," Theo said.

Stella shook her head as she tended to Eva. She got a jug of water and damped a towel. Very tenderly, she wiped Eva's forehead, where bits of ceramic, water, and flower had settled.

"What happened?" Stella asked the young man, who had managed to crawl to the side of the kitchen and braced himself against the kitchen cupboard. Blood was dripping from a cut on his neck, and he was holding his shoulder.

"Crazy woman attacked me!"

"Eva is not crazy, you half crazed idiot!" Zoe screamed and kicked at him, while trying to break from Theo's grip.

"Not her, you," the young man yelled.

"Hush, the both of you." Stella turned on the lights and then knelt beside the young man. "What possessed you to creep on Eva like that, Thomas?"

"I wasn't creeping," Thomas whined as Tessa examined his neck.

"It's just a small cut. You'll live." Stella unbuttoned Thomas' shirt and looked at his shoulder. "I think you just bruised it. As soon as Ma is finished with Eva, you're next." She patted his cheek. "That's some entrance, Tommy."

"I was trying to surprise you."

Theo, still holding Zoe back, shook his head. "You are lucky my sister didn't have good aim or else your head would have exploded."

"I'm an idiot."

"Yes, you are," Theo agreed. "Zoe, will you stop trying to attack him? We know him."

"Who is he?" Zoe growled, her eyes fixed on Eva while Stella loosened Eva's nightshirt. "Aunty, is she okay?"

"She will be," Stella said. "Theo, let go of Zoe and come pick up Eva so we can take her to the bedroom."

"Zoe, don't attack him," Theo whispered and let go of her.

Zoe stood her ground, glaring at Thomas, who was still seated on the floor.

Theo knelt down, picked up Eva, and cradled her in his arms.

Zoe hovered nearby as they all went into the bedroom, where Theo laid Eva down.

Stella shooed Theo outside and closed the door. She returned to Eva, who was now stirring. Zoe scrambled to the other side of the bed and held her hand. Stella removed Eva's nightshirt to wash a small amount of blood. She wiped the blood with the damp cloth.

Zoe brought the blanket up with one hand.

Stella tucked the blanket around Eva, whose eyes fluttered open. "Shh. You had a fall."

"I . . . I . . ." Eva stammered and tried to get up and then moaned in pain.

"Please, stay still," Zoe whispered and kissed her forehead. "You're hurt."

"Tell me what hurts."

"My back," Eva replied through gritted teeth. "My head."

"You knocked it on the stone floor. It's bound to hurt," Stella said as she gently felt the back of Eva's head. "Stone floors would do that to you. You've got a nasty bump back there. Look at me."

Eva blinked and stared into Stella's eyes.

"What's your name?"

Eva winced. "Eva Haralambos."

"Where are you?"

"Larissa."

"How many fingers am I holding up?" Stella held up two digits.

"Two."

"Alright, so you don't have a concussion, but you do have an almighty bruise on the back of your head. Let's turn you over so I can see your back."

Stella very gently turned Eva on her stomach, causing her to moan. She felt along Eva's lower back. "Bad news is that you strained your back. There's some bruising here from when you fell. Zoe, go to the kitchen and tell Theo to break off some ice from the icebox. Have him crush it with the meat tenderizer and put it in a towel."

Zoe took a moment to kiss Eva on the cheek before she scrambled off the bed and went into the kitchen, where Theo was sitting at the table.

"Aunty Stella wants some ice. She said to smash it and to put it in a towel," Zoe said, and glared at Thomas."

"How is Eva?" Theo asked as he knelt beside the icebox and sheared a large part from the block of ice with a knife.

"She got a bruise on the back of her head when she landed on the floor, but Aunty Stella says she doesn't have a concussion. Her back is bruised."

"Oh, dear." Tessa gave Zoe a hug. "She's going to be alright."

"I know, I know, but seeing her like that over something so stupid is driving me crazy. You are so lucky that Eva isn't seriously injured or you would be dead," Zoe said to Thomas.

Theo gave her the towel with the ice. She threw another murderous glare at Thomas and left the kitchen.

Zoe entered the room and gave Stella the ice-filled towel. She went around the bed and lay down next to Eva. Eva turned her head and grimaced.

"This is going to be cold." Stella applied the ice onto Eva's lower back. "We will keep this on for twenty minutes and then I'll strap you in so you will be a bit more comfortable."

Eva drew in a breath and exhaled slowly. "Good thing it's summer," she said, her voice strained.

TWENTY MINUTES LATER Stella walked out of the bedroom with the wet towel and found the others in the living room. "Tessa, did we pack your back brace?"

"Yes," Tessa replied, and left the room.

"While I'm here, let me look at you." Stella went to Thomas.

He took off his shirt, and Stella felt along his shoulder, and asked him to raise and lower it.

"It's just bruised, Ma," Thomas said.

"You're lucky the vase didn't hit you on your head," Stella muttered as she gently tapped her son's head.

"You're lucky my sister didn't have a gun," Theo quipped, and got a wry smile from Thomas. "You are also lucky I'm a big, strong boy because she may be small, but she was really fighting me to get loose."

"I owe you my life, again," Thomas said quietly.

Tessa came back with the brace and handed it to Stella, who walked back to the bedroom.

TESSA STOOD WITH her arms akimbo. "Thomas, what are you doing here?"

"Surprise?" Thomas got off the sofa. "I'm sorry, Mama, but I thought it was you."

"You thought it was me?"

"It was dark, she was tall so it wasn't Ma, so it had to be you," Thomas explained, getting a dubious look from Tessa. "I got off early for my vacation and here I am."

"You startled Eva?"

"Yes. She was drinking some water. She dropped the glass and got startled by that as well, and then she took a step back and hit her head on the open cupboard door."

"How did she end up on the floor?"

"She slipped," Thomas explained. "I was going to see if she was alright when the banshee from hell—"

"Hey, that's my sister," Theo said.

"I know, but, Theo, she came at me like a demon. Doesn't matter that I'm twice her size, she just attacked me."

"I SHOULD HAVE killed you," Zoe said as she and Stella walked out of the bedroom and into the living room. "Who are you?" She glared at Thomas. She frowned at his familiar features. "What the hell?" She turned to Tessa.

Tessa put her arm around Zoe's shoulders. "Zoe, this is my not-thinking-clearly son, Thomas."

"Your son? Eva has a cousin?"

"She does, and at the moment he's not too bright."

Zoe was amazed. She was staring at the male version of Eva. He was as tall as her, if not slightly taller, with thick black hair and sky blue eyes, and even though he was unshaven, she could see the dimpled chin.

"Hi, I'm Thomas Lambros." Thomas grimaced and offered his hand to Zoe. "I'm sorry I scared Cousin Eva."

"Sweet Jesus," Zoe exclaimed in absolute shock. "She has a cousin? Wow."

"You are so dead." Theo slapped Theo on the back. "Once my sister stops comparing you to Eva, you are dead."

"Shut up," Thomas mumbled.

Zoe narrowed her eyes at him.

"Oh, boy," Thomas said.

"What in God's name did you do?" she asked.

"I put my arms around her and kissed her cheek," Thomas explained. "I thought she was my mother."

"Zoe, sit down, we have much to discuss," Tessa said.

"I want to go to Eva." Zoe turned.

Tessa gripped her arm. "Zoe, sit down."

Zoe looked back.

"I've given Eva a sedative and she's out cold, so just sit down," Stella said.

"Alright." Zoe sat down.

"There's something we have been keeping from you and Eva."

"You have a son," Zoe said, and looked up at Theo. "You knew about this, right?"

"Um, yes."

"You knew about Eva having a cousin and you didn't say anything. Theodore Lambros, I could kill you," Zoe muttered darkly. She turned her attention back to Tessa.

"There is one more important thing that needs some explaining. I know you are angry, you are frustrated, and you want to be with Eva right now, but you have to hear this."

"Alright."

"It has to do with Eva's time in Aiden."

Zoe sat up straight. "Aiden? What does this have to do with Aiden?"

"In 1917 when Stella rescued me from the asylum, I found out I was pregnant."

"Oh no, because of what they did?"

"No, darling, no, they didn't do that." Tessa patted Zoe's hand. "That was all my own doing. I had fallen in love with Stella but I thought my feelings were from the treatments I was getting for my disease. There was one porter who was very sweet and gentle with me. I thought if I had relations with him, then those feelings for Stella would be gone."

"I don't think that worked," Zoe said.

"No, it didn't. The day that Stella took me out as a treat, the asylum burnt down. Unfortunately, most of the patients in my ward perished. The porter who had so kindly let me out for my birthday also died."

"He was Thomas' father," Zoe said.

"Yes, Karl Steigler. A German who was a very sweet and gentle man."

"If you had gone back, the baby would have been taken from you."

"Yes. More than likely my parents would not have wanted the child because he may have had the same disease as me."

"Oh."

"Stella didn't want me to go back because she had fallen in love with me, and we decided to have this child, to raise him as our own."

"And nine months later this ugly boy was born," Theo said.

Thomas stuck out his tongue at Theo.

"Boys, behave," Tessa admonished. "My son is a nurse and I sent him to Aiden."

"Because you had the vision?"

"Yes. My son is half German, which allowed him to gain employment at the Aiden hospital. I sent him there to help Eva."

"Oh, dear God." Zoe put her hands over her face. "When were you going to tell Eva?"

"Tommy was supposed to arrive tomorrow, and we were going to sit down and talk to the both of you then."

Zoe got up. "Because Tommy decided to be stupid, I have my wife in pain the other room, and she has bruised her back because of nothing."

"I'm sorry . . ." Thomas began.

"I don't know you but you make a lousy first impression," Zoe said. "I know how important this is but I also know keeping this from Eva was wrong."

"We were trying to find the right time, Zoe. We just didn't know what the right time was. You can't spring this on someone," Stella tried to reason.

"Oh no. You can't spring this on her, but that's exactly what was done." Zoe sighed. "I'll have to explain this to her. 'Oh, Evy, you know last night when you hit your head and your back? That was done by your crazy cousin. The cousin you didn't know you had *and* the cousin that was your nurse in Aiden." Zoe worked to keep her voice low.

Tessa put her arm around Zoe. "Darling, I know you are angry, but I think it has more to do with your fear at the moment that something happened to Eva. Tommy was in the wrong, and Stella and I were in the wrong."

"Aunty Tessa, this has been a trial from the moment we sailed into Athens. I know you want the best for Eva and for me, but something like this . . . This is just incredible news."

"I know. In the morning you can tell Eva and then Stella and I will be in to have a word."

CHAPTER 5

ZOE OPENED HER eyes and immediately closed them against the glare. Sunshine streamed in through the curtains and flooded the room with light. The previous evening's thunderstorm had disappeared. They had finally gone to bed just a few hours earlier.

Zoe tenderly stroked Eva's cheek. Even in slumber, the stress and fatigue over the last few days had taken a toll on her. She tucked the blanket around Eva. The pillow that Stella had placed between her knees was still there and the black back brace stood out against her pale skin. Zoe was annoyed with herself for having forgotten to pack Eva's own brace.

Zoe rolled out of bed, trying not to make it squeak. Eva didn't move and was peacefully asleep.

Zoe put on her robe and slippers and left the room. The house was quiet as she walked into the kitchen. One of the cupboard doors was missing. She imagined Eva's head colliding with it and winced. Tessa was at the kitchen window, looking outside while cleaning potatoes. Zoe cleared her throat and walked up to her.

"Good morning, sweetie." Tessa dropped the potato in the sink, picked up the towel, and dried her hands. She kissed Zoe on the cheek. "How are you?"

"I'm tired." Zoe sat down at the table. "Evy's still asleep."

"The sedative will keep her asleep for a little while longer. I'll make you some tea."

"Thank you." Zoe tried to stifle a yawn. "Where are the boys?"

"They went into town to bring back the boxes from Theo's house," Tessa explained. "Stella went with them. She had to pick up some groceries."

"Is Thomas's shoulder okay?"

Tessa smiled. "Yes, he's fine. He's had worse. He shouldn't have been so reckless. He actually does know better."

"What kind of nurse is he?"

"He's a mental health nurse." Tessa smiled wryly.

"So he was really a nurse when he worked in Aiden?"

"Oh, yes." Tessa nodded. "He was fully qualified."

"Hmm." Zoe accepted the tea cup and poured some tea from the teapot. "How does he know Theo?"

"They were on the Albanian border fighting the Italians. Tommy got captured along with Theo and they spent the war in a POW camp. When they got out, they fought during the civil war."

"Did you know they were alive?"

"No." Tessa shook her head. "Sometimes my gift helps and other times it falls down on the job. They both ended up wounded and found themselves at Stella's hospital. Eva's going to be okay."

"She's hurting, Aunty Tessa. Not just last night but since we arrived in Greece. I can see her just willing herself to get up and face another day of being here."

Tessa came to the table and sat down opposite Zoe. "Darling, Eva has been willing herself to get up and not stay down and die since Aiden. She's been hurting since then, mentally and physically. She hasn't started to heal in her mind or her body."

"It's exhausting. I see her try and just deal with her memories. She doesn't want to say anything, but sometimes she opens up and will talk and other times she just clams up." Zoe shook her head slowly. "She's better at talking about how she is feeling." She smiled. "Sometimes she will tell me before I have a chance to ask."

"What do you love about her?"

"She has never given up, even when everything was against her, she has never given up," Zoe said. "I love her courage, her strength, and her faith. She never lost her faith."

"You see the person most people don't see."

"Yes. Everyone else sees this aloof and cold person, but that's not Eva."

"That's the persona that was born in Aiden." Tessa touched Zoe's hand and gently squeezed it. "People can't hurt you if you don't let them in."

"What truly amazes me about her is that despite what they did to her, she still opened her heart to me," Zoe said shyly. "She gives herself to me. Unconditionally."

"Do you think that's hard for her?"

"She doesn't like not having control."

"That's because in Aiden she had no control. Her life was in someone else's hands. She trusts you, Zoe, more than anyone in the world. In Eva's mind she's still in Aiden, and she needs to have control."

"Hasn't she left?"

"No. In her mind she's still there."

"How do I get her out of that place?"

"You can't." Tessa stroked Zoe's cheek. "I have seen you in my vision, but meeting you in person, you amaze me. You have a tremendous amount of love to give, but sometimes love is not enough. Eva needs to forgive herself and learn how to deal with Aiden and her pain."

"How do we do that?"

"You both get some help. Stella and I are here for you and we think that Stella can give Eva the help she needs."

"But you live in Thessaloniki and we are going back to Australia."

"I know." Tessa smiled. "I hear Sydney has a nice weather, which would be good in the summer. I can't stand the cold winters."

"You're coming to Australia?" Zoe grinned. "Really? Doesn't Aunty Stella have a practice in Thessaloniki?"

"Are people so healthy in Australia that they don't need a doctor?" Tessa joked.

"Oh, Evy is going to be thrilled."

"We are not going to Sydney just for Eva, but for you as well."

"Why?"

Tessa smiled. "You try and hide your pain, but it's there. Eva supports you and gives you the unconditional love you give her but there must be days when it becomes unbearable for you."

Zoe took a deep breath and exhaled slowly. "There are days when I see children with their mothers and I want to scream. I want that—I want my mother back." Her voice wavered. "I didn't have enough time with her."

"Of course you didn't, sweetheart." Tessa pulled Zoe into her arms and held her. Zoe sobbed into Tessa's shoulder and Tessa rubbed her back. "I know. You've wanted to cry since you got here but you were being stoic for Eva's sake."

"I just couldn't fall apart. She wouldn't be able to deal with that right now." Zoe sniffed back the tears.

"I know." Tessa wiped Zoe's tears with her apron. Their eyes met, and she smiled. "That's why we are going to Australia. For the both of you."

"I'm really happy. We now have family instead of being just the two of us."

"You two have done a remarkable job in surviving." Tessa smiled and cupped Zoe's cheek. "It's time you both got a little help and started to heal."

"That would be good."

"Of course. When you both are ready I'll bring in some breakfast." Tessa looked up at the wall clock. "Make that lunch. You can have that chat with your darling and tell her about Thomas."

"Oh, that's going to be interesting. I've been thinking about how I'm going to tell her."

"Well, when you are ready, let me know and I'll come in and join you."

"When will Thomas be back?"

"The boys won't be back for a while. I told them to take their time. The last thing Eva needs is to see Thomas before you've told her."

"Something that should have been done when we got here?"

"I know, I'm sorry," Tessa apologized.

"It's alright." Zoe put her arms around Tessa. "Thank you."

"You're welcome, darling. I'm sure Eva will also welcome a nice cool bath after being doused with roses and two days old stinky water," Tessa gently teased.

Zoe smiled. "That's the only thing I could find that was heavy enough."

"It's alright. We can get another vase and some more roses." Tessa laughed lightly, causing Zoe to smile. "Now go back to your darling wife."

Zoe kissed Tessa on the cheek, and took a glass of water and a damp towel with her.

CHAPTER 6

ZOE ENTERED THE bedroom and quietly removed her robe. She came around the bed and put the water and the damp cloth on the bedside table. She looked down at Eva, then got into bed and lay down facing her. Eva was snoring ever so quietly, and Zoe smiled. She wiped her eyes and sighed.

For the last ten years she had been either alone or with Eva. Father Haralambos came into their lives but only stayed for a little while. It was just the two of them trying to deal with their life. Now they would have Tessa and Stella with them. She sniffed.

"Why are you crying?"

Zoe opened her eyes and gazed into Eva's sleepy blue eyes.

Eva cupped Zoe's cheek. "Are you alright?"

"Yes. I got a little emotional earlier." Zoe took Eva's hand and kissed it. "How's the head?" She felt the sizeable bump on the back of Eva's head and winced. "Ouch."

"Aren't you going to tell me what happened?"

"Yes, but not right now. Stella told me to ask you some questions."

"Alright." Eva nodded. "I already know my name."

"What is it?"

Eva smiled. "Eva Lambros."

Zoe smiled and kissed Eva's lips. "You got that one right. Recite the words to my favorite song."

"My heart goes flitter flutter when I gaze into your eyes." Eva gazed lovingly at Zoe. "My heart goes flitter flutter for you."

"There is absolutely nothing wrong with you." Zoe hitched herself up on her elbow and braced her hand next to Eva's head. She kissed her again.

They parted and smiled at each other.

"That song is imprinted in my brain, love, and even if I had a concussion I would still remember the words. You've played it often enough."

Zoe chuckle. "You are adorable."

"I'm sorry."

"What for?"

"I can't even get some water without making an idiot of myself. First with Stella in the cabin and now this."

"It's not your fault, Evy."

"Yes, it is." Eva took Zoe's hand and intertwined their fingers.

"No, it's not. You were startled by an intruder."

"A what?"

"Someone else was in the kitchen with you."

"There was only me, Zo, no one else. I didn't turn on the light," Eva explained as she rolled onto her back and winced. "Argh, that hurts."

"Please, stop blaming yourself." Zoe got out of bed and went over to Eva's side. She sat down, took the damp cloth, and tenderly wiped Eva's face. She playfully cleaned her dimpled chin, and Eva smiled.

"I smell." Eva sniffed.

"Dirty rose water." Zoe wiped Eva's neck and chest. "I'll give you a nice cool bath after we've had a chat."

"You're back to being my maid?" Eva asked as Zoe took the pillow and put it aside.

"When did I ever lose that job?"

"I'm sorry."

"Evy, stop. Your stupid cousin is to blame." Zoe kissed Eva tenderly and got into bed next to her. She hitched herself up on her elbow and took Eva's hand.

"My what?"

"Shh, let me tell you a story. Once upon a time . . . Last night, while you were getting a drink of water, someone else was in the kitchen." Zoe put her fingers to Eva's lips. "Shh, let me finish. Your cousin decided to be funny and surprise Tessa."

"My cousin?"

"Yes, you have a stupid cousin."

"I have a cousin called Stupid?"

Zoe grinned. "No. He has a name, but he was stupid."

"You've met him?"

"Oh, yes." Zoe nodded. "I heard you go down like a sack of potatoes—"

"That's not fair. I didn't go down like a sack of potatoes, more like a giant boulder," Eva joked.

Zoe giggled. "Well, my giant boulder, you went down and I came out and . . ."

"And you panicked," Eva said quietly.

"Um, yes." Zoe nodded. "A little."

"Is that how I got the dirty rose water on me? Did you throw it on me?"

"Um, no. I saw a man standing over you, and I grabbed the first thing I could find."

"You grabbed the vase?"

"Yes."

"Your aim was a little off."

"I was aiming for his head but I hit his shoulder and the side of the cupboard, which shattered the vase," Zoe said, a little disgusted with herself.

"Ah, so that's why I got nicked," Eva said as she looked down to her chest.

"Yes. Sorry."

"It's alright, love." Eva gently squeezed Zoe's hand. "What happened after that?"

"Aunty Stella and Tessa came out, and Theo too. It was quite a ruckus. Stupid Cousin was on the floor and you were out cold."

"Oh, dear."

"I was so mad. Lucky for Stupid Cousin that Theo wouldn't let me go."

"Stupid Cousin owes Theo his life."

"I know." Zoe sniffed.

"Does Stupid Cousin have a name or do I call him Stupid Cousin?"

Zoe laughed. "He has a name. Thomas."

"Hmm, nicer name than Stupid Cousin." Eva chuckled. She stroked Zoe's tear-stained cheek. "Why were you crying?"

Zoe closed her eyes and swallowed. "I was speaking to Tessa, and it just got a little emotional."

"She has that way about her."

"I like her."

"Me too. What made you cry?"

"We were talking about you and how it is for you here."

"It hasn't been easy but I'm used to it being a little hard."

"I know, but it shouldn't be like that. We're hurting too much."

"I know it's hard for you too to be here," Eva said. "You have to deal with your memories and have me falling apart—it's just overwhelming."

"I would have fallen apart if I had been shown that picture too. Aunty Stella wasn't thinking."

"What did Aunty Tessa say?" Eva asked.

"She said we both need help in dealing with everything from our past."

"Isn't that what I'm doing with Dr. Hannah?" Eva asked. "Hannah has helped me. I'm not going to some other doctor for him to tell me what I already know. I'm not going to talk to some stranger."

"Shh," Zoe said. "I know Hannah has worked miracles but she's no longer with us. I know it's been hard for you with Hannah gone. It's been hard for me as well. We're not going to anyone else. I know you hate doctors and I know you don't trust them. Stella and Tessa are the ones that will be helping us."

"What? How?"

"They're moving to Australia."

"Really?" Eva asked in a childlike voice that Zoe found endearing.

"Yes, really."

"Oh." Eva's smile widened. "Wow."

"You like that?"

Eva nodded. "We will have family with us."

"We also talked about Aiden."

"Argh." Eva made a face and covered her eyes with her hand. "Does she think I'm a complete lunatic?"

"No, she doesn't think you're a lunatic," Zoe gently chastised. "Aiden is so much a part of you."

"It's forever in my head."

"Were there any good things to happen there?" Zoe asked.

"Good? Other than I got out alive?"

"Other than that. Was there anyone kind to you in there? Were the nurses kind?"

"Why are we talking about Aiden?"

"Because I want to know," Zoe said.

"No, most of the nurses were women and they were banshees from hell. They were truly horrible people. One was nice."

"She was?"

"Not a she." Eva shook her head and winced. "Ow."

"Don't shake your head," Zoe said as Eva gave her a mock glare. "You had a male nurse?"

"Hmm." Eva closed her eyes. "Karl Stiegler was his name."

"Why have a male nurse?"

Eva turned her head to Zoe. "So I wouldn't get sexually aroused by having a woman care for me. I don't know."

"Sick bastards," Zoe muttered. "You remembered his name, so he must have made an impression on you."

Eva looked at Zoe. "I remember everything about that place, at least the times I wasn't drugged."

"Is this hurting you?"

"No. You want to know," Eva replied. "Karl was a nice man."

"What did he look like?"

"Um, he was tall, and very strong, since he did pick me up a few times. He had blue eyes and wore really thick glasses. He reminded me a little of Kaiser Wilhelm II."

"Was he old?"

Eva looked at Zoe with a smile. "No, love, he wasn't old. He had a beard with a moustache that curled at the side like Wilhelm II's."

"Wow, that is a very clear memory."

"Hmm. He would come in and talk to me like I was a human being and not some lab experiment."

"Sounds like a nice man."

"He was married," Eva said, staring at the ceiling. "I think, because I remember he had a wedding ring around his neck. He was the one who introduced me to his friend Erik."

"Your Erik?"

Eva smiled. "Yes, my Erik."

"So that's how you met Erik. I wondered how you met him. I thought your uncle had introduced you."

"No." Eva shook her head. "Erik was another one who was nice to me."

"He didn't touch you, did he?"

Eva frowned. "Who? You mean the nurse? He had to touch me, he was my nurse."

"No, I meant in other ways."

"Oh," Eva exclaimed. "No. He did kiss me on the cheek once. He must have thought I was asleep and he kissed me and said 'stay strong,' or I may have dreamed it. I don't know."

"Sounds like Karl cared about you."

"I don't know why, but he did care," Eva said quietly.

"Evy." Zoe took a deep breath. "There's something I need to tell you. Your cousin Thomas was Karl."

Eva blinked. She opened her mouth and then shut it. "Wha . . . I . . . oh . . ."

"That's who I met last night."

"No, can't be," Eva said. "No."

"Yes, it is. Aunty Tessa told me. They wanted to introduce you to him, but Thomas came early and everything went to hell."

"Oh. Are you sure?"

"Yes."

"How? I mean, how was he there?"

"Tessa wants to come in and explain, alright?"

Eva nodded. "Oh."

"First, let's get you sitting up. I'll get you a shirt and then I'll call Tessa. After that I'll give you a bath so you won't stink."

"Zoe?"

"Yes, love?"

"I have a cousin?"

"Yes." Zoe smiled. "He looks exactly like you. Once I stopped wanting to kill him, I got a good look at him."

"He looks like me?"

"Yes." Zoe grinned. "Tall, dark hair, very blue eyes. You have the same smile, the little I saw of it. He doesn't have a beard or a funny moustache like Wilhelm."

"Oh."

"And," Zoe tweaked Eva's chin, "He has a dimpled chin just like you. Very sexy."

"Oh," Eva repeated.

"Hmm, time to call Tessa." Zoe kissed Eva.

CHAPTER 7

"COMFORTABLE?" ZOE ASKED.

Eva, wore a light cotton shirt and propped up in bed, her back braced by the mountains of pillows Zoe had managed to locate.

"Yes," Eva said quietly.

Zoe knew exactly what Eva was doing. It was what Eva always did when presented with something that was out of her control. She retreated into herself. Zoe sat down as Eva played with the bedspread.

Zoe placed her fingers under Eva's chin and tilted her head up. "These people won't hurt you, they are your blood. Tessa is as close as you are going to get to having your mother beside you. Don't push them aside."

"Everything just feels like it's spinning out of control."

"I know." Zoe cupped Eva's cheek. "You have been feeling that way since we saw the vision on the ship. We know what it was now, there's another mystery solved. We know that your Aunt Tessa loves you, so that's not something you need to fear."

Eva shrugged. "I know I'm impossible some days."

Zoe smiled. "No, you're not impossible. It's just when you are not feeling well, you are grumpy."

"My back hurts and I'm just feeling sorry for myself."

"You do not make a good patient," Zoe gently teased. "I trust these people, Evy."

"You do?"

"Yes. Give them a chance to explain."

"Alright." Eva nodded.

Zoe took Eva's hand and kissed it. "Be right back,"

She left the room and closed the door. She stood outside for a long moment and exhaled.

"Right." Zoe made her way to the kitchen, where Tessa was sitting and sipping a cup of tea.

TESSA AND ZOE entered the room to find Eva where Zoe had left her and looking a little annoyed with herself.

"What's wrong?" Zoe asked.

"I have an itch between my shoulder blades," Eva said.

"Did you try and scratch it with the pillows?" Zoe asked as she looked around. "Is that why half the pillows are on the floor?" She picked them up and laid them on the bed. She gently pushed Eva forward a little and scratched between her shoulder blades. "That better?"

"Yes." Eva looked up at Zoe with a wry smile. "Thanks."

Tessa smiled at their interaction. Zoe's tender and very careful handling of Eva was intuitive. She didn't make Eva feel like she had to hide anything, even something as simple as an itch. The dynamic was interesting to watch.

Tessa sat down on the bed and waited. "Well, that was quite an evening's entertainment."

"I'm sorry."

"What for, darling? It wasn't your fault. The only thing you could have done better was turn on the light."

"Didn't want to wake you. You had the door open."

Tessa chuckled. "Oh goodness, no, I'm a light sleeper but a little light wouldn't wake me, and Stella would need an atom bomb to fall before she wakes."

"How's . . . um . . ."

"You don't know what to call him, right? His name is Thomas Karl Stiegler Lambros. His father's name was Karl Stiegler."

"He really is half German?"

"Yes." Tessa nodded. "My son's father was a gentle man. He was the only one, other than Stella, that I truly cared about."

"I thought you were . . . um . . ." Zoe looked embarrassed.

"You mean a lesbian?"

"Yes."

"I'm not a lesbian."

"You're not?"

Tessa looked at Zoe. "Zoe, darling, I love the person's heart, their soul. It doesn't matter to me if they are male or female."

"Does that mean if a man came along you would leave Aunty Stella?"

Eva looked like she was about to answer, but Tessa put her hand on her knee. "Let me ask you a question. Do you love Eva because she is a woman, or do you love Eva because of her heart?"

"Her heart," Zoe quickly said. "Not just her heart but the person she is."

"Does it matter that she's a woman?"

"Um." Zoe looked at Eva, who was smiling at her. "Yes. I don't feel that way with men, not that I've had a lot to do with men that way, but if I did I don't think I would, maybe I never really . . ."

Tessa and Eva smiled.

Tessa touched Zoe's arm. "Zoe, darling, there is no right answer or wrong answer."

"There isn't?"

"No. You love Eva because she is a woman and because you are attracted to her."

"Yes."

"I love Zoe because she is a woman." Eva grinned. "All woman," she added, making Zoe blush.

"Everyone is different. There is no right way or wrong way to love. You just do. I found myself having feelings for Stella when I didn't know I could feel that way about a woman."

"That must have been confusing."

"Were you confused?" Tessa asked Zoe.

"Oh, yeah," Eva answered for Zoe. "She was stealing looks when she thought I wasn't looking."

"Eva Theresa!" Zoe gave Eva an outraged glare.

Tessa chuckled. "It's alright, sweetie. The first time is always the hardest. You're not sure if you are coming or going."

"How did you tell Aunty Stella?"

"Aren't we supposed to be talking about my son?"

"Yes." Eva nodded. "But I want to hear this story too."

"Alright. It was my eighteenth birthday, and Stella wanted to make it special because she was leaving the next day. Her rotation was going to end and she was going back, so she somehow arranged with Karl to take me out when things were a little quiet."

"Ooh, that was naughty."

"It was, and Karl would have been sacked had we been found out. He let Stella take me out, and we went into the gardens. Someone had left the asylum gate unlocked. I suspect it was Stella who arranged that but she won't admit to it." Tessa grinned. "Stella looked at it and said she wanted to show me a little of the spring flowers."

"Nice move," Eva quipped.

"That's my angel." Tessa chuckled. "We went for a stroll and somehow we ended up at Stella's apartment, which was nearby."

"Oh, very nice move, Aunty Stella," Zoe said.

"Her next door neighbor saw me, and Stella introduced me as her sister, who was visiting her from Thessaloniki. I was her younger sister Tessa Lambros. We went inside and I won't bore you with all the boring parts of this story." Tessa chuckled.

"Zoe likes boring parts in love stories," Eva teased. "She reads those romantic serials all the time."

"Eva!"

"Yes, love?" Eva blew Zoe a kiss.

Zoe wagged her finger at her. Eva just smiled.

"You do? I suppose I have to tell you now?" Tessa tapped Zoe on the leg. "Alright, well, Stella told me how she felt about me."

"And?" Zoe leaned forward.

"And I brought along a drawing."

"Did you have a vision?"

"No." Tessa shook her head. "It was just an image of what I wanted to happen. It was of Stella kissing me."

Zoe sat back and clapped her hands. "Wow. I should have done that."

"Oh, Fräulein Muller, I have something to show you and this is what you are going to do, *now*!" Eva mimicked Zoe's accent.

They all doubled over laughing.

"What a smarty pants." Zoe got out of her chair and kissed Eva on the lips. "Behave."

"I'm behaving, Miss Lambros."

"You two just make me laugh." Tessa tapped Eva on the blanket-covered knee. "One thing led to another and I won't tell you what happened but we lost track of time."

"Oh, dear."

"Indeed. I knew Karl was going to be in so much trouble so we rushed to get dressed." Tessa glanced at Zoe, who was smirking. "Next thing we know there is a knock on Stella's door. I actually thought we had been found out."

"Were you found out?"

"No, it was just the next door neighbor. She wanted to tell Stella that there was a fire at the asylum and asked if we had heard about it."

"Wow."

"Yes, indeed. Stella told me to stay inside and not move. She ran to the asylum and it was pandemonium. Fire had engulfed half the building. Stella stayed to help those who made it out. She came back in the early hours of the morning totally exhausted."

"What had happened?"

"Fire had somehow broken out. We don't know how but it ran through the old wards and trapped many of the patients. They burnt to death."

"Oh, what a horrible way to go," Eva said quietly.

"Poor souls, they were there for severe mental problems, and for them to die in such a way . . . it was horrible. Most of those who died were restrained or in locked rooms," Tessa said quietly. "Many of them I knew."

"Had Stella not broken the rules, you would have been killed."

"Yes." Tessa nodded. "Stella told me when she came back that Karl had tried to save as many as he could and went in time and time again to rescue people. That was Karl, my friend. He truly cared about the people inside that asylum while many just thought they were beyond help."

"Karl was a very courageous man."

"He was. Unfortunately, every time he went into that burning building, he inhaled smoke, soot, and all the other poisonous gases fires produce. Stella told me that was worse than being burnt. He passed away from smoke inhalation."

"Oh, wow," Eva whispered.

"So here I was, alive and well, and the asylum half burnt to the ground. Some bodies were so burnt you couldn't tell who was who."

"Did you decide not to go back and tell them you were alive?"

"Well." Tessa looked down at her hands for a moment. "As the morning wore on I felt sick. I had been feeling unwell during the week and I hadn't told Stella because she wouldn't have taken me out. I was throwing up and feeling nauseous. Stella decided to keep me at her home. She came home the next day from her normal hospital with a grim look on her face."

"Did she get found out?"

"Oh, no." Tessa shook her head. "Stella had drawn some blood and taken it with her to be tested to see what was wrong with me. She told me I was pregnant."

"Oh, wow."

"That made matters far more serious than just taking me out of the asylum without authorization. What would we do? If she took me back, we knew that I would never see my child. I knew my parents would never keep the child."

"Were my grandparents so heartless?"

"No, darling." Tessa squeezed Eva's hand. "Your grandparents were not heartless in any way. They loved me. They wanted me to get better and they thought I was suffering. I thought I was suffering. It's not like what happened to you at all. You had no say in the matter and were forced against your will."

"You weren't forced?"

"No." Tessa shook her head. "I wanted to be there. I thought that this was something that could be cured but I also loved the life that was now growing within me. Two people who liked each other conceived this child. Karl gave his life to save others and I didn't want to lose the little child he had given me."

"So you decided to keep the pregnancy a secret?"

"Yes. Stella was going to move to Thessaloniki to finish her residency after her time at the asylum so we decided to do that immediately."

"That's where Thomas was born."

"Yes, at home." Tessa smiled. "The minute I saw him, he looked so much like my older sister that if he had been a girl, I would have named her Daphne. I named him Thomas."

"My grandfather was called Thomas." Zoe smiled.

"Yes. We named him after Stella's father and gave him his father's name as well. So that's how Thomas came into the world."

"How did you find out that your visions were real and not an illness?"

"Sister Irene." Tessa smiled at Eva. "Irene is a very special nun, a little odd, a little bossy, very direct but very wise. Stella had gone into a church and was worried about our son and me. She was approached by one of the nuns and they started to talk. It was then that the nun revealed she knew all about us."

"Did that alarm Stella?"

"By that stage Stella was used to the unexpected." Tessa chuckled. "Sister Irene visited us and we found exactly what was wrong with me. She looked at Thomas and said 'this boy will heal many wounds,' which was rather cryptic."

"Did you tell Thomas about his father?" Eva asked.

"Yes. When he was old enough to understand, we told him how brave his father was and that he should always be very proud of him."

"That's beautiful," Zoe said quietly.

"When he grew up, Thomas wanted to help the people his father had tried to help, so he studied and became a mental health nurse."

"How did he come to Aiden?"

Tessa sighed. "One day Thomas was looking for some papers and he accidently found some of my art. By then Thomas was well aware of what electroshock therapy looked like so he asked me about them."

Tessa got up from the bed and came around to the other side. She got into bed, rested her back against the headboard, and took Eva's hand. "I told him that a young woman was going to be suffering."

Eva looked down at their interlocked hands and took a deep breath.

"He said 'Mama, she looks like me.'" Tessa's voice wavered for a moment. "That's when I told him that he had a cousin, that her name was Eva Theresa and that she was in Aiden."

"Wow." Zoe got up and sat down on the other side of Eva. She took Eva's hand.

"Why didn't he tell me?" Eva asked.

"Darling, if we had told you, what would you have done?"

"I don't know," Eva said, shaking her head. "It would have given me hope. It would have made me feel that I wasn't alone."

"They would have let him go and then, what good would that have done? No good at all. Sister Irene and I tried to get that message to you, but in the condition you were in, there was no way of knowing how it was going to be achieved."

"I thought I had convinced them."

"There was no way you could convince them that you had somehow changed who you were without help," Tessa explained. "Thomas was there but he also needed help."

"How?"

"He was the one that whispered very loudly about the man with amnesia."

Eva stared at her, shocked.

"He gave you the idea after Sister Irene visited you in a vision."

"I always thought that was a dream."

"You were supposed to think it was a dream," Tessa said. "It was up to you now to try and convince them that their treatment was working. Thomas found out that you talked constantly when you were under the influence of those drugs."

"She does," Zoe said.

"I do not." Eva faced Zoe, who was nodding.

"Yes, you do. Remember when you were working at the factory and you injured your shoulder? Remember the doctor who came after you spent days not being able to sleep because of it and driving yourself crazy with no sleep? I couldn't shut you up after he left. You kept talking and talking."

Eva worried her bottom lip in thought. "Oh, I remember that."

"The lack of sleep drove me crazy," Zoe replied. "You talk in your sleep as well."

"Hmm," Eva grumbled.

"It's true. You do talk in your sleep and you don't react well to narcotics. There was no chance of them believing you if you didn't have help. Who introduced you to Erik?" Tessa asked.

Eva frowned. "Thomas."

"Thomas knew that he had to do something in order for them to believe you, so he asked his friend Erik to help."

"Erik knew?" Eva exclaimed. "He knew I was faking it?"

Tessa smiled. "Darling, he knew. Erik was a good man. Thomas told him what was going on. My son is a good judge of character and he knew he could trust his friend. Now do you see why you were not told?"

Eva nodded. "That poor man knew I didn't love him and he married me. Was it out of pity?"

"No. It was done out of love. Erik loved you. He knew you didn't love him but you cared deeply for him."

"I did, but that's not enough. Thomas and Erik worked together?"

"Yes. My son is a loving, caring man who loves you very much. It hurt him to know that he was somehow hurting you. He never wanted to. When he wasn't on duty, he worried about you. When he was on duty, he worried about you."

"Was he married?"

"He was, but his wife left him for another man, that . . . Jezebel. She was a very disagreeable woman." Tessa scrunched her face. "Argh, I disliked that girl. She was not worthy of my son. I shouldn't speak ill of the dead . . ."

"She died?"

"Yes, a few months later she was in an accident and died."

"I'm sorry about Tommy's horrible wife."

"Not your fault, darling, it was just the way it was. Thomas deserves much better and one day he will find the right girl." Tessa grinned. "One that deserves his love."

"Mama bear," Zoe teased.

"Oh, darling, if you are ever in that enviable role," Tessa leaned across Eva to pat Zoe on the leg, "you will become a fierce mama bear and will want to protect your children from everything that can hurt them."

Eva smiled as Tessa squeezed her hand.

"Now." Tessa kissed Eva on the cheek. "You need to go and have a bath and then Stella wants you to be up and about. You can't laze in bed, since that's not good for your back. I should know."

"How did you hurt your back?" Zoe asked.

"Electroshock therapy does that. It creates stress fractures," Tessa explained. "Soon after Thomas was born I contracted polio. It was mild but left me with weakness in my legs."

"That's why you are using the cane?"

"Yes. My back and my gift don't like each other all that well, so when I get a vision my back hurts and my legs get very weak. I also did something quite silly the first week I was here."

"What did you do?"

"I went riding for the first time in my life." Tessa chuckled. "Stella warned me but I didn't listen. I was feeling very proud of myself after riding a big horse. I dismounted, landed in a pile of horse manure, and twisted my knee. Let's just say Stella was none too happy with me."

Eva and Zoe looked at each other and snickered. "Sorry," they said in unison.

"Yes, so am I." Tessa chuckled. "Bath time for you," she said to Eva, and she left the room.

CHAPTER 8

EVA SAT ON a wicker garden chair, enjoying the sun upon her face. Beside her was a small table with her cup of tea. She closed her eyes, tired and quite lethargic after the events of the past few days. The cool bath also made her want to go back to bed but Zoe had orders from Stella not to let that happen and to get her outside. She was outside and none too happy about it.

She opened her eyes at the sound of a car approaching. Theo's car pulled up and stopped short of the house. After a few moments, Thomas got out from the passenger's side. He briefly said something to Theo and opened the rear passenger side door. He removed a small box and shut both doors. Thomas turned and caught Eva's eye. They looked at each other for a moment before Thomas smiled.

Thomas approached Eva with the box under his arm. Without a word, he leaned down and gave her a kiss on the cheek. "What I promise, I deliver." He grabbed a nearby chair and sat down. He placed the white box on Eva's lap and waited.

Eva gave him a quizzical look. She opened the box. She smiled when the pink nose of a rabbit touched her fingers. "Jasper." She chuckled and looked at Thomas, who was grinning.

"I knew you would remember that." Thomas laughed and took Eva's hand.

Eva watched the rabbit sniff her hand. She leaned back on the chair and laughed.

ZOE AND TESSA watched Eva and Thomas laughing and talking quietly from the kitchen window. "What is that?"

"A rabbit." Tessa chuckled.

Zoe put the towel she had in her hand and gave Tessa a kiss on the cheek before she went outside to join the cousins.

Thomas looked up as Zoe approached them and got up from his seat. He put his hands up in mock surrender.

Zoe gave him a mock glare and he chuckled. She sat down next to Eva. "That's a bunny," Eva said.

"Yes, I can see." Zoe touched the soft fur. "They make a great stew."

Eva picked up the rabbit and held it against her. "You are not killing Jasper."

Thomas burst out laughing, making Eva laugh.

Zoe blinked at them. "What's so funny?"

"I have to tell you this story" Thomas said. "It's just going to make you laugh so much. I can almost guarantee you will not want to harm Jasper by the end of it."

"Really?" Zoe gave him a dubious look, but she smiled at the sight of Eva cradling the white rabbit.

"Alright now." Thomas brought his chair a little closer to the rabbit. "This happened in Aiden."

Zoe sat up straighter and glanced at Eva who was grinning at the rabbit. "Alright."

"I'm a nurse. I think my mother has already explained that to you so I'm not going to rehash everything because I really want to get to my story."

"Your story?" Eva giggled a little.

"Our story. This happened on Eva's eighteenth birthday."

"How do you remember that it was her birthday?" Zoe asked.

Thomas smiled. "Eva and I share the same birthday. I was born on January twentieth 1918, two years before Eva. I remember that day. I had come in a little late in the morning and was told that Eva had been given a new medication and to be on the lookout for some changes."

"Hmm." Zoe made a noncommittal noise. Eva was happily playing with the rabbit.

"I came in and the night nurse just looked at me and laughed. That's all she did when we changed shifts. Eva was in a room of her own." Thomas covered his mouth trying to suppress the giggles. "I came to the door and announced myself. I heard this almighty yell coming from the bed. Eva was sitting up and trying to motion to me to stop. The whole bed was moving in her enthusiasm to get my attention."

Eva chuckled and put her hand over Zoe's.

"There's Evy." Thomas waved his hands near his waist and jumped up and down on the chair.

Zoe smiled at the silliness.

"She yelled out 'Wait Karl! Wait!' So I waited at the door. I very quietly asked why I was waiting. Eva yelled . . ."

"The rabbits, Karl, the rabbits!" Eva dissolved into a belly laugh. She put her hands on the small of her back. "Oh ow."

"I looked inside the room and there was no animal in sight," Thomas said. "Nothing. It was just Eva. Eva was hallucinating the rabbits so I decided to play along. I asked if she could tell the rabbits to move aside for me. She got this really wide-eyed look and started to marshal the invisible rabbits by name. She named the rabbits."

"She named the invisible rabbits?" Zoe giggled.

"She was calling them out. I think all the Greek gods were there, and the Roman gods. It was just hysterical, and I was still standing at the door. So Eva yelled again and told me to hug the walls because the rabbits did not like the walls. 'The walls, Karl, the walls! You won't hurt them if you hug the walls.'"

Zoe burst out laughing at Thomas's almost perfect mimic of Eva's voice.

"So there I was hugging the walls and walking sideways to avoid the imaginary rabbits that were filling the room. I got to the bed and Eva turned to me, her eyes glued to the imaginary rabbits just over my shoulder. She said, 'jump on the bed, Karl, jump on the bed, it's safe on the bed, no rabbits there.'"

Zoe bent forward laughing.

Thomas flayed his hands about. "So I jumped on the bed and I got to do my job all the while listening to Eva telling the rabbits what they needed to do and to stop fighting." He slapped his thigh as he roared with laughter. "Oh goodness."

Zoe couldn't stop laughing as she held her head. "Oh, this is hurting my head."

"I finished what I had to do and then I hugged the walls and got out again. I was in the corridor and I heard this scream. I rushed back in and there was Eva flailing one hand, which she had managed to get out of the restraint, and marshalling the rabbits, which had now completely taken over the room."

Zoe wiped the tears from her eyes. Eva was also crying from laughing so much. The poor rabbit in her lap looked a little confused.

Zoe wanted to hug Thomas and kiss him for lifting Eva's spirits.

"I had to go and do something else but a few hours later I was back and this time I looked through the window and there was Eva, just sitting there with this huge grin on her face. Doing nothing but smiling. I called out and asked if I could come in and she yelled back that it wasn't safe to hug the walls anymore. She ordered the rabbits to make a path for me." Thomas giggled. "Right! Wilhelm. Artemis. Cleopatra. Out of the way. Out of the way." He wiped the tears from his eyes. "They must have listened because I was allowed to hug the walls again and then I jumped on the bed."

"Oh, my god. Oh, my god. You killed Jasper," Eva yelled out. She threw back her head and laughed.

"You killed Jasper." Zoe pointed at Thomas and giggled.

"How was I to know the damn rabbit was now on the bed? I got off the bed and then she yelled again that I had just stepped on Hera."

"Oh, my god." Zoe tried to catch her breath.

"Eva was yelling, 'You killed him. You killed him.' Which brought the other nurses in to find out what the ruckus was about. They came bursting in and Eva yelled, 'My rabbits. They're escaping. Stop. Stop.' My colleagues were laughing and I was standing there, with Eva shoving an imaginary rabbit at me."

"What were you going to do with it?"

"Resuscitate it, of course. I had squished him so now I had to bring him back to life. I gave this imaginary rabbit mouth-to-mouth resuscitation." Thomas guffawed.

Eva and Zoe laughed hysterically. They looked at each other, stopped for a second, and then laughed uncontrollably.

"I guess I wasn't really good at it because Eva stopped yelling at the escaping rabbits to tell me I was trying to give it the breath of life through its ass."

Zoe fell out of her chair onto her knees. She thumped the ground with her hand and laughed until she was gasping for breath.

"So when things calmed down a little I promised Eva that I would get her a new rabbit and he would be as white as the Jasper I had squished." Thomas wiped the tears from his eyes. "Since I couldn't quite see what Jasper looked like, I think this one will have to do."

Eva kissed Thomas on the cheek. "Thank you." She took his hand. "I think the squished Jasper was a little bit whiter."

"Yes, almost transparent in color," Thomas quipped.

They all looked at one other and spluttered with laughter.

"I'm just going to tell Mama I'm here and I'll be right back." Thomas got up and trotted to the house.

Eva giggled and played with the rabbit. Zoe watched Thomas through the open window.

Tessa approached Thomas and cupped his face. "I have a very loving son. You make me so proud." She tenderly kissed his cheek.

Thomas smiled and shyly looked down. "Thank you, Mama." Tessa embraced him.

You are a very smart man, Thomas Lambros. Zoe turned back to Eva and their new found pet.

CHAPTER 9

"THOMAS," STELLA CALLED out as she came into the kitchen and gave him a kiss on the cheek. She passed Tessa, who was leaning against the kitchen sink. "Didn't I ask you to stay off that knee?"

"You did and I will," Tessa said.

Stella scowled and Tessa smiled. She kissed Stella, who shook her head and turned to Thomas. "I want you to take Eva and go for a walk."

"Ma, she's very comfortable out in the sun."

"That's why I want you to take her for a walk—she needs to move around a little bit," Stella explained and then left the kitchen.

ZOE CAME INTO the kitchen with two empty tea cups and put them in the sink. "Are you taking Eva for a walk?"

"It seems so. Doctor's orders," Thomas replied, getting a mock scowl from Tessa.

"There's a riverbank close by that is just gorgeous this time of year. She likes rivers." Zoe looked out the window. Eva had her head back, enjoying the sun on her face. "There's a huge overhanging tree as well with a tree house."

"Do you want to come with us?" Thomas asked.

"No. I think you and Eva need to be alone," Zoe replied as she washed the cups. She looked over her shoulder at Thomas. "Eva needs this. That story you recounted about the rabbits really made her laugh. We both needed a good laugh and it's the only funny thing I've heard about that god awful place."

Thomas nodded. He approached Zoe and hesitantly put his hand over hers. "I'm sorry I called you crazy. That's not a word I should have used."

"That's alright. You got a shock and you were hurting."

"Still, that's not something I should have said."

"The Australians have a very nice way of letting you know that everything is alright. No worries, she'll be right."

"Huh? I understand the 'no worries' part, but 'she'll be right?'"

"Don't even try to understand it. Australians are a little strange." Zoe chuckled. "I'm sorry I hurt you. How's the shoulder?"

"Sore," Thomas admitted. "I was lucky the vase hit the cupboard or else Ma would have had to stitch my head back together."

"I go a little crazy when I see someone attacking her."

"A little?"

"I was shocked to find her on the floor, and even more alarmed by you over her. I didn't know who you were and we had her stepfather attack her in Sydney. I jumped to the wrong conclusion."

"That's how we found out that Eva was still alive."

"She was responsible for getting Muller arrested by the War Crimes people. He and his friend Rhimes paid us a visit and then we had that evil bitch ex-girlfriend." Zoe shuddered. "When I saw you over her, I just wanted to protect her."

"Greta?"

Zoe snorted. "Evil Nazi bitch," she muttered under her breath.

"But you didn't know how big I was or what my intent was."

"No." Zoe shook her head. "I was there to stop you and that's all that matters."

"It is," Thomas agreed. "I would like to get to know you a little better, with you being my cousin and everything."

"Of course. It's not every day I gain a cousin. Now go and walk my wife." Zoe giggled as she walked out of the kitchen and back outside.

"SHE'S NICE," THOMAS said. Tessa gazed at him affectionately. "She is."

"She is very nice, although I would offer you some advice, my son," Tessa said. "You should not get Zoe angry. Just underneath that seemingly gentle nature is a very formidable woman. Don't let her height fool you."

"Thomas, what are you still doing here?" Stella walked into the kitchen and gave him a gentle slap on the behind.

"Yes, walking with Eva, going now," Thomas replied. He kissed both of his mothers on the cheek and left the kitchen.

"He's so sweet." Stella took Tessa's hand.

Tessa smiled. "I think he likes Zoe."

"He does. I'm just worried about him."

Tessa put her arm around Stella's shoulders. "He will find someone who will love him for the wonderful man that he is. It's just a matter of time."

"It would be nice. He has to find the right one."

"I'm not worried." Tessa gazed at Stella.

"Ah, I see my calm and serene wife has returned from her short vacation." Stella chuckled. "Tessa, darling, can you please go sit down and get off that knee?"

Tessa looked down. "You tell Eva to go for a walk and you tell me to go sit down. You're going to get us confused at some point and send me out for a walk."

"I may make that mistake because you are as beautiful as the day I met you, and I could easily confuse you for young Eva." Stella looked up into Tessa's eyes. She stood on her toes, gave her a quick kiss, and walked out of the kitchen.

Tessa grinned happily. "I love you too, angel."

THOMAS WALKED OUT of the kitchen and went to Eva, who was quietly chatting to Zoe. They looked up as he approached.

"I've been told that you are going to take me for a walk?" Eva shielded her eyes from the sun's glare.

"I am. My mother says you should go for a little exercise and Zoe thinks you might like to go down by the river."

"Which mother?"

"Stella." Thomas grinned.

Eva rose from her seat with Zoe's help.

"Well, I won't argue with my doctor." Eva put her hand on her back and winced. "Sitting down doesn't seem to be a good idea." She blew Zoe a kiss.

"Make sure she's home by midnight," Zoe joked.

Eva looped her arm around Thomas's elbow and they walked off, the sound of her cane tapping lightly on the ground.

"Ah, the young'uns." Zoe chuckled. "They grow up so quickly."

THOMAS SLOWED HIS pace as he and Eva walked quietly along the dirt track leading to the river. He held back the overgrown brush so Eva could pass.

They came to a well-hidden clearing. Large overhanging trees surrounded the river as it bubbled quietly. A makeshift tree house sat in the branches high above the clearing, and a swing, with a plank for a seat, hung down from a sturdy branch.

"I can see Zoe playing here," Eva said. "She probably got her brothers to build the tree house."

"Zoe is—"

"A lioness." Eva grinned. "If you are ever in trouble, she's the woman to have in your corner. She will fight for you no matter the odds. If you're not in trouble, she's the woman to have by your side."

"She protects you and you protect her."

"Yes." Eva leaned against the tree and smiled. "Your mother didn't say anything about me not leaning against trees, did she?"

"No, she didn't say anything like that."

"Good. I'm not moving." Eva played with her cane.

They stayed quiet for a while.

Eva looked at Thomas. "Thank you for saving my life."

Thomas looked down a little shyly. "You needed me, and I was there for you. When Mama told me who you were, well, I had to do something."

"You must have been scared."

"Not as scared as you were. That place terrified me and all I did was look after you. It was evil."

"There wasn't just me they were doing those things to, right?"

"They had other people they were using as guinea pigs." Thomas looked up at Eva. "They were evil people and they just didn't care."

"My grandmother owns that place."

"What?"

"Aiden Spa is owned by AEMullerStahl, my grandmother's company," Eva said. "I wonder if she really knew the inhuman acts that were being done under that roof."

"That would be hideous."

"She did allow my stepfather and my uncle to do that to me."

"Maybe she didn't know. I do remember reading your chart and it did say you were there because of a traffic accident and severe melancholy."

Eva looked at Thomas with a sad smile. "A traffic accident? Is that what they called being beaten half to death by your father? They falsified records. How shocking."

"You were their prize guinea pig."

"I know." Eva nodded. "My uncle told me."

They fell silent for a few minutes.

"Tommy," Eva said.

"Hmm?"

"Why did they give me a hysterectomy?"

Thomas gazed at Eva for a moment, his brows furrowed. "You had uterine fibroids, which causes massive amounts of blood loss. Your uncle chose to give you a hysterectomy after they grew too big."

"Uterine fibroids? Not because my stepfather didn't want me to have children?"

"Goodness, no, who told you that?"

"My stepfather."

"That man was a sadistic evil bastard." Thomas put his arm around

Eva. "Dr. Muller said you had them before you came to Aiden and they continued to grow, so he had no choice. In this instance he was right."

"Oh."

"You believed all this time that Muller had ordered that to happen?"

"Yes." Eva nodded. "He knew I had always wanted children. I kept telling him that when I grew up I would have a dozen children."

Thomas smiled. "A dozen? What were you going to be? A baby factory?"

"Hadn't thought that far ahead. I was an only child so I thought having brothers and sisters was special."

"Hmm, yes, so did I."

"I remember coming home one day and I felt so alone being the only child, like you, and saying to mutti that I was going to get married and have a dozen children with my prince." Eva laughed.

Thomas smiled. "I like hearing your laugh."

"Better than my crying."

"That's true." Thomas brushed the hair from Eva's eyes. "It's a good thing you won't be going to the wedding. There will be lots of crying there."

"I am going."

"I thought you said you weren't before you . . . um . . ."

"Before you scared years off my life?" Eva teased. "I'm going because of Zoe."

"When did you change your mind?"

"When Theo came over and told us that the church altar had part of the roof collapse onto it and they are moving the wedding to the plaza."

"Why is that a problem for Zoe?"

"The plaza is on the edge of a field," Eva said as she tapped the cane against an overhanging branch. "That's Maragos Field."

"I don't understand."

"It's where her mother was murdered." Eva struck the branch with the cane in anger. She watched it swing. "I can't let Zoe face that alone."

"You have trouble standing. She will have—"

"I would crawl on all fours if I had to," Eva said, and gave the branch another whack. "Zoe is going to need me."

"Alright," Thomas said quietly.

They fell silent for a few moments.

"I'm sorry," Thomas said. "I should have realized that you would want to be there for her."

"I would eat porridge for her." Eva glanced at Thomas and smiled.

"That is love." Thomas chuckled. "My god, I remember I had to do choo-choo noises for you to eat it."

"I only ate it because you were so silly and you made me laugh."

"Ah, Cousin Eva, but you ended up eating the pile of goo." Thomas wagged his finger and they both chuckled.

"Tommy, what does it feel like having two mothers?"

"I didn't know it wasn't normal not to have two mothers. That is until I went to school. That's when it was the hardest. I didn't have a father and you know how children can be so vicious."

"Bastard child." Eva had heard that phrase coming from her own stepfather.

"Bastard child. That was the kindest taunt. I've had a lot worse thrown my way. Why do you ask?"

Eva tapped the cane against her foot. "Zoe and I want to have children."

"Ah." Thomas nodded.

"What do you think?"

"Children who are wanted? It's pure love."

"Oh." Eva looked at the leaf-strewn ground.

"Do you have a man?" Thomas shook his head. "I mean, do you have someone who wants to help . . . Now, that didn't sound right either."

Eva chuckled. "No, we don't have a man. We were thinking that one of our friends in Australia, Earl, might help us out."

"Ah." Thomas played with the leaves on the ground with his foot. "What if I volunteered?"

"You're a Catholic, Tommy. Doesn't that . . ."

"I'm a Catholic during Christmas and Easter and that's about it. I don't have a great love for the Church. Is this important to you? You're a Catholic girl, aren't you?"

"Yes, I'm Catholic. Zoe is Greek Orthodox. Faith is important to both of us but not the Church, if you know what I mean."

"Of course. You're lesbians and that's a gross sin in the eyes of the Greek Orthodox and Catholic Churches."

"I would rather commit the gross sin of loving Zoe than condemming someone like me to hell. I don't believe in their version of God."

"Me either," Tommy replied.

They stayed silent for a moment before Eva looked up. "Why do you want to volunteer?"

"You are my cousin and I love you. Earl? What does his wife think of that?"

"He's not married," Eva said as she tapped the cane against the tree stump.

"Forget this Earl. I want to do it."

"A little hard to do if you are in Greece and we are in Australia."

Thomas scratched his chin. "Yes, it would be difficult if I were going to be living in Greece."

"You're not?"

"Mama told me that they are going to Australia to stay," Thomas replied, smiling broadly. "Theo and I have been chatting and he doesn't want to be away from his sister now that she's back, and I don't want to be the one left behind."

"Wow."

"Yes. Who is going to cook for me and where do I take my laundry?" Thomas joked.

Eva smiled at the realization that her family was coming to Australia.

"To be serious for a moment, I want to be with my family," Thomas said.

"That is just amazing,"

"Well." Thomas dragged a tree stump over and sat on it, facing Eva. "As I said, I want to help. Is it so hard to believe?"

"No, I know you. I trust you, but I'm curious why you are so quick to volunteer when you haven't had time to think about it. This is a life-changing decision."

"I love you. You're my cousin. Do I need any other reason?"

"Can I ask you a personal question?"

"Of course."

"How involved would you want to be?"

"Eva, I don't want to be the child's father. That's your job." Thomas smiled. "You know what I mean. You and Zoe are going to be the parents. You don't need a third wheel. I want to give you what you are not able to do yourself."

"That's very generous of you. I would give you a kiss if I was able to bend over, but since I'm not . . ."

Tommy rose and kissed her on the cheek.

"Or you can give me a kiss."

Thomas doffed his imaginary top hat and smiled. "It's a good thing you want to do it in Australia and not here."

"Why?"

"Unwed mothers are pariahs. You know what happened to your own mother when she was pregnant with you."

"Yes. She was sent away in the middle of the night so as to not scandalize the sensibilities of the good Christian souls," Eva said. "My mother was pregnant, she didn't have the bubonic plague."

"Is it like that in Australia?"

"Yes. We get women coming to the interpreter service seeking our help because the State deemed they were unfit mothers. There isn't anything we can do because once the State decides they are unfit, they have an uphill battle to try and prove they do love their children."

"Have you thought about what this will do to Zoe?"

"I have thought about this and it worries me." Eva nodded. "Zoe says she doesn't care—it's her life, her choice, and it doesn't have anything to do with the government."

"What if I found a solution to that problem?"

"What's the solution, marry Zoe?" Eva chuckled.

"Yes, I get to marry Zoe," Thomas suggested.

Eva stopped smiling.

"What do you think?"

"You just asked me if you could marry my wife."

"Yes."

Eva closed her eyes and laughed. "Tommy, you are asking for my wife's hand in marriage."

"Should I have asked Theo instead?" Thomas teased.

Eva tapped his arm lightly with her cane.

"Ow." He grabbed his arm. "Think about it. The child or children will not be born out of wedlock, thus avoiding Zoe being immoral or the State wanting to take the child away. It does make sense. The other factor to consider is that the children will be legally your next of kin."

Eva smiled. "My second cousins."

"Exactly." Thomas nodded.

"Hmm."

"Is that a good hmm or a bad hmm?"

"There's another reason to go with your plan."

"What's that?"

"Zoe wants children that look like me." Eva waved her hand in front of Thomas. "You look like me."

"Actually you are wrong. You look like me. I'm older than you." Thomas chuckled and moved out of the way of Eva's cane.

"I'll have to talk to Zoe about this."

"When?"

"When do I talk to Zoe?" Eva asked, and tried not to laugh at the look of expectation on Thomas's face. "When we get back."

"What do you think she will say?"

"I don't know. It's not every day I ask my beloved spouse to marry my cousin so we can have children."

"That is a little odd."

"Just a little odd." Eva laughed and shook her head. "We have another issue to deal with."

"What's that?"

Eva scratched her ear. She wasn't sure how to broach the subject. "Sex."

"Hmm. Do you want to know how babies are made?" Thomas teased.

Eva whacked him again with the cane. "I'm serious. Zoe wants to try doing it the way her father did it with the animals."

"Pardon?"

Eva smiled. "That's what Zoe said. She said that her father used some method to impregnate the sheep."

"And you want to use that method on Zoe?"

Eva shrugged. "It's what she wants."

"That's not going to work, Eva."

"We were going to ask Stella how we could do that. She will know the best way to do it."

"I'm afraid to say that my mother will tell you the best way to do it would be to have sex."

Eva leaded back against the tree trunk and shut her eyes. "Oh god."

"But you knew that, didn't you?"

"I knew it but hoped Zoe was right that it would work."

"It might work but . . ."

"I know. Sex is the only way."

They fell silent for a long moment before Eva turned to Thomas and stared at him. "Zoe has never been with a man. She's never . . . um . . ."

"Are you sure you want this to happen?"

"Zoe wants a baby and she wants to give me what I can't have."

"What do you want?"

Eva took a deep breath and released it slowly. "I wish I had never mentioned wanting children to Zoe. The idea has taken root in her mind and there is nothing I can do to make her change her mind."

"Ask her. Ask her if she wants this and then if you both agree, I'll will help you if you want me to."

"Do I want you to have sex with Zoe?" Eva replied with a small shake of her head. "No, of course not, but Zoe wants to have children."

"Why don't you ask her if she really wants to? She may say no, that sex is not going to happen. Let's go back so you can talk to her." Thomas scrambled to his feet and reached out to steady Eva as she pushed herself off the tree.

Eva threaded her arm around his elbow as they made their way back to the farmhouse. "It was a good idea."

"For the animals it's a great idea."

"We were going to get our friend Earl to volunteer."

"That is for family only. Is he family?"

"Uh, no."

"Problem solved. Can you walk a little faster?" Thomas asked.

"No."

"Just a little?"

"No."

CHAPTER 10

EVA WENT INTO the bedroom, thankful that her little walk was over. She was in pain and just wanted to lie down. When they returned from their walk, Zoe took one look at her and suggested she needed a nap. Thomas's proposal could wait.

Eva sat down on the wicker chair in the bedroom and sighed. Zoe came into the room and shut the door behind her. Eva gazed at her as she sat on her haunches and started to remove Eva's shoes. They were used to the routine when Eva wasn't able to bend over and do it herself.

"I don't know why you wear these things. Going without stockings is not going to be in the Larissian Fashion News, not that we have one of those here," Zoe chatted while she unhooked the stockings from Eva's garter belt. She smiled. "What's on your mind, Miss Lambros?"

"I've been asked for your hand in marriage."

Zoe's eyes widened and she fell to the floor with one stocking in her hand. She looked up to find Eva quietly chuckling.

"You did that on purpose."

Eva shook her head. "No, but your reaction is funny."

Zoe sat cross-legged and motioned for Eva to continue. "Did you find a husband for me on the riverbed?"

"Yes."

"How nice. I hope it wasn't old man Yiannis."

"Before I tell you about the marriage proposal . . ."

"Yes, that's not very important."

"I asked Thomas why I was given a hysterectomy," Eva said quietly.

Zoe got off the floor and sat on the bed. "Don't we already know why?"

"No. I was wrong."

"You were wrong? How were you wrong?"

"I had uterine fibroids and they grew too large, so my uncle chose to operate."

"Is Thomas sure?"

"Yes." Eva nodded. "He said it wasn't my stepfather who ordered it."

"But the bastard said he did. He was playing some vicious mind games with you?"

"Yes."

Zoe ran her hand through her hair and looked up at the ceiling. "I know this man was a bastard but this just proves what kind of sadistic son of a bitch he was."

"It does," Eva replied.

"I don't know a lot about what uterine fibroids are, but it sounds pretty serious if the solution is to have a hysterectomy."

"It is very serious, but with everything else going on, it was just one more thing to deal with. If there is a positive here, a lot of women get them and they have this operation."

"Isn't it strange that we find comfort in you having a disease that wasn't the dummkopf twins' fault?"

Eva chuckled and Zoe smiled. "You like saying that word, don't you?"

"Yes. And boofhead. I like the sound of both words." Zoe tapped Eva's knee. "Now tell me who proposed."

"He didn't propose to me, they just asked me for your hand in marriage."

"Uh huh."

"I asked Tommy what it was like to have two mothers."

"Ah. He would know. What is it like?"

"He said it was good until he went to school and he was taunted by the other children for being a bastard child."

"Children can be so vicious."

"Tommy asked me why I wanted to know and I told him we wanted to have children. I hope that was alright. I wasn't going to say anything, but I was curious."

"That's alright. I like Thomas."

"One question led to another and Tommy asked if we would like him to be the father."

Zoe's eyebrows rose and a smile slowly creased her face. "Hmm. Would I want sperm from a man who looks like you, is your cousin, and has volunteered? That's difficult." She chuckled. "I hope you said yes."

"I wouldn't say yes without talking to you first. That wouldn't be right."

"So how did that become a marriage proposal?"

"Zoe, we've discussed this before . . ."

"Oh no, not again." Zoe got up from the bed and paced. "I don't want to be married. I can have a child without being married."

"You know how society views unmarried mothers. I've told you about the poor ladies that come—"

Zoe went over to the chair and put her arms on the handles, and leaned over inches away from Eva's face. "I don't want to get married because I already am married."

Eva smiled at Zoe's very aggressive posture. "If anyone else did that to me, it would be confronting, but I just find you so adorable. I love your passion." She cupped Zoe's face and kissed her.

Zoe sighed and sat back down on the bed. "I don't want to get married."

"Then we won't have children."

"That's not fair."

"I'm not trying to guilt you into doing this, Zo. I'm not willing to have you in the crosshairs of some government agency. I've seen it too many times and that's not what I want for you."

"But you want children."

"Yes, but not at the expense of your happiness." Eva took Zoe's hand. "I won't sacrifice you so we can have children."

"That sounds like a really bad plot in a romance novel."

"Like the ones you read?" Eva gently teased.

Zoe stuck her tongue out at her.

"Why?"

"He said he loves me and he wants to give me what I can't do for myself."

"Wow, well, I'll give him full marks for that. Won't that be hard to do with him being in Thessaloniki and us being in Sydney? Is he going to send us his sperm by air mail?"

"About that . . ."

"About what? I thought you said he wants to give his sperm."

"He does, but we talked about how your father got the animals pregnant and he doesn't think it will work for you."

"He doesn't? Why? He's a nurse, not a doctor and what does he know, anyway?" Zoe crossed her arms across her chest.

"He knows a lot."

"So what does that mean? I have to have sex?"

Eva nodded. "Yes."

"I think we should ask Aunty Stella. She's a doctor and, as much as I like Thomas, I think Aunty Stella will know more about this."

"Has she impregnated a lot of women with turkey basters?"

"No, but she is a doctor."

"What if she says we can't do it that way?"

"We will then talk about it." Zoe took Eva's hand and they fell silent. "If we can't do it the turkey baster way, how does Tommy think he can do it the other way? I mean if we are in Australia."

"Thomas and Theo have decided they want to go to Australia with Aunt Tessa and Stella."

Zoe shook her head. "So that's why Theo was all cryptic with me when you went on your walk. He said he had a secret but he would tell me when you got back."

"Yes, that's probably it."

"If Thomas wants to marry me, what happens when he finds a girl and wants to get married?" Zoe asked.

Eva looked down at their interlocked fingers. "He's not into girls."

"Well, the former Mrs. Lambros hurt him by running off with her new man but that's no reason not to want—"

"Zoe, slow down." Eva playfully put her fingers over Zoe's lips. "He doesn't like girls like you don't like boys."

"Oh! He's like Earl? Why didn't you just say that?"

"He told me on the way back, after I kept asking why he didn't want to get married."

"Wait." Zoe put her hand up. "You were asking questions about someone's private life? You? The woman who never wants to intrude on anyone's privacy?"

"Yes, me. You're rubbing off on me." Eva stroked Zoe's hand, making her giggle.

"Oh, my god, do his mothers know?"

"He said he suspects Tessa knows and Stella doesn't. That's why his wife left him—he couldn't lie to her."

"Oh, Sweet Mary Mother of God," Zoe exclaimed as her hand flew to her mouth. "Why hasn't he told his mothers?"

Eva sighed. "He said he disappointed Stella by going ahead with the wedding even though she didn't like the girl. She told him she wasn't good enough for him, but it was his choice to do it and she would support him. When Kaila left him, he was expecting his mother to tell him he had made the wrong choice, but she didn't."

"Is that her name? I want to call her Jezebel, since no one has called her anything but that. Aunty Stella or Tessa wouldn't hurt Tommy by doing that."

"He did make the wrong choice. He thought that getting married to Kaila would put an end to his feelings."

"Oh, the poor man."

"I don't think we will have the problem of him wanting to marry someone else."

"Yes." Zoe nodded. "How do you feel about this?"

"I'm not overly thrilled but we want children. Let's see what Aunty Stella says first, alright?"

"I'm not thrilled by the idea of having sex with Tommy but I want to have children. So what do we do now?"

"I told Thomas he would have to ask Theo, since he is your older brother," Eva said with a straight face.

Zoe gently slapped her hand.

"Ow, don't hit the infirm."

"Theo is going to find this very strange. Back to Thomas. How would he be involved in the children's lives?"

"He doesn't want to be involved other than doing . . . um . . . his duty."

"So we are the children's parents and he has nothing to do with the decisions we make? I don't want anyone else other than you and me involved in that."

"He assured me he will not interfere."

"Hmm." Zoe looked down to the floor, lost in thought for a few minutes. "I want that in writing. If he changes his mind, I don't want to have this huge fight over our children."

"That's putting the cart before the horse, isn't it?"

"Maybe, but normally you are the cautious one. You're rubbing off on me." Zoe grinned and stroked Eva's cheek. "I want that in writing, that he relinquishes all parental control."

"You sound like Friedrich."

Zoe clucked her tongue. "You just insulted me and called me a lawyer."

"You and I will have full parental control. Tommy won't be involved. One of the benefits of Tommy being our sperm donor is that I'm related to the children by blood."

"Second cousins." Zoe grinned. "They will be fully ours."

"I love you," Eva whispered, and she captured Zoe's mouth for a passionate kiss. They parted and gazed at each other. "I can't wait for our children and I hope they look like you—red, curly hair and green eyes."

"That's something I hope you never get. Black hair, blue eyes, and a dimpled chin is the order I'm going to place with God," Zoe said, and tweaked Eva's chin. "Aunty Stella and Tessa are going to be grandmothers."

"Tommy is talking to them now."

"Do you think they knew?"

"I don't know, but I guess we will find out."

"Eva." Zoe got up from the bed and went down on her knees to finish removing Eva's other stocking. She looked up with a mischievous look in her eye. "Would you be my matron of honor?"

Eva stared at Zoe for a moment and they laughed.

Eva tried not to jar her back as she rocked back in the chair. "I did tell Tommy that Earl was our first choice as a sperm donor and he was now out of a job."

"Hmm." Zoe looked up at the ceiling with a thoughtful expression on her face.

"No."

"No, what?"

Eva shook her head. "Whatever your pretty mind is up to, forget it. You are not going to play matchmaker between Tommy and Earl."

"Who said anything about that?"

Eva shook her head. "Zoe, you are not going to do that. Earl can find his own boyfriend. He doesn't need help from you."

"Of course he doesn't." Zoe giggled.

Eva sighed and then laughed at Zoe's wicked little smile.

CHAPTER 11

ZOE CLOSED THE door to the bedroom after she had settled Eva in bed for a nap with Jasper sitting quietly on the edge of the bed. She kept her hand on the doorknob as she went over the life-changing events that were to occur. Having sex with a man. She involuntarily shuddered at the thought. She shook her head as if to remove the mental image that had lodged in her mind as she made her way down the corridor and into the living room. No one was there, so she poked her head into the kitchen.

No one was in the kitchen either, so she decided to go outside, hoping to find Thomas.

"Hmm, where has everyone disappeared to?" Zoe said.

"I'm here."

Zoe followed the sound of Theo's voice to the side of the house, where he was sitting and sipping a cup of coffee. A cigarette was in a makeshift ashtray at his feet.

"I see you still drink that sludge." Zoe patted Theo on the shoulder and sat down on an upended drum.

"This is real coffee."

"If you say so. Where has everyone gone?"

"Tommy took his parents for a walk. Is Eva taking a nap? She looked exhausted when she came back."

"Yes, the walk drained her, so she's in bed having a bit of a rest."

Theo turned to Zoe. "Tommy had a word with me earlier."

"Oh?"

"He said something very strange and at first I thought he was drunk."

"What did he say?" Zoe picked up a twig and started to draw in the dirt in front of her.

"He asked me for your hand in marriage." Theo watched Zoe, who was busy with her ground drawing. "Can you stop that and look at me?"

Zoe looked at Theo, who had a very serious look on his face. "What's wrong, Theodore?"

"Did you hear what I said?"

"Yes. Thomas has asked you if he could ask me for my hand in marriage. I heard you."

Theo scowled.

"Don't scowl." Zoe smoothed the furrowed groove between Theo's eyes. "What did you say?"

"I said no," Theo exclaimed angrily.

Zoe suppressed a smile. *He is just so adorable.* "Why did you do that?"

"You don't love him, Zoe. You just met the man."

"Hmm. He's very handsome. Don't you want him as your brother-in-law?"

"He's already my brother. I don't need a brother-in-law. I have a sister-in-law that does a stellar job at it." Theo picked up several pebbles and chose one. He looked at Zoe with a puzzled expression. He threw the pebble and hit the chicken shed with a dull thud.

"What did you say?"

"Are you deaf? I said I have a sister-in-law that does a stellar job. I thought this thing you have with Eva is real. You told me it was. Eva loves you and you said you loved her. I don't understand it but you said this is what you wanted. Why would you hurt her like that?" Theo threw another pebble. "She loves you."

"You are just so . . ." Zoe stopped and sighed happily at Theo's words. She realized her brother's feelings were very genuine, and at that very second she loved him more than ever. She took a hold of his bicep. She put her arms around his neck and kissed him. She smiled and she almost got up and raced into the house to cuddle up to Eva with the news of Theo's reaction.

"Yes, but Zoe—"

"Stop. I'm going to explain. Eva and I are not breaking up."

"You're not?"

"No." Zoe shook her head. "Thomas asked you for my hand because Eva and I want to have children."

Theo dropped the pebbles and turned to Zoe. "You want to have children."

"Yes."

"You want to marry Thomas because you just want to have children? You don't love him or anything like that?"

"I just met him." Zoe grinned. "I'm not leaving Eva for a man."

Theo exhaled and leaned back against the house. He swore under his breath. "I thought you were going to leave Eva for Tommy."

"I know." Zoe giggled. "Sorry, I was going to play along but you are seriously upset by it."

"Sweet Jesus." Theo shook his head. "That's not nice."

"Sorry, brother." Zoe rested her head against his shoulder.

"What's the story?"

"Eva and Tommy went for a walk and they talked about how we want to have children. Eva doesn't want me to be unmarried because—"

"It's immoral."

"If you say so. I don't see what the fuss is about but Eva thinks it makes a big difference. She doesn't want to have children if it means putting me in what she calls the government crosshairs."

"She's right. If you are going to have children then you need to be married. That's just the way it is. Eva wants to have children but you are carrying them? Is that because you are younger?"

"Eva can't have children," Zoe quietly said. "She had some woman thing and they had to operate."

"What's this 'woman thing'?"

"You wouldn't know it. Uterine fibroids."

"I know what that is. Mama had them just after you were born. They had to operate and she couldn't have any more children after that."

"Oh." Zoe gazed at Theo. "I didn't know that."

"Hmm. We nearly lost Mama. So Eva can't have children but you can."

"Yes. Thomas said he wanted to be the father of those babies and he asked Eva if he could marry me."

"So why did he ask me?"

"Because you are my brother and that's the traditional way of doing things, isn't it?" Zoe wanted to laugh at Theo's confused look.

"Yes, it would be, but Aunty Stella told me that you and Eva are a couple and it's like you are married. She's your head."

Zoe suppressed the urge to smile. "We don't have that kind of relationship. It's not like a man and a woman, where the man is the head. She's not my head. We do things together."

"So who makes the decisions?"

"We both do."

"Isn't that confusing? Someone has to decide."

"Sometimes when Eva knows more about something than I do, she does, and if I know something Eva doesn't, then it's me. We both decide on things. Remember how Mama and Papa used to sit and talk about everything?"

"Yes, I remember."

"Well, it's like that."

"Oh." Theo nodded and picked up his cigarette. He took a drag and exhaled. "So do you want to marry Thomas?"

"No, I don't but that's the only way to have children."

"Are you sure that's what you want to do?"

"No," Zoe shook her head. "No, I'm not sure. It would mean marrying a man and . . ."

"Sex."

Zoe sighed heavily as she picked up a pebble and threw it. "I have a plan. Remember how Papa used to impregnate the animals?"

"I remember, but you're not a cow."

"This is very true but the same idea—"

"You're not a cow, Zoe. I don't think that works with women."

Zoe glanced at her brother. "Tommy doesn't think so either, but I'm going to ask Aunty Stella. If it can be done, she will know how."

"What if Aunty Stella says the only way you can have these babies is by having sex?"

Zoe stayed silent and stared down at the ring on her finger. "Eva wants children. She's wanted them for a long time. She loves children and she can't have them."

"I haven't known Eva for a long time but I can see she loves you. However, sharing you . . . How does Eva feel about that?"

Zoe stayed silent for a long moment. "It will hurt her deeply and she will more than likely cry a lot."

"So why do it if it's going to hurt her?"

"A lot of horrible things have been done to her, Theo. Things that would make your hair stand on end. I want to give her something that she's always wanted," Zoe replied softly. "Something she can't do herself."

"How do you feel about having sex with a man?"

"I don't believe we are having this conversation." Zoe half smiled and bumped her shoulder against Theo's. "I don't want to have sex with a man, but if I don't, Eva won't get what she wants."

"Is that what you want?"

"I want Eva to be happy. It may not come to that. Aunty Stella may know of a way so that I don't have to have sex. I don't want to think about it now."

"I can accept you wanting to live with Eva, but as your older brother and head of this family, I don't approve you having children without being married."

"Even if my marriage is a sham?"

"Does Tommy know that it's a sham?"

"Yes."

"Right then. I don't know where it says in the Bible that a marriage can't be a marriage of convenience. Tommy can't love you because he's not into . . ." Theo stopped and looked away. "Well, he's not in love with you."

"Do you know what I love about you, Teedore?"

"What?"

"You are the second finest man I have ever met," Zoe said fondly, and kissed Theo on the cheek.

"Who is the first?" Theo grinned.

"Papa beats you to that honor. He was the finest man ever."

"He was. He loved us all so much. He would be so proud of you, of the way you kept yourself alive and battled against the war criminals. You were his little girl. Imagine him as a grandfather?"

"I hope he would have been accepting of me."

"He accepted Aunty Stella."

"He called her crazy Aunt Stella. That's not accepting."

Theo chuckled. "That wasn't because she loved women. That's because she wore those crazy outfits and did some crazy things like wanting to work in lunatic asylums. It had nothing to do with Aunt Tessa. He loved Stella so much. You didn't meet Uncle Timothy, but he was such a nice man, and when he died, Aunt Stella just went to pieces. She was here for a long time and she could barely get out of bed. It was really bad."

"He died at Skra?"

"Yes. Horrible, but that's war. I remember I overheard Papa talking to Mama about how Aunty Stella had finally found a reason to live again because of Tessa. Uncle Timothy was her first love. Uncle Dion, the jackass, called her all sorts of names when he found out and tried to run her out of town. He is a terrible man."

"I didn't know Papa knew about Tessa."

"He didn't say anything. What's there to say? And you were too young to understand."

"I like how Tessa took on Aunty Stella's name. That was nice," Zoe said. "Thomas was our grandfather's name."

"What is Eva going to do?"

"Huh?"

"Are you teasing me like you did earlier?"

"No." Zoe shook her head. "What do you mean?"

"Will Eva take on Lambros? She changed her name from Muller to Haralambos. Will she do it again?"

"It's a little bit more difficult because this time there isn't a reason to do this. Father H was her father after all. She had to fill out forms, go through immigration . . . She has a War Crimes folder, do you believe that?"

"What for?"

"She's the stepdaughter of a war criminal. They investigated her to see if she was connected with Muller and his crimes. So every time she does something with a government department they find that file and we begin the explanations. We want to do it, but it's going to be difficult."

Theo nodded and picked up his coffee. "What if I married Eva?"

"Eh?" Zoe blinked in surprise. "You want to marry Eva?"

"Yes. I can give her my name and then she becomes Eva Lambros.

She wouldn't have to go through all that government idiocy. What do you think?"

Zoe sat back against the weatherboard beams of the house and gazed at Theo. "Erm . . ."

"Is that a yes or a no?"

"Why do you want to do that?"

"Because I love you. You are my sister and it's something I can do for you and for Eva."

"Do you not like women?"

"What?"

Zoe sighed. Theo was giving her a very puzzled look. "Do you like men? I mean . . . erm . . . for sex . . ."

"What? No." Theo dropped his cigarette in the dirt.

"So you like women?" Zoe asked. "I mean to have sex."

"Zoe!" Theo turned away from his sister. Zoe found it endearing that his ears had turned pink. "Yes."

"Alright then. So what happens if you fall in love with a woman and you want to marry her, maybe have children? What's going to happen to Eva?"

"I can't," Theo said quietly. He stretched his long legs out and crossed his feet at the ankles. He rocked them back and forth for a few moments. "I can't have children. I don't want to talk about it, alright? But I don't want to get married."

"Oh." Zoe threaded her arm around Theo's bicep and leaned against him. "I'm sorry, Theo."

"I know you are." Theo tenderly stroked Zoe's head.

"I'm alive, that's all matters. Let's not talk about this."

They fell silent for a long moment.

Theo looked down at Zoe. "Zo?"

"Yes?"

"Can I marry your wife?"

Zoe chuckled and nodded. "Wait until Eva wakes up to find out I am going to marry her off."

They looked at each other and laughed.

CHAPTER 12

"ALEX, MOVE THAT beam."

"I've got it, Father."

Father Panayiotis Haralambos looked over the debris that littered his church and shook his head. His black over-cassock was covered in white dust. His long salt-and-pepper hair was tied at the back in a ponytail. It bopped up and down as he surveyed the damaged altar and ceiling.

"Boys! Take care of our Savior," Father Haralambos called out as two young men took down the icon of the crucified Christ. The other icons had been removed to protect them from further damage.

"Father Haralambos?"

Father Haralambos turned around to see a man standing hesitantly just inside the church. He motioned him to come forward and then turned to watch a young man remove a timber beam from on top the altar.

"How can I help you, my son?" Father Haralambos asked.

"Father, I could come back if you are busy."

"No, I'm not busy. I think I've seen enough of the damage," Father Haralambos said. He looked the young man on the roof. "Alex . . ."

"I know, Father, don't worry," Alex said.

"Hmm, yes. Every time someone tells me not to worry, I worry," Father Haralambos mumbled and stroked his long beard. He walked to the back of the church.

The man bowed and kissed his hand.

"Come to the residence. There's too much dust here and I need a drink of water." Father Haralambos took the man's arm and led him into the house next to the church. "Let me get out of these dusty clothes and then we can talk, all right?"

"Of course, Father."

Father Haralambos left the man in the living room, changed to a clean black cassock, and returned a few minutes later.

"Please, sit," he said.

"That roof collapsing is a sign, Father."

"Yes, it's a sign. A sign that I should have fixed the roof. We should at all times take steps to fix a potential problem before it becomes a real problem. I should give a sermon on that, but first I have to learn that lesson."

"I'm sure we are all guilty of that."

"How can I help you?"

"My name is Dionysius Lambros."

"Any relation to Zoe Lambros?"

Dion nodded. "I'm her uncle."

"Ah. I knew your brother, Nicholas, and his wife, Helena, as well as their sons and of course Zoe. Very faithful family."

"Yes. I'm afraid that's what I came here to talk to you about."

"Oh?"

"I know you don't know me, but I came here over this government property law," Dion said. "I'm going to be in Larissa for a short while before my family and I go to Volos. My wife has property there we need to attend to."

"Of course."

Dion nervously curl the rim of the hat in his hands. "Father, I have a very serious problem."

"You do? How can I help?"

"I have to tell you a little story first. Do you have the time?"

"Of course."

"My older sister Stella was married to a man named Timothy Andronikakis. He was a very well-respected doctor in Thessaloniki. Unfortunately he was killed at Skra in 1916."

"A terrible loss of life in Skra."

"Yes. My sister, as you can imagine, was devastated. She had lost her unborn child before Timothy was sent to war and then her husband died. She lost her mind."

"That is a great deal of suffering."

"It is. The tragedy of this is that Stella has never recovered from those two deaths. I'm her only living brother."

"What makes you believe that she has not recovered?"

Dion sighed heavily. "After Timothy died, Nicholas looked after our sister until she decided to go to Athens to finish her medical studies. She's also a doctor."

"That's not something one does if they are still grieving the loss of her husband and unborn child."

"That's what I thought, but she then started working with insane people in those lunatic asylums."

"My son, those lunatic asylums are filled with very ill people who need your sister's help. They have lost their way and ability to find the way out. I don't think Stella working there is a sign that she is suffering."

"You don't?"

"No, to the contrary. It shows she wants to help others. That's a good sign."

"It could be, but that leads me to the second reason I think she needs help. Do you know of Petros and Eva Mitsos?"

Father Haralambos smiled. "Of course."

"They had two daughters . . ."

"Daphne and Theresa. I know of them. I was going to be married to Daphne, so I'm very aware of the family."

Dion squirmed in his seat and looked embarrassed. "You know of Theresa's problems."

"I do. I don't understand what this has to do with Stella."

"Stella worked at the same lunatic asylum where Theresa Mitsos was a patient. That's where Stella completely lost her mind."

"I know the story of the fire. So tell me what concerns you about that."

"I believe this Theresa is a witch," Dion whispered. "She somehow blinded my sister and made her believe that she was a deviant."

"A what?"

"A deviant, Father. Sodom and Gomorrah deviant."

"Oh. You mean a lesbian?"

"Yes. She survived that fire. The fire did not touch her. You know what that means?"

"It means that she was very fortunate to have escaped when many did not."

"That only happens to witches."

"You must be very careful about accusing someone of witchcraft. It's a heavy accusation."

"I know. I don't know how an educated woman like my sister could become a deviant overnight. It's not possible. She was married, she nearly had a child and then this?"

"I don't understand what you wish me to do. Do you want me to perform an exorcism?"

"No, Father. I fear it's too late for my sister. I have come here to ask you for help with my niece."

"Zoe."

"Yes. It's not too late for her. She's twenty-two and I think we can save her."

"I've known Zoe all her life. She is a very faithful and courageous young woman."

"I know. I've heard all the stories from the village of how she also nearly lost her mind when her mother was murdered. She pulled through but I fear for her soul."

"Why is that?"

"I don't know if you have heard of the rumors about Zoe and . . . uh . . ."

Father Haralambos sat back and folded his hands on his lap. "You are talking about my daughter, Eva?"

"There is a lot of talk in the village about Eva and Zoe during the war."

"Yes, I know. They were both working with me to save the Jews from the Nazis. That was a very courageous thing to do."

"It's not that."

"No?"

"No. This is a great sin. This involves immorality and gross sin."

"Does it?" Father Haralambos sighed.

"She's a deviant. Like my sister Stella. Somehow your daughter convinced Zoe that she should follow her . . . um . . . immoral ways. It's the Mitsos curse. They are all cursed. You know that Petros' great great great grandmother was tried for witchcraft and was stoned to death."

"Uh huh." Father Haralambos stroked his beard. "I was not aware of that."

"It's true. Now that curse has been passed on to your daughter."

"Uh huh."

"I know you love Eva, but I'm trying to save my niece's soul."

"What do you want me to do?"

"Talk to your daughter. Maybe Christ will give you the power to remove the curse from her and thus release Zoe's mind and heart. I want her to get married, to have children, and be happy."

"Well." Father Haralambos paused and nodded. "I will see what I can do. I can't promise that it will work but I will talk to them."

"Thank you, Father." Dion grinned and got up from the chair. He wiped his hand on his trousers, took Father Haralambos' hand, and kissed it. "You have no idea how much this has lifted the heavy weight off my heart."

"I'm sure," Father Haralambos replied as he escorted Dion to the front door and watched him leave.

Father Haralambos stood in the middle of the room and sighed heavily. "Now I wish the damaged roof was the only thing I needed to worry about."

CHAPTER 13

ZOE ENTERED THE bedroom to find Eva sitting on the edge of the bed. She was using her cane to try to maneuver her slippers onto her feet.

"They should invent a game like that." Zoe laughed when Eva got the right slipper on.

"I just invented it," Eva replied as she tried to get the left slipper on her foot. She missed. "You should have seen me earlier. I'm getting good at this."

"Evy." Zoe sat down on the bed and stilled the cane. "Look at me. Have you taken your pain medication?"

"Hey, I was nearly there."

"Yes, I know, but this is important."

"Yes, I have. I'm being good and listening to my doctor."

"And they say miracles never happen anymore," Zoe teased. "I need to speak to you about something."

"Alright." Eva sighed and put the cane across her lap. She faced Zoe and played with her red curls. "What's on your mind?"

"Your surname."

"Haralambos or Lambros?"

"Lambros."

"Yes. I haven't changed my mind—I'm changing it when we get back home."

"Why not change it here?"

Eva frowned. "Getting it changed here would be impossible. I would have to go to the British Consulate, fill out a million forms and then—" Zoe put her finger on Eva's lips. Eva smiled and kissed Zoe's finger.

"I have an easier way."

"You do?"

"Theo said no when Thomas asked him for my hand in marriage." Zoe closed Eva's lips with her fingers, and Eva tried to bite them. "Behave. I want you to listen."

"I'm lithening," Eva said with her lips half closed.

They laughed.

"It's good that you're lithening because there is much to lithen to." Zoe giggled. "Theo didn't want to give his consent because he thought I was leaving you for Thomas."

"Aw, what a sweet boy."

"Yes, he is. He agrees with you about children and being married."

"You know we are right, Zo."

"I finally convinced him that I'm marrying Thomas so you and I can be parents. Theo wanted to know what you were going to do with your name. I told him you were changing it even though it's going to be difficult."

"It shouldn't be this hard, but I think it's going to take longer to change my name this time."

"It would take months, but there is a way to do it quicker."

"Will Stella adopt me?" Eva chuckled.

"No. Theo will marry you."

Eva stopped smiling. "What?"

"Theo wants to marry you."

"No." Eva shook her head. "I'm not marrying your brother."

"Eva, I'm marrying Thomas."

"Yes, but that's for a good reason. We want to have children, love. The only way I'm going to be able to sleep at night is knowing that the government is not going to step in and take our babies away. Thomas is not going to want to have a relationship with you other than a sisterly one."

"You do worry too much."

"Do we really need to discuss this again?"

"No. Everyone agrees with you. Back to Theo."

"Your brother is a fine man, Zo, don't mistake me, but he is a heterosexual man."

"You've noticed?"

"I'm serious. I can't marry him."

"Why?"

"One day he will fall in love with another woman and he won't be able to marry her because he is already married."

"Ever heard of divorce?"

"Yes, of course, but—"

"Listen to me. Theo doesn't want to get married to any girl."

"Not now, but in the future."

"He can't," Zoe said quietly. "He doesn't want to. He can't have children, and to my brother that means he can't be a proper husband."

"That's just not right. Many men can't father children and they are in loving relationships with their wives."

"I understand that, but that's a Lambros for you. He wants to give you his name."

"He does?"

"Yes. I know you like Theo, and this is similar to what I'm doing with Thomas."

"Well, Theo is coming to Australia."

"Yes." Zoe grinned as Eva warmed up to the idea. "I think I need to send a telegram to Earl and ask him to rent those two houses at the end of our street that have been empty for a long time."

"Yes, that would be a good idea. Don't tell Earl why just yet."

"So what do you think? You become a Lambros by marriage. You don't need to have yet another appointment with another government agency or have to explain Hans Muller to them all over again."

"And I'd also be your sister-in-law." Eva giggled. "What a crazy life we have."

"So do you accept my brother's proposal?" Zoe tried to be serious but she got the giggles. "That sounds so funny."

"Yes, I'll marry Theo." Eva nodded. "We can have a double wedding."

There was a knock on the door. They turned as Tessa entered.

"I see you are up," Tessa said.

"She's taking her pain medication."

"Well, that's really good. Stella will be happy you are listening to her. She likes it when her patients do that."

"That's me, the obedient patient."

"Well, obedient patient, your presence and that of your loving spouse is requested at the family meeting."

"What's a family meeting?"

"You have never had a family gathering where everyone is present to discuss something important?" Zoe asked.

"Uh . . . no."

"Come on, you're in for a treat." Zoe knelt down to put on Eva's left slipper and then helped her up. They looked at each other for a moment then Zoe kissed her tenderly. "Welcome to the Lambros clan."

"WE ARE HAVING two weddings now?" Thomas made a face at Theo. "You just had to steal my day, didn't you?"

"I was jealous."

"Of course you were. Now we have to find matching outfits."

"Boys!" Stella sighed in exasperation. "Will you two please be quiet?"

Eva giggled. "Is this normal?" she whispered to Zoe.

"Yes. You should have seen all three of my brothers during family meetings. Papa let them have their silliness and then they settled down after he threatened them with doing the washing for the week. I'm not quite sure why that worked."

"It worked because we had to go down to the river and get in it to do the washing." Theo grinned. "It was cold."

"Your father had the patience of a saint," Stella said with a mock scowl. "Now. Wedding number one is Tommy and Zoe, and wedding number two is Theo and Eva. Do we wait until after you come back from Germany?"

"No." Eva shook her head. "We want to do it before we go to Germany."

"We do?" Zoe asked.

Eva turned to Zoe and nodded. "I want to do this before we go, love. I just feel it's important."

"We won't be making babies before we come back."

"I know but . . ."

"It's a little extra security?" Tessa touched Eva's hand. "Do you feel a little more secure knowing that Theo and Thomas will be with you?"

Eva looked down at the table and worried a splinter with her fingernail. "Having family around helps with what may happen."

"What do you think may happen?" Tessa asked.

"I want to confront my grandmother."

Zoe blinked in surprise. Tessa had a hint of a smile on her face.

"You want to confront your grandmother?" Zoe asked, not quite believing what she was asking.

"Yes. I have questions and she has the answers."

"Are you going to go to her?" Tessa was watching Eva carefully.

"No. She's going to come to me."

"Are you sure you want to do this?" Zoe asked, even more surprised.

"Yes. I'm sick and tired of feeling this way, Zo. I want to know the truth."

Zoe smiled. "Well, then we are going to see Frau Muller."

"Here I thought we were going to discuss what suit I'm going to wear for my wedding." Thomas put his arm around Eva's shoulders. "Frau Muller is far more interesting."

Silence descended at the table for a moment.

Theo tapped his hand on the wood. "Can I just say I want to wear blue for my wedding?"

Everyone chuckled.

Zoe put her hand under the table and grabbed Eva's hand. They looked at each other and Zoe mouthed "Proud of you."

"Sister Irene has arranged for us to stay with her and her brother Johan." Stella looked through a pile of papers. "In Dahlem."

"Dahlem?" Eva asked as she glanced at Tessa and then at Stella. "How does a nun afford a house in Dahlem?"

"What's wrong with Dahlem?" Zoe frowned at Eva's smile.

"It's a very expensive area."

"Well, it's handy," Stella quipped.

"Alright, now I'm missing something," Theo interrupted.

"Zehlendorf is where Eva grew up," Zoe explained. "I'm going to guess that Dahlem is right next door?"

"Yes."

"Well, that won't be too far for Frau Muller to travel," Stella said as she shuffled some more papers. "Sister Irene will like to meet you."

"I'm going too because I haven't seen Aunty Irene for a long time," Thomas said. Zoe looked at Eva and saw that she also noticed the "aunty" attached to Irene.

"This is going to be an interesting visit," Eva said.

"We go to Germany, we go to the cemetery, catch up with Sister Irene, and we wait to see if Frau Muller will show up."

"My grandmother will show up," Eva said definitively. "She went to the trouble to hire Mrs. Muldoon, she went to the trouble to spy on us. She will come."

"We need to stop now. We are going to have a guest," Tessa said softly, Everyone looked at her.

Tessa looked at Eva. "Your father is coming."

"At this time of night?" Eva glanced at the clock in the living room. "It must be important if Father is out at night."

CHAPTER 14

EVA OPENED THE door to reveal Father Haralambos, dressed in a black overcoat over his black cassock. The light glistened off the gold cross that dangled from his neck as he came into the living room. His anxious face transformed into a smile when he saw Eva, and then he noticed the cane.

"Eva. Were you hurt?" Father Haralambos asked, his attention focused on Eva. "The tree didn't hit you?"

"No, no, no. I slipped here at the house." Eva made a face. "Hit my head and my back. Not that I'm not happy to see you, but what brings you out this late at night? You know you shouldn't be out with your bad heart."

"Tree? What tree?" Zoe came up from behind Eva and stood on her toes to kiss Father Haralambos's cheek.

Father Haralambos put his arms around Zoe and kissed her. "Oh, thank God, you two are all right. I went to the cabin and saw the damage . . ."

"We decided to stay down here."

"It's a good thing you did. That old tree near the cabin decided the perfect time to come crashing down to earth was during the storm. Crashed right on top of the cabin."

Eva turned to Tessa, who had a neutral expression. She realized that talking about Tessa's abilities with Father Haralambos would not be a good idea.

"You mean the cabin has been flattened?" Eva asked.

"Unfortunately the tree went right through the bedroom," Father Haralambos said. "Poor Theo. Just when he had finished it as well."

"Wow." Zoe squeezed Eva's hand and they looked at each other for a moment. "It's a good thing we decided to stay here."

"Yes, a very good thing. Ah, Tessa." Father Haralambos Tessa hugged Tessa. He held her for a few minutes and then kissed her cheek. "So good to see you again."

"Panayiotis, how are you?" Tessa smiled.

Father Haralambos saw Thomas, who was standing just inside the door. His eyes widened. "Oh my, who is this young man?"

"This is Thomas, my son."

Father Haralambos's eyebrows rose as Thomas came forward.

"Good evening, Father," Thomas said, and kissed Father Haralambos's hand.

"Well, this is quite a surprise. I'm pleased to meet you, Thomas. I was not aware you had a son, Tessa."

"He was born after the fire," Tessa explained. "He looks like my father, doesn't he?"

"He looks very much like your father. Daphne, Eva, and Thomas all look like him."

Tessa put her hand on Father Haralambos's shoulder. "I nearly called him Dafnis."

Father Haralambos's eyes crinkled in delight. "Oh, Daphne would have hated it."

Tessa's gentle laugh made Eva sigh. It reminded her so much of her mother's laugh that if she could close her eyes, she would think her mother was right there in the room.

"So you named him Thomas. Much nicer." Father Haralambos turned to Stella, who was hovering nearby. "Dr. Lambros."

"Father Haralambos, welcome to our home." Stella took Father Haralambos's hand and kissed it.

Father Haralambos smiled. "Welcome to Larissa, Dr. Lambros. I missed you a few days ago when I dropped in."

Father Haralambos sat down on the sofa. Zoe sat at his left and Eva tried to get comfortable in the hardback chair. Stella and Tessa took a seat at the table, while Thomas stood nearby. Theo entered the room and also greeted Father Haralambos by kissing his hand.

"Would you like some coffee?" Zoe asked.

"Oh, no. That would keep me up all night. Just some water, please." Father Haralambos faced Eva. "The reason I was coming to see you is that I had a visit from Zoe's uncle."

"What did he want?" Zoe asked from the kitchen.

"He is concerned about you."

"Where was he during the war? How concerned was he then?" Zoe couldn't mask the bitterness and contempt she had for Dion. "Where was he, Father?"

"Well, we both know he wasn't here then, but he's here now."

"It's too late for that." Theo took the water from Zoe and offered it to Father Haralambos. "Why does he want to interfere in my sister's life now?"

"She's twenty-two and unmarried," Father Haralambos explained. "Your uncle Dion is concerned that you are not happy."

"Zoe is very happy," Eva replied with a smile.

"Do you have any complaints?" Zoe sat down and looked at Eva.

"Oh, no." Eva shook her head. "No complaints." She chuckled.

"What did my brother want? Was it just about Zoe?" Stella asked.

"No. Your brother believes you are under a terrible influence and he asked me to help. In addition he wants Zoe to find the right man."

"I think we solved one problem for you, Father," Thomas said.

Father Haralambos chuckled. "Zoe is getting married to a man?"

"Yes," Zoe answered.

Father Haralambos gave her a puzzled look.

"You see, your problem is solved," Zoe said.

"Pardon? I thought I heard you say you were getting married to a man."

"Isn't that the only wedding you recognize?" Stella asked. Tessa gave her a warning look. "Well, the Church does."

"I'm sorry, I'm getting old and my hearing is going. Did you say Zoe is getting married to a man?" Father Haralambos looked at Eva and then at Zoe.

"Yes, Zoe is getting married to a man."

"Oh, I see." Father Haralambos stroked his beard. "Well, yes, that would solve Dion's problem."

"I don't understand why it's his problem."

"He is the head—"

"No," Theo said. "I'm sorry, but he is not the head of the family. I am. Zoe is my sister. I am the head of the Lambros family from Larissa. Uncle Dion does not speak for me and I don't acknowledge his authority over my sister."

"I'm sorry, you are right."

"I know I am."

"Who is the groom? Who is this brave soul?"

Eva and Tessa laughed.

Eva gently tapped Zoe with the cane as they shared a smile. "He is a very brave man."

Zoe stuck her tongue out at her and Eva giggled.

"Yes." Theo pointed to Thomas. "Meet the groom."

"Ah." Father Haralambos nodded. "Well, that wouldn't be hard to guess. So are you . . ." He looked at Eva. "Did you two split up?"

Eva smiled. "No, we haven't."

"But why are you letting Zoe marry Thomas?"

"I never thought I would hear an Orthodox priest ask why a lesbian couple have split up and be upset by it," Tessa said, a note of warmth in her voice.

"The priest isn't asking—the father is."

Zoe giggled. "Father H, you are one of a kind." She kissed him on the cheek. "Please, tell me you didn't walk all the way here."

"No, no, no. Kiriakos brought me with his buggy after we got to the cabin and found it destroyed. Of course I was very concerned, but when we didn't find you there and then saw your suitcases were gone, I was not so worried."

"So you came here?"

"It was the only place you would be." Father Haralambos looked at Eva affectionately. "I didn't think you would be in town."

"Is Kiriakos outside?"

"No, I sent the young man home. I'm sure Theo can drive me back." Father Haralambos smiled at Theo. "Now tell me, what is this about Zoe getting married?"

Eva glanced at Zoe, who gave her a subtle nod. "Father, you're going to be a grandfather soon."

Father Haralambos stared at Eva for a long moment. "I thought you couldn't have children?"

"I still can't. Zoe will be the one giving birth."

"Zoe is pregnant?" Father Haralambos' voice rose as he stared at Thomas darkly. "What have you done, my son?"

Eva put her hand on Father Haralambos's arm and got his attention away from Thomas, who was looking quite uncomfortable. "Tommy didn't do anything. He hasn't touched Zoe."

"He didn't touch Zoe and yet she's pregnant? Do we have a miracle on our hands that I need to let the Bishop know about?"

Eva laughed. "No, Zoe is getting married to Thomas so she can have children."

"Ah!" Father Haralambos nodded. "I still don't understand why you are letting Zoe do this, but getting married and then having children is always the correct order in God's arrangement."

"I don't want her getting pregnant without being married."

Father Haralambos shook his head. "I still don't understand but that is all right. There are some things I really don't need to know."

"I'm getting married as well," Eva said.

His white bushy eyebrows shot up as he stared at her. "Why are you getting married?"

"It seems everyone is doing it, thought I might try it."

Everyone laughed.

"Theo asked me."

Father Haralambos turned to Theo and his features softened. "I see. I'm going to assume you asked the person in charge if you can marry my daughter?"

"Ah, no sir, I was going to come and see you . . ."

"Not me, my son. I'm talking about your sister." Father Haralambos chortled and slapped his thigh. "All kidding aside, what is the real reason you are marrying Eva?"

"I want to make Zoe happy," Theo honestly replied. "Eva would become a Lambros."

"Ah, no more Haralambos? Not that I should be proud of this, but I thought that name would be still alive once I have passed."

"I'll always be your daughter." Eva rested her head on Father Haralambos's shoulder. "With Zoe having children, we wanted everyone to have the same last name."

"Yes, that does make sense, although it's a very strange way of doing things."

"Will you marry us?" Eva smiled at the adoring look she was getting from her father.

"Hmm." Father Haralambos sighed deeply. "No, I can't do that."

"Why?"

"Theo is agnostic and you are a Catholic. The Church would want you to convert."

"I can't," Theo said. "I won't go back to the Church, not after what it's done." The tone in his voice made it quite apparent that he wasn't going to relent on that issue.

Zoe looked at Theo for a long moment. "Can you conduct the service, Father?"

"No, I'm not allowed. The Church and the State forbid me to marry anyone who isn't of the faith."

"That's rubbish. We're getting married. It's not like we are going to have a party in the church. What happens to all those people who don't want to convert?"

"They remain single in the eyes of the law."

"That's so unfair."

"Yes, it is." Father Haralambos squeezed Eva's hand.

"So how do we do it if we can't get married here?"

"In Germany," Tessa said quietly. "We will all go to Germany and we will have the weddings there."

"Do you want to come to Germany with us, Father?" Eva whispered. "I want you there."

"It would make me very happy to be at your wedding, but I can't. The damage from the storm on the church is quite extensive." Father Haralambos put his arm around her shoulders. "I know why you are doing this and I think you are doing the right thing."

"But?" Zoe said.

"There is no 'but.' I expect to be seeing you back in Larissa as soon as this trip to Germany is over."

"Well, we have a lot to do to get ready."

"Dr. Lambros . . ."

"Please, call me Stella."

"Stella, can I talk to you privately?"

"Of course. Let's go into the kitchen."

Father Haralambos kissed Eva on the cheek. "Are you coming to the wedding tomorrow?"

"Yes." Eva nodded.

"Zoe will need your strength," Father Haralambos whispered in her ear before he rose and followed Stella into the kitchen.

"What was that about?" Zoe asked.

"The wedding tomorrow."

"Ah. You're not coming, not with that back of yours."

"I am."

"No, you're not."

"Are we going to argue?"

"You went for a stroll and you needed a nap. I don't think a wedding is that important for you to attend."

"It's final. I'm going. My back is feeling much better."

"Hmm." Zoe looked around the room. Theo and Thomas were talking and Tessa had joined Stella in the kitchen. Zoe picked up a cushion from the sofa and dropped it to the floor. "Pick that up for me."

Eva looked at the pillow and then slowly raised her eyes to Zoe. She stood and smiled grimly as she flicked the pillow to the side with the cane.

"Yes, your back is much better." Zoe shook her head and picked up the pillow.

"I didn't say I could bend over." Eva smiled and put her arm around Zoe's shoulders. "I'm not going to miss this wedding, love. You need me there and I'm going to be there."

Zoe looked into Eva's sky blue eyes. "Have I told you how much I love you?"

"Do you still love me even if you are getting married to my cousin?" Eva laughed.

Zoe brought the footstool to Eva and stood on it.

"What are you doing?"

Theo and Thomas stopped talking and looked at them.

"This is the only way I'm going to kiss you when you are standing up, Miss Lambros." Zoe looked at Theo and Thomas and shrugged before turning back to Eva, who was gazing up at her. She cupped Eva's face and tenderly kissed her on the lips.

CHAPTER 15

STELLA CLOSED THE door from the kitchen to the living room and turned round to find Father Haralambos and Tessa embracing. She watched them affectionately.

"Hello, Tee," Father Haralambos said as he cupped Tessa's face. "It's been a long time."

"Too long, Pani," Tessa replied, and kissed him tenderly on the cheek. "Look at you —you got old and priestly."

Father Haralambos chuckled. "Unlike you, I can't color my hair or beard. Do you like the priestly look?"

"I do not color my hair . . . yet." Tessa ruffled Father Haralambos' beard. "It suits you, my friend, it suits you." She took Father Haralambos' hand and sat down at the kitchen table.

"What happened to your knee? Eva's sore back and your knee—is it some sort of secret Mitsos bonding ritual?"

Stella chuckled as she brought a chair from across the room and sat next to Tessa. "She was riding a horse."

"Oh, no, Tee, you can't ride. What were you doing on the horse?"

"The problem is not her riding, but her dismounting. She slipped in some horse manure."

Father Haralambos burst out laughing. "That reminds me of when you were chasing that goat."

"Stop." Tessa put her hand over Father Haralambos's mouth. "Don't you dare. I thought priests were supposed to be all secretive and not reveal anything."

"Oh, no, I want to hear this," Stella said.

"I wasn't a priest then, but a simple shepherd boy. However, because I love you, I won't tell Stella that you chased that goat around the farm as he was chewing your panties."

"Panayiotis Haralambos!" Tessa playfully slapped him on the shoulder.

"I can honestly tell you I have never laughed so hard in all my life. The goat lived, which is always a good thing." Father Haralambos chortled. "Ah, the good days."

"Were they good days?"

"Yes." Father Haralambos nodded. "They were the good days. All I had to worry about was chasing goats to get back the panties of my future sister-in-law."

"You have a very selective memory." Tessa patted his hand.

"It's the only way I can deal with what came next."

"Yet here we are, back in Larissa and reminiscing about goats and panties."

Father Haralambos sighed heavily. "Ah, for those days. A lot has happened since then."

"You should have been allowed to marry Daphne."

"Yes, but I wasn't and that German fellow was. He gave them everything I couldn't."

"He also tortured your baby girl," Stella quietly added, trying to take the sting out of her words. She mentally slapped herself at his furrowed brow.

"Yes, he did." Father Haralambos stroked his beard.

"There are more things in heaven and earth, dear Pani," Tessa said gently.

Father Haralambos smiled. "There you go quoting some dead writer again. There are things we have no control over and this is one of them. The other was your premonitions."

"What premonitions?" Stella asked as she glanced at Tessa, who didn't appear to be all that disturbed by Father Haralambos's words.

"It's alright, angel, Pani was the only one who truly believed, even when I didn't."

"You did?"

"I did. There was nothing an exorcism or treatment at a lunatic asylum could cure."

"What made you believe when the others did not?" Stella regarded Father Haralambos with interest.

Father Haralambos looked down at the cup of tea on the table. "Daphne and I were looking for something that would account for the demon possession, something that would seem out of place. We knew that if it was demon related, we would find the source of Tessa's visions. Then I found something that I didn't tell Daphne or anyone else about."

"You found my artwork."

"Yes. It was of me and Daphne kissing."

Tessa grinned. "I did like that one."

"Yes, so did I when I saw it. I was about to call out to Daphne that her little sister was spying on us when I noticed the date."

"What was the date?" Stella glanced at Tessa and smiled.

"Two years before I plucked up the courage to talk to Daphne. Right next to Tessa's initials was the date."

"You believed me because of that?"

"Not just that." Father Haralambos shook his head. "I had a great aunt who they all said was crazy. I believed everyone until I went to see her. That woman was the sanest person I had ever met."

"What was her gift?"

"She looked at me and I thought she was looking straight into my soul," Father Haralambos replied quietly. "I remember her words so clearly. She looked at me and said, 'Panayiotis, son of Constantinos Haralambos, you are a man of God. Believe in the unknown; believe there are things it's impossible to believe are true. You will know great joy and you will know a pain so deep that nothing will remove it. You will meet your one true love and her name is Eva, but she will not be yours for long. You will be forever connected and the bond will never sever.'"

Tessa's eyes widened. "When was this?"

"I was doing my army training and I was about to be discharged. The lunatic asylum was near Thessaloniki so I went to pay her a visit."

"She said Eva, not Daphne?"

Tessa and Father Haralambos looked at each other and smiled. "Daphne's first name was Eva, but because our mother was named Eva, everyone called her by her second name."

"Daphne."

"Yes." Tessa nodded. "Daphne liked the name Eva, but it got confusing with mother and daughter having the same name. It's a Mitsos tradition. Our mother was named Eva Maria, and her mother was called Eva Theodora."

"That is just confusing." Stella chuckled. "Most Greeks don't have two names."

"For some reason we had that tradition. Daphne called her daughter Eva Theresa." Tessa smiled. "So the tradition continues."

"So what happened after you saw your aunt?"

"I found a job as a shepherd in Larissa about six months after I saw my great aunt at the asylum," Father Haralambos said.

"Did you know Daphne's name was Eva?" Stella leaned forward, intrigued by his story.

"No. She introduced herself as Daphne and it was only after we started to court in secret that she told me her first name."

"What did you do?"

"I did nothing. I didn't believe my great aunt could tell the future or know about Daphne so I chose to ignore her words. I was called to the lunatic asylum because she was dying and I went to see her. I was too late and she had passed away before I got there." Father Haralambos sighed and took a letter from his pocket. "I was given this letter as part of the little she had left. I have kept it all these years because I believe that there are things I can't explain. I don't believe my great aunt was demonized. I do believe God has given faithful women of the past the ability to be prophetesses."

"What does the letter say?"

Father Haralambos unfolded the creased old letter and put his glasses on. "'My dearest great nephew, this letter is for you, and you are reading this because I am no longer of this world. Forgive me for being so melodramatic, but being here in a lunatic asylum, melodrama is the only thing I have left.'"

"She also had a sense of humor," Stella said.

"She was right," Tessa said softly.

Father Haralambos looked over the top of his glasses at Tessa with a sad smile before he dropped his gaze back to the letter. "'I did not reveal the whole truth to you, Panayiotis Constantinos. Your love is Eva but her initials are EDM. You will have already learnt this by now. Follow your heart, great nephew. You will know of great joy and great pain. Become the man that you are, become the spiritual man that you want to be. It is not with sadness that I leave you this letter, but with joy, for I will be seeing my loved ones in heaven. Be well, be brave and remember that your little one will have your strength.'"

"Wow," Tessa whispered.

"I read that letter a few weeks before I found your artwork. I told Daphne and I showed it to her."

"So Daphne believed?"

"She said she knew there was nothing wrong with you, but you and your parents were convinced there was."

Tessa turned to Stella. "Pani came to see me in Athens."

"I was studying at the Theological Seminary and it was near Saint Gregori," Father Haralambos said.

"Do you remember the big German man who was the porter?"

"Yes, he was an imposing fellow and I felt like I was a little boy when I stood next to him."

"That was Thomas's father," Tessa said. "He died in the fire."

"You are a very unusual priest," Stella said, softening her words not to be rude to Tessa's friend.

"I am." Father Haralambos nodded.

"Aren't you conflicted by what you see before you, what you know to be the truth, and the fact that the Church teaches you that all of this," Stella pointed at Tessa, "is demonic in some way?"

"Stella!" Tessa said.

"No, Tessa, Stella is correct." Father Haralambos put his hand up to stop Tessa's objections. "It is a conflict, but not for me. I choose to believe that God has chosen certain people to have the ability to foresee the future. The Apostles and other Saints did have that ability. I don't understand it. I don't know how it works but I also don't know a lot of other things in this life. I am a simple shepherd boy. I don't know why my daughter loves a woman, but she does. Do you know what faith is?"

Stella nodded. "It's believing in something you can't see."

"The Bible says, 'Now faith is being sure of what we hope for and certain of what we do not see.' I have faith in God even though I cannot see Him. I choose to believe in things that I cannot see and yet believe they are real. I believe my great aunt and Tee have the gift of prophecy."

"You are a very enlightened soul that belongs to a Church that is in darkness," Stella said.

"I am a man who has faith, Stella. I don't need to understand why things are the way they are."

"You are extraordinary," Stella exclaimed. "I have never met a priest like you."

"I do not think there are many priests who have a lesbian daughter, a former almost sister-in-law who has the gift of prophecy or a great aunt who was a prophetess. It is a little out of the ordinary." Father Haralambos chuckled.

"I know what you did for her during the war."

"I did what any sane person would have done, and that is help a wounded soul."

"You knew she was your daughter, right?" Tessa asked.

"I knew the minute I saw her in that field," Father Haralambos replied. "The way she stood. Everything about her was Daphne. The first time I heard her speak, I nearly called her Daphne."

"Tessa was having the same problem."

"It is hard for the both of us to see her, and yet it is not her," Father Haralambos explained. "It is also hard for your brother, Stella, to see you and know that you are not what he wants you to be."

"It's not up to him what I am. My husband, Timothy, and my brother Nicholas were best friends and he introduced me to Timothy. When he was killed at Skra, I fell apart. It was over. Everything just didn't matter anymore." Stella took Tessa's hand.

"How did he die?"

Stella took a deep breath and exhaled slowly. "He was shot saving my brother Nicki's life."

"'Greater love has no one than this, that he lay down his life for his friends,'" Father Haralambos quoted.

"Yes." Stella nodded. "I was angry with the world, and angry with

Nicholas for living, but my brother showed me so much kindness and love. He was the one who urged me to fulfill Timothy's dream of caring for the mental health of soldiers. They needed help in dealing with the death that was around them. It is why I went to Athens to finish my studies and it is how I ended up going to Saint Gregori Lunatic Asylum."

"That's where she fell for my charms," Tessa gently teased as she squeezed Stella's hand.

"Dion doesn't understand what Tessa means to me. She brought me happiness and joy. He thinks grief has turned me into a deviant."

Father Haralambos nodded. "Yes, he did mention that when he came to see me."

"I don't know what to do to change his mind nor do I want to waste my time in trying."

"I will tell him that I came, that I counseled you, and that he doesn't need to worry about Zoe, since she's getting married." Father Haralambos shook his head. "Zoe getting married." He chuckled.

"Are you sure you can't perform the ceremony?" Tessa touched Father Haralambos' arm. "Are you certain?"

"Yes, Tee, I am."

"What a shame. Is there any chance you may be able to travel to Germany with us?"

"Unfortunately, I can't. As I said to the girls, I would love to travel with you but the church has suffered extensive damage in the storm, and I want to stay and oversee the repairs."

"The church was damaged so much?"

"Yes, the ceiling collapsed over the altar and there is other damage to the building. It wouldn't be right for me to leave. I would have loved to have caught up with my old friend, Father Faber—he lives in Berlin."

Stella looked at Tessa in surprise. She turned back to Father Haralambos. "Is that Father Johan Faber from Berlin?"

"Yes, do you know him? I met him in Athens when I was at the seminary. Of course he's Catholic, but I bumped into him at St Gregori when I went to see Tee."

Tessa's smile grew. "There are more things in heaven and earth, dear Pani."

"Pardon?"

"Father Faber has a fleshly sister."

"Yes, I believe he does. She's also in God's service."

"Father Faber's sister is Sister Irene," Tessa quietly said. "She was the one who convinced me I wasn't crazy."

"She believed you?"

"Yes. She also convinced Stella that I wasn't crazy or possessed."

"Well, goodness me." Father Haralambos gently laughed. "It is such a small world."

Tessa touched Father Haralambos' hand. "Sister Irene was also the one who helped save Eva's life."

Father Haralambos's eyes widened. "It was no coincidence that Johan and I met that day at the Asylum."

"I don't know. It may have been. There is something else you need to know. Sister Irene and Father Johan are Eva's great aunt and uncle," Tessa said.

"God works in mysterious ways and there is a plan. I don't know what it is but He knows. There is no other way to explain it." Father Haralambos shook his head in wonder. "There are indeed more things in heaven and earth."

CHAPTER 16

EVA LEANED ONE-HANDED against the wicker chair, using it as a brace, and put on one stocking over her foot with her other hand. She smiled.

"This isn't so hard," she mumbled.

Her stocking snagged against the chair. She sighed. She heard the door open and didn't need to turn around to know Zoe was standing just inside the doorway looking at her.

"Go on, you can say it."

"You have a great ass."

Eva chuckled.

Zoe came around the chair and looked up at Eva. "When did I get fired from being your dresser?"

"I can do this myself."

"Yes, I can see." Zoe held up two torn stockings. "It's been quite a success, although your range of movement has improved. You can bend a little."

"Yes, but not enough to put on my stockings without snagging them."

"Sit," Zoe said.

Eva put both hands on the wicker chair and lowered herself down.

"This is the part I like," Zoe said as she rolled the stocking up the long leg and snapped the garter into place. "I really like the sound that makes."

"You also like taking it off."

"Yes, that too." Zoe rolled the other stocking up and did the same to the garter. "Right, I think you are ready. What do you think of what I'm wearing?"

Eva nodded her approval at Zoe's emerald green satin dress with black Chantilly lace. It brought out her eyes. Zoe's chestnut-colored hair cascaded over her shoulders in long rivulets. She wore a tilted emerald green hat and her gold cross around her neck.

"Green is my favorite color and I love that dress on you." Eva crooked her finger and beckoned Zoe to her.

Zoe put her hands on each side of the wicker chair and smiled before she tenderly kissed Eva on the lips. She helped her out the chair.

"Blue is my favorite color," Zoe said as Eva looked at herself in the long mirror.

Eva was wearing a navy blue dress with a beaded and rhinestone collar. Her hair was up, which accentuated her long neck, and she wore a dark blue hat with a feather on the side. She also wore her gold cross around her neck.

"I think we are ready," Zoe said.

"Not quite, love. Hand me my cloak."

"It is warm out there. You sure you want to wear that?"

"Yes."

Zoe sighed and went around the bed, picked up the cloak, and handed it to Eva, who quickly put it on. Zoe looked at Eva for a long moment and then turned away.

"Now we are ready," Eva said with a smile. She grabbed her cane, which was leaning against the dresser. She took Zoe's hand and they left the bedroom.

"My, don't we all look nice. I think we're going to a wedding," Stella said as she walked out of the bedroom and into the kitchen. She was wearing a bright pink dress with a bright yellow hat that made Eva's eyes hurt.

"Ooh, I like what you are wearing," Tessa said to Eva and gently poked her. Tessa's outfit was a little more subdued than Stella's—black lace, a hot pink drop waist and long lace sleeves.

Thomas and Theo, dressed in their Sunday best suits, were sitting on the sofa. They looked uncomfortable but presentable.

"Alright, are we set?" Stella clapped her hands and led the way through the door.

"I know you're nervous." Eva looked at Zoe with a gentle smile as they went outside. "How are you?"

"Good. You?"

"Almost as good as you," Eva replied with a lopsided grin. "I'm invited to the wedding of the Resistance Leader during the War, in a town where I was part of the occupying force."

"You weren't the occupying force."

"No, just the Butcher's daughter. More importantly, I'm worried about you."

"I went past the field the first day, Evy. I'm fine."

"You would tell me if you weren't, right?"

"Of course. Now can we get to the car? Because Theo is giving us his hurry-up-we-haven't-got-all-year look."

"Ah, yes, the famous Lambros patience."

"It's a gift." Zoe giggled as she helped Eva into the car.

FATHER HARALAMBOS SMILED at Thanasi and Althea before him. He led them around a small table three times to signify their oath to preserve their marriage bond forever. "May you love each other, take care of each other, and have God in your lives," Father Haralambos said.

He lifted the white crowns that signified that the newlyweds would receive the grace of the Holy Spirit and would be the founders of a new generation that would live their lives to the glory of God off their heads and gave them a smile.

"I now pronounce you man and wife." Father Haralambos's deep voice boomed.

The assembled wedding guests broke out in a cheer as Thanasi kissed his new bride. He looked very handsome in his black suit. Althea wore a beautiful wedding gown of ivory white and looked radiant as she gazed up at him.

Eva had enjoyed her first Greek Orthodox wedding, and was quite intrigued by the white crowns that had been placed on the groom and the bride. They reminded her of the laurel wreaths that the athletes from the ancient Olympic Games wore after they won. She looked around the congregation and sighed when she saw a familiar face coming towards her.

"Eva!" Mrs. Kalmias said.

Eva smiled at the petite elderly lady. "Hello again, Mrs. Kalmias."

"Goodness me, what happened to you?" Mrs. Kalmias asked on seeing Eva's cane.

"I slipped and hurt my back."

"Hmm, tall girls like you . . . That would cause quite some damage."

"It did, to the floor." Eva smiled. Mrs. Kalmias looked puzzled for a moment then burst out laughing. "I'm already on the mend."

"That's good." Mrs. Kalmias reached into her bag. "At the train station I promised to give you this photo."

Eva took the photograph and a smiled at her mother's face. A young Daphne Mitsos was standing next to another teenage girl, their arms around each other.

Zoe leaned into Eva for a look at the photograph. "Wow. You look so much like your mama, even the dimpled chin. No wonder Father H recognized you. If I didn't know better I would have said this was you."

"I lost the photo of her and I didn't have any other." Eva smiled at Tessa, who put her arm around her and looked at the photo.

Eva looked at Mrs. Kalmias, who was giving Tessa a very perplexed look.

Mrs. Kalmias's eyes widened and she tapped Tessa with her cane. "Young Tessa Mitsos. Goodness me."

"Hello, Yiayia Kalmias." Tessa smiled.

"My sweet Lord Jesus. Tessa. You're alive," Mrs. Kalmias exclaimed as she tugged on Tessa's dress. "What happened to your knee?"

"I fell down," Tessa admitted.

Mrs. Kalmias laughed. "Was it the cow again?"

Tessa smirked and shook her head. "No, a horse."

Mrs. Kalmias chuckled. "Well, you take care of that knee. Are those terrible visions all gone now?"

"Yes Yiayia, they are all gone. I'm much better."

"Oh, I'm so glad. We were all so worried about you. I told your mama that someone had given you the evil eye. I knew it—such terrible people. Your mama said you had died in a fire."

"It was the wrong person, Yiayia, I'm sure Mama must have told you."

"Probably, but my memory is like an old rusty bucket with holes." Mrs. Kalmias chuckled. "Come by the house and we can talk. I've got to greet the new couple." She turned and walked to the bride and groom.

"She is a character," Eva stated, watching Mrs. Kalmias greet Thanasi with the same tugging motion, until he went down on his haunches to speak to her.

"Zoe!"

"Oh God, please take me now." Zoe groaned.

Eva suppressed a giggle as Zoe's cousin, Maria, bounded towards them. She couldn't quite believe that the two were related. Whilst Zoe was redheaded and green eyed, Maria's hair was dark blonde, and had hazel-colored eyes.

"Zoika!" Maria grabbed Zoe into a hug. Zoe made a face at Eva over Maria's shoulder. "I thought you had died."

"No, I'm very much alive," Zoe said.

"Yes, I can see that. Weren't you at the cabin?"

"No, we went to the farm and stayed with Aunty Stella."

"Crazy Aunty Stella? Really?" Maria noticed Tessa. "Who are you?"

"I'm Eva's Aunt Theresa," Tessa said.

"Oh. You're Greek."

"Yes." Tessa nodded. "So is Eva."

"I don't understand. Her aunty is Greek, but she's German."

"Maria, she's standing right next to you," Zoe pointed out.

Eva turned around, unable to suppress her grin. She had to compose herself before she faced Maria. Zoe was glaring at her cousin.

"Can she speak Greek?" Maria whispered.

"She speaks Greek, German, Italian and English," Zoe explained, trying not to burst out laughing.

Maria looked at Eva, who smiled at her. "Hello."

"Hello, Marika." Eva lowered her voice a decibel, exaggerating her German accent. She stood to her full height and looked down at the woman who was much shorter than Zoe. "I think I need to have a bit of a walk," Eva said in German to Zoe.

"My name is not Marika," Maria replied slowly, enunciating every word. "It's Maria."

"Ja, Marika." Eva patted her on the head and walked away.

"SHE DOES KNOW my name is not Marika, right?"

Zoe wasn't sure whom to look at—Eva, who was walking away, or her irritating cousin. "What?"

"Your friend, who just called me Marika. Aren't you paying attention? Speaking of your friend, why did you leave Larissa with *her?* Wasn't she the enemy?"

"What were you doing during the War?"

"You know what I was doing, silly. I was in America."

"Safe and sound." Zoe tried to keep the bitter tone out of her voice. "Eva was here, helping the Resistance while you were playing with your dolls and having play tea parties."

"We can talk about that later. Papa says that there are some really nice boys here that would be perfect for you. Do you remember Kiriakos? Well, he is here and Papa was saying that he—"

Zoe put her hand over Maria's mouth. "Stop talking."

"Why?"

"I'm already engaged," Zoe replied.

"You are? To who?"

Zoe turned Maria around. "Do you see that tall, dark, very handsome . . . man over there?" Zoe said as her eyes were glued to Eva, who was leaning on her cane talking to Thomas.

"Wow. Who is that?"

"Thomas Lambros."

"Huh? You're going to marry our cousin? Do we have a cousin that gorgeous?"

Zoe sighed. "No, he's not our cousin."

"But he is a Lambros."

"Yes. Steigler-Lambros." Zoe decided to embellish just a little since she didn't want to tell Maria the whole story.

"What a funny name. Is that German?"

"Yes, he's half German."

"When are you getting married?"

"Next week in Germany."

"Why there? Why not here?"

"He's a Catholic and he doesn't want to convert." Zoe feigned exasperation with the decision, and Maria looked at her sympathetically.

Thomas put his arm around Eva. "Are they related? They look like brother and sister."

"No, they're cousins."

"Does he have any brothers?"

"No. Just one of him."

"What a shame. I'll let Papa know of your upcoming wedding. I'm sure he will want to give you away."

"Oh, how kind." Zoe forced herself to smile at Maria. "My brother Theo is giving me away."

"Oh, that's right, he didn't die. We have to get together and talk about wedding dresses, but now I have to go and see my boy. Did I tell you I'm also getting married? You should meet him. He is such a gorgeous boy." Maria gave Zoe a kiss on the cheek and bounded away, leaving Zoe opened mouthed.

"Oh, dear god, thank goodness that is over," Zoe muttered.

A light misty rain began to fall. Zoe stepped under one of the large awning that covered a large part of the plaza for the wedding.

Zoe looked around at the guests who were chatting amicably and smiled. Familiar faces smiled back at her and waved when they caught her eye. She walked a little down the cobblestone street and stopped dead. She swallowed when she saw Eva on the edge of the plaza leaning on her cane. Eva was looking out at the field with a faraway expression on her face, which was half covered by the cloak's hood.

A firecracker exploded above Zoe, and it made her heart race. Her knees wobbled at the sound, the rain, and Eva's dark cloak. She needed to sit down or she would collapse.

She was transported back in time to that horrendous day. Like this day, it was raining. The heavy pelting rain and the sound of German soldiers sloshing through the mud would stay with her forever.

Her gaze fell on the field and she could see the new commander in that gray-and-black uniform she despised so much, the crowds parting for him.

Another firecracker went off and Zoe jumped. Another gunshot, another death. Major Hans Muller striding through the villagers brandishing his gun, stamping his authority of the terrified villagers.

Eva stood in an almost identical stance to the first time Zoe had seen her in the field. Eva leaned on the cane. Zoe gasped. This time no guard held an umbrella for her as in 1942.

Zoe stared at the angular face she knew so well. On that fateful day the gloom made it difficult to see, and Eva's face had been barely visible under the hood of her cloak. The memory of that one gunshot made Zoe shudder.

> *The major had stepped in front of Zoe and her mother and looked at them. Helena put her arms around Zoe and held on tight. All Zoe could feel was the sound of the beating of her heart and the look of utter hatred in the man's eyes. She could see the tall woman's gaze turn towards her. Sky blue eyes met her stare for a long moment. Ice. Cold. The woman turned away and stared off into the distance, devoid of any emotion.*
>
> *Zoe wanted to hide her face from this madness. She held tight to her mother and closed her eyes, hoping against hope. But will alone could not stifle the sound of the gun popping so close that she felt the bullet pass when it exploded.*
>
> *Zoe felt her mother's arms release their grasp and she opened her eyes to see her mama slump to the ground. A dark crimson stain spread across her chest. The madness continued around her as she held her dying mother to her chest, the blood mixing with the mud, caking her legs. Oh, dear God, Mama!*
>
> *Zoe was oblivious to everyone but her mother, but in that instant between life and death, her purpose in life was crystallized. She looked down at her mother's face and rocked her back and forth.*
>
> *"I promise I will kill them, I will," she said, over and over.*
>
> *Nothing else had meaning any more. She was going to exact her revenge for her mother's death and kill the woman that laughed as her mother lay dying.*
>
> *"I promise you, Mama, I will kill them. I promise," Zoe kept repeating as her mother passed away.*

Zoe took a shuddering breath and felt a presence. She glanced back to find Tessa, who put a protective arm around her waist.

"I want you to turn around and walk with me," Tessa said.

"I can't." Zoe's voice wavered.

"Yes, you can, sweetheart." Tessa took Zoe's hand and led her away from the crowd and into a small alley away from the noise. She used her cane to pull two overturned boxes to her. She gently pushed Zoe down onto one of the boxes.

"Look at me."

Zoe opened her eyes and gazed into Tessa's light gray eyes.

"I want you to breathe, that's all you have to do," Tessa said.

"I have to go to Eva." Zoe's voice broke as she bent over, covered her face with her hands, and sobbed.

Tessa took her in her arms and let her cry against her chest. "It's all right, Zoe, let it out, it's all right." She gently rubbed her back.

Zoe's sobs diminished to sniffles and the occasional body-shaking hiccup.

Tessa brushed away Zoe's tears and looked into her eyes with concern. "You were due for a good cry."

"I'm sorry."

"Nothing to be sorry about."

"It's just . . ."

"I know," Tessa said quietly. "You were back to when your mama was killed."

"How did you know?" Zoe looked up at Tessa and sniffed back the tears that threatened to spill again.

"I saw it," Tessa replied. "I saw you and I saw your mother."

"I couldn't do anything to save her. Nothing."

"Did you think you could do something to stop what happened?"

Zoe took a deep breath and exhaled slowly. "Muller told us to keep our eyes on the ground. That's what he was yelling. Keep your eyes on the ground."

"You didn't?"

Zoe shook her head. "No. I was too inquisitive, too stupid. I looked up."

"At Eva."

"Yes. I couldn't take my eyes off her. I wanted to know who she was, why she was there. She was so ice cold that day." Zoe held onto Tessa's hand and took a deep sigh. "I thought she was indifferent to the suffering before her. She was made of stone. Her eyes were just dead. I looked into her eyes and I just couldn't see compassion or horror. Nothing."

"You looked at Eva. Do you think that's why Muller shot your mother?"

"Yes."

Tessa pulled Zoe to her and kissed her tenderly. "No, that isn't what happened."

"Yes, it is, Tessa, it is."

"No, sweetheart, it's not. There was no rhyme or reason for Muller's butchery. He didn't choose your mama because you looked up. He didn't care."

"But I looked up . . ."

"Yes, you did, and so did everyone else. Others were running for their lives. Some were shot, others were not. It was random acts of senseless violence. Did Eva look at anyone else?"

"Yes."

"Did they get shot?" Tessa asked gently. "Who did she look at?"

"She looked towards Mrs. Kalmias. Muller had just shot Alexandra. Eva wasn't really looking at Alexandra, but at the blood-stained dirt instead."

"You had nothing to do with your mama's death. You didn't cause it by looking up when you were told not to. You didn't cause it by staring at Muller's daughter."

"Why then? Why did my mama have to die?"

"The Bible says that 'time and unforeseen circumstances befall us all.' It was just that."

"You saw it. You saw it years in advance. Doesn't that mean it was destined?"

"I don't know. Sometimes I see things that don't work out the way I envisioned them. We all have free will, Zoe. We change our destiny. How do we do that? I don't know."

"Does that mean if we had been there minutes before or minutes after we could have changed history?"

"Yes, possibly, maybe. I don't know. Death is senseless. You had no control over it. You can't control what others do. How were you going to control what Muller was going to do?"

"I couldn't. I should have killed that bastard when he came looking for Eva."

"You didn't."

"No, but I should have. I should have smashed his head like a pumpkin with that fireplace poker instead of giving it to Eva."

"What would that have achieved?"

"Justice."

"Isn't he dead now? Hasn't justice been served?" Tessa asked as she took Zoe's hand. "It was not your job to mete out justice."

"Vengeance."

Tessa shook her head. "No, sweetheart, that's not your role. God says 'Vengeance is mine; I will repay.' Your mama has been avenged. All those poor unfortunate souls who perished have been avenged or will be when their murderers are all caught. You cannot kill another human being without a part of you dying."

"That's not true." Zoe shook her head. "I didn't feel anything other than relief when I shot Reinhardt."

"You didn't have any nightmares over that, did you?" Tessa looked into Zoe's eyes. "Not one night's sleep did you miss because you couldn't get his image out of your mind?"

Zoe averted her eyes but Tessa gently tipped her head up and met her gaze. "You died a little. You did it to save Eva but a little part of you died."

"She was worth it. I would do it all over again. I have no regrets over that."

"I didn't say you had regrets. As a loving human being you still had nightmares over killing that man. Butchers like Muller did not have nightmares. They were devoid of what makes us human—empathy."

"You should have seen Eva . . . She was just so—"

"She was dead inside. What you saw was Eva just existing—a shell. She didn't know how to deal with so much death. She didn't know how to deal with her own broken soul. That's why she looked cold and indifferent to you."

"How do you come back from that? I don't know, but she did."

"She found a way to guard her heart and you saw it that day," Tessa explained. "What was she wearing that day?"

"What was Eva wearing?"

"Yes. You have a photographic memory. You know exactly what everyone was doing and what they were wearing. You looked at her."

Zoe stared at Tessa's, astonished at her empathic ability. "Yes."

"It's that cloak that keeps reminding you, every time Eva wears it."

"Yes."

"Have you told her?" Tessa gazed at Zoe. She brushed the hair from Zoe's eyes. "Have you told her how much it hurts you?"

"No."

"Why not?"

"She feels secure wearing it, like some sort of protection. She wears it at home as well."

"She doesn't know what it's doing to you. She doesn't know that when she wears it, the most devastating moment in your life is being replayed."

Zoe shook her head. "I don't want to tell her."

"Why? Do you think she won't understand? Eva loves you so much."

"I know she does but she's got enough to deal with without me adding to it."

"That, sweetheart, is not giving Eva a chance to prove to you how much she loves you. You are not adding to her pain. You are giving her the ability to remove something from that horrible memory. She has the ability to change this and you are denying her that chance."

"Every time I see her in that cloak, I see her face on that day. She looked so heartless in that thing. A soldier held an umbrella over her and the look in her eyes . . ."

"You remember that so clearly, don't you?"

"Yes. I was so scared of what was to come, but my attention gravitated to her. I kept wondering why they would have brought this woman there. She wasn't in uniform, wasn't SS, or Gestapo. She wasn't anything but a woman in the rain. Her eyes were so cold."

"You have to tell her. You can't continue to hide this from her."

"I don't want to hurt her."

"You are hurting yourself as well as her. Do you think she doesn't think about that day almost as much as you do? Have you spoken about that day?"

"No, not really."

"I think it's time."

Zoe went to stand up but Tessa grasped her arm. "I want to go to her."

"No, she will come here."

"But—"

Tessa closed her eyes for a moment, then looked at Zoe with a heart-warming smile. "Eva will come here soon."

CHAPTER 17

EVA LOOKED OUT at the once blood-soaked field and shivered at the very clear memory that surfaced in her mind. She closed her eyes and swallowed as she recalled the memories of the villagers, all huddled together in the rain.

She could still hear the awful sloshing noise her boots made as she traipsed through the mud as she followed her stepfather through the field. She tried not to look at the villager's faces. She couldn't cope with knowing they were soon to die and reappear in her nightmares. She kept her eyes down.

She was wet and cold. The rain sleeted sideways and hit her in the face. She shivered uncontrollably. Henry, her most trusted guard, had an umbrella over her but it was useless.

Eva closed her eyes and the happy sound of the wedding guests faded into the background.

Eva swallowed and closed her eyes as Muller screamed orders. He was enjoying the terror he was inflicting; she could hear it in his voice.

Eva opened her eyes and focused on the first villager that stared back at her. Green eyes met her blue ones. Defiance stared back at her, daring her to do something, but she held back. She tried to not to look at the green-eyed girl. Tried to look away but she couldn't. The young girl's hatred was palpable. They both jumped when a shot rang out and the woman beside the green eyed girl slumped to the ground.

Eva looked away, unable to watch the heart-rending scene before her. She gazed out into the horizon and watched the rain come pelting down—anything but the ugliness before her.

A firecracker went off nearby, causing Eva to gasp in shock. She put her hand on her heart and wasn't surprised to find it beating so fast she could actually hear it. She looked at her shaking hands. She drove her cane into the ground to steady herself.

"Breathe." Stella came up behind Eva and put her arm around her waist. "Breathe in, breathe out."

Eva swallowed and took a deep, shuddering breath. Her head dropped to her chest as she tried to calm her racing heart.

"That's it, just breathe." Stella's voice was soothing. "Let's get out of the rain." She took Eva's hand and led her to a vacant taverna table, away from the crowds that were milling about.

Stella poured some water from the water decanter that was at the table. Eva took the glass in both hands and lifted the shaking glass to her lips.

"I fall apart every time you see me," Eva said with a slight tremor in her voice.

"Not every time." Stella tenderly cupped Eva's cheek. "You have been through a lot of trauma. I would expect you to have memory triggers. That's what we doctors call shell shock."

"I hate this, Stella. Please, help me."

"I know you hate this, but you will get through this. It's going to take some time but you will."

"I want to go to Zoe." Eva tried stand up, winced, and sat back down. "I need to go and see Zoe."

"You will, just take a few minutes to calm down." Stella put her hand over Eva's larger hand. "Tell me what you were seeing in your mind."

Eva took a deep breath. "It was cold and wet and I was trying so hard not to look at their faces. I was in so much pain because I hadn't taken my pain medication. I could barely stand up because of it but he wanted me there. Wanted me to see his brutality."

"Knowing that you were in pain, Muller had you go out in the field with him?"

"Yes. I angered him because I wasn't taking my medication, and by the time we got to the field, his rage took over. It was my fault," Eva said, giving voice to the guilt she had held within her heart since that fateful day.

"You think because you angered him . . . you think he shot them because of you?"

Eva looked into Stella's dark eyes and nodded. "I shouldn't have disobeyed him."

"What would you have done differently?"

"Listened to him, taken my medication. Behaved like I was supposed to. I resisted him every chance I got," Eva replied. "I don't know."

"Was Muller a man who didn't anger easily?" Stella gently probed.

"No. It didn't take much for him to explode."

"So if you had listened to him, do you think you would have prevented him from getting mad?"

"Maybe."

"Why were the villagers at the field?"

"The Resistance had blown up the train tracks the night before and he lost some officers that had come up from Athens. Some that he knew personally." Eva stared at the glass of water.

"The Germans usually exacted retribution for any Resistance activity. Was this their retribution?"

Eva nodded and swallowed as another firecracker went off in the distance.

"That dreadful day the Germans were retaliating for the Resistance bombing. If you had listened to your stepfather, had obeyed his every word, would it have stopped him from pulling the trigger and murdering Zoe's mother and all those other villagers?"

"I don't know. Maybe he wouldn't have been so brutal with them. He was enraged that I didn't listen to him and together with the train bombing . . ."

"How was it your fault that Muller murdered Zoe's mother? It couldn't be. Whether you had angered him or not, the outcome would still have been the same. Their lives were forfeit the moment the Resistance bombed the train tracks."

Eva closed her eyes and shook her head. "What if—?"

"There isn't any 'what if,' Eva," Stella said gently. "You didn't do anything to make him kill or to be more vicious." She covered Eva's hands and gently squeezed them.

"I didn't act."

"If you had acted to save their lives, what would have happened to yours?"

"They wouldn't have killed me. I was his daughter."

Stella shook her head. "Darling, you had just survived being beaten by him, had survived Aiden. What makes you think Muller wouldn't have killed you where you stood?"

"Because he didn't kill me when he had the chance after my mother was killed." Eva's voice wavered as she closed her eyes. "He could have done it then but he didn't."

"Oh, sweetheart." Stella brought her chair forward and tenderly kissed Eva on the cheek. "He would have killed you. There was nothing you could do. You couldn't have done anything to save those villagers. It was out of your control."

"It was so senseless."

"Death doesn't make any sense. You didn't commit any crime by your inaction. You could not have saved their lives. You saved your life by not doing anything."

"That's reassuring," Eva said bitterly. "I save my own life but watch as others are butchered."

"Have you been feeling guilty all these years because you lived?"

"I didn't do anything when a rabbi was being beaten and his synagogue was being burnt to the ground during Kristallnacht, I didn't do anything when villagers were being killed. I just didn't do anything," Eva confessed as she played with the gold cross around her neck.

"You didn't do anything to save anyone, is that right?"

Eva nodded and looked up to meet Stella's eyes. "I did nothing."

"Was it some other Eva Muller who forged her stepfather's signature on identity papers? Was it some other Eva Muller who risked her life to help people she didn't even know?"

"No."

"Where did that Eva come from? Did she materialize out of thin air? Were you transported to another time, another place, and this Eva took your place?" Stella put her hands on either side of Eva's chair and gazed into her eyes.

"No, that was me."

"That's right. You have always been there. Aiden almost destroyed you, but you fought back. You fought back against your stepfather here in Larissa. I would say that was doing something."

"Yes."

"So tell me about this." Stella touched Eva's cloak. "I see you like wearing cloaks. You've got them in different colors."

"Yes," Eva said, relieved that Stella had eased up on probing her memories.

"Hmm. Does Zoe own one? I haven't seen her wearing it."

"No."

"What makes you like them so much? I would find them so constricting." Stella's voice was even, a little conversational.

"I like the look of them."

"I'm sure Zoe would look quite funny in a cloak with her height. You look a little intimidating in one."

"I do?" Eva asked in puzzlement.

"Why do you like it?"

Eva blinked and furrowed her brow. "It makes me feel secure," she said quietly.

"It covers you and you can hide."

Eva bowed her head and nodded. "I'm tall enough as it is."

"So you disappear as if you were wearing Hades's Invisibility Helmet."

Eva nodded. "That would be handy."

"Yes, it would for a tall girl like you. You don't want people to look at you. You don't want them to see you."

"It's a bit hard not to see me."

"Right. So you wear this cloak thinking no one can see you."

"I know they can," Eva reasoned. "I'm not silly enough to believe they can't."

"No, you are not silly. You are a very intelligent woman, but you choose to hide behind that cloak."

"It's not hurting anyone."

Stella took Eva's hand. "How do you know it's not hurting anyone, Eva?"

Eva stared blankly at Stella for a moment and then shrugged. "You don't know."

"No."

"Let's go back to that day you were in the field."

"Do I have to?" Eva asked, her voice trembling. She rocked the cane between her hands.

Stella stopped the cane. "Yes. Can you do that for me?"

"Yes."

"Good, now close your eyes and breathe deeply." Stella gentled her voice. "Now, describe to me what you were doing."

"I was trying not to see the villagers' faces," Eva replied in an almost whisper.

"But you did see their faces. You tried not to focus on them?"

"Yes."

"You didn't want to see their faces because they would haunt your dreams."

"Yes."

"Whose face did you focus on?"

"Zoe's." Eva opened her eyes and looked down at the silver ring on her finger. "I stared at her. Something made me stare at her."

"Why were you looking at Zoe?"

"I don't know. There was something about Zoe. I don't know. Maybe because she was staring at me, daring me to do something."

"She was daring you to do something?" Stella said. "What could you have done?"

"I don't know, but she was looking at me, expecting something."

"What was Zoe wearing?"

Eva blinked at Stella, puzzled. "Why?"

"Eva, just close your eyes." Stella put her hand on Eva's shoulder and gently squeezed. "Tell me what Zoe was wearing."

Eva sighed and did as she was asked. "Um . . . A green blouse with a dark green skirt."

"Your favorite color."

"Yes. It was forest green, like her eyes."

"With everything going on around you, you remember what Zoe was wearing. You remember she was wearing a green blouse and a green skirt?"

"Yes. I don't know why I remember that."

"What were you wearing?"

"Um . . ."

"Close your eyes. If you were Zoe looking back at you, what did Zoe see when she looked at you?"

Eva thought for a few seconds and opened her eyes. "My black cloak."

"Could Zoe see anything else apart from that cloak when she looked at you?"

"My face, my eyes. Everything else was covered," Eva whispered.

"That would be quite intimidating for her. There's this tall German woman watching the massacre of her countrymen and just staring at her."

Eva nodded, not trusting her voice. She bowed her head and shook it slightly.

"What do you think Zoe thinks about when she sees you wearing that cloak?"

Eva looked at Stella, her mouth dropped open in shock.

"To you it's your invisibility helmet. To Zoe . . . what do you think it is?"

"A reminder of that day." Eva swallowed. "She has never said anything."

"What did you want her to say? She must know why you wear that cloak, doesn't she?"

"Yes."

"You've told her, haven't you?"

"Yes."

"She knows it's important to you and that's why she doesn't say anything. What would you want to do, knowing Zoe can't bear to look at that garment?"

"Never wear it again," Eva said resolutely. "I just didn't think." She unclipped the cloak from around her neck, shucked out of it, and dropped it onto the seat next to her.

"That's alright. It's not as if you knew and wore it anyway." Stella cupped Eva's cheek. "You have a kind heart. I know you wouldn't want to hurt Zoe by doing something that would cause her pain. I want you to remember something for me."

"What's that?"

"Sometimes telling someone how you feel doesn't make you weak," Stella said. "I used to think like that. I thought I could handle my Timothy's death but I couldn't. I had to rely on someone else to guide me through. You have to learn to trust yourself and trust those who love you to find your way."

Eva stayed quiet for a long moment. "It's hard for me to trust people."

"I know, but that doesn't mean you don't. You trust Zoe with your life. You trust your real father, you trusted Tommy."

"Yes."

"Tommy has never told us what fully happened and we have never asked him to. Tessa knew because of her visions but Tommy never said much and I don't expect him to do so. There are people you can trust."

"I trust you and Tessa," Eva admitted.

Stella smiled. "Even if I do bully you in taking your medication." She grasped Eva's hands. "Trusting family is not going to weaken you."

"I know."

"Good. Now I think we've sat here long enough and you know how I feel about you not moving about." Stella got up from her seat. She took Eva's hand, and they walked towards the party.

Eva saw Tessa standing near the alley.

"Do you know where Zoe is?" Eva scanned the sea of faces around them, her height helping to look over people's heads.

"Yes, just over there."

Eva put her head down and walked arm in arm with Stella as they made their way across the plaza.

CHAPTER 18

ZOE'S HEART SKIPPED a beat when she saw Eva heading her way. Stella's animated hand gestures were in stark contrast to Eva's subdued responses. Stella had her arm looped around the crook of Eva's elbow and was chatting and greeting people, obviously trying to get Eva to talk. She wasn't having a lot of luck there but Stella was trying.

"Something is wrong." Zoe tilted her head, wondering what was different about Eva. She was slouching and it wasn't because of her back.

"How can you tell?" Tessa asked.

Zoe glanced at her. "Do you know when Aunty Stella is upset?"

"Oh yes, I can hear her clearly across the house." Tessa put her arm around Zoe's shoulders. "'Theresa Rosa Lambros!' is her usual battle cry. There is nothing subtle about your aunt when she's angry or when she's happy."

Zoe couldn't help but grin at the description of her mercurial aunt. She watched as Eva came closer. "Eva doesn't yell. The angrier she gets, the quieter she becomes."

"That must make for a very quiet argument."

Zoe gave Tessa a lopsided grin. "Eva did scream at me once. She lost her temper with me in Egypt. She had told me not to go to the market on my own, but I didn't listen. She was so angry with me she was shaking with rage when she found me. I think that shocked me more than anything else. It shocked her as well."

"She was scared that she might have lost you. When someone like Eva loses control like that, then you know it's fear."

"That's what she said," Zoe replied, her attention still on Eva. "It terrified her that something would happen to me."

"How do you know when she's just being quiet?"

Zoe smiled. "Most people think Eva is this quiet mouse who doesn't say much, but she's not. She's talkative, very affectionate, and playful. She has a wicked sense of humor, but only a few people see it."

"Does she only let the people that she trusts see that side of her?"

"Yes. Like Earl. Earl is our closest friend and she trusts him. I think he reminds her of her best friend, Wilhelm."

"Ah yes, Willie."

"You know Willie?"

"I know of him, yes," Tessa replied. "Very few men have that kind rapport with Eva. Willie and Thomas have it." She smiled at Zoe. "I'm going to guess that Eva knows when you are upset."

"I'm not subtle but I never yell at her. Early on in our relationship I found out that yelling at Eva just had a horrible effect on her. We argue, what couple never argues, but we try and resolve things quickly. Eva hates to go to bed if she's upset. It took me some time to figure that out."

"That's a good thing, isn't it?"

"Yes. I learned if I wanted to sleep, I had better resolve our argument or else we would be up till the early hours of the morning."

"Why do you think there is something wrong now?"

Zoe watched Eva for a moment, then turned to Tessa. "Eva has developed a way to deal with people's attention. She stands ramrod straight and appears distant. She uses her height when she doesn't want people to approach her. That usually works because it can be intimidating."

"Yes, I've used that technique." Tessa nodded.

"Well, she isn't doing it now. She's slouching and it's not because of her back. Eva will stand straight even if her back is hurting. Something else is going on . . ."

"You can see it but you're not seeing it," Tessa said.

"She's not wearing her cloak," Zoe said quietly as Eva reached the alley. Eva looked up and met her gaze. *Oh, she has been crying. Goddamn this place.* "Hey."

STELLA AND TESSA exchanged glances as Stella let go of Eva and took hold of Tessa. "The rain has stopped, and you need to stretch your legs."

"Don't you want me to sit down and take the weight off my knee?" Tessa joked.

"No, you can stand," Stella replied.

Eva took a few steps towards Zoe and embraced her. Tessa and Stella left the alley and positioned themselves at the entrance. Somehow Theo and Thomas found themselves there as well and took up their place on the other side, completely blocking the tiny alley from the wedding guests.

"We have two very smart boys," Tessa whispered. She met Thomas's gaze and nodded her approval. "How did it go?" she asked Stella.

"Rough. Eva feels guilty for surviving. We made some significant progress though," Stella whispered back. She beamed at Tessa with a wide grin. "She asked for my help, Tessa." She jumped a little with glee.

Tessa laughed lightly at Stella's obvious joy. "I wish I could take a photograph of your face. You look so ecstatically happy."

"I am. She actually said, 'Help me.' She said the words, Tes. She reached out to me and that is such a huge step. I'm so proud of her. It usually takes soldiers longer to accept help. How was Zoe?"

"It was very emotional. She feels guilty that she didn't obey Muller when he ordered everyone to look down. She didn't listen and kept looking at Eva. You were right about the cloak—Zoe loathes it. I see you had success with that wretched thing."

"It took a little bit of time but she figured it out. Once she did, she took it off and left it there."

"Just like that?"

"She let go of the one thing that made her feel secure. Just like that. She didn't even think about it—took it off and left it. That girl has got so much courage and she loves Zoe so much there was no question about it. I'm so proud they are our babies."

Tessa smiled. "We are truly blessed, angel." She put her hand on Stella's arm and stopped her from turning towards the alley. "Leave them alone. They just want a kiss and a cuddle."

"I know, but they are so cute together."

"Incurable romantic," Tessa whispered. Stella blew her a kiss and Tessa chuckled as they leaned against the whitewashed walls.

EVA WALKED STRAIGHT into Zoe's open embrace and held on to her. Zoe felt Eva's body tremble and wondered what had really happened.

"You're wet."

"I was standing in the rain," Eva said, barely audible.

"I saw you. You were looking at that godforsaken field. I thought we agreed we weren't going to do that."

"I just found myself there," Eva said hoarsely. "I couldn't get that day out of my mind."

"I don't think anything can wipe that day out of our minds, Evy. Can I ask you a question?"

"Anything," Eva replied.

"It was something Tessa said that got me thinking. Why did you only look at me?" Zoe asked. She had always wanted to ask Eva but always had a nagging feeling she didn't want to know the answer. "You were unfocused for most of that horrible ordeal but you focused on me."

Eva swallowed. "You stared at me. You were the only one to really notice I was there. Everyone else was looking at Muller but you were looking at me. Your eyes . . . I couldn't take my eyes off you—"

"Until Mama was shot."

"I . . ." Eva took a deep breath and slowly released it. "I was standing at the edge of that field and I might as well have been back then—I didn't hear the party or anyone else. I just remembered how terrified you were and how terrified I was. I remember your screams, Zoe, and the look on your face."

"We were both thinking the same thing," Zoe replied, intertwining her fingers with Eva's. "I still remember the sloshing noise Muller's boots made as he walked past us. He was heavy, and the mud squished under his weight."

"You remember that black cloak as well, don't you?" Eva asked and looked into Zoe's eyes. Zoe looked away but Eva tenderly turned her face towards her. "Why didn't you tell me?"

Zoe was unable to stop the tears from running down her cheeks. "I couldn't."

"Why, love?"

"It's not fair on you. It's not fair to take away something that makes you feel secure. It would be selfish of me to deny you that."

"That wasn't your call, love. It wasn't. I didn't know how you felt. If I had, I would have burnt that piece of rubbish." Eva's voice trembled with emotion. "I would never want to hurt you. We promised each other we were not going to have any secrets."

"Yes, we did."

"This wasn't just a secret. This was something that was making you sick every time you looked at me with that thing on. I don't ever want you to feel that way about me."

"I don't, Evy. I just thought that this is what makes you feel safe."

"It did. It doesn't anymore."

"I thought I could just think of it as just another coat."

"But it's not. It would be like me wearing a miniature gun around my neck. How vile would that be?"

"Your cloak didn't kill my mama." Zoe looked into Eva's eyes, which were glistening with unshed tears. "There's something about that cloak that reminds me of that horrible day, but it's not just that."

"I'm not wearing it ever again."

"I can't let you do that."

"Do you remember when I took off my shirt at the beach? I was so scared that people would look at my scars. I was terrified, but I told you I didn't want to let my stepfather win. Isn't that what I've been doing? I'm letting him win because I'm reopening your scars. I wore that cloak for the last five years, love. I hate to think how many times I've caused you pain."

"It's not the same."

"It is, Zo. It is. It's an open wound. We have so many, but this one we can stop. All it takes is for me to stop wearing that cloak. It's exactly like the beach."

"Yes, I remember the beach." Zoe smiled through her tears. "I was so proud of you. You didn't let that bastard win."

"I'm not going to let him win now either," Eva said resolutely. "That son-of-a-bitch has tortured us enough." She cupped Zoe's cheek and brushed away a tear with her thumb. "No more."

"Tessa says it's going to take a while."

"I want to heal. Up here." Eva tapped the side of her head. "And here." She placed her hand over her heart. "I can't do it on my own. I asked Stella for her help."

Zoe grinned in delight. "I love you so much." Zoe stroked Eva's cheek.

"I love you too. I don't want to hurt like this. I don't want you to hurt. We have just one more hurdle to jump through. We have Germany to look forward to, and dealing with my grandmother."

"Yes, Germany is waiting for us, but you are not a teenager anymore, and I'm not some cowering fourteen year old. If she comes, she will not only have to contend with you, but with me as well. Where you go, I go. You are a strong woman."

"Yes, so strong I fall apart in the rain." Eva sounded disgusted with herself. "I was so worried about you, worried that all this would bring up those terrible memories, and then I fall apart. When you needed me the most."

Zoe stepped up onto the overturned box and cupped Eva's face. She gazed into her eyes. "You weren't only taking on your bad memories, Evy, you were taking on mine as well. That is far too many bad memories for one person."

"I wanted to be there for you."

"You are always here for me. I never doubted you would be by my side."

"I want to get this over and done with. I want to go back home. I want to have our babies and start a new chapter in our lives that doesn't involve lunatic murderers."

"Is that all?" Zoe's smile grew as Eva ran her hands down her back and squeezed her cloth-covered backside.

"No." Eva kissed Zoe passionately as Zoe entangled her fingers in her hair.

They parted, gazed at each other, and smiled. Eva gently brushed her fingers across Zoe's lips and then kissed her again. Zoe moaned into Eva's mouth at the gentleness of the kiss.

"What else do you want?" Zoe breathlessly said.

"You. Just you. That's all I've ever wanted."

"GIRLS, WE HAVE company," Tessa said.

Eva straightened her dress and quickly checked Zoe's before stealing a very quick kiss.

Eva picked up her cane and walked down the alley with Zoe to join Tessa and Stella.

"Isn't it a good thing you stopped kissing me?" Zoe bumped Eva with her hip. "Here comes Father H."

"Hello, girls." Father Haralambos kissed Eva and Zoe on the cheek and embraced Stella and Tessa. "Eva, I have someone I would like you to meet."

Father Haralambos brought forward a young man, a woman, and their two children.

The young man stepped forward. "Vangelis Pavlidis," he said and shook Eva's hand. "You don't know me, do you?"

Eva shook her head.

"There isn't any reason you should." Vangelis brought his wife and his boys forward. "This is my wife, Anna, and these are my sons Erastus and Damos."

Eva nodded, not quite knowing what to say.

"You are responsible for this." Vangelis pointed to Eva and then to his family.

"I am?"

"Yes." Vangelis smiled as he took a piece of paper out of his pocket and handed it to Eva.

Eva went from complete puzzlement to absolute astonishment. She handed the paper to Zoe, who had the biggest grin on her face when she read it. Zoe gave the paper back to Eva.

"I had to come back to Larissa for this property law and I went to the church to seek out Father Haralambos to thank him, to tell him I survived," Vangelis said. "He told me you were coming back here and I just had to stay and meet you."

Eva didn't know what to say. She looked down at the creased identity papers. Papers she had forged and handed to her father to distribute.

"Do you know what that little piece of paper did?"

Eva shook her head, still unable to speak.

Vangelis smiled and nodded. "I lived just outside of Larissa, a nice little village where I thought I would grow old and die like my father and his father before him. The Germans came and my life changed, like it did for everyone. One night I prayed to God and asked him for a way out before they realized where I was. I was going to pack my life in a suitcase and leave, and then something happened." He smiled. "I was walking down that dusty road and I met a priest. I must have looked like the whole world was crashing down around me because he asked me what was wrong and if he could do something to help me."

"Father Haralambos?" Zoe grinned.

"Father Haralambos, yes. God truly brought that man to me that day. I didn't know if I could trust him because some priests sold out the Jews in other villages. I told Father Haralambos my story and at the end of our walk he told me he had a way for me to escape. That very night I was hidden in a Christian church right under the Nazis's noses. About a week later he gave me new identity papers and I left thinking I would never return to the land of my fathers ever again." He looked down at the dirt under his feet and nodded. "I was met by Resistance members and secreted away. I found myself in England, where I met my Anna, and there we stayed until the war ended."

"That's incredible," Zoe said and glanced at Eva.

"Yes, it is very incredible. I don't believe in luck. It was God's direction that I met Father Haralambos that day, because if I hadn't, I would have been killed. The rest of my family all perished when they were sent to the concentration camps. I was the oldest in a family of twelve children and everyone has died except me." He paused as if collecting his emotions. "I cherish this piece of paper, Miss Muller, because it saved me. You saved me. By your actions, I met my Anna and we have two beautiful sons."

"Two and a half," Anna said. "We have one on the way."

"I'm happy for you." Eva was at a loss to what to say.

"Miss Muller, you don't understand. I wouldn't have had all of this if it weren't for you. I came here today to thank you for my life, for my wife, and for my children."

"I'm a little overwhelmed."

"What you did was God's work. You saved my life and many others. Oh behalf of those who can't say thank you to you, thank you, my dear woman, thank you so much." Vangelis took Eva into his arms, kissed her tenderly on the cheek, and held her.

They both broke down and wept in each other's arms. They finally parted and smiled at each other.

"Before I go, there is something I want to do for you," Vangelis said.

"What's that?"

"I don't know if that little life my wife is carrying is a boy or a girl, but if it's a girl, I would like to name her Eva. Can I do that?"

Eva nodded, not trusting her voice.

"Lovely! We are leaving Larissa tomorrow to head back home, but if you give me your address I will send you photographs of the baby."

"I would like that," Eva said, and took Vangelis' hand. He brought her in for another hug.

"Thank you, my guardian angel," Vangelis whispered in Eva's ear before he walked away with his family, leaving Eva stunned into silence.

CHAPTER 19

EVA BLINKED AND smiled sleepily. Zoe was sprawled half on top of her, her red-gold hair fanned out over Eva's chest and her face resting against her shoulder. The white sheet was pooled down to Zoe's lower back, and her right leg was curled up over Eva's. Zoe's fairer skin contrasted with Eva's tanned leg.

Eva let her hand wander over Zoe's smooth skin. She felt contented and safe with Zoe's body against her. Their bare skins touching sent tingles up her spine.

Eva could hear, albeit barely discernible, activity in the kitchen through the half-open window. A gentle breeze fluttered the lace curtain and just moved the drapes ever so gently. She didn't want to disturb Zoe and didn't want this tranquil moment to end. She was completely drained, emotionally and physically, from the previous few days. She needed this respite. Everything outside that door needed to stay outside even if it was only for a few hours.

She looked down at Zoe and shook her head slightly. In her arms was the only person who truly understood what she was going to face in Germany. Tessa may be aware through her gift but Zoe was the one who stayed up at night listening to her, holding her when the nightmares resurfaced or when she couldn't sleep. It was Zoe who got up, despite her own tiredness, and asked her to teach her German in the wee hours of the morning so she would have something to do other than think. Zoe's unconditional love and support kept her mentally strong and she hoped she had reciprocated in her devotion to her.

They both knew Larissa would be a minefield and it had lived up to their expectations. It was tough, it was emotional, and it was completely draining. Germany was not going to be any different.

The sound of the rooster crowing woke Zoe with a start. She raised her head slightly.

Eva gazed down at her. "Good morning, my little naked drunk." She kissed Zoe's head.

"Shh." Zoe touched Eva's lips. "You're talking too loud." She looked up again. "Am I hurting you?"

"No, not at all," Eva whispered in deference to Zoe's apparent hangover. "I love having your naked body against mine. Don't move."

"Good, I don't want to move," Zoe mumbled.

She groaned at the rooster's constant crowing and pulled the covers over her head. After a moment, she pulled the covers off and looked up at Eva, who was grinning.

"You're not wearing your brace." Zoe pointed to Eva's naked body. "Not that I'm complaining, but why did you do that?"

"I didn't." Eva chuckled. "You did."

"Are you sure? Why would I do that?"

"You wanted to touch all of me and the brace was in the way. You took off my dress, my stockings, my brace, and everything else." Eva giggled. "You don't remember, do you?"

"No." Zoe shook her head and winced. "Eh, I shouldn't do that. It hurts."

"You and Maria were in a drinking contest with Theo and Tommy."

"I was what? Maria and I were trying to outdrink the boys?"

"Oh, yes. Theo was egging you on and he got Tommy involved. It was so funny."

"You watched me get drunk? Why didn't you stop me? You know I can't drink more than a glass or two."

"I didn't want to stop you," Eva replied quietly. "We've had some rough days so I wanted you to have some fun."

"You didn't get drunk."

"I had a glass but I wanted to watch you enjoying yourself. You were drinking one glass after another, trying to beat Theo. Maria was trying to beat Tommy."

"Did I win?" Zoe sighed and played with Eva's belly button.

"Not exactly." Eva tried to laugh as quietly as she could so that Zoe didn't shush her again. "Maria threw up, but you continued until Theo gave up because you were not going to stop. You went dancing with him, Tommy, and Stella.

"I danced?"

"Oh, yes." Eva nodded. "You, Theo, Tommy, and Stella were dancing in a small group. Tessa and I were enjoying the show."

"I don't remember anything after Father H left us."

"As Earl would say, you were 'off your face and down the gutter.'" Eva laughed and put her hand to her mouth.

"I was drunk and dancing." Zoe sighed. "Thank goodness I didn't do anything more embarrassing."

Eva snickered.

Zoe groaned. "All right, what else did I do other than get drunk, dance, and strip you naked?"

"You also sang. I think poor Tommy was in pain because you were singing really loud and off key."

"Tell me that wasn't in front of the entire village."

"No, that was in front of our family, which doesn't count. You were singing 'My Eyes Are Watching You.'"

"Is that all?"

Eva shook her head. "Um . . . no." She looked away, trying not to laugh at the look on Zoe's face.

"Eva Theresa, you tell me what I did."

Eva turned back and giggled. "Um . . . you finished singing 'My Eyes Are Watching You' and then went on to 'I Gaze Into My Love.'"

"Oh no, no, no, no." Zoe sat up in bed and covered her face. "No, no, no."

"Yes, yes, yes and oh, definitely yes." Eva chuckled. "Heidi and Helga were very happy. I mean they were very, very happy and standing to attention."

"Oh, Evy." Zoe buried her face against Eva's chest and laughed. "Oh, my god. I touched the girls in front of my future husband. My brother as well. They are never going to forget this."

"Heidi was upset you touched Helga more. You loved Helga a lot." Eva guffawed. Tears ran down her face as Zoe groaned. "Theo wasn't sure who to look at—the road or you."

"Wasn't Theo drunk?"

"He was, a little. Tommy was worse than you. He was lamenting the lack of good looking men in Larissa and trying to get Theo to stop as we passed some farmers."

Zoe fell back against the pillow and laughed. "Theo is *never* going to let him forget that."

"Theo was having a great time." Eva giggled. "He was laughing so much it was a good thing he didn't drive us into a ditch. Stella was kissing Tessa in the back seat until Tommy started to give a running commentary. He stopped when he realized he was watching his parents kissing. Then he started to kiss the back of Theo's neck, which only got Theo laughing more. It was just hysterically funny. The back of my head hurt from laughing so much."

"Oh my god, oh my god, oh my god." Zoe rocked back and forth. "Why didn't you stop me from touching the girls?"

"You were very determined." Eva placed the pillow on her face and roared with laughter. "Oh, my goodness, Zoe, your hands were everywhere."

"Eva!"

"Not my fault."

"I am never going to hear the end of this from my brother."

"It's not just your brother."

"Or Tommy."

"Or Stella and Tessa," Eva added. She snickered at Zoe's wide-eyed look. "I think they all know how much you love Helga over Heidi now."

"Oh, dear God, please tell me I didn't talk to the girls?"

Eva nodded slowly, and grinned. "Theo wanted to know who Helga was and why Heidi was less loved."

"No!" Zoe buried her head under the pillow. "At least I waited till we got to our room to start undressing you, didn't I?"

"Yes, and then you decided to give me a private show. You danced the *tsifteteli* for me when we got back here." Eva chuckled. It was one of the most erotic Greek dances she knew—a combination of belly dancing and some very suggestive hip thrusts and shaking. "You were very good. I didn't know you could dance it."

"It's my Eva Special." Zoe grinned and ran her hands through Eva's hair. "Did you enjoy it?"

Eva nodded. "Especially the part where you improvised. You took a shirt and used it in a very inventive way."

Zoe's grin broadened and she waggled her eyebrows. "Did I at least do this in our room?"

"Yes. You dragged me into our room, slammed the door shut, and told me you were going to dance."

"You didn't join me, right? I did have the presence of mind that you were hurt."

Eva shook her head and chuckled. "No, you wouldn't let me. You wanted the performance to be just for me."

"Did we make love?" Zoe asked, keeping one eye open and scrunching up her face. "Not remembering making love to you would be just horrible."

"Well." Eva giggled. "You took off my dress, my stockings, my back brace, you gave Heidi and Helga some attention, thank you very much, and then you said you were too hot, kissed me, and fell asleep." Eva laughed at the relieved look on Zoe's face. "I wouldn't worry about not remembering doing that because I'm sure the boys will remind you about what you did to me in the car."

"Eva. Are you going to let them do that?"

"Yes." Eva giggled. "Theo just about killed himself laughing so much. It's too bad you don't remember the dance."

"It was a waste of a dance."

"I enjoyed it, thank you," Eva whispered. She nuzzled Zoe's neck. "You do know what you were drinking, right?"

"Retsina?"

"It was homemade Retsina. That was a potent brew. I was feeling it after one drink so I don't know how you managed to stay upright. I heard Theo say it would grow hairs on your chest." Eva pulled the sheet away to look at Zoe's chest. "Nope, no hairs."

They looked at each other and laughed.

"Phew." Eva wiped the happy tears from her eyes. "That was a good laugh."

"Sure beats waking up crying."

"That's true."

"Well, I think our family knows how much I love all of you now." Zoe giggled. "I can't believe I did that."

"You needed that as much as I needed to laugh," Eva said quietly. "Before I forget, I asked Theo to see if he could go to the house and see if your mama's painting was under the rubble."

"Was it?"

"No. Unfortunately the office had caught fire and everything was destroyed. That included the photograph I had of my mutti. I'm really happy that Mrs. Kalmias had that photograph," Eva said as she wrapped her arms around Zoe.

"I was thinking about this last night . . ."

"Is that before or after the Retsina?" Eva teased as she tweaked Zoe's nose.

"Ha Ha. Before the Retsina." Zoe rested her head against Eva's shoulder. "I think I'm going to paint a mural of all those we have lost. It would be a way to honor them and never forget their faces."

"I don't think we can forget them, can we?"

"No, not really, but our babies won't know them. If they see them every day, they will know who everyone was. It would be good for them to know their heritage."

"It would also be good for them to know how much they are wanted and loved," Eva replied. "Maybe you can put your bedroom into some use other than a glorified storage room."

"I don't know why we have to keep up that charade since the only people coming into our home are people we know."

"Just one of those things." Eva kissed the top of Zoe's red hair. "I'm going to be really happy to get out of here."

"I know this has been hell for you. Thank you for doing it for me." Zoe snuggled against Eva and put her arm around her belly. "You didn't have to, but you did it for me."

"It wasn't all horrible."

"Watching me get drunk and lecherous doesn't count." Zoe giggled.

"Oh, that was the best part," Eva said as she faced Zoe.

They gazed at each other for a long moment.

"Those hands of yours are legendary." Eva smiled broadly.

Zoe pulled the sheet off them in one fluid motion and positioned herself on Eva's side, her elbow bearing her weight. She entangled her fingers in Eva's hair. Eva looked into Zoe's eyes—they had darkened to a deep forest green.

Zoe leaned over for a long passionate kiss and slid her hand down the soft skin of Eva's stomach. She swirled her fingers with a teasingly light touch into the dark curls between long, quivering legs. She massaged and caressed Eva's back.

Eva moaned, felt her own need, and reluctantly pulled away. "Uh . . . n . . . no."

"I know," Zoe said breathlessly.

Eva heard footsteps and doors closing just outside their room.

"Oh, I know," Zoe said.

"Oh god, love, I want you right this minute, but we can't," Eva said.

Zoe groaned, rolled over, and found the bed sheet. Eva raised her head and grinned at Zoe.

"You are such a beautiful, sexy woman," Eva whispered.

Zoe looked back at her with a bashful smile.

"Come here." Eva said, and crooked her finger.

Zoe scrambled back in bed. She paused in tucking the sheet around. "I forgot to greet the girls."

Zoe leaned in for an intense and passionate kiss, while running her hands over Eva's skin. Eva drew in a sharp breath and held it as Zoe barely touched the circles around her nipples. She released the breath with a small exclamation when Zoe, at last, pressed against the sensitive flesh.

"Good morning, Heidi and Helga," Zoe said breathlessly. She impishly looked up between Eva's breasts and winked.

"Whoa." Eva fanned herself. "You are going to kill me."

"I forgot you are an old lady now." Zoe giggled as she tucked the sheet around Eva. She looked around and found her singlet on the floor. She leaned over, nearly falling out of the bed, much to Eva's amusement. She put her singlet on and settled back down next to Eva.

There was a gentle knock on the door.

They looked at each other and smiled.

"Come in," Eva called out.

Stella entered with a tray and a towel draped over her shoulder. "I thought you two might like to have breakfast in bed." Zoe made a face. "Or maybe not Zoe." Stella put the tray on the dresser.

She nearly tripped over the back brace lying on the floor on top of Eva's dress and stockings. She raised an eyebrow, and a smile creased her face as she turned to Eva. "How are you feeling today?" She picked up the brace, the dress, and the stockings and put them on the dresser.

"My back is feeling better," Eva said.

"Hmm. I would suggest keeping that on for another day to give your back some time to heal properly." Stella sat down on Eva's side of the bed.

Zoe looked away, and Eva snickered when she realized Zoe was trying not to catch her aunt's gaze.

"How are Heidi and Helga this morning?" Stella asked.

Eva shut her eyes and laughed lightly. "They are doing just fine."

"Good. We don't want them to be ignored, not that Zoe will allow that to happen." Stella ruffled Zoe's hair. "You are just adorable. You both are."

"Thank you for your help yesterday." Eva looked into Stella's eyes.

Stella cupped Eva's cheek. "Darling, you did all the work. I just guided you through it. I suggest you both spend the morning lying in bed, just enjoying each other's company. There isn't much to do around here. I'm sending Theo to the train station to book our tickets for Germany."

"Zoe and I wanted to ask you a question and um . . . it's been a little busy over the last few days and all but . . . um . . ." Eva felt a little shy about broaching the subject with Stella.

Stella smiled. "You can ask me anything you want."

"We want to have a baby and um . . . we wanted to know how best to do it." Eva glanced at Zoe, who was intently studying a spot on the bed sheet.

"I see. You want to know how you go about it."

"Uh . . . yes," Eva said.

"Well, you get a woman and a man and then you leave them alone so they can have sex. If everything works, nine months later you have a baby," Stella joked.

Eva grinned sheepishly. "We want to know how to make that happen without Tommy and Zoe . . . uh . . . having sex."

Stella nodded. "Ah, I see."

"We have been thinking about this and Zoe says her father used to impregnate the cows using a syringe."

"Hmm. Yes, that is one way of doing it, but Zoe is not a cow. I wouldn't recommend it. The only way to make babies is by having sex."

"Are you sure?" Zoe looked up at her aunt expectantly. "Are you sure that is the only way?"

"Yes, I'm sure."

"Can't we try it with the syringe? If that doesn't work then—"

"Zoe, you can't do it that way. It just doesn't work."

"We don't normally discuss our sex life with other people," Eva said bashfully.

"I'm not just any other person, I'm your aunt and your doctor. I know you two are very private and I'll respect your privacy, alright?"

"Yes."

"You have to decide what you want to do, but whatever you decide, your Aunt Tessa and I will support you. One more thing and I won't mention this again. The next time we discuss sex and babies, I hope Zoe is pregnant." Stella gave Eva a kiss on the cheek and went around the bed to kiss Zoe. She went to the door and stood there for a moment. "One more thing. Twins run in the Lambros family." She chuckled as she left the room.

Silence descended on Eva and Zoe as they sat in bed. It was Zoe who spoke first. "I want to do it."

"No," Eva replied softly.

"Evy, I want to do this for you. Let me do this."

Eva leaned back against the pillows and closed her eyes. A mental image of Zoe in Thomas' arms made her shudder. "I don't want you to do it. I can't stand the thought of you with anyone else."

Zoe rested her head against Eva's chest and placed her hand on Eva's stomach. For a long moment she didn't say a word. "The thought of being with a man makes me sick, but it's Tommy. He is the man who saved your life in Aiden."

"Yes but—"

"Shh." Zoe placed her fingers against Eva's lips. "I don't want to do it because he saved your life but I want to do it because I can give you something you can't do yourself."

"There's a lot of things I can't do myself, love. It's just life."

"Yes, but I want this for us. I want to have a baby as well. It will make us both happy. The 'making the baby' part is going to be icky."

"You have no idea how icky," Eva replied as she gazed down at Zoe.

"What's it like?"

"It's not the same as making love to me. It's very different."

"Do you want to have children?"

Eva sighed and closed her eyes. "My heart says yes and no. Yes, I want children, but no, I don't want to think about you having sex with Tommy."

"If I do have sex with Tommy, will you still love me the same way?" Zoe asked quietly. Eva looked down and blinked. She wasn't expecting that question.

"Of course! Of course I would love you the same way." Eva kissed the top of Zoe's head. "You know I will always love you."

"If I have sex with Tommy, you—"

"Please, don't ask me to be in the same room because I think that would just make me want to throw up."

Zoe giggled. "No, I don't think I can handle you being in the room, but I want you to be with me afterwards."

"I don't think you would be able to keep me out."

"So we are doing this?"

Eva reluctantly nodded. "I sure hope you are one of those women that have sex and get pregnant after the first try."

"It didn't happen to you after you had sex with Wilhelm."

"No, but then you might get lucky."

Zoe grinned. "Let's hope I get lucky," she said and snuggled against Eva's chest.

CHAPTER 20

Germany

ZOE CLOSED HER eyes and tried to stay calm as the train made its way into Germany. She anxiously glanced at Eva, who was seated next to her wearing a sleeping mask.

Eva moved her hand over and gently squeezed Zoe's hand.

They had, together with the Lambros clan, boarded the train in Larissa for Athens, and the trip to the city hadn't taken as long as their tortured journey to Larissa had. The train to Germany felt like she was venturing into the enemy's lair.

Zoe was feeling more than a little anxious, and was tired as well. She had tried not to take any notice of the two young German soldiers who boarded the train and sat nearby. The harder she tried to ignore them, the more she found herself staring at them, since they were seated a few rows in front. One of the soldiers got out of his seat and walked towards her.

"Hello, I'm Gunther," Gunther said with a smile as he leaned on the vacant seat in front of Eva. "My friend and I couldn't help overhearing you reading aloud the book about Berlin."

Eva removed her mask and put it aside. Zoe didn't want to talk to the soldier and kept quiet. She glanced at Eva, who gave her little nod.

"Is this the first time you've been there?" Gunther asked.

"No," Eva replied. "Berlin's my home town."

"Really? Ha, I win my bet with Dieter. He said you sounded German but your friend wasn't."

"I am German." Eva smiled at Gunther. "My friend is Greek."

"Ah, what are your names?"

"I'm Eva and this is Zoe."

Zoe smiled that Gunther looked more than a little disappointed that Eva was doing all the talking. His very blond hair and blue eyes reminded her of the posters she had seen of the perfect Aryan the Nazis had used. Six years was not enough time for her to forgive or forget.

He glanced at Eva, smiled and then faced Zoe. "You have pretty eyes."

"She does." Thomas came up the aisle and put his hand on Gunther's shoulder. "She's my fiancée, my friend."

Gunther grinned and backed off. "Sorry."

"It's alright, you have good taste." Thomas chuckled as Gunther went back to his seat. He put his hand on Eva's shoulder and dropped down to his haunches. "So how is my fiancée feeling?"

"A little anxious," Eva replied. She turned to Zoe and took her hand.

"Hmm, Theo is a little anxious himself. Must be a Lambros thing." Thomas chuckled.

Thomas reached across Eva and kissed Zoe's hand. He smiled at Eva and then walked back to his seat.

"Dion is a right proper bastard," Eva whispered. "Theo was right to throw him out of the house."

"Should have kicked him in the behind on the way out," Zoe muttered darkly. "Uncle Dion should worry about his daughter getting married and leave me alone. Where was he during the war? Hypocrite."

"Well, we won't have to worry about him. He's gone to Volos. You're getting married and his burden is off his shoulders."

"It's not that, Evy, it's the way he spoke to Aunty Stella. You wouldn't speak to a dog that way."

"It's quite all right. I'm used to my brother speaking like he had just come out of the sewer," Stella said as she leaned over from her seat. "Your uncle Dion is a bit—"

"He's a big bully."

"Yes." Stella nodded. "He always was a bully, but what can you do?"

"He was very surprised when you told him about your wedding to Tommy." Eva chuckled. "He looked very relieved he didn't have to worry about you anymore."

The conductor was making his way through the train and alerting the passengers of the next stop.

Eva squeezed Zoe's hand and they touched heads.

"I know you're scared," Eva whispered.

"In the valley of death we ride . . ."

"That's a bit melodramatic."

Zoe smiled. "I'm Greek, we do melodrama really well. I wish I had Dorothy's red shoes right now."

Eva looked down at Zoe's feet as Zoe tapped them together. "We need red shoes."

They looked at each for a moment before they started to laugh. Zoe leaned over and whispered, "I want to make love to you."

"Here?"

"No, but when we get to where we are going."

"Hmm. Most definitely. Are you sure you are alright with our family nearby?"

"I'm not going without touching you for the next few weeks. That would drive me crazy." Zoe laughed lightly. She wanted to passionately kiss Eva, but kissed her chastely on the cheek instead.

"You need to rehearse how to kiss." Eva giggled.

"You are just too funny. How are you feeling?"

Eva looked down at their intertwined hands for a long moment. "I was trying not to think about it, but the closer we get, the more butterflies I have. This was my home. A part of me wants to be here but the other part of me knows it's going to be hell."

"We've going to face this together."

"Even if—"

"Shh." Zoe put her fingers on Eva's lips. "We will talk about this later, but I want you to enjoy coming home. You've waited twelve years to come back. I'm going to be fine."

"I love you." Eva's voice wavered as Zoe rubbed her thumb against her hand.

"I love you too." Zoe smiled, and very deliberately took Eva's hand and kissed it. She didn't care if anyone was watching.

EVA GLANCED AROUND the bustling train station. There was something so familiar, something so right. She was home. No matter how she wanted to believe that Sydney was her home—it was not the same. This was home. Even the loudspeaker announcements made her feel welcome, something she found very strange. She couldn't help the grin on her face while they waited for Theo and Thomas to collect their bags.

Tessa put her arm around Eva and smiled. "You're happy to be back home, darling?"

"Yes. I thought I wouldn't be, tried to tell myself that Sydney was home, but it's not."

"Yes, I felt the same way when I went back to Larissa," Tessa admitted. "I had been in Thessaloniki since I was seventeen years old. It's a long time to be away."

"Things are never the same, are they?"

"No, they're not. You change, people you left behind change. It's just the way it is."

"Do you think my grandmother still cares?" Eva asked.

"Do you still care what she thinks?"

Eva turned to Tessa with a sad smile. "Unfortunately, yes."

"It's alright to still care, Eva."

"Do we know where we are going?"

"Yes, we do." Tessa held up a slip of paper. "I have the address." She glanced at Stella, and they quickly made their way out of the station into a murky afternoon.

A man approached them with cap in hand. "Good afternoon. I'm Louis, are you Theresa Lambros?"

"Yes," Tessa replied.

"This way please. We have two cars waiting to take you to the villa." Louis directed them to the waiting cars. Theo and Thomas loaded the cars with the luggage and they got in and away from the train station.

Zoe took Eva's hand and as the car made its way through streets lined with army personnel and littered with partially destroyed buildings. Eva stared out of the car window. The war had ravaged the city. Many of the buildings had been reduced to rubble.

"It looks so . . . bad," Zoe said quietly.

"It was once a very beautiful city, very green and with so much history," Eva replied. She put her hand on Zoe's knee and squeezed it gently, conveying the message loud and clear that she appreciated her restraint in commenting about the war. Zoe caught Eva's reflection in the window looking at her and smiled.

The car made its way through the city, and Eva smiled at the very familiar landmarks. She leaned her head against the window as they crossed into Dahlem.

"Hey." Zoe tapped Eva's shoulder. "Home?"

"No. Dahlem, next borough from home."

The car slowed and turned into a driveway that led to twin properties. Huge trees afforded privacy from the road and obscured the road from the villas.

"Welcome to my former life," Eva whispered.

Zoe's eyes widened, and Eva smiled at her shocked reaction. They got out of the car and waited for the luggage to be offloaded.

Zoe did a one-eighty turn. "Wow, I think I just fell down the rabbit hole."

One of the doors to the villa closest to them opened and a short, older woman came out. Her white hair was in contrast to the black tunic she was wearing. As she came closer Eva could see her more clearly.

"Hello, hello!"

Tessa ran towards the woman and engulfed her in a hug, much to Eva's surprise.

"Well, look who is here. Theresa Rosa, you are looking as beautiful as the last time I saw you. Where is that woman of yours?"

"Right here." Stella approached the old woman and hugged her.

"Did you have a good trip? Where is my boy?"

"Right here." Thomas approached and picked up the woman in a bear hug. "I'm so glad to see you, Aunty Irene."

"Ah, you sweet boy, what is with this facial hair? Need to shave that off." Irene patted Thomas' cheek. She looked at Theo. "Who is this?"

"This is my friend Theodore."

"What a strong name."

Theo offered his hand, but Irene ignored it and brought him down for a hug. "We don't shake hands here, young man. We hug," she said in Greek.

Irene then approached Eva and Zoe, who were standing near the car.

"Hello there, shy girls, come here." Irene tilted her head a little and regarded Eva. "You must be Zoe?" Eva couldn't help but smile. "Oh silly me, oh, yes, the blue-eyed girl is Eva." She nodded. "And the redhead with the beautiful green eyes is Zoe."

Irene, much shorter than Eva, looked up at her.

Eva stood to her full height and looked down.

"I can't reach you all the way up there." Irene pulled on Eva's shirt until she leaned down for an awkward hug. "You're not a hugger, are you?"

Eva didn't know how to deal with Irene. Despite the woman's short stature, she felt intimidated.

"My, you are very tall." Irene patted Eva on the cheek. "Come down here for a moment." Eva bent her knees and lowered herself down. Irene looked into her eyes. "Welcome home, sweet child."

Eva's eyes welled up as she smiled and hugged Irene. "Thank you." Tears ran down her face.

"You're Sister Irene." Zoe said.

"I am."

Zoe kept staring at Irene with an amazed look. Irene stared back. Eva watched them both, intrigued.

Irene smiled as she waited for Zoe to say something. Eva wasn't sure why but Irene patiently waited.

"I know you," Zoe said.

"You do?" Eva asked, and looked at Irene and then at Zoe. "How?"

"She does," Irene replied.

"In 1942, Mama's funeral. An old lady came up to me and comforted me. She said, 'You will find your everything,' and walked away. You were in Larissa for the funeral."

"So." Irene gazed affectionately at Zoe. "You found your everything, didn't you, little one?" She cupped Zoe's face and her eyes crinkled in delight. She kissed Zoe on one side and then on the other cheek.

"Now, I'm sure you are hungry from your long trip. Let's have something to eat and then we can talk."

Irene put her arms around Eva and Zoe and led them to the main villa. Eva looked back at the car and the surrounding gardens and slowly shook her head in amazement.

CHAPTER 21

THE REGISTRY OFFICE was small, much too small for Eva's liking. She stood in the back and waited for the clerk to arrive with their marriage certificates. Tommy and Theo were both dressed in dark suits with a small flower in their lapels, which she found amusing. Zoe had thought it would appear quite normal for grooms to have flowers.

"Hey, are you alright?" Zoe asked.

"I am. This is my third wedding."

"My second."

Eva smiled at Zoe, who smiled back at her. "And our last."

"What is taking that man so long?"

"Patience, Zoe." Stella put her arm around her shoulders. "He will be back with the paperwork soon and everything will be done."

"He did look at us a little oddly."

The door opened and the Registry clerk entered. He pushed up his glasses and glanced around the room. "Mr. and Mrs. Thomas Lambros and Mr. and Mrs. Theodore Lambros, congratulations."

Zoe rolled her eyes. "Do I introduce myself now as Mrs. Thomas Lambros?" she whispered.

"Yes," Stella replied.

Eva chuckled at Zoe's objections at being now only known by her husband's name. She watched Thomas put his arm around Zoe's waist.

Theo put his arm around her, and she scowled. All for show or not, she still found it rather unsettling to see Thomas with Zoe.

Thomas and Theo let go of their new wives and accepted the marriage certificates from the clerk along with the congratulatory handshakes while Eva and Zoe stayed silent.

They left the Registry office and walked out into brilliant sunshine.

Zoe turned to Eva, who was quietly walking beside her. "Are you alright?"

Eva glanced at Thomas and Theo, who were talking. Stella and Tessa were walking ahead of them. "I am fantasizing about making love to you," she whispered.

"Oh." Zoe fanned herself. "Let's celebrate our wedding back at the house. You need all the practice you can get in baby making," she said with a slight chuckle as Eva gave her a lopsided grin.

"OH GOD, ZO . . . E," Eva stammered as Zoe captured her lips one last time. She groaned into Zoe's mouth as her climax took control of her long-limbed figure, her muscles jumping and quivering in irrepressible spasms of delight.

Zoe planted a soft kiss on Eva's sweat-soaked brow.

"Open your eyes," Zoe said breathlessly. "I love you."

"Oh, you are going to kill me." Eva panted.

After a few moments, Zoe gently rolled to her side and hitched herself up on her elbow. She lightly traced Eva's nipple, which hardened at her touch. She kissed it and then kissed Eva again.

"Oh, dear god." Eva put her hand over her eyes and laughed weakly.

"Sex in Berlin." Zoe giggled and gazed into Eva's eyes. "Elena collects postcards and I keep score of how many times—"

"You're keeping score of how many places we make love?" Eva turned her head to look at Zoe.

Zoe gave her another deep and passionate kiss.

"We have to celebrate our weddings," Zoe said with a chuckle.

"I'm quite sure the boys are not celebrating this way."

"Well, one of them isn't." Zoe giggled. She scrunched her face up. "If only it was possible to create our babies by magic."

Eva brushed Zoe's tresses out of her eyes. "Unfortunately you need a man and a woman to do that. It's the first time in my life I wished I was a man."

"I'm glad you're not a man," Zoe replied, which earned her a kiss. "You heard Aunt Stella say that twins run in the family. Maybe, if we get lucky, I'll only have to have sex once."

Eva sighed. "That would be great, but somehow I don't think so."

"It's going to be really difficult, but I want us to have children, Evy."

Eva glanced at Zoe and nodded. "I know. You have to promise me that if at any time you change your mind, you will stop. You won't continue just for me. I don't believe I'm saying this to you but you have to promise me."

"I promise," Zoe replied solemnly. After a beat she said. "What does it feel like?"

"Do you want to try and see how you feel?"

"You have a penis handy?" Zoe quipped making Eva laugh.

"No but I have one of your father's syringes that I found in the barn. It's almost as big er as a penis."

"Why do you have that?"

Eva sighed. "I found it when I went looking for Theo and was looking around the barn. I thought maybe we could use it if Stella thought it would work."

"Ah . . . since you have it and there isn't a penis to practice with . . ." Zoe fell back on the bed, chuckling as Eva closed her eyes and laughed.

"Alright, I'll be right back." Eva rolled away and off the bed. She padded to their luggage, knelt down, and took out the syringe that she had packed in her toiletries. Zoe stared as Eva put the syringe under her armpit. "What are you doing?"

"I'm warming it up." Eva looked at the syringe for a long moment. "I want you to relax, alright?" She lay down alongside Zoe. Zoe looked down the length of her body at Eva's hand. She scrunched up her face and closed her eyes.

With her free hand, Eva cupped Zoe's face and brought her lips down for a passionate kiss, which turned into two, and then three, until Zoe was moaning. She moved her kisses across Zoe's jaw and down her neck and Zoe slipped one hand into Eva's locks to hold her closer.

Eva lavished Zoe's body with exquisite attention and eventually Zoe squirmed and groaned.

"Spread your legs wider for me, love," Eva said in Zoe's ear.

Eva teased a small earlobe with her tongue. "Alright. Ready?"

"Uh huh," Zoe exclaimed.

Eva slipped a hand under Zoe's neck and the back of her head and kissed her. She thrust her tongue past lips that parted for her. She gently pressed the syringe against Zoe, not pushing it in but holding it in place. "Okay, love, I'm going to insert it, alright?"

"Did I hurt you?" Eva dropped the syringe on the bed and rolled off Zoe, who was looking quite pale. "Zoe, talk to me."

"Take it out, Evy!"

"Did I hurt you?" Eva asked as she cupped Zoe's cheek.

"Uh . . . no, you didn't hurt me." Zoe buried her head against Eva's chest. "I got scared."

"It's alright." Eva pulled Zoe to her and kissed the top of her head. "It's alright." Zoe sniffed. "It's different from what you are used to."

"It's big.I've seen what a penis looks like, I'm an artist but um . . ."

"Seeing a penis and having one inside you are two very different things."

"Is it like that with a man?" Zoe asked in a quiet voice.

"A penis is larger than this syringe." Eva pulled Zoe tightly against her body. "It will be different."

"How different?"

"What do you love about making love to me?"

Zoe grinned. "Everything. Your softness, the feel of your hands, your kisses, your breath against my skin. The way you say my name. Everything."

"Tommy is a well built young man, he's muscular and his chest will be hard. His hands are rougher. He will smell differently."

"How long does it take for him to do his business?" Zoe asked making Eva smile.

"It will take him minutes to do it. Men don't take their time. At least that's been my experience."

"I don't know how you could have sex with a man," Zoe muttered, and realized what she had said. She looked into Eva's eyes apologetically. "I'm sorry, Evy, that just came out wrong."

"It's okay, love. I don't know how I did it either, but I had to convince my uncle that he had cured me. I had no choice but to have sex with Erik."

"How did Mengele Junior know you were having sex?"

Eva sighed and closed her eyes. "He watched us the first time."

Zoe stared at Eva, shocked. "He what? Oh, Evy." She cupped Eva's face and kissed her. "That evil son-of-a-bitch bastard."

"That's how he knew that his treatments worked," Eva replied softly. "He found out that Erik was visiting me and caught us a few times kissing."

"So he spied on you?"

Eva nodded. "I was in the normal part of the hospital by then and was taking daily walks with Tommy, and Erik would drop by. In hindsight Tommy would have arranged for that to happen at the same time as my uncle would do his rounds."

"That was smart."

"Yes, but I didn't figure it out back then. I had my plan and this was working to my advantage. I didn't know Tommy and Erik were working to that same plan. Erik would show up and spend some time with me."

"So you had to have sex with him in front of your uncle?"

"No. Tommy told me back in Larissa that my uncle approached him to tell him that he approved of Erik seeing me and wanted to make it easier for us by giving us a private room."

"Argh," Zoe exclaimed, thoroughly disgusted. "I'm so sorry I brought this up now."

"It's alright, Zo. I know you wanted to ask. Actually I was waiting for you to ask."

"You were?"

"Yes. I thought you might ask when we talked about Erik but you never did."

"I did, but didn't." Zoe stroked Eva's cheek. "I don't want to hurt you and it made me jealous that this man was married to you for two years."

"You of all people can ask me anything."

"Oh." Zoe nodded. "Next time you want me to ask something, can you give me a nudge?"

Eva smiled. "I'll try and remember that." They gazed at each other for a long time before Eva kissed Zoe tenderly on the lips.

"You thought Erik didn't know and believed you were cured. He obviously knew you weren't, yet he played along. Why did he marry you if he knew you weren't in love with him?"

"He was in love with me. To him it was real, and he may have thought that all I needed was the love of a good man and everything would be right."

"Was it . . . um . . ."

"Terrible. Yes, but I tried to convince myself that this was the right thing to do. I had to get . . . used to it."

"That must have been so horrible for you. Did any part of it get easy?"

"No." Eva sighed as she intertwined her fingers with Zoe's. "It never got easy. It was something that I needed to just endure.

"You know how I've been reading that book and some of the drawings—"

"I know. I saw it on the bed stand. Some of the positions in that book would break my back if we ever tried them." Eva chuckled. She gazed at Zoe for a long moment.

She ran her hands up Zoe's body, stopped at her face, and gently brushed her fingers across her lips. She smiled, and captured Zoe's mouth with her own.

"I love you so much," she said breathlessly as they parted.

"Um." Zoe looked into Eva's eyes.

They laughed.

"I was reading the book about how . . . um . . . a man . . . it looks painful," Zoe said.

"It can be," Eva replied truthfully. "Some days I just had to stop myself from screaming because he would be on top of me and I felt trapped. The tenser I became, the worse it got, and the more painful it was physically." She closed her eyes and sighed deeply. "I can't bear the thought of anyone dominating me like that."

"You let me be on top when we make love."

Eva tenderly touched Zoe's face and smoothed her thumb against her cheek. "I love you. I trust you and you don't dominate me—you love me."

"Erik was trying to dominate you?"

"Most of my sexual experiences with men haven't been pleasant and men like being on top. They like it that way or . . ."

"Or?"

Eva shook her head. "That's the part you don't want to hear about, love. Sometimes Erik would want to . . . uh . . . um . . . He liked oral sex."

Zoe screwed up her face in horror. "That's just so . . . argh. Did you . . . um . . . have an orgasm with him?"

Eva looked into Zoe's eyes. "You've been wanting to ask me that for years, haven't you?"

"Yes, but I never knew how to ask without sounding like a bit of a jealous shrew."

Eva smiled. "You do sound jealous and I like it."

"Forget the 'bit' jealous. I am jealous that he had you for two years."

"Erik never had my heart, love. You're the only one who has all of me. Did I come? My body responded to his touch but more often than not I would fake it. To me it wasn't love making—it was just sex."

"Was Erik blind?"

"No." Eva shook her head. "Sex is very quick with men, Zoe. Something I was most grateful for."

"How in the world did he believe you weren't faking it? Didn't he ever look into your eyes when you were coming? Didn't he see that your whole body spasms or that you couldn't talk for a few minutes?"

"No. He didn't know what to look for. He didn't know what you know about me."

"Show me."

Eva looked at her, surprised. "You want me to show you how I faked it?"

"Yes."

"Alright. You have to be Erik, but don't try and kiss me or I won't be faking anything." Eva giggled as she reversed their positions so that Zoe was straddling her.

"How am I not supposed to make love to you?" Zoe asked.

She slid her hand down the soft skin of Eva's stomach, grinning as she swirled her fingers with a teasingly light touch into the curls between Eva's legs. Eva bit her lip and closed her eyes tightly.

"You're not making this easy," Eva said in a calm voice.

Zoe gently entered Eva, who arched her back and moaned loudly. Zoe stopped with a puzzled expression on her face.

"Erik was blind and stupid," she muttered. "Evy, open your eyes for me."

Eva opened one eye and grinned.

"I just can't believe how you did that. Did you just stop your body from reacting?"

"It's very hard to do with you on top of me, Zo, but yes."

"How?"

"Years of experience," Eva mumbled as Zoe rolled off her and settled next to her.

"Your eyes haven't gone that gorgeous deep shade, your body isn't responding to anything. How could he not feel that you were faking that?"

"He was pleasuring himself. He thought I was responding to him."

"Are all men so self-involved when they make love?" Zoe asked.

"I've only ever been involved with one man willingly. That was Erik, so my experience says yes, but I'm not the best person to ask."

Zoe opened her mouth then shut it.

Eva gave her a sad look. "The other men were more about domination, fear, and control. Tommy won't be like that. Tommy loves you and it's not about control with him."

"I don't ever want to find out."

"I sure hope you don't. Erik was not a bad man. He saved my life." Eva pulled Zoe close to her. "I cheated on him by not giving of myself to him."

"Did you at least like him?"

"I liked him, but not enough that I wanted to give myself to him."

"You agreed to marry him."

"Hmm. I did. I couldn't see a way out. It was just this awful life ahead of me. I could submit to a marriage with a man who was nice or going back to Aiden or death."

"You chose submission."

"Yes. My stepfather ordered me to Paris then Larissa and my choices improved." Eva took Zoe's hand and kissed it.

"I don't believe I'm saying this, but thank you, Hans Muller, for being such a controlling paranoid bastard." Zoe gave Eva a quick kiss. "What happened to Erik?"

"About six months before heading for Larissa, Erik was sent to the Eastern Front."

"Where is he now?"

"Whilst I was recovering from the bomb blast in Paris, I got word he was killed. Erik wasn't a soldier—he was a young doctor."

"That's sad," Zoe said quietly. "I've never really asked you, but what was Erik's surname?"

"Hoffman. I was Eva Hoffman." Eva smiled when Zoe scrunched up her face. "You don't like it?"

"It sounds strange."

"You like Muller instead?"

"I don't like either of them. I like Lambros. Eva Lambros sounds much nicer. Why didn't you use Hoffman in Larissa?"

"Muller didn't want me to," Eva replied with a tiny shrug.

"What a strange man," Zoe said. She got out of bed.

"Where are you going?"

"I just remembered I brought some scented oil from Larissa."

"Right. What are you going to do with it at this hour of the night?"

"Give you a massage," Zoe replied as she rummaged through their luggage. "Found it. You have a choice, m'lady. Which shall it be? Rose scented or lavender oil?" She returned to the bed.

Eva pointed to the lavender and rolled over onto her stomach without a word.

CHAPTER 22

EVA STOOD AT the window and watched the twinkling lights of the sleepy borough as she dried her wet hair from her bath. She brushed her long hair while staring at the full moon that was still up in the pre-dawn sky as the city started to rise. Her city—it was her home. She was in Berlin after a twelve-year absence. The city had been changed forever. The scars were everywhere. The war had left indelible marks on its façade, but underneath it was the same. The same but different. Just like her.

Eva blinked at the realization that she was like this city. Despite every-thing that had happened, she was still who she had always been, but she was scarred by the experiences of the past. The scars would eventually heal but they would be with her in her psyche.

Eva looked down at the bed where Zoe was sprawled on her back, fast asleep. Red-gold hair fanned out like a halo on the white pillow. Zoe's face in slumber was relaxed and her full lips just slightly parted. A white sheet was pooled around her legs—Zoe was notorious for kicking off any bedding during the night. She was naked except for the gold cross that rested in the hollow of her throat.

Eva sat down on the bed and watched Zoe sleep. "I am the luckiest woman alive," she whispered as she tenderly kissed Zoe.

Zoe stirred. Her eyes fluttered open and she smiled.

"Good morning." Eva kissed Zoe.

"Good morning." Zoe took Eva's hand. "What were you doing?"

"Watching you sleep," Eva replied. "Sleep well?"

"Um, yes, but you didn't."

"Huh?"

"You were talking in your sleep again."

"Oh." Eva looked down at the bedspread. "Was I telling off my grandmother?"

"No, not this time." Zoe brought Eva's hand to her lips and kissed it. "You were talking to Willie."

"Oh."

"I wonder if Willie is here in Berlin." Zoe smiled. "You may be wrong."

"He didn't make it, Zo. I just know."

"I'm sorry."

"What for? About Willie?"

"Last night . . . about Erik."

"Oh. Erik is part of my past. It's just what I had to do."

"I know, but reminding you about it, that's just poking another wound. You tossed and turned, you talked and—"

"No, it wasn't about Erik, love. I couldn't sleep because I was excited to be home, not because of Erik or Willie." Eva smiled. "I'm home."

"Are you sure?"

"Yes, quite sure. I didn't realize how much I missed home until we got here. It's familiar, it's—"

"It's home," Zoe said.

Eva kissed her tenderly on the lips. "I've also been thinking about that syringe."

"Argh. What about it?"

"If we put some lubricant on it, it can—"

"Evy?"

"Yes, love?"

"Don't tell me how you are going to do it. Just do it." Zoe scrunched up her face. "If we talk about it, I'm going to get anxious. I don't want to see it."

"You know I can't do that without your help. It's a little difficult for you not to notice a large syringe." Eva tried to suppress the smile as she met Zoe's gaze.

"I'm being silly, aren't I?"

"A little bit." Eva chuckled. "We will find a way. I'll just have to get you to the point where you don't notice that a giant syringe is in you."

"You're so funny." Zoe giggled and patted Eva's belly. "I think you need to eat some breakfast. You didn't eat any dinner."

"I am hungry."

"Well, go downstairs and have some breakfast before your grumbling belly gets louder and wakes up the neighborhood. I'll go and have a bath and join you soon."

Eva cupped Zoe's face and brought her lips down for a passionate kiss, which made Zoe moan. They parted and looked at each other until Eva's stomach rumbled, causing them to start laughing.

"Go feed yourself, Mrs. Lambros," Zoe said as Eva let go of her and left the room reluctantly to go to the kitchen.

EVA WANDERED DOWN the hallway and down the steps into a large kitchen. She looked around and saw the refrigerator in the corner. A pot was on the boil on the stovetop. She leaned over to see what was boiling and then padded to the refrigerator.

Eva opened the door and contemplated what to eat. Hands encircled her waist. She screamed, took a step back, and crashed into someone behind her.

"Oh, Father in the heavens. Oh, Virgin Mary," the woman screamed.

Eva turned around and stared astonished at Katarina, who engulfed Eva in a tight hug and nearly picked her off her feet. Eva's heart was beating so loudly she could hear the whooshing in her ears and she tried to free herself from Katarina's grasp, but she couldn't, which only terrified her more.

Irene rushed into the kitchen.

"Katarina, stop, put her down," Irene said. "I think you may want to let her go, Katarina, she can't breathe."

Katarina let go of Eva, and Eva sank down onto a chair. She heard footsteps bounding down the steps. Zoe ran into the kitchen, a towel wrapped around her and dripping wet.

"What the hell." Zoe stopped in front of Irene.

Eva had her hand on her heart in obvious distress.

Zoe went down on her knees in front of her. "Hey, I'm here."

Eva nodded. "I'm o . . . okay." She took a deep breath. "I'm okay."

"You don't look okay to me." Zoe tilted Eva's head and looked into her eyes. "You got startled."

"This is getting embarrassing. At least this time I didn't slip."

"That's a good thing because I don't see any vases lying about, and she's a lot bigger than Tommy." Zoe brushed Eva's hair from her eyes.

Eva sat straight in the chair and smiled weakly at Zoe, whose towel had opened. "That's one way to resuscitate me," she whispered.

Zoe stuck her tongue out and closed her towel. "Are you going to be okay so I can go and start my bath?"

"Yes, mother, I don't need hand holding."

"Alright then." Zoe stood and looked down at Eva, who was gazing up at her. She kissed her tenderly then walked past Irene without saying a word. Katarina followed her out of the kitchen.

"Dear god, I have to stop reacting like a scared child," Eva muttered, and blew out the breath she was holding. With her shaky hands, she took out her cigarette case and removed a cigarette.

Irene held out the lighter and lit her cigarette. Eva looked at her surprised.

"Take a couple of puffs. It will settle your nerves," Irene said quietly.

Irene picked up her cigarette case, took a cigarette for herself and lit it. "Do you smoke?"

"Indeed, it's one of my many vices." Irene chuckled. She took a drag of the cigarette. "Has your heart stopped racing?"

Eva nodded. She felt embarrassed that she had been taken by surprise and by her reaction.

"You don't need to be embarrassed. When you suffer from shellshock that is what happens. It's very common to get startled by even the slightest of things."

Eva gazed at Irene for a long moment. "Did Aunt Tessa tell you?"

"No, you just did by the way you reacted. I've worked with soldiers who suffered from shellshock, and that is one of the signs," Irene said. "There is a great deal we need to discuss, Eva. When you are ready . . ."

"I'm ready," Eva replied. "I keep getting told that the story with my aunt Tessa will be revealed, and I hear little bits and pieces, but I don't get the full story."

"I'll tell you the full story once I explain why my maid went a little crazy. The house was robbed recently and Katarina caught the men looking for whatever they were looking for. She saw you, and you are not exactly petite, so she thought you were robbing the place."

"I was standing in front of the refrigerator. Do robbers steal food?"

"As I said she went a little crazy." Irene put Eva's cigarette in her mouth. "Smoke it. You need to calm your nerves."

Eva puffed on the cigarette and exhaled. "You are not like any nun I've ever met."

"Good. I wouldn't want to be like any nun I've ever met, and I've met quite a few." Irene chuckled.

Katarina walked back into the kitchen a little hesitantly. She was taller than Eva, a rotund woman in her late fifties. Her hair was up in a bun and she wore a dark blue uniform and a white apron.

"I'm so sorry, Fräulein."

"It wasn't your fault, Katarina. I'm a little jumpy."

"You're a little jumpy, I'm a little jumpy, it makes for a very interesting morning," Katarina said, and smiled shyly. "What would you like me to make you for breakfast? A big girl like you would probably like some *bauerfruhstuck*?"

Eva grinned at her favorite breakfast.

Katarina laughed. "I think I have my answer. I will call you when it's ready."

Eva stood up along with Irene and they walked out of the kitchen and into a small study. Irene shut the door.

CHAPTER 23

"SO, WHY DON'T you finish your cigarette and tell me about Zoe?"

Eva sat down on a comfortable overstuffed chair. She picked up her cigarette from the ashtray and took a drag. She then stubbed it out, half-smoked.

Irene smiled at Eva's impatience. "Or you could stub it out. Now where do I start?"

"We can talk about Zoe as soon as you answer some of the thousand questions I have."

"Only a thousand?"

"How was it possible for me to see you in Aiden?" Eva asked.

"That's going to be in the middle of the story. I'll start at the beginning," Irene said.

Eva looked up at a gentle knock on the door. Zoe entered with a tray containing three mugs. Her hair was slightly damp but she was fully clothed.

"Katarina thought you might like some tea." Zoe placed the tray on the nearby coffee table. She handed a cup to Irene and another to Eva. Then she dragged a chair to next to Eva and sat down.

"Sister Irene is about to answer some questions," Eva said.

"Ah, all right," Zoe said.

"I was born on January tenth, 1880 to Rudolph Faber and Theresa Petra Frei, a German couple from Dahlem. My name is Irene Eva Faber. Actually I was born in this room." Irene smiled.

"Can—" Eva started.

Irene held up a hand.

"You're not Greek?" Zoe asked.

"No. My parents had three children. I was the oldest daughter. My sister was Eva Theresa and Johan is my brother."

Eva stared at Irene as the words sunk in. "My grandmother was your sister?"

"Yes." Irene nodded. "Your grandmother was my sister, which makes me your Great Aunt."

Eva closed her eyes and exhaled. "This is a story within a story within a story . . . It never ends."

"Our family history has many layers, Eva. It is important to know how you are connected for this to make any sense."

"Johan? Is that Father Johan that Eva's father befriended in Athens?" Zoe asked and glanced at Eva.

"Yes. Johan and Panayiotis did strike up a friendship . . ."

"You know my father?"

"Do I know him? No. Have I met him? Yes," Irene replied a little too cryptically.

"So you used him?"

"Who? My brother? Heavens, no. They became friends quite by accident."

"I'm coming to believe nothing in this family happens by accident." Eva ran her hand through her hair.

"Hey." Zoe put her hand on Eva's knee. "This is a good thing."

"Is it?" Eva asked, and turned to Zoe. "I go from having no family other than the Mullers to having an aunt who is very much alive, although I thought she was dead, a first cousin, an adopted aunt and cousin, a great aunt and a great uncle, and a husband."

"It's going to be fine, love, it will." Zoe turned to Eva. "There's so much that's happened to us since we've been back, but let's hear what your great aunt has to say."

"Well, there isn't much I can do other than listen."

"You know of Theresa's gifts, is that right?" Irene's blue eyes gazed into Eva's eyes. Eva nodded. "Theresa is blessed with something that only God can give. All the women in our family line possess this ability, but sometimes it will jump a generation."

"What is it?"

"Some have had the gift of prophecy, others possess the ability to project themselves to another time or place, and others will dream dreams and have visions and other gifts. I traced our family lineage to the day of our Lord."

"The Day of our Lord?"

Irene turned around and found the Bible. She opened it and flipped through several pages. She put on her glasses and looked over the rim at Eva. "Acts 2:15 says, 'In those days Peter stood up among the believers.' That was a group numbering about a hundred and twenty. In Acts 2:17, it reads: 'And in the last days,' God says, 'I will pour out my spirit upon every sort of flesh, and your sons and your daughters will prophesy and your young men will see visions and your old men will dream dreams.'"

Eva covered her mouth in shock. "You are telling me that my ancestor was one of the women who received the Holy Spirit along with the disciples?"

"Yes. A woman by the name of Theresa Eva was one of the first Christians to receive the Holy Spirit on the day of Pentecost in 33 AD."

"Pentecost? We are talking about one of the most incredible miracles in Christianity."

"Well, next to bringing the dead back to life, yes, that's the one."

"Eva Theresa . . . that's your name," Zoe explained. "Is the name significant?"

"I don't know, but over the centuries, the names of those that were gifted had either Eva or Theresa in them. There may have been gifted ones named differently but it was tradition to pass on those names."

"Damn. Eva was given both names, what does that mean?" Zoe exclaimed. She looked apologetically at Irene. "Sorry."

"It's alright. You should have heard your aunt Theresa when I told her. We are getting to that part."

"I . . . I . . . wow." Eva took a cigarette from its case, lit it, and took a drag. "I think I need something stronger than tea, Zo."

"For many generations this gift has been a blessing and a curse. Among many of those hundred and twenty that were originally given the Holy Spirit, it only lasted until they passed away or soon after as its influence on their descendants waned. For others it got passed down from generation to generation."

"Only the women in the family get it?"

"Not all the time," Irene explained. "I'm not sure you can predict what God intends for you and who the gifts will go to."

"Are you gifted as well?"

"Yes. I had always been an inquisitive child and ever since I could remember, I saw visions. I told no one about this, thinking they would think me mad. I had heard family stories of aunts who had been sent to lunatic asylums—far too many down the generations to really be an accident," Irene said with a wry smile. "One lunatic aunt was feasible but not in every generation going back hundreds of years."

"I need something to drink," Eva got up and walked to the liquor cabinet. She opened the nearest bottle of alcohol she could find and poured herself a drink. She turned and leaned against the cabinet. She shook her head and took a drink of the wine.

"What do you think?" she asked.

"I plan on getting us both drunk tonight. That's the only way we're going to go to sleep," Zoe replied.

"It's evening in Sydney," Eva said with a half smile, and filled her glass, shook her head, and drank the entire glass in one gulp. "All right, please continue."

"I never told anyone about my gifts. I really didn't want to end up in a lunatic asylum. I chose to go where miracles are considered acts of God."

"You joined a convent?"

"I did. It was also a way to help the poor, which appealed to me, and I could use my gifts without arousing suspicions."

"That's clever."

"Yes, but I'm not that clever." Irene chuckled. "My great aunt Erika Theresa told me about my gifts because she had them."

"How did she know you had them?"

"I went to visit her in the lunatic asylum," Irene replied with a sad smile. "She was an incredible woman; she could see the future. I remember she said to me that I wouldn't have children, not because I couldn't but because I'd choose not to."

"That's not shocking."

"It was to me, so I asked her why. She looked at me with a smile and she said, 'You know why Irene, you have the gift of prophecy. Don't deny it, you do. I know you do and so does our Lord.'"

"You became a nun to hide the gifts?" Eva asked.

"Yes, I did. My sister didn't know, but I suspect my mother did and chose not to say anything. When my sister was pregnant with Theresa, I knew that Theresa was the one that would have that gift."

"Why didn't you tell them? Why didn't you stop them from sending her to the lunatic asylum?"

Irene closed her eyes for a long moment. "When Theresa's visions began I was struck down by polio and was very ill. It was touch and go if I lived. When I finally regained my strength, I was told that Theresa had been killed in a fire at the asylum."

"Oh, wow."

"I was devastated that my beautiful niece was gone and I grieved for her. A few months after that terrible news, I began to have visions of Theresa. I dismissed them thinking that was because I was grieving." Irene took a cigarette from Eva's case and lit it up.

"A nun who smokes?" Zoe turned to Eva with a bemused expression on her face. "What kind of family have I married into?"

Eva smiled for the first time since they had gone into the study.

"I was asked to help where there was a need in Thessaloniki. They had had some polio deaths and needed some extra hands to help in the hospice. While I was there, a young woman walked into the church." Irene took a drag of her cigarette. "She was sitting alone in the pew and I was drawn to her."

"Aunty Stella."

"Yes. I sat down to talk to her because she looked like she could use some company. We started talking about what she was doing and about the war. It was then that she started to tell me about her work at Saint Gregori and her experiences there."

"Oh, wow."

"Yes, indeed. What was more remarkable for me was that right in the middle of her telling me about her work, I saw my niece's image in my head. Clear as day and it wasn't a vision of her as a teenager but as a grown woman. I took a big risk but God was sending me a message."

"Did you come out and ask her about Tessa?"

"I did. To say Stella was shocked would not have been a lie. She was scared but when I proved to her who I was, she invited me to her home. Imagine my surprise not only seeing my beautiful niece, who was exactly as I had seen in my vision, but that gorgeous young boy as well."

"Oh," Eva exclaimed.

"I know this is a lot to take in, darling." Irene put her hand on Eva's knee. "If you want to stop, we can take it up tonight—"

"No. I want to know."

"When I visited Theresa and we talked about her gifts and how to deal with them, she showed me some drawings. I believe you've seen them?"

"Oh yes, we saw them," Zoe replied as she rested her hand on Eva's thigh.

"I had a panic attack."

"Darling, when I saw those drawings I was disturbed, so I don't blame you. They are very realistic. You lived it, so seeing them again made you relive it. I would have been worried if you hadn't reacted."

"That's not much of a gift . . . um." Zoe paused.

"Call me Irene. Not all of Theresa's artwork is so gruesome. The art is not part of her inherited gift from God, but another gift which is quite common. She is a very talented artist. She combines these two gifts."

"This sounds more like a curse than a blessing," Eva said quietly.

Irene smiled cryptically. "Do you really think so?"

"Yes."

"Yes, it could seem like a curse because of the pain and anguish your aunt went through knowing her niece was going to suffer so much, but there is the knowledge that you can do something to help," Irene said. "She had the power to help you."

"She sent Tommy."

"Yes, that dear boy. He saw those drawings and he didn't hesitate to help you. One day he will find the right soul for him."

"What kind of soul?"

"Zoe," Eva warned and shook her head. "Stay out of it."

Irene laughed lightly. "Yes, he will find the right man."

"You know about that?"

Irene laughed. "Oh goodness, I knew long before he did. I'm sure Tommy would not like us to be discussing him in this way, but he will find that special man."

"Oh, boy." Eva shook her head in disbelief. She pinched herself and winced. "Ow, yes, I am awake." She poured herself another drink.

"So was it you that came to Eva with the idea to fake her recovery?"

Irene smiled. "Sort of."

"Sort of?"

"It was me but it was also you, Eva."

"I . . . I . . . what?"

"It was you and I. We both shared that vision."

"How is that even possible?"

Irene looked at Eva and for a moment hesitated. "You have inherited these gifts."

"I . . . I . . . what?" Eva looked at Zoe, who looked stunned. "Did you hear what Irene just said? I'm not the only one hearing this, right?"

"Yes, Irene said you have these inherited gifts," Zoe said.

"Fuck me dead," Eva cursed, not caring if her great aunt would be outraged by the expletive. Zoe's eyes widened. She looked up at the ceiling. "Fuck."

"That's an expletive I heard a few times from your Aunt Theresa when I told her about her gifts. It must be the curse of choice."

"S . . . sorry," Eva apologized as she stared at the wine bottle.

"It's quite alright. You allowed me into your mind, Eva, that's how you were able to see me."

"But I didn't know . . ."

"No, you didn't, but somehow you trusted me even though you didn't know who I was, and allowed me to do what I did."

"What about on the ship? Was that was you on the ship?"

"Yes." Irene smiled. "That was me."

"Wow."

"So what are Eva's gifts?" Zoe asked as she leaned forward.

Irene looked at Zoe for a long moment. "My dear girl, I think you may need to have a drink yourself shortly."

"I would do it now, Zo."

"No, I'm fine," Zoe replied as she turned to Eva. "Are you alright?"

"No, but I will be."

"I want to take you both back to Larissa, back to that field," Irene said. "I know it's going to be hard but this is important."

"No, I don't want to do that." Eva stood and turned for the door. Zoe grabbed her arm and stopped her.

"Evy, come back here," Zoe said. "It's important."

"No." Eva walked to the door, put her head on the doorknob, and rest her head on the door.

Zoe went to Eva. "This is going to hurt. It always does, but you have to know. We can't hide from this. I need to know."

Eva sighed. She returned to her chair and sat down heavily, head down but still holding Zoe's hand.

"When Muller was yelling and cursing on that muddy field, why did you look at Zoe?" Irene asked.

Eva looked up and blinked. "Zoe looked at me."

Zoe turned her attention to Eva and shook her head. "No, I didn't. I was looking at Muller but when he passed me, I turned and found you staring at me."

Irene watched Eva's face closely. "You don't remember that?"

"I don't know," Eva honestly replied. "I remember trying not to focus on anyone."

"I want you to think back, I want you to think back to that very moment in time when you chose to look at Zoe."

Eva closed her eyes as the visions came flooding back. Eva grimaced. She could smell the stench of blood all around her as if she was back there again. She had focused on the horizon, not wanting to see the faces of those that would be killed. She didn't want to remember their faces. One girl stood out from everyone else. Zoe.

"I remember being mesmerized by this young girl who wasn't cowering as Muller was coming towards her. She wasn't doing what everyone else was doing and trying to hide. Zoe almost dared Muller to come her way."

"I did what?"

"You watched as Zoe met Muller's gaze without fear—" Irene said.

"Oh I was afraid," Zoe said. "I was terrified . . ."

Eva's eyes popped open and she stared at Zoe in amazement.

"What?" Zoe asked.

"I knew something was going to happen to you," Eva whispered.

"What?"

"I knew."

"Like you knew that you had to get home instead of staying with your friends on Kristallnacht. You knew your mother was in trouble," Irene said. "Like you knew that your grandfather was dying or that your friend Wilhelm didn't survive the war."

Eva's head fell forward. She felt her chest constrict as memories of Kristallnacht flooded back—that one night that changed everything for her. She did know. She knew there had been something wrong, begged off from going with her friends and ran home as fast as she could. She knew.

"Like you knew that I would fall off my motorcycle. You kept warning me to be careful and you knew when I had fallen off my motorcycle even before Earl rang you," Zoe quietly added. "Or you knew when someone was watching us at the park or you know when I'm sick before I get sick."

"I . . ." Eva opened her mouth and froze. She nodded. "I do."

"Why did you look at Zoe, Eva?"

Eva blinked. "I knew Zoe was going to die that day."

Zoe gasped.

"You knew Zoe was going to die that day. At that very moment in time, you knew that Zoe was going to be shot dead. You looked at her to distract her from—"

"From doing something so completely stupid that it would have gotten me killed," Zoe exclaimed. "I remember what I was thinking as Muller was coming towards me. I was going to rush him."

"But you didn't. Why?"

"The tall German woman in a black cloak, standing in the rain, looked at me. She stared at me that I didn't move," Zoe said in amazement. "Evy, you saved my life."

"I . . ." Eva looked to Irene and then to Zoe in shock and disbelief.

"Zoe and her mother were destined to die that day," Irene said quietly. She took out Tessa's drawing and put it on the table.

Zoe's eyes welled up and tears tracked down her cheeks, but she didn't turn away from the image.

Eva looked down to see two bodies in the mud. She was in shock. She blinked back tears on seeing mud and blood caked on Zoe's teenage face.

"You changed Zoe's destiny, Eva," Irene said.

"Dear God," Zoe exclaimed and wiped her eyes.

Eva got up and faced the wall. She rested her head on the paneling as she tried to process it all.

Zoe went to her and put her arms around her. "You saved my life."

Eva turned and gazed down into Zoe's eyes. "You saved mine." Her voice broke as the tears ran down her cheeks. She cupped Zoe's face and kissed her. They held each other for a long time.

Zoe took Eva's hand and led her back to their seats.

"You have that ability, Eva, but there is more," Irene said.

"Isn't that enough?"

"It's God's will, Eva. We all say 'isn't it enough' but God has a plan. You went through the fires of hell in Aiden. It's going to take time to heal, and once you do, those gifts will come to the surface."

"Like what?" Zoe asked. "Apart from Eva's knowing when things will occur before they happen."

"I don't know, but we will have to wait and see."

"Wow." Eva scrubbed her face. "Did my mother know?"

"I don't know if your mother knew you had these gifts. I know she didn't believe Theresa was possessed, but other than that, I don't know."

"What happens next?"

"You start to heal. You finally walk out of Aiden and learn to accept who you are. It will take time, but Stella tells me you have made great progress in the short time she has been helping you. Allow Stella and Theresa to help you and help Zoe." Irene smiled. "You're going to the cemetery to see your mother, is that right?"

"Yes, we were going to go today but I don't think I can handle that now."

"No, I don't expect you can, but knowing why is better than not knowing. It's a lot to process and we will talk again, alright?" Irene tapped Eva on the knee. She got up and kissed Eva's head, then walked out of the room.

Zoe picked up the drawing and gazed at it for a long moment before she looked at Eva. Eva was slouching in the chair and staring at Zoe. "Evy?"

"Hmm."

"Thank you," Zoe quietly said and dropped the drawing on the table. She got up and sat in Eva's lap. "You changed our lives."

Eva gazed at Zoe for a long moment before she buried her head against Zoe's chest and wept.

CHAPTER 24

A GENTLE, WARM breeze blew the fallen leaves across the court-yard as Tessa sat on the stone bench under a large weeping birch tree. She watched the leaves swirl around and settle before another breeze would carried them further across the ground.

Tessa glanced at the house, knowing that Irene was giving Eva the news. The door from the villa opened and Irene walked out. She stood at the top of the steps for a long moment and crossed herself.

Irene slowly made her way down the steps and followed the walkway to where Tessa was sitting.

"You told her?" Tessa asked and shifted sideways to let Irene sit beside her.

"I did."

"What did she say?"

"Fuck me dead," Irene replied.

Tessa looked away grimly towards the house. "There isn't a lot she can say to that news."

"It's a word I used many years ago when I was told about my gifts," Irene said.

"That would sound funny coming from you."

"I do like the sound of those words although I don't quite understand why they are curse words. If you fuck yourself dead, wouldn't you die happy? Not that I would know, and that shouldn't fascinate me, yet it does. I have a fellow sister in Great Britain that likes to use the word 'Bollocks' every now and then," Irene rambled.

Tessa gave her an affectionate smile. "She didn't realize she had the gift, did she?"

"No. You were right about that. She thought it was because Zoe was looking at her that she stared back. Are you going to tell Zoe about Athena's Bluff?"

"Zoe did ask me if I was the one who said 'no, don't' to her on Athena's Bluff, thus distracting her from pulling the trigger. I've come to know Zoe quite well, and one thing I've realized is that she will continue to dig if she has questions, and she has a lot of questions.

"Eva doesn't?"

"I don't know. Eva keeps things close to her chest. She doesn't say much unless you get it out of her." Tessa shook her head. "Zoe will be the one to ask me."

"You know this or . . ."

"I'm guessing." Tessa smiled. "Experience with Zoe tells me that Zoe will ask."

"Yes I'm sure Zoe will ask. Don't tell them about their firstborn."

"Yes, I agree. Now is not the time and telling them may make them change history." Tessa shook her head. "Aunty, um . . ."

"It's been on your mind for a while, hasn't it?"

"Yes. I can't help but wonder. Are our gifts more powerful now than in previous generations? Surely they can't be more powerful because Eva Theresa was given these gifts directly from the Holy Ghost."

"Your great great aunt Erika Theresa told me that there was great darkness coming. I don't know what that means or if we have gone through it already . . ."

"The Last Days that Jesus talked about?" Tessa asked. "Is that what she meant?"

"Could be. I don't know. Saint Peter did say 'I will pour out my spirit upon every sort of flesh, and your sons and your daughters will prophesy and your young men will see visions and your old men will dream dreams.' I don't know."

"It's been quite a morning. Any more visits from our friends?" Tessa picked up a twig from the ground and twirled it around her fingers. She gazed at it for a moment and the twig snapped in two. She dropped the twigs to the ground.

Irene looked at the twig and then at Tessa. "Show off," she said with a smile. "Katarina is primed with a bat for anyone who breaks in again. She thought Eva was an intruder. Luckily for Eva, Katarina didn't have her bat."

"They are coming, right?"

"Oh yes." Irene nodded. "Tonight."

"When is Uncle Johan coming home?"

"He was at the hospice last night giving the Last Rites to a young man with cancer—he passed away this morning. I expect him to be home tonight."

"Aunty, what do you think Eva will say to them?"

Irene glanced at the house for a moment and then back to Tessa. "Fuck off," she said with a mischievous grin and a twinkle in her blue eyes.

"DID I SAY 'fuck' to a nun?" Eva turned to Zoe, who was slumped in a chair.

Zoe smiled and nodded.

"I said 'fuck' to a nun and not any old nun . . . my great aunt."

"You didn't say fuck any old nun—that's different and a little icky," Zoe joked, trying to get Eva to laugh.

Eva turned to her looking shocked, then a smile creased her face and she laughed.

Zoe fell back on the lounge chair, shaking her head. "Your mother would be so proud. I'll tell her tomorrow you told her aunt to go and do naughty things."

"Oh, god." Eva held her head in her hands. "I think facing my grandmother would be like taking a walk in the park compared to this."

"Are you going to tell your grandmother to get fucked?" Zoe said mischievously. "I would love to see that."

"Why not? I'm on a roll, great aunt, grandmother . . ."

"So." Zoe took Eva's hands. "What are we going to do?"

"I don't know. I can't give this gift back, can I?"

"I don't think so. So what do we know?"

"The women are inheriting this gift that was handed down by that silly woman who was in a room with the Apostles." Eva leaned forward, inches away from Zoe's face. "We know that gift didn't die with her as it should have."

"She was one of one hundred and twenty to get this gift, right? So what happened to the other one hundred and seven minus your gift giver? We know what happened to the twelve Apostles. Did those one hundred and seven give their gifts to their children like Theresa Eva? There must be others like you, your aunt, and great aunt."

"That makes me sound like a leper." Eva scowled.

Zoe smoothed the deep furrow between Eva's eyes. "What if she didn't die?"

"Who?"

"Theresa Eva. What if she didn't die and she's still alive after two thousand years?"

"That's impossible. No one is immortal."

"Really?" Zoe smiled. "How do you know? As far as we knew, you didn't have any gifts, you didn't have any family other than the Mullers before we left for Europe. How do we know that this woman is not the head of some big organization?"

Eva looked at Zoe for a moment and then grinned. "You read too many stories, Zo."

Zoe grinned back and nodded. "Got you to smile. She might be Frau Muller."

Eva fell back on her chair, laughing. "Oh god, you just make me laugh."

"That's my job." Zoe kissed Eva tenderly. "Are you feeling better?"

Eva shook her head. "No, but I don't think I'm going to feel better for a long time. That was a shock."

"I was going to be shot in the head," Zoe said quietly. "That would have messed up my day and my pretty green blouse."

Eva laughed. "Zoe, stop."

"If we don't attempt to find humor in this, I think we will both be ready for the lunatic asylum just like all those poor women."

"You may be right."

"You know what I think? I think your aunt Tessa hasn't been telling us the truth about her gifts," Zoe said seriously. "I think she may have been hoping we were too bamboozled by what was going on with her visions and that whole eye thing to question her any further."

"I think that vision thing and her eyes was enough to shake us."

"Yes. She didn't lie to us but she didn't tell us the truth either. I was so shocked by what she could do when her eyes changed color."

"Do my eyes change color?"

Zoe smiled. "Only when we make love, and that," she buffed her nails against her shirt, "has everything to do with me and not you." She gave her a devilish grin.

Zoe got up and looked out at the garden, where she could see Irene and Tessa talking under the tree. "Ever since Irene told us about these gifts, something Tessa said to me in Larissa makes me wonder about something."

"What?"

"Remember I asked her if it was her that said 'no, don't' up on Athena's Bluff and that didn't give me enough time to rush you? She said it was her."

"So what's wrong with that?"

"That wasn't the only thing that happened up on the mountain. Eva, that gun I had with me did work, but it jammed when I saw you."

"I don't understand. The gun jammed and what?"

Zoe turned away from the window and gazed at Eva. "I killed a rabbit with that gun right after you left. There was nothing wrong with that gun."

Eva stared at Zoe for a long moment. "Tessa jammed the gun? How? She was in Thessaloniki."

"Yes. She could send a message to me that only I could hear, I had a gun that worked but didn't . . ."

The two remained silent for a moment before Eva slapped herself on the head. "Oh dear."

"What?"

"Do you remember when Father brought me down to the church cellar and you were there?"

"Yes, after I executed my collaborator cousin—that worthless piece of shit," Zoe exclaimed.

"Do you remember what happened?"

Zoe frowned in thought, then turned to Eva in astonishment. "The gun jammed."

"You saw me and you pulled your gun and fired. It jammed. Zoe, your gun jamming once up in the mountain could be a faulty gun but jamming twice and both times I was on the other end . . ."

"Holy Mother of God!" Zoe exclaimed. "Evy, that gun jammed twice up the mountain and twice in the cellar."

"Wow," Eva exclaimed quietly. "Who are these people? What if they are possessed?"

"Are you possessed?"

"I don't know. One minute everything is fine and the next I just know something is wrong. Where does that come from?"

"Do you see visions?"

"No. I just feel that something will happen."

"Have you ever had visions?" Zoe asked as she sat on the coffee table book and gazed at Eva. "Think back to before you were sent to Aiden."

"Not really."

"Not really means yes, I think so but I'm not sure," Zoe reasoned.

"I don't remember." Eva shook her head slowly. "I've always known when something was going to happen but I didn't think anything of it."

A gentle knock preceded the door opening and Tessa walked in. She closed the door. She carried a plate with Eva's breakfast, and a towel was draped over her arm. She put the plate in front of Eva.

"Eat something."

"I'm not hungry," Eva replied as she poured herself another glass of wine. She drank from it and put it down.

"You are going to feel absolutely awful in an hour."

"How do you know that? Your gift?" Eva asked with a nervous laugh.

"No." Tessa shook her head and sat down. "When Irene told me what I had inherited, I drank a full bottle of Retsina on an empty stomach." She smiled. "Poor Stella had to clean up after me because I threw up all over the place."

Eva stared at Tessa for a moment before she picked up a fork and cut off a piece of the *bauerfruhstuck* and gave it to Zoe. Zoe accepted the morsel then gave Eva a pointed look. With a resigned shrug, Eva ate some of her breakfast.

"I know what you are going through," Tessa said. "I know the questions running through your mind."

"No, you don't," Eva mumbled as she put another forkful of her breakfast in her mouth.

"I have a question." Zoe quickly glanced at Eva and then back at Tessa. "What are your powers?"

"They're not powers."

"Gifts, powers, whatever they are called. What are they?"

"As you know, I have visions."

"What else?"

Tessa tilted her head and smiled. "I was just saying to Irene that you would figure it out. I can move objects with my mind."

"Huh?" Eva mumbled with a mouthful of food.

Tessa exhaled slowly and closed her eyes. She placed her hands on her lap, opened her eyes, and looked at Eva.

Nothing happened for a moment, Then Eva and her chair moved sideways by a few inches.

"Argh!" Eva screamed. She bolted up and the plate with the *bauerfruhstuck* came crashed to the carpet. She stood staring at the chair, the fork still in her hand.

Zoe stood with her mouth agape and her hand over her heart in shock. "Fuck."

"That word seems to be getting a good workout today." Tessa smiled serenely. "Katarina is going to get so mad at me," she muttered as she knelt by the upturned plate and picked up the remains of the food. She placed the plate onto the table and resumed her seat.

"You jammed the gun," Zoe said.

"I did. Every time you pulled that trigger and you were aiming at Eva, it jammed, and yes, it was me." Tessa nodded. "Eva was going to die by your hand. I wasn't going to let that happen."

The study door was flung open and Stella came running in to find Tessa smiling and sitting in the comfortable leather chair. Stella glanced at Eva, who was still looking at the carpet in shock, an upraised fork in her hand.

Irene peered around Stella at the occupants of the room. "Show off," she said, shaking her head, and walked off.

CHAPTER 25

EVA DECIDED SHE needed to walk. Anywhere. It didn't matter where as long as she was alone and able to think.

Eva found herself walking in the gardens surrounding the villas until she got to a garage. She sat down on the wooden bench and stared off into the sky as if seeking answers to her many questions. She heard noises coming from the garage, so she got up and went to investigate.

"Hello?" Eva said as she spied a couple of legs sticking out from under a vintage car.

The legs moved as the person they belonged to slid out from under the undercarriage of the car.

"Hello," the man said as he got up and picked up a cloth to wipe the oil from his hands.

"Who are you?"

"I could say the same to you but I already know." The man chuckled.

Eva couldn't see him clearly in the dark garage. She took a step back to allow him to exit.

"Great, another seer," Eva muttered.

The man smiled and walked out into the sunshine. Eva stared slack jawed up at him. He was taller than her, and broad shouldered, and he had salt-and-pepper hair and a dimpled chin.

"I'm Father Johan Faber. I'm also known as Uncle Johan." He engulfed Eva in a hug that she enthusiastically reciprocated.

"Wow."

"Yes, your great aunt Irene did draw the short stature straw." Johan chuckled. "My, my, my, let me look at you." He held her at arm's length. "You have the Faber dimple, black hair and blue eyes. You are the spitting image of—"

"My mother?"

"Yes, you do look like Daphne." Johan nodded. "But the template for this look belongs to your great great grandmother Eva Louisa."

"I've never heard of Eva Louisa."

"There's a lot you haven't heard about." Johan led Eva to the bench. "So has Irene dazzled you yet?"

"Dazzled isn't the right word. Bamboozled, puzzled, confused, bewildered, baffled, perplexed, and—"

"Are you going through the whole thesaurus?" Johan asked.

Eva nodded.

Johan smiled. "You're trying to find the right word to describe the indescribable?"

"Yes, that's it."

"Hmm. Don't." Johan stretched out his long legs and folded them at the ankles. "Sometimes it's best to just accept what God has given you."

"That's the problem. I don't know what God has given me."

"You don't?"

"No. I just found out about this inherited gift. I don't even know how much I want to believe is true."

"What is faith?"

"Faith is the substance of things hoped for, the evidence of things not seen." Eva recited the Bible verse she knew by heart.

"Yes, that is what the Bible says, but what do you think faith is?"

Eva took a deep breath and exhaled slowly. "Believing in something so profound, something that is bigger than you, and knowing that it's true even though you can't see it."

Johan smiled. "This gift is profound, bigger than you, and you can't see it, but it's there. If you can accept that this is what faith is, then why can't you accept that God gave you this gift as a sign of His love?"

Eva looked down at the ground and tracked an ant as it went around her foot. "How does a woman who goes into a room with one-hundred-and-twenty people, a normal, average woman who just happened to believe in Jesus Christ, come out totally transformed?"

"That, Eva, is called being touched by The Holy Spirit. They were normal people, they had every day jobs, every day concerns like you and me. They went into that room to congregate together, to find solace in each other's company. The Lord promised them that he would send help. He did. It was The Holy Spirit."

"They walked out totally transformed."

"They did." Johan smiled. "Everyone outside thought they were drunk. They were speaking in tongues. People who could barely speak their own language spoke with great authority and in a different language. The power of God."

"I understand that, but why has this gift come down through the generations to today?"

"I don't know," Johan replied. "Why do the descendants of Eva Theresa receive this gift? I don't know."

"If this is from God, why does the Church condemn people like Aunt Tessa and think she is possessed?"

Johan took out a small bible from his top pocket. "The Church has lost its way."

Eva turned to him, astonished at such sentiments coming from a priest. "Are you saying the Church is wrong?"

"Yes, I am. They fear what they do not know."

"Good thing we are not living through the Inquisition," Eva quipped.

Johan put his hand on her shoulder. "We would have been in a lot of trouble."

"So what do I do?"

"Nothing," Johan replied. "You do nothing. Have you experienced anything out of the ordinary?"

"Other than knowing when things are going to happen? No," Eva replied with a wry smile.

"How long have you known things were going to happen before they happened?"

"For as long as I can remember," Eva admitted. "I knew things would happen and they did."

"You didn't think that strange?"

"No. I thought everyone thought this way. I just never questioned it."

"Interesting." Johan a cigar from his pocket.

Eva raised her eyebrows.

"I like cigars."

"Me too."

"You do? Wonderful. Wait here." Johan went back into the garage. Moments later he came out with another cigar. "Here you go."

Eva chuckled while Johan lit her cigar. "I wonder if I'm dreaming all of this."

"Nah," Johan said as he took a puff of his own cigar. "Life is far more interesting than dreams."

"Not if you have visions, it's not."

"Ah yes, those."

"Am I supposed to have them too?"

"Yes, I believe visions do come with the knowing everything before it happens part of the gift."

"Are you joking?"

"Yes." Johan chuckled. "Everyone has different gifts. Some foresee events before they happen or know they will happen. Others move objects with their minds, although I'm not quite sure what good that does in spreading the word of God. Others project themselves to another time and place."

"Like Aunty Tessa."

"Oh yes, Tessa is something else." Johan smiled knowingly. "She has to be the most powerful of all the generations so far. Has she shown you yet?"

"She moved me and my seat while I was eating."

Johan laughed lightly. "That's her favorite. Gave me a few extra grey hairs when she did that to me. Did she do that whole sitting down and concentrating? She can do it with a blink of an eye."

"What else can she do?"

"Ah, Eva, that's not for me to tell. That's for your Aunty Tessa. When she was a child she suffered a great deal because she truly believed she was possessed."

"I'm incredulous and I'm thirty. I can't imagine what that would do to a child."

"It doesn't do anything good. Tessa possessed the ability to foresee events that hadn't happened, and because she was an artist, she drew them. You can imagine her horror in drawing something and then finding out it was true."

"I can imagine," Eva said quietly. "I've seen her art."

"Hmm, yes. That wasn't one of Stella's brightest ideas."

"You heard?" Eva asked, feeling a little apprehensive at what Johan would think of her.

Johan took Eva's hand and gazed at her. "There is no shame in showing those you love how you feel. You have gone through a terrible ordeal but you are stronger for it."

"I am, sometimes."

"I think you underestimate yourself. Did you believe you would survive Aiden?"

"No."

"Even with your gift, you didn't believe it?"

"No."

"But you have. You are sitting here, in the lovely garden, with your great uncle, smoking a great cigar." Johan held up his cigar and smiled. "Are you sure you didn't know this was going to happen?"

"Quite sure."

"No. I think you are wrong. I think you did know this would happen but you believed it wouldn't. Believing in something requires faith. You lost your faith."

Eva stared at Johan open mouthed. "How—"

"We all lose faith. Even Saint Peter lost faith. Remember when Jesus asked him to join him on the water? Peter was full of faith and he stepped out of the boat." Johan smiled. "But once his brain caught up with his faith, it said 'oops, what are you doing, stop,' and down Peter went. He lost faith that he could walk on water just like Jesus."

"But he couldn't walk on water."

"But he did," Johan replied. "He walked on water with Jesus. He had so much faith in the Lord that he was the only second mortal man to ever do it. What does that tell you?"

"I don't know."

"Sure, you do. God calls us to do impossible things by faith. He asked Peter to come and Peter came. Peter kept his eyes on Jesus and by doing that he believed. Looking around and believing the storm was going to defeat him, his faith wavered for a moment and he lost the ability to walk on water."

"He actually walked on water?"

"He did. He also uttered the words you said many times while in Aiden."

"Lord, save me," Eva whispered.

"Yes, and what did the Lord do?"

"Saved me," Eva replied as she closed her eyes.

"He did. He sent Tessa, Irene, Tommy, and your own father. When you found the strength, you opened your heart and he sent Zoe."

"You know about Zoe?"

Johan laughed heartily. "Have you forgotten who my sister is? I've been hearing about that young woman for a long time. Eva, God sent you people who could help you because you asked Him."

"He did."

"You said to Him, 'save me,' and He did. Don't question why He gave you this gift. Accept it for what it is."

"But Uncle Johan, I have no idea what it is."

"Many didn't know why they were given those gifts or how to use them, but in time they were shown. Give it time and He will tell you."

Eva sighed. "I'm normally a very patient person but Zoe must be rubbing off on me because I want to know now."

Johan put his arm around Eva and smiled. "My dear Eva, all will be revealed when He wants it to be revealed."

"Spoken like a priest," Eva joked, and for the first time that day she felt a calm descend on her. "Talking to you about this has been good."

"I actually think it's the cigar. I find it calms my nerves, but I'll take the compliment." Johan chuckled.

"What were you doing in there?"

"That is my lost cause. When I have something on my mind, I find it relaxing to tinker with the car."

"Do you fix it?"

"No, it's unfixable, but I tinker with it anyway, hoping by some miracle I can actually fix it. I may take it apart again just to reassemble it." Johan leaned back against the garage wall and sighed contentedly. "A young man passed away last night from that dreaded cancer. I was with him before he passed on."

"I'm sorry."

"Hmm. He is now with the Lord and not in pain anymore. What is your favorite scripture from the Bible?"

"Psalm 23," Eva replied without hesitation. "'Yea, though I walk through the valley of the shadow of death, I will fear no evil: for thou art with me; thy rod and thy staff they comfort me.'"

Johan nodded. "Why do you think you like that?"

"I walked through the valley of the shadow of death."

"Yes, indeed, and the end of that chapter says, 'Surely goodness and mercy shall follow me all the days of my life: and I will dwell in the house of the Lord for ever.' God has shown you mercy and a whole lot of goodness.'"

"He has."

"My favorite is from Revelation 21: 4, where it says, 'And God shall wipe away all tears from their eyes; and there shall be no more death, neither sorrow, nor crying, neither shall there be any more pain: for the former things are passed away.' That young man is with God and there is no more pain." Johan brought out the gold cross that hung around his neck and kissed it.

"We're going to get a couple of visitors," Eva said surprising herself. She glanced at Johan, who didn't seem fazed at all.

Johan stubbed out his cigar and put it in his pocket. He stood and took Eva's hand. "The Mullers are going to be paying us a visit."

"I'm not even going to ask how I knew that or how you knew that."

"Irene tells me they are going to pay us a visit. When? I don't know but it's going to happen in a few days."

"I knew I would have to face my grandmother at some point."

Johan took Eva's arm as they walked away from the garage. "Everything is going to be fine."

CHAPTER 26

"WHAT THE HELL was that?" Zoe yelled as she stormed into the kitchen. Eva had been positively rattled by Tessa's display of her telekinetic powers, to the point where Zoe could see Eva just needed to walk away and be by herself.

Stella looked up from her cup of coffee with a startled look. "Zoe, what is the matter?"

"What's the matter?" Zoe asked, incredulous. "For the love of God, are you people insane?"

"Zoe, please calm down," Tessa said calmly as she entered the kitchen. "The neighbors can hear you."

"I don't fucking care who hears me." Zoe turned to Tessa. "I have kept my opinion to myself ever since Aunty Stella showed up." She turned to Stella. "You waltzed into the cabin surprising Eva, who had no idea who the hell you were."

"Zoe—"

"Let her talk, angel. She needs to get this off her chest," Tessa said.

"Get it off my chest?" Zoe whirled around to Tessa. "Where do I start? It's not the fact that Aunty Stella undid all the work to get Eva to the point where she could, somehow, try and not let Larissa completely overwhelm her, but the fact that she brought that drawing. What in God's name were you thinking?"

"I did apologize."

"Yes, wonderful. We have an apology, and that is going to solve what? I'm having sleepless nights over that damned drawing. Eva hasn't had a decent night of sleep since we arrived in Athens. What did you expect her to do? Just sit there and look at it like it was some damned flower arrangement?"

"You do have a point."

"Yes, I have a point. I don't know why you felt the need to show us those damn drawings. What the hell did you want to achieve? I don't understand."

"I wanted to show—"

"I don't care." Zoe put her hand up in frustration. "You are a middle-aged woman that should know better, for God's sake. You are a doctor. Do

you treat your patients with so much disregard for their feelings? What
if you showed artwork like that to one of your soldiers? Do you think he
would thank you?"

"No, but—"

"There is no excuse," Zoe said. "There just isn't. You know Eva knew
how being at the wedding would affect me. It took her all of seconds to
make the connection. She was feeling battered and sore from Tommy's little
surprise, but she still made this heroic effort to be there for me. You're a
doctor, Aunty Stella, you deal with trauma like the one suffered by Eva,
and you should have known better."

"Yes, you are right, but—" Tessa started.

"Don't." Zoe pointed at Tessa. "Don't get all this calm and serene with
me. I know you have powers, gifts, whatever the hell they are, but what
you did in the study was beyond . . . I don't know what." Zoe threw her
hands in the air in frustration. "What the hell did you think you were going
to achieve?"

"You asked me for—"

"So you thought you would show off? You couldn't just move the wine
bottle? That would have been impressive, but no, you had to terrify Eva
by moving the damned chair and her in it." Zoe balled her fists up and
punched the wooden table, rattling the plates on it. "Is that your favorite
party trick when you get together with the others like you?"

"Zoe, that is unnecessary," Irene said quietly as she stood up.

"You think so? You even said 'show off' and left. It seems this is so
common for you all that you think Eva and I would be used to it." Zoe
gripped the table and glared at Irene. "Well, we are not. The only time I
ever heard of this is in the Bible two-thousand years ago."

"We know and we could have handled this better."

"Really? You're thinking you could have handled this better? Wow."
Zoe shook her head in disbelief. "Didn't your second sight, or whatever
you call it, give you a little hint that springing this on someone who is
feeling emotionally fragile might be a little, oh I don't know . . . *stupid*?"

"I understand why you are angry," Tessa said.

"I have *never* seen Eva drink almost an entire bottle of wine on her
own. *Never*."

"I'm sorry, we—"

"I don't want to hear it." Zoe turned away from them and took a deep
breath to try and calm herself. She faced them again. "You've had years
to get used to this thing. You know how this works and you understand
it. Eva and I don't. We've never heard of this before other than what we
have heard in church. Personally, I've always thought of this as demon
possession." She took a deep breath. "When I was little, Theo and I saw

a woman who was possessed. There was no earthly explanation for her behavior. She terrified me. She was wild and did things that I'm scared just thinking about. You now come to me and tell me that this isn't demon possession but something left over from Pentecost? How is that even possible?"

Thomas and Theo entered the kitchen. They looked at Zoe and then at the other three women.

THEO DIDN'T NEED to be told what Zoe's glare meant. He did an about face and took Thomas's arm and pulled him out of the kitchen.

"What?" Thomas asked. "I want some lunch."

"You don't want to be in that room with my sister in that mood."

"Why?"

"Let's go to forage for food elsewhere." Theo pushed Thomas away from the kitchen and out the door.

Eva and Johan were just about to enter.

"Where are you going? Aren't you boys going to have lunch?" Johan asked.

"No, I think it would be safer . . ." Theo stopped when he heard Zoe's raised voice coming from the kitchen. "Safer if we were not near the kitchen."

ZOE OPENED HER mouth to let loose again but she felt Eva's presence and stopped.

"Hey," Eva whispered. "Let's go and talk."

"How was your walk?" Zoe asked through gritted teeth.

"Much better than what is going on here. Come with me."

She took Zoe's hand, and led her into the study. She closed the door.

Eva put her arms around Zoe's waist. "You were waking the dead."

"I bet they walk at night around here as well," Zoe muttered as she snuggled up against Eva's chest. She took a shuddering breath and let it out slowly.

"Hey." Eva tipped Zoe's face up and smiled. "Did that make you feel better?"

Zoe nodded vigorously.

Eva laughed lightly. "I thought it might." She kissed the top of Zoe's head.

"It's just not fair."

"I know, love, but it's normal for them."

"They should keep it to themselves."

"They can't." Eva sighed. "I met my great uncle Johan."

"The priest? Is he like them?"

"No, he appears to be normal like you."

Zoe rolled her eyes.

Eva grinned. "That's not quite right. No one is as normal as you."

"Ha Ha. What is he like?"

"Hmm, he's alright. There's something about him that's a little . . . odd," Eva said quietly. "I don't know. He talks about these gifts and he's very calm."

"I think these gifts cast a spell over everyone and that makes you calm and serene."

"Well, we can safely say you don't have any inherited Pentecost gifts."

Zoe buried her head against Eva's chest and laughed.

"You do have an enormous amount of artistic ability, which is probably inherited from your mama."

"More than likely."

"I love you. I know you've been trying not to get upset, but you were loud. I could hear you all the way across the courtyard."

"Good. They were toying with you and it drove me insane."

"They're not toying with me, love. I'm not sure what they want to do, but it's not that."

"Whatever they were doing, they started it in Larissa."

"You kept your temper for quite some time." Eva looked at Zoe with a slight smile. "I think I was the one who snapped first."

"No, I did that in the bathroom this morning," Zoe admitted. "I yelled at my reflection in the mirror."

"Hmm, did that help?"

"No."

Zoe looked up at Eva's glazed eyes and furrowed brow. "How are you feeling?"

"Um, I've got the beginnings of a migraine," Eva admitted. "I can't believe I drank so much."

"It's not that you drank, although alcohol for breakfast is not that great, but you drank a Merlot." Zoe scrunched up her face in distaste. "You always get a migraine after drinking red wine. For what it's worth, you would have drunk a bottle of ouzo if they had had it handy."

"I really hate red wine, and ouzo would have sent me to the floor." Eva stuck her tongue out. Zoe giggled. "I'm going to need to sleep this off. Uncle Johan said that my grandmother is coming soon—just what I need right now."

"Great. Just what we need to be added to the craziness . . ." Zoe noticed Eva's distant, faraway look. She blinked in surprise at Eva's eye color. Zoe shook her head and looked up again to find Eva's eyes the normal sky blue. "Evy, what just happened?"

"Huh?" Eva looked down. "What do you mean?"

"Where did you go just now?"

"Um." Eva hesitated for a moment. "I was just thinking there is something weird about what Irene said—that they had a burglary and the thieves didn't take anything. I find it odd.

"I don't know, maybe inept thieves? What worries me now is that I thought I saw your eyes go completely black before returning to normal. You better sit down." Zoe gently pushed Eva to the nearest seat. She tipped Eva's face up to the light and looked into her eyes. They were their normal color except for a tiny spot of black in the blue irises. "Hmm. I've never seen this before."

"Are my blue eyes still there?"

Zoe smiled. "Yes, still sky blue and they are still gorgeous but . . ." She tried to find the black spot but couldn't. Both eyes were clear. "I think I'm seeing things and I haven't drunk anything."

"I think we both need to get home to Sydney," Eva said quietly. "I've had enough of this adventure."

"You're right, but now I'm going to put you to bed." Zoe stood and held out her hand. "Come on, my lady. Let's take you upstairs so you don't throw up here."

"I'm not going to throw up." Eva stood up and swayed a little. "Oh, that wasn't good."

Zoe shook her head. "You should have grabbed a bottle of white."

"Beer. That's even better."

"Pentecost gifted ones don't drink beer like common folk." Zoe chuckled as she put her arm around Eva and walked to the stairs. She looked back at the study for a moment. She was pretty sure of what she had seen but it might have been the light playing tricks.

ZOE CLOSED THE door to the bedroom and contemplated the morning's mayhem. She had yelled at her aunt and her adopted aunts.

"Oh, good job, Zo" she muttered as she sat down on the top step of the staircase and leaned against the wall.

Tessa stopped at the bottom of the steps and looked up at Zoe. She went up the stairs and stopped a few steps down from Zoe.

"I owe you both an apology," Tessa said as she sat on the step and braced her back against the wall.

"Yes, you do," Zoe replied. "You all do."

"I'm sorry. We didn't handle it correctly. Stella would never do what she did to a patient and she knows that. She didn't think."

"I'm not sorry I got angry."

"I know. I was surprised you kept your temper for so long."

Zoe glanced at Tessa. "You don't know me. You may think you do, but you don't."

"No one knows anyone all that well."

"I know Eva and she knows me. I'm sure it's the same for you and Aunty Stella."

"It is. Do you accept my apology?"

Zoe closed her eyes and leaned back against the wall. "Of course."

"Thank you." Tessa smiled. "Why are you sitting up here?"

"Thinking."

"Can I ask what about?"

"Eva. Something happened in the study. I don't know what but something happened."

"When?"

"When she came back from her walk. I thought I saw something but it may have been the light."

"What was it?" Tessa leaned forward and looked at Zoe.

"I don't know," Zoe said, a little bewildered as to why this was bothering her. "We were in the study and there was a lot of sunlight in the room. It may have been a shadow or something."

"What did you see?"

"That's just it, I don't know. I thought I saw her blue eyes darken. Either that or you have me completely spooked and I'm seeing things that are not there."

"How long did it last for?"

"Seconds," Zoe responded. "When you have a vision, the change in your eye color lasts for a long time, doesn't it?"

"Yes. It usually lasts for two or three hours. This doesn't sound like it was a vision."

"Hmm." Zoe nodded. "I don't know what I saw. This is exhausting."

"Do you want some ice cream?"

"Yes."

"What flavor?"

"Any flavor as long as it's ice cream," Zoe replied as she got up from the top step and followed Tessa into the kitchen.

CHAPTER 27

SITTING IN THE shadows of an overhanging tree on the balcony of their bedroom, Zoe had a good view of Irene and Johan's property. Situated on a large block of land, the house was L shaped in design and each bedroom had a balcony. The room she shared with Eva overlooked the entrance to the property and the large courtyard.

She was impressed by the grandeur of the estate and a little bit dumbfounded at how a nun and a priest could afford such a property.

"So much for a vow of poverty," she muttered, resting her forearms on the railing and gazing at the birds in the trees.

Zoe sighed. This portion of their trip was scheduled for only three days but it seemed that it was going to take longer. "Nothing is ever easy. Nothing. One day I'm going to find that something goes according to plan and probably fall down in shock." She turned away from the railing and leaned to the side to see if Eva was still asleep.

Eva was indeed asleep, a slight smile on her lips. Her dark hair had flopped down over her eyes.

"I have got to paint that when I have some time." Zoe turned away and stood in the middle of the balcony.

Since her angry outburst this morning, Stella and Irene had kept their distance. Zoe smiled. People often underestimated her, and it seemed even those with these Pentecost-inspired gifts were not immune. Tessa had been the only one that had apologized to her and for their behavior towards Eva. Zoe was fully aware that they didn't want to hurt Eva, but the ham-fisted way they went about revealing everything was appalling.

Tessa's apology both surprised her and endeared her to Zoe. Her father used to say that you could tell the character of a man (or in this case woman) by how well they apologized. Tessa did not try to excuse herself or be mealy mouthed about the apology. She said she was sorry and that was worth more to Zoe than Tessa realized. It wasn't until Zoe had time to think that it occurred to her that Eva also never made excuses and simply said she was sorry.

A bird flew overhead, casting a shadow on the wooden balcony floor. "Shadows. I did not see shadows." Zoe was certain Eva's eyes did change color, albeit very briefly. "Does she know this happened? This must have happened before. For as long as I've known her she would say, 'I know this is going to happen,' and it did." Zoe slowly paced along the balcony.

"So when did this all start?" Zoe stopped and looked up into the sky, which was littered with little tuffs of cloud that ambled slowly across the blue expanse. "When does this happen?" She closed her eyes and tried to meditate.

She opened her eyes and she smiled. "It can't be that easy, can it?"

"What isn't easy?"

Zoe whirled around to find Eva leaning against the French doors watching her. She couldn't help but look lovingly at Eva, whose tousled hair, combined with the sunlight hitting her blue eyes, took Zoe's breath away. Eva's jet-black hair glistened in the sunlight and Zoe could only gaze at her.

"Zoe." Eva came forward and put her arms around her. "Where did you go?"

"You take my breath away."

Eva kissed Zoe tenderly. "You do that to me every time I open my eyes and see you."

Zoe buried her head against Eva's chest. "We are just addicted to each other."

"At least my addiction to you doesn't give me migraines." Eva chuckled. "What are you doing up here?"

"Did I wake you?"

"I felt the vibration of the floor boards and heard you muttering."

"Oh, I'm sorry. I should have taken my pacing to the garden."

"Nah, it's alright. So what were you muttering about?"

"Alright, well, I've been thinking about something that happened in the study. I want to try something."

"What and why?"

"In the study your eyes changed color."

"Alright." A tiny smile played on Eva's lips. She sat down on the wicker chair and brought Zoe down to sit on her lap. "Is the experiment to see if you get lost in my eyes?" she asked with a slight chuckle.

Zoe jokingly slapped herself. "No. Keep your eyes open."

"Okay."

"We are going to get visitors tonight?"

"Yes, but not my grandmother, at this point. Someone else is coming."

"Hmm. Do you know anything else about them?"

"No."

"Alright, that's a good place to start. I want you to concentrate on them, but don't shut your eyes. You always shut your eyes when you're thinking."

"Do I?" Eva asked as she stroked Zoe's hair and played with the red curls.

"Evy, please," Zoe begged.

Eva pouted.

"Did I just ask you to stop touching me?"

"Yes. Mark it down. It's a historic event." Eva giggled. "All right, I'm to concentrate and not close my eyes. What am I concentrating on?"

"Our visitors."

"Fine, and then what?"

"Just concentrate. I want to watch your eyes."

Eva shrugged. She didn't look at Zoe, but a little to the left. Zoe stared into Eva's unfocused eyes. For a few minutes nothing happened. Zoe continued to stare. Eva's irises went dark blue, bluer than Zoe had ever seen them, and then she started to count. At five seconds, the dark blue broke up just as quickly as it had formed. She continued to count and the sky blue irises were back.

Eva refocused on Zoe and smiled. "Something happened, didn't it?"

"Oh, yeah," Zoe replied quietly. "All seven seconds of it."

"Really?"

"Hmm, your irises went navy blue."

"Is that what happens when we're making love? That's what you say, isn't it?"

"Please, tell me you weren't thinking of that," Zoe teased.

"Pfft," Eva responded with a grin. "You wouldn't be still dressed if that happened." She gently laughed. "So what did happen?"

"You tell me. Nothing happened for a few minutes and your eyes didn't change color, but then boom, they went navy blue and then back to normal." Zoe tilted Eva's head back. "You still have a dark blue speck floating in a sea of sky blue."

"How pretty."

"Yes, it is. What were you thinking?"

"For a few minutes nothing much, other than I liked sitting in the sun with you on my lap," Eva replied. "While I was thinking about that, I don't want you to be alarmed . . ."

"You do know that when you say that, I am alarmed?"

"No need to be, Zoe. I feel someone is watching us."

Zoe gazed at Eva for a long moment. "I shouldn't turn around, right?"

"No. Get off my lap and don't react."

"But—"

"There isn't any point. They have already seen us."

"I don't like this," Zoe replied as she got off Eva's lap and walked back into the room. "So this works, just like that?"

"Just like that," Eva repeated. "That's how it's always been for me. Just a thought, a feeling. No big 'ta da' big reveal."

"Just very quietly. That's just the way you are. No mess, no fuss, no big dramas."

"Yes, so far."

"So that's when your eyes changed color, because for a few minutes they remained sky blue."

"So." Eva nodded. "What does that mean?"

"It means that your gifts are very different from Tessa's gifts. Her eyes change color but they take hours to change back. That also means that there may be other gifts we are not aware of."

"Oh, goodie," Eva said. "Just what we need to complicate our lives."

Zoe grinned. "You would be bored if things went according to plan."

"Less gray hair," Eva said, and then laughed as Zoe came back out and tipped her head down to check for any white in her black hair. "Find any?"

"No, it looks all black to me." Zoe kissed the top of Eva's head. She tipped Eva's face up to meet her eyes. "So who are these people who are spying on us?"

"I don't know."

"Why send someone to spy on us?" Zoe asked. Eva merely shrugged. "Your grandmother?"

"Why did she send Mrs. Muldoon? I don't know, Zo. All of this is one giant puzzle and every time we try and work it out, something else happens that completely changes things."

"How strange."

"Hmm, we have visitors," Eva said as she got up from her chair and leaned over the balcony.

Zoe followed her and saw that a black sedan had come to a stop in the courtyard. She couldn't see any markings on the car. "Were they the ones looking at us?"

"No," Eva replied quietly. "Let's go find out what these people want."

CHAPTER 28

EVA CAME DOWN the steps followed by Zoe to be met by Tessa.

"Yes, I know, I saw them as they arrived," Eva said before Tessa said anything.

"They're War Crimes Unit agents."

"What do they want?"

Tessa looked back to the living room before she turned to Eva. "They want to talk to you."

"Well, let's not keep them waiting," Eva muttered as they entered the living room.

"Eva, these are Herr Isaac Abels and Marco Geitner from the War Crimes agency," Stella said and they sat down.

Eva greeted the men and noticed the concentration camp tattoo on Abels' arm.

He followed her gaze and looked up. "Thank you for agreeing to talk to us, Mrs. Hoffman."

Eva glanced at Zoe before she turned her attention back on the agent.

"How can I help you? My name is not Hoffman or Muller anymore. It's Lambros. I recently got married," Eva said with a slight smile.

"You got married?"

"Yes, here in Berlin just after I arrived back home."

"Oh. We were not aware of that." Abels scribbled in his notepad. "Do you mind if I ask you some questions?"

"Please go right ahead."

"Your father was Major Hans Muller, is that correct?"

"No. He was my stepfather. My father is Panayiotis Haralambos."

"Major Hans Muller was a high-ranking Nazi officer during the war and he recently was tried and convicted at Nuremberg for crimes against humanity and sentenced to death. Your father isn't Major Hans Muller?"

"No, as I just said he was my stepfather."

"Your birth certificate states Hans Muller as your father," Abels said without looking up from his notes.

"It's wrong. My mother was a single woman in Austria. When I was born my mother met Hans Muller and they got married."

"So your birth certificate was falsified?"

"You could say that, yes. My natural father was Panayiotis Haralambos from Larissa, Greece."

"So in 1946 you immigrated to Australia from Greece?"

"No, from Egypt. I was in Egypt for a year and then sailed to Australia in 1946."

"Why did you decide to go to Australia?"

Eva glanced at Zoe. "I was shot before the Americans liberated the town. When I was well enough we decided to leave for Egypt and then took a ship to Australia."

"Who is the other party in the 'we'?"

"My friend Zoe Lambros."

"Ah." Abels sat back. "Mrs. Lambros, where were you during the war?"

"In Aiden from 1938 to 1942, and in France and Larissa from 1942 till 1944."

"You have a good memory."

"I'm sure you can remember where you were during those years, Mr. Abels."

"Before the war, you were in the Hitler Youth?" Abels asked, ignoring Eva's pointed question.

"Yes, as all German children were."

"As long as you weren't a Jew," Abels muttered. "Did you become a member of the Nazi Party?"

"No."

"Are you sure?" Abels looked up and met Eva's eyes.

"Quite sure. I never signed up as party member."

"Yes, a lot of Germans say that now."

"Maybe they felt that way to begin with. Not all Germans were Nazis," Eva replied reasonably. "Although some were and still are members."

"No, just the majority. So you were in the Hitler Youth up until what date?"

"November ninth, 1939."

"You are quite certain of that date."

"Very certain." Eva met Abels' eyes and was aware they both knew the significance of that date.

"November ninth, 1939 was Kristallnacht, was it not?"

"Yes." Eva took a sip of water that Tessa had placed near her hand.

"Can you please tell me what happened on that night?"

Eva took a deep breath. "It was the night that systematic looting and assaults on Jews took place. Synagogues and shops were burnt. Why are you asking me when you already know?"

"Who took part in that assault?"

"The SS, members of the Hitler Youth, and the general public in some areas."

"Since you despised the Nazi party and what it stood for, you obviously stayed at home?" Abels asked.

"No, I didn't stay at home."

"Where were you?"

"I was with my friends."

"From the Hitler Youth?"

"Yes."

"Ah, so I see. Now a moment ago you told me that members of the Hitler Youth participated in the wonton destruction of Jewish property and lives. Did you take part in that destruction?"

Eva looked down at her hands and took a moment before answering. "Yes, I did."

"So, as someone who despised the Nazi regime, you chose to destroy Jewish property and kill innocent people. Why is that?"

"I didn't kill anyone, Herr Abels," Eva said quietly. "I was present at the torching of a synagogue and then I ran back home."

"You were present when a house of worship was destroyed. Did you do anything to stop this torching? Did you partake in this torching?"

"No, I didn't stop my friends from torching it, and no, I didn't participate."

"Why do you remember this date so well then? Surely it's not because of the torching of a synagogue?"

"No," Eva whispered.

"I'm sorry, I didn't hear you. Can you repeat that?"

"I said no, it's not because of just Kristallnacht."

"Why is this event so important?"

"My mother was killed that night," Eva said quietly, and for a moment she saw some compassion in Abels' eyes before he looked down at his notes again.

"Is that why you hated the Nazi party?"

"No. I did not like Hitler."

"I see." Abels tapped his pen against his chin. "Since you didn't like Hitler, why did you join the Nazi Party?"

"I didn't."

"Can you explain why your signature appears on a registration form for the Nazi Party dated November 9, 1939?"

"That's not my signature."

Abels looked down at the paper and then back up at Eva. "I haven't shown it to you yet—you have to wait to see it before lying to me."

"I've already seen that registration paper."

"Yes, I know, Mrs. Lambros. You saw it when you added your name to the Nazi party. You claim that you never registered as a Nazi member but your signature appears on this membership form. How is that?"

"As I told you, it's not my signature," Eva replied. She glanced at Zoe, who got up and left the room.

"It was witnessed by your father Major Hans Muller . . ."

"It's not my signature," Eva responded just as Zoe came back and handed Eva her passport. Eva gave it to Abels.

Abels took the passport and compared the two signatures. He looked at Eva over the top of his glasses. "Hmm, you are right."

"I know."

"Were you ever at the AEMuller Medical Research Facility?"

"The what?" Eva glanced at Tessa, who was staring intently at the investigator. "I don't know where that is."

"It's in Aiden, Austria."

"No, I was never there."

"Yes, you were there, Evy," Thomas said.

Eva lifted her eyes and met his gaze. "I was?"

"Yes. That's what it was called, but everyone knew it AMRF Aiden Spa."

Eva took a deep breath and exhaled. She looked at Zoe, who had a lit cigarette in her hand. Without a word, Zoe gave her the cigarette and she accepted it gratefully. Taking some time to compose herself, Eva took a drag of the cigarette.

"I'm sorry," she said. "I was there. I knew it under a different name. I was sent there for my injuries and subsequent incarceration."

"According to your medical records you were at the hospital recovering from a car accident and melancholy."

"Don't you need my permission to look at those records?"

Abels looked at Eva and nodded. "You were not in the country at the time and I received authorization from your grandmother Mrs. Beatriz Muller."

"I see."

"Your medical records say you were at the Aidan Spa Hospital and then you were discharged. Approximately three months after your discharge you went to work for your uncle, Dr. Dieter Muller."

"No. That is wrong."

"Are you sure about that?"

"Quite sure."

"What were you doing there from November 1939 to June 1940?"

Eva paused, annoyed that Abels was leaning in towards her. "I was held against my will and tortured."

"You were at your uncle's health spa and you were a prisoner?" Abels asked. "Are you sure about that? A car accident and melancholy is not a cause for you to be held prisoner. Do you even know what that really is? It may have felt that way but—"

"Quite sure," Eva replied. "How many times do I need to say this?"

Abels went back to his notes on the table and retrieved four pieces of paper. "The Nazis were notorious for keeping notes. I think they prided themselves in their bookkeeping abilities and that was the only thing they did right. I have in my hand records that were found at the AEMuller Medical Research Facility. It lists the staff which was employed from November 1939 to July 1943." He took a sip from a glass of water. "Can you tell me why a Miss Eva Muller, born January 20, 1920 and a member of the Nazi party, is listed on this staff list when you claim you were a prisoner?"

"I was never a staff member."

"The records state you were a member of staff from November 1939 to June 1940. You resigned from the area you were working in because of medical reasons."

"That's a lie. Your records are wrong." Eva's voice rose as she tried to calm her rising anxiety.

"It says so right here." Abels held up the sheet of paper. "Germans are many things, Mrs. Lambros, but they are meticulous about paperwork."

"I'm sure, but that's falsified."

"Just like your birth certificate and party registration?"

"Yes."

"Of course it is," Abels replied. "Were you aware that your AEMuller Medical Research Facility was a place of torture, experimentation on Jews, homosexuals, and retarded individuals?"

Eva bowed her head and nodded. "I am aware of that."

"You just told me you didn't know about this place. Now you do know what happened there?"

"No . . . I mean yes . . . umm" Eva looked directly at Abels.

"How are you aware of this if you did not work there?"

"Because I was one of those being experimented on," Eva replied quietly.

"I don't believe you, Mrs. Lambros. I have the paperwork in front of me and it clearly says you were a staff member. How can you prove otherwise? Can you prove you weren't?"

ZOE WAS NOT liking the direction the interrogation was taking. The investigators were very direct with their questioning. She glanced at

Thomas, who had taken a position at the back of the room. He gave her a reassuring nod.

"I can prove it," Thomas stated.

"And who are you, sir?"

"My name is Thomas Lambros. I worked at the hospital and I was responsible for nursing Miss Muller . . . I mean Mrs. Lambros, from her injuries," Tommy said. "You will find my name under Karl Steigler."

"Is that your real name sir?"

"It is. My full name is Karl Thomas Steigler. I was a nurse."

"You worked in the AEMuller Medical Research Facility?"

"No sir, I worked in the Aiden Spa Hospital."

"I see." Abels flipped through several papers and looked up when he found what he was looking for. "You were a nurse at the Spa Hospital but not in the research facility."

"Yes, sir."

Zoe pursed her lips in thought at Abels' choice of words. Research facility sounded mundane and innocuous.

"Eva was a class AF1 patient."

"What are AF1 patients?" Abels asked and looked over the top of his glasses at Thomas. "I don't have any notes about patient types."

"People who had a severe mental defect and were admitted by a doctor or family member," Thomas replied as he met Eva's gaze.

"I don't have that on my notes here," Abels muttered and turned to his partner who was also looking at his notes. "We don't have that information."

"I still have notes from when I nursed Mrs. Lambros."

Abels gazed dubiously at Tommy. "You kept notes and you still have them after so many years?"

"I keep notes on all my patients. I am a certified mental health nurse and I keep methodical records, both for my benefit and for those that I care for."

"Do you have those notes with you?"

"No, sir, I don't. They are back in Greece."

"Can you send them to me?"

"No, sir. I can't. The German Criminal Code article 203 states that it is a crime for me to give you any medical records without authorization from the patient. I will not do that."

"Do you authorize those notes to be given to the War Crimes unit, Mrs. Lambros?"

Eva glanced at Thomas and nodded. "Of course, if it will clear my name."

"Good. I expect to receive those notes and a statement from you as soon as possible." Abels grunted as he packed up his files and stuck them into his bag. "Mrs. Lambros, if you come in contact with Dr. Muller, please inform me." he produced his card.

"That's it? You go through all those questions and all you were after was if she had been in contact with her uncle?" Zoe asked incredulously.

"Yes. We have reason to believe that Dr. Muller is in Berlin. We think he may try to contact you."

"Why would he do that?" Eva asked as she got up.

"There are a number of reasons," Abels replied. "If you come in contact with him and don't tell us, you will be arrested."

"Of course," Eva replied as the two men were shown to the door. She waited by the door until they were back into their car and had driven off. She turned to find Zoe leaning against the wall.

"That was strange," Zoe exclaimed. "You were in no condition to sign membership papers and all that rot about you working for the hospital . . ."

"That's the least of our worries. There must be a reason, with my uncle being here."

"Why all those questions. Where did they get their information? Could it be from your grandmother?" Zoe asked.

"I don't know." Eva shrugged.

"Tommy, you really don't have notes, do you?" Tessa asked.

"Yes, I do." Thomas nodded. "I keep notes on the patients I treat but it's nothing more than just things I need to remember."

"I don't know what it all means but I'm going to say something is going to happen in the next day or so," Stella muttered. "I'm not even gifted and I know that."

CHAPTER 29

ZOE SAT OUTSIDE on the balcony, enjoying the quiet. A sketchbook lay across her lap as the light from the full moon shone down onto the paper. The pencil flew across the paper, and Zoe sighed at the tranquility and peace this brought her.

Eva's gentle snore in the bedroom and Zoe glanced inside. They had been through so much, and Eva was mentally and physically drained from all the revelations about her family and the interrogation of the previous evening. Zoe felt tired of all the secrets that had come tumbling out as soon as they reached Larisa.

Zoe turned back to her sketchbook and continued to draw until she looked up and saw a shadow near the gate and then a silhouette up against the wall in the darkness. She slid down onto her knees and left her sketch-book on the chair. The balcony's wooden railing afforded her some privacy and she could easily see the gate and the intruder.

The intruder stood still for quite some time, much to Zoe's annoyance. She wanted him to move into the light but the mystery trespasser was taking his time. After what seemed like an inordinate amount of time, he moved.

Zoe waited very impatiently as the intruder stealthily made his way to a large tree near the kitchen. Just as he reached the tree, the moonlight caught him. The man was dressed in black, with a black beanie and black gloves. The moonlight caught his face before he crouched down into the brushes.

Zoe sneered. "Oh hello," she whispered. "I bet you have blond hair underneath that beanie. Come into my parlor, said the spider to the fly. I've been waiting for you for years Dr. Dieter Muller."

Zoe crawled backwards and into the bedroom. She hit one of their shoes and cursed silently as she made her way further inside the room. She knew the layout of the residence and could easily find her way, navigating in the dark without any problems.

Zoe glanced at Eva, who was still asleep, and went to the balcony door to see if their unwanted guest was still there. She couldn't see him from the angle she was standing in but she could see his shadow. She left the bedroom and closed the door quietly behind her. She padded down the steps and into the kitchen, where she thought Muller would likely enter. She unlocked the door.

"We might as well make our visitor feel welcome."

Zoe went into the living room and looked around for the perfect weapon. She grinned. "Oh, this is perfect."

She went to the fireplace and chose the smallest poker and practiced a swing. "Nice. This should do some damage."

Zoe took the poker and placed herself between the living room and the kitchen and waited. Several minutes passed and she was getting impatient at the man's tardiness. Just as she was about to cross the living room to look out the window, she heard the window in the kitchen slide open.

Dumkompf, I left the door open. Zoe heard a gentle thump in the kitchen. She could see the man's reflection in the cupboard's glass panes. He crouched for a moment, as if he was aware someone was in the room with him. Zoe held her breath.

A mouse scampered across the kitchen floor and Dr. Dieter Muller jumped. Zoe grinned. She never did like mice but this time she would make an exception. Muller crept along until he was flush with the pantry.

Muller stepped into the living room, and Zoe swung the poker. The blow made a sickening crunch as it connected with Muller's face. He screamed in agony as blood spewed from his nose. He squeezed the trigger of the gun in his hand. Zoe stared, shocked at the flash from the weapon. She swung with the poker as hard as she could, and crunched it down on Muller's head.

Muller crashed head first into a glass coffee table and the gun fell out of his hand.

Zoe exhaled slowly. The realization that she could have been killed sank in as she slid to the floor next to Muller. With her back against the wall, Zoe tilted her head a little and rested it on the pantry sideboard. She wasn't sure if her heart, which felt like a runaway train, was going to run off the rails.

After a moment, she pushed herself up and stood over Muller. She saw that he had some blood near his ear where the second blow had hit.

"Asshole," she muttered darkly and spat at him. She crouched down, placed her fingers against Muller's neck, and grimaced when she felt a strong pulse. "Why don't you Muller bastards ever die?"

She went in search for the gun in the darkness.

EVA WOKE WITH a start at the sound of what sounded like a gunshot. She blinked in the shadows and scowled. She saw the bed was empty and frowned. The open balcony door brought the sounds of cars passing in the

quiet of the night. She shook her head and wondered if the sound was a car
that had backfired. *Where have you gone, Zo?*

She threw back the covers. She put on her robe and was about to leave
the room when another two shots rang out in succession followed by
agonizing screams and cursing.

"That was not a car backfiring."

She raced out of the bedroom. Her bare feet making a thumping noise
as she ran down the stairs.

She reached the bottom of the stairs and saw that the living room light
was on, but Theo was blocking her view. He was standing just inside the
living room and appeared to be holding a gun.

"What the hell . . . ?"

Theo turned completely around and blocked Eva's entry. "I don't think
you want to be here."

"Where's Zoe?" Eva asked, trying to see past Theo. What she saw was
a lot of glass, broken bits of wood, and blood. "Where's Zoe, Theo!"

"I'm here."

Eva turned to the kitchen. She ran into the kitchen.

"Zoe!" Eva screamed and rushed forward to grab her. Zoe was sitting
on a chair covered in blood. Stella was kneeling beside her and trying to
stem the flow of blood from her thigh.

"Hello there," Zoe greeted Eva with a smile.

"Zo, you're bleeding." Eva knelt beside the chair.

Stella wrapped a towel around the knee. Eva checked Zoe's face for
any sign of injury and started to unbutton Zoe's top.

Zoe took Eva's hands, which were now trembling. She wasn't sure if it
was rage or fear. "It's okay. Stop, I'm alright."

"You don't look alright. You're bleeding."

"Well, that's what you get when you don't turn on the light and run right
into the credenza," Zoe replied as she cupped Eva's cheek. "I'm alright."

"You're not hurt?"

"No. I'm fine."

Eva exhaled and sat back on her heels in relief. She saw the
blood-stained poker lying across Zoe's lap. "What the hell is that?"

"That's a poker."

"Zoe," Eva exclaimed as she touched the poker.

"It's not her blood on it, Evy," Stella said. "We have a visitor."

"What . . ." Eva went to the kitchen door and looked into the living
room. She covered her mouth in shock and her knees nearly gave out.
Sprawled against the wooden display cabinet was her uncle. Dr. Dieter
Muller's face was covered in blood—his nose was shattered and blood
was freely flowing, and his mouth was covered in blood.

Tessa appeared beside Eva and turned her away from the carnage inside the living room. Eva sat down on the chair with a thud, not quite believing her uncle was in the next room.

"Hey, hey," Zoe quietly said as she hobbled to where Eva was sitting. Eva bowed her head and was trying not to let the fear overwhelm her. Her uncle was in the next room. She despised him for what he had done to her and she feared him more than anyone else.

"He isn't going to hurt you."

"Zoe—"

"No, he isn't going to hurt you," Zoe reassured. Eva looked up into her very concerned face. "I made sure of it."

Tessa approached Eva and Zoe and went down on her haunches. "Zoe, give me the poker." She took the poker from Zoe's hand.

Eva took Zoe's face into her hands and looked into her eyes. "He didn't shoot you?"

"No. The blood is all his except for my leg but that's all my fault. I ran into the credenza in the dark and hit myself. He didn't touch me."

"What happened?"

"Well, it started with me having a sleepless night and wanting to sketch. I went out to the balcony because I didn't want to wake you." Zoe grinned as she took Eva's hand and kissed it. "I was minding my own business when this dummkopf came over the wall. I thought I might welcome our guest the proper way."

"You could have been killed, Zoe," Eva gently admonished. "You should have woken Theo or Tommy."

"Nah." Zoe shook her head. "This was personal and I wanted to deliver the message myself."

"Losing you is not worth the risk for that asshole," Eva replied.

"He didn't stand a chance. My only regret is that I missed."

"What did you miss?"

"I was aiming for his dick," Zoe said and then chuckled. "He's taller than I thought he was."

"Zoe, my love, he would have had to be Goliath for you to aim so high."

They looked at each and caught Tessa and Stella's amused expressions. All four glanced towards the living room and laughed.

Eva exhaled. "I really need a drink." she looked at Zoe, who was sporting a beaming smile. "Oh, Zoe, you could have been killed."

"But I wasn't. Come and have a look." Zoe got up and took Eva's hand and led her to the door.

Eva surveyed the room—shattered coffee table top, blood all over the carpet. Muller was sitting on the floor. She stared, transfixed by the sight.

"Help . . . me!" Muller tried to scream but the blood bubbled out of his mouth.

Stella quickly went back into the kitchen to get some towels. She came back and approached Muller, who glared at her.

"Shut up. Don't say another word or Theo is going to shoot you, and he won't be as gentle as Zoe was," Stella said as she took Muller's hand away from his nose. Blood gushed out. "Well, I can safely diagnose that your nose is broken. What's your name, you stupid man?"

"Diether Multher."

"What?" Stella asked with a slight smile.

Muller sighed and just pointed to Eva. "Her uncthle."

"Oh. That bastard." Stella shook her head. "You are a lucky bastard. If I wasn't a doctor and didn't take my Hippocratic Oath seriously, I would finish the job that Zoe started." She smiled menacingly and Muller's eyes widened.

"From one doctor to another doctor, you are fucked," Stella added. She took the towel and tied it around his knee. "That should keep until the ambulance gets here."

"My knee!"

"Yes, it's shot." Stella wrapped up the knee in another towel.

"Has someone called the police?"

"Phone is dead," Theo replied, still holding the gun.

"Well, of course it is." Irene shook her head as she entered and glared at Muller. "Tommy, go to the neighbors and alert the police and an ambulance from there."

"We can safely say that our War Crimes people will get their man," Tessa observed.

Eva nodded. "I need some ice cream."

"Me too. Vanilla with nuts," Zoe quipped and leaned to the side to look at Muller. "I should have aimed lower . . ."

Eva's felt her knees tremble and was thankful for the long robe that covered them. She leaned against the doorjamb and blinked. She couldn't focus all that well on her uncle and she felt light headed. *Don't let the bastard win, Evy.* She was startled to hear Tessa's voice in her head, and she turned to find Tessa beside her glaring at Muller.

Eva took a deep breath and despite the overwhelming fear that gripped her, she stepped forward to look down at her uncle. Muller had his eyes closed. He opened them and looked up at Eva. Eva did not disguise her disgust and contempt.

"Efa . . ."

Eva took a hesitant step towards the man that was responsible for so much of her pain. She looked back at Zoe, who was standing next to Tessa, the poker in her hand.

Show no fear. Tessa's words echoed in her mind.

Eva went down on her haunches. She stared at him for a long moment. "I had hoped I would never see you again, but here you are." Her voice trembled a little. She steadied herself by leaning on the overturned chair that was lying next to her. "The last time Zoe shot a man, she shot him in the face so many times that no one could recognize him. That slip of a girl over there," she pointed to Zoe, "brought you down." She glanced at Zoe before she turned back to Muller. "The last time she did this, it was to protect me. You were lucky. You get to live, the other bastard didn't."

"Whath?"

Eva couldn't help but sneer at her uncle's obvious discomfort. She glanced up at Theo, who was pointing the gun at Muller. She faced Muller, who was glaring at her.

"When they take you to the gallows, you might want to think about what I'm about to tell you." Eva sat down on the floor next to him in what seemed like a very casual pose. She braced her back against the fallen chair. She took a deep breath and tried to hide her anxiety over being so close to him. "You see those two women? One is my mother's sister. The other, the one you have already met." She could see Muller was grimacing in pain. "She's my lover. Reinhardt tried to stop her but he couldn't. Father tried to stop her but he couldn't. Her name is Zoe Lambros. *My* lover."

Muller made a gurgling sound which only made Eva more determined to follow through in telling him what she thought. She had been telling him for years in her dreams and now he was here. She didn't understand what he was trying to say and didn't care. "Remember me when they tie the noose around your neck and you take your last gasping breath." She sighed and went up on one knee and looked back at Muller. She gently cupped his blood-splattered cheek, remembering vividly how he had done that to her when she left Aiden. "I was not your prized trophy. You did not win. When that rope tightens around your neck, may you feel the same pain I felt, the same terrifying fear should grip your heart. I hope your death is slow and agonizing, and when you're dead, I hope you go to hell."

Eva stood and went to Zoe, took her hand, and together they walked into the kitchen as she heard the sound of a police siren in the distance.

CHAPTER 30

STEAM ROSE FROM the water that enveloped Eva as she rested her head on the rim of the tub and closed her eyes. Tiredness overtook her and she felt quite lethargic. It had been quite a morning, with the police arriving with sirens blaring and then the ambulance. The police questioned them about the break-in and then about her relationship with her uncle. They deemed it an act of self-defense but the neighborhood was in quite an uproar in the early hours of the morning.

Zoe had eaten a half-bucket of ice cream followed by Katarina's cookies. Eva had sat at the kitchen table, watching Zoe eat and talk. After a couple of hours, Zoe finally settled down and went straight to sleep, leaving Eva wide awake.

Eva opened her eyes and watched the steam rise from her body. She turned towards the knock on the door. Hoping it wasn't anyone but Zoe, she smiled when Zoe appeared with a hot cup of tea.

"Oh, this is good." Eva accepted the tea and a kiss before bringing the steaming mug to her lips. She blew on the hot beverage and took a sip. "Are you going to have more ice cream?"

Zoe giggled. "No, I don't think I can eat for the rest of the day." She sat on the floor with her back to the wall. "When I woke and didn't see you in bed, I thought you might have escaped and headed for the first train station."

Eva chuckled. She stopped when she realized it wasn't such a bad idea. "One problem with that plan."

"I wasn't with you?"

"Yes."

"See, that's how I knew you hadn't escaped, so you must have been here."

Eva smiled. "How are you feeling?"

"Bloated." Zoe laughed lightly. "You mean about Muller? I'm feeling great. I won't have any nightmares about putting a bullet in him . . . or three."

"You could have been killed."

"Yes, I could have." Zoe knelt beside the tub, gazed into Eva's eyes, and smiled. "But I wasn't. Do you know what the best thing about last night is?"

"Other than you caving his face in?"

"Yes, other than that." Zoe cupped Eva's face. "One of the proudest moments of my life was watching you go to him and face him. I was so proud of you that I thought my heart would jump out of my chest."

"Oh." Eva smiled shyly. "He had to know who did that to him and I had to tell him that you were mine."

"You did more than that, Evy. You faced down the man who hurt you so badly. Why did you cup his cheek like that?"

Eva closed her eyes and rested her head on the rim of the bathtub. "When I was discharged from the hospital, he came really close to me and cupped my cheek. He said I was his most prized patient and that he was a miracle worker."

"Bastard."

"I wanted him to know that he didn't win. I wanted him to know your name so that when he went to the gallows, he would know he failed," Eva said quietly and opened her eyes to see Zoe's tears track down her face. "Hey, don't cry."

"You are just incredible." Zoe's voice broke and she leaned in for a kiss. "What you did was just so awe inspiring."

"You were right there beside me, love," Eva replied with a beaming smile. Zoe kissed her tenderly. They parted and Eva splashed a little water at Zoe, who tried to jump back but fell on her backside on the tiles and laughed.

"You've been in this bath for over an hour."

"Do I have to get out?"

"Yes." Zoe grabbed a towel. "Come, Mrs. Lambros, let's get you out and dressed."

Eva reluctantly raised herself up from her comfortable spot and stepped out of the tub and into Zoe's embrace and the towel.

"Do you want to go and see if Elena's shop is still there?"

"I nearly forgot about that," Zoe replied, and handed Eva a towel for her hair. "Yes, I want to do that."

"We may not find anything but we have to try." Eva put her arm around Zoe's shoulders as they walked out of the bathroom.

"ELENA'S SHOP WOULD be just down the road from here," Eva said as they walked past bombed-out buildings.

At one building Eva stood for a long moment, staring at the charred remains. "That was one of the oldest libraries in Berlin," she said quietly. She had spent many hours reading in the grand old library with its ornate ceilings and stained glass windows. It had had an old world charm about it.

"You know, I never really thought about what the war did to Germany," Zoe said as she gazed at the building. Three US soldiers walked past, laughing and making bomb noises. Eva watched them for a moment and then walked away.

They continued to chat as Eva played tourist guide to a city she knew so well and pointed out various buildings and landmarks. Zoe asked questions, which made Eva appreciate the city even more, even though it wasn't at its best. Eva stopped talking when they reached an intersection and looked up at an unremarkable burnt building, its roof caved in.

"What's this?" Zoe asked.

"A synagogue," Eva whispered. Memories of *Kristallnacht* came flooding back. From this corner she'd watched the building go up in flames, watched as her friends beat the old rabbi.

"Evy? Are you okay, love?"

"Old memories," Eva whispered and let her tears run down her face. She said a prayer, asking for forgiveness for having taken part in such a crime. "Greta, Jurgen, a few others and myself were here burning down this synagogue."

"You didn't—"

"No, love, I didn't, but inaction is sometimes worse than committing the crime," Eva replied. "It was here that I got this feeling that I needed to be home. I just needed to leave."

"What did the others say?"

"Greta called me soft." Eva sighed. "Let's not talk about it."

Zoe put her arm around Eva's waist. Eva looked down and then back up at her. "About a block from here is where Elena's shop should be."

"I don't like it here," Zoe said.

"I know. It's horrible to look at. There's something sinister about it. Elena's shop is nearby. Let's go quickly over there. I really don't like being here."

"Is that your PentaSense?" Zoe took Eva's hand.

Eva looked at Zoe and smiled. "My what?"

"Pentecost Sensitivity," Zoe replied. "PentaSense."

"No, not my PentaSense." Eva chuckled as they crossed the road. "This is it, Zoe."

They stopped in front of a grocery which seemed to be open for business.

Zoe pointed at the shop front and smiled. The name on the store was Mannheims. "This is it."

"There are a lot of Mannheims in Germany. It may not be Elena's family."

"But it's their store."

"I wouldn't get your hopes up," Eva replied quietly as they entered the store. They tentatively approached a man who was stocking cans on a shelf. "Good morning."

"Ah, good morning, Fräulein, how can I help you?" The storeowner said with a smile. He left the rest of the cans on the counter and turned his attention to Eva.

"Your store is called Mannheims . . ."

"Yes, I'm the owner. My name is Josef Gerber. That's what the store was called."

Zoe looked about to jump in her excitement. Eva squeezed her hand to indicate to take it nice and slow.

"My name is Eva Muller. I wonder if I can ask you who owned this store before the war."

"Why do you need to know this?"

Eva glanced at Zoe, who was doing her best not to jump into the conversation. "I have a friend back home in Australia and her name is Elena Mannheim. Do you know her?"

Josef scratched his beard for a moment. "Elena Mannheim, you say?"

"Yes, sir."

Josef looked at Eva for a moment and then walked around to the front of the counter. He went over to the door and turned over the open sign to "closed" and pulled the heavy drape that covered the window. He came back to Eva and Zoe.

"Come with me," Josef said, and led them to a small room behind the shop front. He offered them a seat and sat down on a rickety old chair.

"Yes, I know Elena Mannheim."

"Are you related?" Zoe leaned forward in her chair.

"No." Josef shook his head. "I was a family friend for many years."

"What happened to Franz Mannheim?"

"I was in Buchenwald concentration camp with my friend Franz," Josef said sadly. He rolled up his shirtsleeve and showed them his concentration camp tattoo. "Franz did not survive."

"Oh." Zoe leaned against Eva.

"Franz died on April tenth, 1945. I remember that day." Josef paused and looked at Eva. "On April eleventh, the Americans liberated our camp. Do you know what happened to Elena's mother?"

"She died in Bergen Belsen," Eva replied.

"Jacob and David also died."

Zoe wiped the tears from her eyes. "Do you know if any of Elena's family is alive?"

"They are all gone," Josef replied. "All gone. When I was liberated and strong enough I came back here. Where else would I go? I heard they had given us a home in Israel but this is my home."

"Don't you want to go to Israel?"

Josef shook his head. "What will I do there?"

"It's your spiritual home," Zoe replied.

Josef gazed at Zoe with a sad smile. "How old are you, Fräulein?"

"Twenty-Two."

"You're not German. What is your name?"

"No, I'm Greek. My name is Zoe."

"Hmm." Josef looked up at Eva. "You are German."

"Yes, sir."

"Hmm. Why would I go to Israel, Zoe? This is my home. I was born here, I grew up here. I lost my wife, my children, my friends. What is in Israel?" Josef asked. "If I leave, they win."

"Who wins?"

"The Nazis. They will drive me from my home, my fatherland."

"These people murdered your family," Zoe said. "Why do you want to stay here amongst people that hate you?"

"I look at you and I see a child that has lost much." Josef touched Zoe's hand. "You have been through the fire. You understand. You young people want to see the world. You want to know, want to explore and change the world."

"What is wrong with changing the world, Herr Gerber?"

"Nothing, but I'm an old man. If I go to Israel, who will remind the Gentiles of the HaShoah?"

"HaShoah?"

"Our destruction, Fräulein. Who will remind them? If we all go to Israel, who will be left?"

"I don't know."

"I came back and I opened the store to remember my friend." Josef took out a handkerchief and wiped his eyes.

"Can we give Elena your address so she can write to you?" Eva asked as she took out a pencil and a piece of paper from her handbag.

"Of course. Is Elena well?"

"Yes. She got married to a wonderful man and they just had their first baby."

"Ah, that's good, a new life." Josef took the pencil and paper and wrote down the address. He handed the paper back to Eva.

"Thank you for taking the time to talk to us," Eva said as she stood.

"You are welcome, Fräulein. It's not often I get to spend a little bit of my morning with two very beautiful girls," Josef said with a little chuckle.

Zoe kissed Josef on the cheek. "That's from Elena."

"Ah, thank you, and now I get a kiss as well—I am a happy man."

Zoe put her hand through the crook of Josef's right arm and Eva took the left as he escorted them out. He bid them farewell.

CHAPTER 31

EVA STOOD OUTSIDE the cemetery walls, which were marred by bullet holes and mortar damage. The façade and the iron gate appeared worse for wear and in need of some attention, much like the rest of the city. She had been there a few times and the last time was to take flowers to her grandfather's grave.

"Are we going in?" Zoe gently bumped her.

Eva glanced at Zoe and smiled. "You would think I would want to hurry in."

"No," Zoe replied and took Eva's hand. She looked down at their locked fingers. "I didn't think you'd want to sprint in there, but the longer we stand out here, the harder it will be."

"Hmm." Eva nodded and stood still for a moment. She took a deep breath and nodded. She walked slowly, with Zoe beside her, their hands still locked together.

The cemetery was a peaceful place despite its gruesome nature. At one time Eva found the place fascinating because of its history and significance. She veered off the walkway to sit on a bench just under the shade provided by the trees surrounding the area.

"Alright, we will sit down." Zoe sat down next to Eva, who was gazing at the entrance to a mausoleum. "Is that the Muller one?"

"No. Becker."

"Ah." Zoe nodded. "Are you going in there?"

"I don't want to," Eva replied quietly. "I don't want to know if Willie is buried there. It would be real."

Zoe nodded and kept silent as Eva gazed at the gate.

Eva turned to her and took her hand. "Larissa."

"Pardon? What about Larissa?"

"That's what we should name our baby when she's born."

"Larissa? Why would you select a place you hate as the name for our baby?"

"It's the place where our lives converged, Zo. We were both reborn there. You heard Tessa. I saved your life and you saved mine." Eva brushed a piece of lint that was perched precariously on Zoe's red hair.

"You may have missed the part about me wanting to kill you."

"I want our baby's name to reflect where we were born again."

"Alright, but we have to give her one of those Pentecost names as well, and my choice is Eva." Zoe grinned. "You get to give her Larissa and I choose Eva."

"Why not Theresa? It is Tommy's mother."

"Pah, I don't like those naming traditions. My papa didn't name me Maria like the others. Anyway, Tommy doesn't have a say in what we call our babies."

"Larissa Eva?"

"Yes. I like it."

"I think if the baby is a boy, it's pretty obvious what it will be."

"Oh? Really? What will it be?" Zoe smiled and patted Eva's knee.

"Nicholas."

"Nicholas? My papa's name? I thought I just said I don't like those traditions?"

"It's perfect. I want to honor the man who brought you into this world. If it wasn't for him, you wouldn't be alive."

"Nicholas . . ."

"Nicholas Karl," Eva said. "I know what you said about Theresa and Tommy, but Tommy is here to give us this gift because Karl loved Theresa."

"Alright, I like that idea. Larissa and Nicholas Lambros. What beautiful names."

"I like them."

"Good, now can you stop procrastinating and let us go to honor your mama? You can honor Willie when we come back."

Eva nodded and got up from the bench. They continued the slow walk down the path. Eva glanced at Zoe, who had a thoughtful look on her face, as a young man walked past them. Eva knew what Zoe was thinking—she was in the middle of enemy territory. To Zoe, the Germans were the enemy even after the war ended.

"I'm alright, you know," Zoe said softly, and looked up at Eva with a slight smile.

"How do you do that?"

Zoe squeezed Eva's hand and smiled. "The same way you do it," she replied and bumped Eva with her hip. "Let's go."

They resumed their walk and came to an area of the cemetery that was walled off. They walked through the gate and headed to the right, where Eva knew the Mullers were buried. She rounded a corner and stopped. Taking a deep breath, she moved forward and through another smaller gate.

"This place has too many gates," Zoe muttered as she followed Eva down a narrow pathway.

They rounded another corner and stopped. Large oak trees acted like beacons where they surrounded the grave sites. At the entrance to the walkway was a large white marble monolith, and beyond that was a small walkway. On either side were graves with white headstones.

"All the Mullers are here?"

"Every single one of them."

Zoe took a few steps forward in front of the monolith. The names of the deceased were inscribed along with the dates of their births and deaths.

"This is impressive," Zoe mused.

Eva read off the other side of the structure. Eva found her mother's inscription, and underneath, her stepfather's name.

Zoe came up behind her and put her arm around her waist.

Eva glanced at her and followed Zoe's stare at her stepfather's name. "I guess they had to bury him some place. You can say it if you want."

Zoe gazed at Eva and shook her head. "No, it's not the time. Go," she urged, and gently pushed Eva towards the headstones.

Eva nodded and headed down the walkway, leaving Zoe near the monolith. She looked back at Zoe. Zoe was sitting cross-legged on the grassy knoll, her back braced against a tree, watching her. Eva came to a stop at her mother's grave. She knelt in front of the tombstone, made the sign of the cross, and kissed the cross that hung around her neck. She took out the letter that Father Haralambos had given her in Greece and placed it at the base of the headstone as she had promised.

"Oh, Mutti, I'm so sorry. I'm sorry I wasn't there like you told me to be." Eva's voice broke. She took control over her emotions before they overwhelmed her. "I visited hell for a while, Mutti." Eva glanced at Zoe, who was still watching her intently. "I know you've been with me and watched how my life has turned out . . . Mutti, you would have been so disappointed in me. The choices I made on that day. I chose to disobey you and went to meet Greta. I know you didn't like her, but I thought I knew better than you did. I was wrong. Willie didn't like her either." She smiled at the memory of her greatest friend and ally.

"Is Willie there with you, Mutti? I miss him so much. He promised me he was going to survive the war and come home. He promised. I don't know to what god-forsaken battlefield he was sent. If he's there with you, tell him I love him." She sighed and swallowed the lump in her throat. She licked her dry lips and gazed around the cemetery. "Father was executed at Nuremberg, and he's buried next to you. I'm sure he's not there with you. I forgive him for what he did to me, Mutti. I do . . . I have to forgive him because if it wasn't for him, I wouldn't have met my prince. I can't forgive him for what he did to my Zoe. I will never forgive him for that."

Eva took out a locket. She opened it and gazed at a picture of Zoe and herself and then glanced back at her beloved, who had her eyes closed and was resting her head against the tree trunk. She placed the locket at the foot of the headstone alongside the letter. "You were right. You told me my prince would come and she has. She's everything you told me to expect in a husband." She wiped her eyes and smiled. "You told me that a prince would come and make me his princess. I found my prince, Mutti. I found her."

Eva bowed her head. "I love her, Mutti, more than anyone in the world. She is the most loving person God ever put on this earth." She wiped her eyes and chuckled. "She is also the most stubborn, whoa, is she stubborn." She sniffed back tears. "She never gives up; even when I go into a black mood she comes right on in after me. God has blessed me, Mutti. He has. I want you to meet her."

Eva looked back to find Zoe smiling at her. She beckoned Zoe to come over, and in one fluid motion Zoe was up on her feet and walking towards her.

Zoe knelt beside her and tenderly brushed the tear-stained cheek. She took Eva's hand as she sat cross-legged on the ground next to her.

She turned to the grave and smiled. "Thank you." She turned back to face Eva. "Thank you for creating my princess."

Eva looked up. Zoe was bathed in sunlight filtering through the trees, and she blinked back the tears.

Zoe put her hand over her eyes to shield them from the sunlight. "Are you alright?"

Eva nodded, unwilling to trust her voice for a moment. "I'm fine." She put her arm around Zoe's shoulder. "I don't know when we'll be back, Mutti, but you are in my prayers every night."

"And mine," Zoe said quietly. "I thank you and God for Eva."

Eva took Zoe's hand and kissed it tenderly. "We are both thinking of you."

"And hope not to meet you up there for a long time," Zoe quipped.

Eva shook her head and kissed Zoe on the lips.

"Ach, not in front of your mother!" Zoe said in mock outrage, then leaned in for another kiss.

Eva got up and held out her hand for Zoe. With her free hand she crossed herself and blew a kiss to her mother.

"Who else do we have to visit?" Zoe asked.

"My grandfather," Eva said and squeezed Zoe's hand. "He's over there." Zoe followed Eva's gaze to the headstone that read, "Alexander Muller."

Eva smiled, opened her handbag, and took out two cigars. Zoe shook her head as Eva took out some matches and lit both cigars. She stuck the cigar in the soil next to the headstone.

"There you go, Opa." Eva sat down next to the headstone and crossed her legs.

Eva took a puff of the cigar.

"What are you doing?" Zoe asked.

"Smoking with my opa," Eva replied, and blew out some smoke. "I did this every time I came to visit him."

"You smoked at his grave?"

"Yep. He wanted me to." Eva patted the grass next to her. Zoe sat down. "When he was sick, before he died, he said to me that when I visited him, I was to bring his favorite cigars and when the time came when he couldn't enjoy them with me, I would smoke them for him."

"How old were you when he died?"

"Fifteen."

"He wanted you to smoke them with him?"

"Hmm, he said that I was going to smoke them anyway so we might as well enjoy them together." Eva grinned. "My grandmother was livid the first time she caught me smoking here after he died. She didn't know who to yell at first, him or me." She chuckled at the memory. "Isn't that right, Opa," she asked her grandfather. "Opa, this is Zoe, Zoe this is my grandfather."

"You let her smoke?" Zoe asked. "You let her smoke?"

"Watch out, Opa, Zoe is not happy." Eva giggled and kissed Zoe lightly, knowing full well Zoe hated the cigar taste on her lips. Eva wasn't sure why, but she was feeling very light headed. Maybe it was the relief of finally visiting her mother's grave or the fact she was smoking her grandfather's favorite cigar at his grave again.

Zoe scrunched up her face. "You did that on purpose."

"Yes, guilty." Eva nodded solemnly before winking at her. "You forgive me?"

"No." Zoe shook her head with a mischievous grin. "But because you promised to smoke that thing here, that's what you have to do."

"I love you." Eva blew a kiss at Zoe. Zoe smiled —the response Eva wanted.

"I'm going to leave you to smoke and talk to your grandfather." Zoe got up and walked a little further down the hill.

"So, Opa, you like her? She's one of a kind." Eva brought the cigar to her lips and puffed away. "I missed talking to you. It's been a long time. You have Mutti up there with you, and Willie. Papa isn't there, he's gone somewhere else . . . I told Mutti I forgave him for what he did . . . I don't want to talk about him. I don't know if I'm ever going to come back here again. I live in Australia now with Zoe. It's nice there, although it's not home. I can't come back here, Opa. Nothing is left here for me."

Eva gazed at Zoe, who was reading the various headstones. "Oma has disowned me and I don't even want to know what the rest of the family thinks. A lot of things have happened, but the best has been Zoe."

Eva looked up at the sky and wondered if she would ever see Germany again. More than likely this was her last visit. "I'm going to say goodbye now." She stubbed out her cigar and put it in her bag. She knew it was also the last she would see of that cigar as soon as Zoe got a hold of her bag. She changed her mind, opened the bag, and lit the cigar. She took another puff and buried it lightly in the soil. "You can't waste a good cigar. "Goodbye, Opa." She kissed the headstone before getting up from the grass to join Zoe.

"Are you ready?"

"Hmm." Eva nodded and took Zoe's hand. "I want to go home."

"Well, you didn't sleep at all last night so—"

"No, I meant home. Our home." Eva turned and took one long last look. "I'm going to be seeing my mother and grandfather when it's time over there."

"I don't want that to happen for a very long time."

"I'll try not to," Eva promised.

"I'm going first."

Eva stopped. "You're going first? Do we need to have this conversation now?"

"Probably not, but I'm telling you, I'm going first."

Eva closed the gate and took a final look before she turned with Zoe and walked away. "I don't want to have this conversation."

"Too depressing?"

"Yes."

"Fine, we won't have this conversation, but I'm still going first."

Eva tapped Zoe on the nose. "I'm older."

"I thought we weren't having this conversation."

"Eva Muller?"

Eva was stopped in her tracks by the very familiar voice and she turned in the direction of the voice. Her past had finally collided with the present.

"Oh, dear God," she whispered. "It can't be."

CHAPTER 32

"WHO'S THAT?" ZOE asked when Eva turned around.

Eva took a couple of steps towards the woman and then set off into a run to her.

Zoe didn't know who to look at first, Eva running or the woman dropping what she had in her hands and opening her arms to welcome her. "I'm going to guess this is a friend." She shook her head and sprinted after Eva.

"My God, it is you!"

"Leila!" Eva exclaimed as she engulfed the woman in a bear hug, nearly lifting her off the ground in her exuberance. "My God, Leila."

Zoe came to a stop near the two friends as Eva cupped Leila's face and laughed. Leila was an elegantly dressed woman, as tall as Eva with fire-red hair and deep green eyes. Zoe's smile broadened when she realized who this Leila could be.

"You're alive." Leila held Eva at arm's length and laughed. "My God, I thought I was seeing things. I saw you and then I thought it couldn't be you, but the more I watched you, it dawned on me that I wasn't seeing things."

Zoe could half follow what Leila was saying—she was talking so quickly Zoe could barely keep up. Her German was good but she got lost when someone was talking excitedly and fast.

"Oh, my God," Eva kept repeating while she hugged Leila.

"Effie, I need to breathe." Leila laughed and took Eva's hands. "You're too skinny."

"And you've got red hair."

Zoe thought that's what Eva had just said but didn't get the connection. She knew that trying to keep up with them was going to be a hit and miss affair, so she sat on a nearby bench and observed.

"We thought you were dead." Leila took Eva's hand and led her to the bench where Zoe was sitting. They were quite oblivious to her presence, much to Zoe's annoyance at first, but then she realized that this Leila woman was seeing Eva for the first time since 1938.

"No, no, very much alive." Eva laughed. "I don't know where to start."

"Well, I have to say Oma kept this a secret from us."

"Oma doesn't know I'm here."

"Really?" Leila laughed. "We are talking about your grandmother, right?"

"I take that back." Eva smiled. "She probably does know I'm here."

"Wait until my mother sees you. Oh, she's going to be overjoyed. I see you've turned into an old hag, Fräulein Muller," Leila teased as she cupped Eva's cheek. "You are so beautiful."

Zoe frowned at the overly intimate gesture. *Hmm Evy, did you leave anything out of that story you told me?* It wasn't just the intimate gesture, but Eva's response as well. Eva never allowed anyone to touch her like that, other than Zoe. Eva's demeanor fascinated her —her normally reserved partner was so relaxed.

"So are we going to be rude toward your friend here?" Leila asked.

Eva blushed at the obvious afterthought. She turned to Zoe and had such an apologetic look on her face that Zoe laughed.

"Old age will do that to you, Evy," she said in German.

Eva looked between Leila and Zoe. "I'm so sorry. Zoe, this is one of my dearest friends, Leila Becker, Willie's sister. Zoe this is my . . ."

"I'm her friend, Zoe Lambros." Zoe stuck out her hand.

Leila leaned over and shook it. "Pleased to meet you, Zoe." She smiled and then turned back to Eva. "Were you visiting Opa? I can smell that awful cigar on you."

Zoe raised her eyebrows at the very personal revelation and the very intimate way Leila put her arm around Eva's shoulders.

Eva chuckled. "I would show it to you but I left it with Opa."

"Good place to leave it," Leila quipped. "You visited your mutti?"

Eva nodded.

"I'm so pleased. You never got the chance to say goodbye. I'm glad you are here. I was just tending to . . ."

Eva's eyes glistened.

"You know, don't you?"

Eva nodded. "I think I've known for a long time."

"Let's wait a moment before I take you in," Leila suggested.

Zoe internally smirked at the way Leila was ordering Eva and at Eva's acceptance. Leila took Eva's hands.

"He's gone, isn't he?"

Leila nodded. "Yes, darling, he's gone." She wiped the single tear that ran down Eva's cheek. "He was injured in France and was brought home but he never recovered."

"Oh," Eva whispered.

"I did take photographs of him." Leila smiled. "His good side, of course." They laughed at what sounded like a very private joke. "When you come to the house tomorrow, I will give you a copy. I've got the negatives and will print some off for you tonight."

"His good side?"

Leila smiled at Zoe. "My brother used to say he looked much more handsome from the left than from the right side of his face. Crazy boy."

"How was he?" Eva asked.

"Let's not talk about that, darling. I want to remember him with you as that crazy boy who climbed your balcony to lie in bed with you when you had chickenpox," Leila said affectionately.

"He climbed the balcony?"

"Oh, yes. He was told he wasn't allowed near Eva because she had chickenpox. I think you were ten or something. My brother and Eva were inseparable, so naturally Wilhelm just didn't want to listen so he climbed the balcony and got into bed with Eva."

"He got his wish of catching chickenpox with me." Eva laughed.

"He did. Your grandmother still tells the story of her coming into your bedroom to check on you and seeing Willie asleep next to you, his cherub face so peaceful."

"He made chickenpox fun."

"Not sure if your mother saw it like that. He started to play join the dots on your arms." Leila chuckled. "The last time I saw you was in Aiden."

"What?"

"You probably have no memory of that, but Papa pulled some strings with Willie's commanding officer and we both went to Aiden to see you," Leila said, and brushed Eva's hair from her eyes. A gesture so intimate that Zoe almost thought Leila was in love with Eva.

"I don't remember that."

"No, I'm quite certain you don't. You had just undergone surgery for the fibroids, and as shocking as that was, we were so glad they saved your life. When we came you had just come out of surgery so you were still asleep."

"You and Willie?"

"Yes, darling, Wilhelm and I came to see you. I went to speak to your uncle and left Willie alone with you. When I returned, what did I see? My little brother, who looked all grown up in his uniform, had taken off his shoes and jacket and was in bed with you." Leila sighed at the memory. "That boy loved you so much."

"I loved him."

"I know." Leila nodded. "He took off his signet ring and put in on your finger. He proposed to you and he claimed you said yes."

"He proposed on the night he was due to leave," Eva said quietly. "I said yes then."

Zoe looked down at the ground and wondered how life would have been like had Eva stayed in Germany and not been forced to come to Larissa. She knew how life would have been for her—she was destined not to survive the war.

"Did you take a photograph of that?"

Leila smiled. "Of course, I don't travel without my camera."

"Can I have it?"

"Of course you can, darling. Tomorrow when you come over. Don't be shocked about mutti's hand, alright?"

"What happened to your mother's hand?"

"Your father didn't tell you? Of course he didn't." Leila sighed. "On the night your mutti was killed, she was together with my mother."

"Our mothers were together?"

"Yes. Those Brownshirts, they came looking for my mother. I think you need to hear the full story from her."

"What's wrong with her hand?"

"They shot it."

"Oh no," Eva exclaimed and turned to Zoe. "Leila's mother is a renowned artist—"

"Becker? *The* Marlene Becker, that's who you are talking about, right? *The* Marlene Becker."

Leila looked surprised. "Yes, have you heard of her?"

Zoe grinned. "Have I heard of her? Yes, absolutely."

"You must be an artist."

"She is. A very gifted artist." Eva smiled at Zoe.

"Wow, Marlene Becker." Zoe whistled.

"My mother was an outspoken critic of Herr Hitler and it reflected in her art, much to the annoyance of the Nazis. Why don't you come to the house tomorrow and I'll introduce you?" Leila suggested and smiled at Zoe's very enthusiastic nod.

"Thank you."

Leila turned to Eva with a sad smile. "Let's go and say hello to Wilhelm, shall we?"

"If I don't, then he's not really gone, Leila."

"You can't do that, darling, because he is gone. I know you can't say goodbye to him, but you have to," Leila said gently. Eva nodded and got up from her seat. "Have you got another one of those horrible cigars?"

"I do."

"Well, Willie did love smoking them with you, so you can leave him one." Leila grimaced when Eva took out a cigar from her handbag. "Let's go, darling."

Leila threaded her arm around the crook of Eva's elbow and started to walk towards the mausoleum. She stopped and looked back at Zoe. "Are you coming, Zoe?"

"Yes," Zoe replied and hurried along after them.

CHAPTER 33

EVA WAS SITTING on the bed lost in thought when Zoe came back from the bathroom wrapped in a towel. She smiled and beckoned her over. She captured Zoe's body between her legs. "You smell nice."

"You're not dressed yet and thank you."

"Hmm. I'll get dressed soon."

"How do you feel about going to the Becker house?"

Eva studied the carpet for a moment, lost in the myriad of memories that swirled around in her head. "I'm nervous."

"Why? They're your family. I know Tessa is family, but you have a history with the Beckers, a good history."

"I know."

"Why are you nervous?"

"I don't know. Marlene Becker was always like a second mother. I was at their house as often as I was in mine so I'm not worried about that. Leila is like a big sister—"

"That you still have a crush on" Zoe smirked at Eva's scowl. "You do, Evy. There's nothing wrong with that."

"Yes, there is and no, I don't."

"You don't have a crush on Leila?"

"No." Eva shook her head. "I grew out of that crush a long time ago. I'm a little hurt you would say that."

Zoe grinned and Eva's pout morphed into a wry smile.

"Aww." Zoe put her arms around Eva's neck and gave her a kiss. "I didn't mean it in a bad way, but you do look up to her. I noticed she's a photographer—she carried that camera in her bag."

"Is there anything you don't notice?"

"Well, it was a little hard to miss. I'm going to make this really hard guess that Leila taught you photography and you wanted to be like her. Now, why don't you get dressed and we can get out of here."

"ARE YOU ALRIGHT?" Zoe asked as they turned onto a tree-lined street.

"Yes," Eva replied a little unconvincingly while they walked along the pavement.

Zoe looked around. She was starting to understand a little of Eva's background. Having Eva tell her about her upbringing and seeing it in person were two very different things.

Eva gave Zoe a knowing smile. "Yes, this is where I grew up."

Zoe looked in amazement at the beautiful homes. "You came from here?"

"Yes."

"Wow."

"It's just another home."

"No, it's not. This is privilege," Zoe replied. "I'm almost speechless. You worked in a factory . . ."

"Almost speechless?" Eva teased and bumped Zoe with her hip. "I worked in a factory. That's not a big deal."

"Yes, it is, it's . . ." Zoe stopped outside a gate that led to one of most beautiful houses she had ever seen, surrounded on either side by gardens. "Oh, wow."

Eva chuckled and put her arm around Zoe's shoulders. "Let's not dawdle here. That's where the crazy old lady lives. I bet she is still around."

"You had one of those?"

"Every neighborhood has one. Remind me to tell you about my tangle with her dog Satan." Eva took Zoe's hand and they crossed the street.

"Her dog Satan?" Zoe asked while still looking behind her at the house.

"Ach! She's here, she's here," a voice rang out in the midday stillness, which caused Zoe to forget the house. A rotund woman wearing an apron was running towards them with her arms open wide.

"Brace yourself." Eva was engulfed in a bear hug. "Isabella!"

Isabella, the housekeeper took a step back and cupped Eva's face in her chubby hands as she grinned with delight. "My baby girl." She kissed Eva on both cheeks. "Leila told me you were home but I didn't believe it."

"I'm here." Eva laughed and kissed Isabella on the cheek. "You're looking good."

"I'm happy and fat." Isabella laughed.

Zoe smiled as they switched from German to Italian. That was a language she knew a little, but not enough to understand what they were saying.

"Isabella, this is my friend Zoe." Eva switched back to German.

"Hello, friend Zoe." Isabella smiled and put her arm around Zoe.

"Is Aunty Marlene home?"

Isabella chuckled. "Aunty Marlene has been worrying what time you would arrive and told me to sit outside and wait. Where did you go?"

"Isabella, are they . . . ?" Marlene Becker stepped out to the street.

Zoe stared in surprise as Eva ran towards Marlene. The look on Marlene's face was one of pure joy and Zoe couldn't help but smile.

"Her second daughter has come home," Isabella explained.

Zoe nodded. Marlene Becker was of average height and had blond hair worn up in a bun. Even from where she was standing, Zoe could see her bright blue eyes and beaming smile. It was obvious to anyone who cared to look that Marlene truly loved Eva and the feeling was reciprocated.

"And who is this?" Marlene stepped forward, still holding Eva's hand.

"This is my friend Zoe Lambros," Eva said with a bright smile.

"Ah yes. Leila did mention you had a friend with you at the cemetery. Let's go inside," Marlene said, and they walked through the gate.

Zoe tried to hide her surprise at the opulent house as they walked up the driveway. She lost the battle as soon as soon as they stepped inside. The floors were white marble and the cream-colored walls were lined with art. She stood with her mouth open in front of a Renoir.

"Breathe," Eva sidled up to Zoe and whispered in her ear.

"Huh." Zoe nodded and continued to gaze in amazement.

"In, out, in, out," Eva gently teased. "Pretty," she whispered.

Zoe turned to Eva, outraged. "That is a Renoir."

"Yes, as I said, pretty."

"You are terrible." Zoe giggled. "I had never seen a real Renoir."

"Now you have." Eva tapped Zoe on the backside and laughed lightly.

"Hmm." Zoe turned her attention back to the artwork.

EVA LOOKED AT the woman she considered a second mother and smiled shyly. Marlene smiled at them.

"Zoe, I'm going—"

"Yeah, yeah." Zoe waved her hand as she went to the next piece of art and stared up in wonder. "Not going anywhere."

Eva shook her head in mirth and followed Marlene into the parlor. Marlene closed the door and led Eva to the sofa, where they sat down. They looked at each other for a long time then Marlene took Eva in her arms.

"You have been gone for too long, darling."

"I know."

"I missed you so much. We all did."

"I didn't want to come home."

"Why? This is your home. No one can take that away from you." Marlene stroked Eva's hair. "Your mama may be gone but I'm here. I will always be here for you."

Eva took a shuddering breath. "Coming back was . . ." Eva paused as she tried not to let the tide of emotions overwhelm her. "She abandoned me."

"It seems that way but I don't think that's the case. You also had me, Evy. You had me and Leila."

"Did Uncle John make it home?"

Marlene took a deep breath and exhaled slowly. "No. He died in Africa."

"I'm sorry, Aunty." Eva put her arms around Marlene and hugged her. "Leila told me about Willie."

"Ah yes, my beautiful boy." Marlene's voice broke. "He asked for you."

"He did?"

"Yes. He gave me something to give you when you came home. I'll give it to you later."

Eva nodded, not trusting her voice. They sat in silence for a long time.

Marlene tipped Eva's face to meet her eyes. "So, tell me about your special girl outside."

Eva blinked rapidly. Not quite believing what she had heard, she gaped at Marlene.

Marlene chuckled. "Goodness, you should see your face."

"Uh . . ."

"You are adorable." Marlene laughed as she cupped Eva's face and kissed her on the cheek. "Just adorable."

"Uh."

"Where did you meet her?"

"How . . . ?"

"How did I know?"

"Yes."

"I didn't, but you just told me." Marlene gently laughed. "Sweetheart, did you think we didn't know?"

"Did Willie tell you?"

"Did Willie know?"

Eva rolled her eyes when she realized she had revealed yet another secret. "How do you do that?"

"Do what?" Marlene asked with a tiny smile. "It's called being a mother."

"Are we talking about the same thing?"

"You like girls."

Eva sighed. "We are talking about the same thing."

"So, where did you meet her?"

"In Greece," Eva replied, and quickly glanced at the door.

"That crazy father of yours," Marlene exclaimed. "I just could not believe he took you to a war zone."

"I couldn't believe it either."

"So you met this girl in Larissa? She obviously likes art." Marlene smiled. "She has good taste."

"She's an artist herself. She's a huge fan of your work. I didn't know that until she found out who you were."

"Really? Hmm, is that all you're going to tell me about her?"

"How long have you known that I like girls?"

Marlene tilted her head a little and regarded Eva. "How long have you known?"

"There is no way you would have known then."

"Actually I didn't . . ."

Eva shook her head. "I just told you, right?"

"No." Marlene took Eva's hand. Eva looked down at their interlocked hands and she couldn't hide the sadness at Marlene's deformed right hand. "Eva." Marlene tipped Eva's face up with her fingertips and gazed into her eyes. "I didn't know, but your mother did."

"My mother knew?"

"Sweetheart, mothers know their children. I know you loved Wilhelm and he loved you. That was real. Your mother knew you also liked girls."

Eva felt her cheeks blush. "I did love Willie."

"I know. You can't fake that kind of bond."

"Did my mother . . . um . . . ?"

"No."

"I hadn't asked the question yet," Eva objected.

"Did your mother think you were a deviant?" Marlene asked, much to Eva's surprise.

"Yes."

Marlene looked down at their hands. "She was scared for you."

"Scared for me? What does that mean?"

"A mother wishes for her child to have a life that is full of joy and happiness. Your mother wanted you to be happy. She knew that your feelings for women were going to cause you pain."

"So she was disappointed?"

"No, I didn't say that," Marlene corrected her. "She knew that once your father found out it was going to be a very bad time for you."

"She wasn't wrong," Eva muttered.

"What Daphne wanted in life was to see you happy. If you had married Willie you would have been happy, but the war had other ideas." Marlene sat back on the sofa and took Eva's hand and held it on her lap.

"If the war hadn't happened, I would have married Willie."

"I know." Marlene smiled. "I know how much you loved him. If we hadn't had that lunatic little Corporal Hitler, we wouldn't have gone to war, he wouldn't have killed my son, and you would have been able to be together."

"I nearly forgot how much you despised Hitler."

"Hmm. I'm constantly reminded of that raving lunatic." Marlene sighed.

"Leila told me not to mention your hand," Eva said as she took the disfigured hand into her own. "What happened?"

Marlene took a deep breath. "I need a cigarette to tell you that story. I want you to promise me that you will tell me about Zoe after this."

"I will." Eva pulled out her cigarette case from her handbag and offered a cigarette to Marlene and took one for herself. She lit both cigarettes with her lighter and she took a drag and exhaled.

"It was on the night the Brownshirts went mad," Marlene related as she gazed at the unlit fireplace. "Your mother and I were together."

"You were with Mutti on that night?"

"Yes. I was teaching her how to draw." Marlene put the cigarette holder to her lips and took a drag. She exhaled and watched the smoke rise. "Your mother was atrocious at it," she said with a slight smile. "But we had fun. We were drinking some wine and attempting to draw."

"Were you at the house?"

"No. Here," Marlene said. "That's when the Brownshirts arrived and started to break the windows."

"They broke the windows here? But you weren't a Jew. Didn't they know this was Colonel Becker's residence?"

"They knew that Marlene Becker, the anti-Nazi artist, lived here."

Eva put her hand over her mouth. "They wanted to kill you?"

"They did. Your mother tried to reason with them and identified herself as Major Muller's wife but they were animals."

"That's why Mama died?" Eva whispered and felt tightness in her chest.

"No."

"They were not after your mother. They were after me. One of them took out his gun and shot my hand." Marlene held up her hand and gazed at it. "He was going to shoot my other hand but your mother pushed him."

"My mother pushed him?"

"Yes, quite forcibly, to the point where his fellow lunatics were laughing." Marlene closed her eyes for a moment. She wiped the tears that streamed down her face. "Your mother was courageous, Evy. She stood up to them for me."

"He shot her."

"Yes. That's when they realized they had gone too far and ran out of here," Marlene said in disgust.

"It wasn't my fault," Eva almost whispered and tried to blink away the tears that fell down her cheeks.

"Darling, how could it be your fault?"

"My stepfather blamed me."

"Muller was always an idiot. I know Daphne loved him but he wasn't a very bright man," Marlene said. "How could he possibly have blamed you when you weren't even in the house?"

"I wasn't in the house."

"How were you going to stop those thugs? Hans Muller was always a brute of a man, and your grandmother told me what he did to you, and he deserves the seven layers of hell."

"I don't want to talk about that now."

"Then we won't, but it wasn't your fault."

"I know that now," Eva quietly replied and wiped her eyes.

"How about we talk about the ring on your finger?" Marlene asked, and held up Eva's hand with the wedding band.

"Oh, that."

"I'm married."

"Hmm." Marlene scowled. "What man could possibly replace my Wilhelm?"

"No man could replace Willie in my heart." Eva smiled. "It's a long story."

"Well, since you are not going back to your hotel tonight but staying here instead, you can tell me this long story."

"I'm not at a hotel."

"You're staying with your grandmother?"

"No."

"So where are you staying?"

"That's a long story as well." Eva laughed gently as Isabella came into the room with a tea tray and Eva's favorite cakes.

CHAPTER 34

"WHAT DO YOU mean there is no phone?" Marlene asked as she sipped her cup of tea. Zoe had entered the parlor and was seated on an overstuffed chair after having feasted on the artwork.

"The phone was cut last night."

"Why?"

Eva glanced at Zoe with a tiny before she turned to Marlene. "Uncle Dieter decided to pay me a visit."

"Dieter Muller? What was he doing at the place you are staying and how did he know you were there?"

Eva sighed. "This is such a long story, I don't even know where to start."

"I know you were sent to Aiden under his care after your mother passed away. Your grandmother told me what happened with your father," Marlene carefully said, as if gauging Eva's reaction. "This is correct?"

"Yes."

"Your grandmother also said that Dieter was working on a treatment for deviant behavior . . ."

Eva's hand froze over a piece of cake on the platter. She sat back down and looked at Zoe, who had a horrified look on her face. "What did you say?"

"I said Dieter was working on a treatment for deviant behavior."

"My grandmother told you this?"

"Yes."

"When?" Eva leaned forward and took Marlene's hand. "Aunty Marlene, when did my grandmother tell you?"

"I asked her where you had been taken and that I wanted to visit. She told me a few months after your mother's death."

"Wow." Zoe put her hand over her mouth. "Wow."

Eva stood and slowly paced. "She knew. I told you, Zo, she knew."

"What was that treatment, Eva?" Marlene went to Eva's side and stopped her from moving away. "What did it involve?"

"Drugs and electroshock therapy," Eva quietly explained as she held back from the pain that overwhelmed her.

Marlene shook her head slowly.

"What?" Eva said quietly. "What is it?"

Marlene sat down and clutched her hands in her lap. "Daphne told me that you were different and that she feared for your safety, and that it involved drugs."

"She was right."

"She was. She was right about a lot of things."

"What do you mean?"

"There was more to Daphne that anyone ever realized," Marlene related quietly. "She used to have a parlor game where she would read an upturned coffee cup."

"Yes, I remember that. She always got it wrong." Eva giggled on remembering how much fun she used to have with her mother when they played the game.

"Did she?" Marlene leaned forward. "You were always there by her side, and you would be the one who turned the cup and she would read it."

"Yes, it was just a harmless game."

"It was a game, but she wasn't doing it for anyone other than you."

"Oh!" Zoe sprang up. "Oh, what a smart woman."

Eva frowned and gave Zoe a quizzical look. "I don't understand."

Zoe went to Eva and knelt in front of her. She glanced at Marlene, who smiled at her. Zoe turned back to Eva. "What was your mother doing?"

"She was just reading the coffee grounds . . ." Eva stopped and blinked. "Oh, god. That wasn't a game."

Marlene smiled. "No, it wasn't. Daphne was teaching you how to harness a power she possessed and one that you also had."

Eva stared at her surprised. "You knew about my mother's gifts?"

"How do you know this?" Zoe asked, and swiveled around on her knee to face Marlene, one hand clutching Eva's shaking hand.

"She told me about the gifts that the women in the family have been given, and she told me that when she was a young woman one of her aunts came to visit—"

"Irene?"

"No, that wasn't her name. Erika something."

"Erika Theresa Faber?"

"Yes, I think that's correct. She told your mother that somehow these gifts were split between herself and her sister Theresa."

Eva exhaled slowly and her heart beating a little faster. "This was unusual?"

"It seems so. From what she was told, what usually happened was that one of the daughters, if there was more than one, would inherit these gifts, but with the Mitsos daughters, both girls received them. She described it as a fork."

"My mother didn't have either Eva or Theresa in her name . . ."

"Of course she did, darling," Marlene replied. "You didn't know your mother's full name?"

Eva grimaced and shook her head.

"It was Eva Daphne but because her mother's name was Eva, Daphne used her middle name."

"Sweet Mary, Mother of God," Zoe exclaimed and crossed herself. "Both girls were given the names."

"That was unusual?"

"It seems so. Theresa is now dead but—"

"She's not." Eva shook her head. "Theresa, my aunt, is not dead."

"She's not?" Marlene blinked in surprise. "Daphne was right." She slapped her hand on the table. "Daphne was right. Your mother never believed that Tessa was dead. Never believed it."

"Aunty Tessa was living in Thessaloniki. My mother didn't know where she was?"

"No. Your mother kept telling me that Tessa was not dead. She couldn't be dead because she could still feel her."

"Wow," Zoe said and shivered.

"How do you know she's not dead?"

"We are staying with her in Dahlem."

"For the love of God." Marlene put her hand over her mouth. "In whose house?"

"My great aunt Irene's. Do you know her?"

"No, I don't believe . . ." Marlene stopped and gazed up at the crucifix hanging on the wall. "Your great aunt was called Erika Theresa Faber?"

"Yes."

"My Wilhelm received his Last Rites from a Father Johan Faber . . ."

Eva stared at her, shocked.

"He is your uncle?" Zoe asked.

"Yes," Eva whispered.

"Alright." Zoe got up and shook her hands. "Now I'm scared."

"There is nothing to be scared about, Zoe," Marlene calmly said. "Father Johan was there for my Wilhelm every night after they brought him home. When he could, my son would talk to him. The priest stayed with him, slept near him. Never left his side. There isn't anything to be scared about. That was an act of love. Wilhelm told him about the letter your mother gave him to give to you."

"Letter?"

"Yes, before Willie was shipped out, Daphne asked him to give you a letter. She told him to hide the letter and when the time was right, to give it to you."

"Willie hid the letter?"

"He did just as Daphne asked him to. Father Johan retrieved the letter. It's still unopened and he gave it to me. He said that one day, soon, you would be back and that Willie had asked for the letter to be given to you."

"Alright, this is just too much," Zoe muttered.

"Did you believe my mother?" Eva opened her eyes despite the migraine that had settled just behind her eyes.

"Yes. I believed her. She hadn't told anyone before but she trusted me to keep her secret. I loved your mother from the moment I met her. She came to Zelhendorf soon after she married Hans with a most precious bundle in her arms." Marlene cupped Eva's cheek. "I remember you were such a chubby baby, with a mop of black hair and those big round blue eyes."

"You knew Hans was not my father?"

"Yes. Daphne married him on the advice of your grandmother Eva Mitsos. It was either that or give you up for adoption."

"They were going to take me away?"

"Yes. She was an unwed mother. Eva Mitsos and Beatriz Muller were friends."

"Ah, that explains that connection," Zoe said. "I always wanted to know what the connection was. How did a young woman from Larissa end up in Vienna?"

"I befriended your mother and we became like sisters."

"Wow."

"Maybe now would be a good time for me to give you that letter." Marlene got up and went to a roll-top desk and unlocked it. She took out two letters and closed it. She went back to her seat and sat down. With trembling hands she gave one letter to Eva.

Eva took it, her own hands shaking so much that she could barely keep the letter in her hand.

Zoe took the letter. She slit the letter open and set it on her lap. "Do you want me to read it?"

Eva swallowed and nodded. She took Zoe's hand and held it tight.

Zoe took a deep breath. "The letter is in Greek," she said in amazement, and gazed at Eva. She bent her head and began to read.

My dearest baby girl,

You are foremost in my thoughts and in my heart, my darling Eva Theresa. I am writing this to you on a beautiful sunny day. The sky reminds me of your eyes and I have to smile as I write because you are reading out in the sun. Your jet black hair is glistening and I can't help but marvel at the beautiful soul I see before me.

Eva, head bowed, tears flowing down her cheeks felt Zoe kiss the top of her head.

I never knew what true love meant until you were born, my darling. Your happiness is all I ever cared about. This is why I am writing this letter. There will be dark days ahead, my love, dark days. I will not be here to protect you or be your guide. You must stay strong, you must believe in God with all your heart . . .

Zoe took a shuddering breath.

I know you are struggling with the feelings you are having, even though you think I don't know. I love you and there is no measure to the love that is in my heart. Do not doubt my love for you. Never doubt . . .

Eva saw Zoe take a sip of water out of the corner of her eye and calmed her own mind as she waited for Zoe to continue.

I want you to do several things. These are important. I beseech you, my darling daughter, you must do these things. I will tell you why. You are a descendant from a very special woman. Her name was Theresa Eva. You have not heard of her until today. She was one of the one hundred and twenty that entered into a room on Pentecost 33 AD and was given God's Holy Ghost. She wasn't a noblewoman, nor was she a titled woman. She was a humble Jewish woman who converted to Christianity after meeting our Lord. Theresa Eva sat at the feet of our Lord, my darling daughter. On Pentecost, Theresa Eva was given the gift of prophecy and a gift for languages. These gifts have been passed on from generation to generation. My darling daughter, you have those gifts. I have seen you grow, and each passing year your abilities get stronger. You are not aware of them but they are there.

Before you can master these gifts you need to understand where you came from. Hans Muller is not your father. I married him to give you the chance for a life that I know you deserve. Not one of misery and despair.

Eva could feel Zoe's eyes on her.

I want you to go to Larissa in Greece. This is where you will start. Go outside the town, past Athena's Bluff . . .

Eva blinked and glanced at Zoe, who stared at the letter in astonishment.

Find a woman named Helena Kalanaris . . .

Zoe stopped again and Eva tightened her hand around hers.

"Do you want me to read the rest?" Eva whispered.

Zoe shook her head. "No. Give me a minute."

Find a woman named Helena Kalanaris. She was my childhood friend and she knows everyone. Not that she was a gossip . . .

Zoe chuckled.

Not that she was a gossip but she will know what to do. Ask her where Panayiotis Haralambos lives. Go there. You will not have to introduce yourself because my darling Pani will know who you are. He has two good eyes and will know when he lays eyes on his own daughter."

"Oh, wow," Zoe exclaimed.

Eva looked up and gazed at Zoe for a long moment. She shook her head in amazement.

Eva, sweetheart, you will then need to leave Larissa and go and find your Aunt Theresa. I believe in my heart she is not dead. She can't be dead. I do not believe she is. I don't know where you need to look but you need to go back to Berlin. Find your great Aunt Irene. She's a wise but a little strange woman. She will guide and teach you. When you find your Aunt Tessa, embrace her, kiss her and then . . .

Zoe burst out laughing. She continued with a giggle.

Kiss her and then slap her for me. She will know why.

I do not want to end this letter, but I must. I will not be there to watch you grow, watch you embrace who you are or see you as you grow into a beautiful woman. You have a gentle loving heart. I wish you, my love, everything, but know I won't see it. Trust yourself; trust your creator, for He knows you from the time you were conceived. I will love you in this life and the next. Be strong, feel joy, embrace life. No goodbyes, my darling baby girl, just a longing until I see you in the next life where I can hold you again.

Your beloved mama,

Daphne Eva Muller

10 October 1938

Zoe continued to gaze at the letter. Eva sniffed back tears as she took the letter out of Zoe's lap and held it to her heart.

CHAPTER 35

"I'LL GO AND get our driver to deliver this message to your aunt that you will be staying with us tonight," Marlene explained as she took the note from Eva and left the room.

Leila entered. "How are you, E?" She put her arm around Eva and leaned in close. "Some days you just want to have a great big bag of sweets." She brought out Eva's favorite candy.

"Oh." Eva grinned and put her hand in the jar.

"That always works." Zoe chuckled as she helped herself to one of the sweet-and-sour candies.

"So did Miss Evil tell you about Satan?"

"Huh?"

"Oh no, Leila, don't." Eva put her hand over Leila's mouth.

"I have to tell Zoe this story. I just have to." Leila laughed and brought Eva in for a hug. "It's good for the soul to laugh."

"At my expense."

"No, at your butt." Leila giggled. "This story is best told by my brother, but since he isn't here, let's pretend I'm Willie."

"Oh god," Eva exclaimed and covered her eyes.

"Evil and Willie went everywhere together. They were sort of like Siamese twins." Leila laughed. "On the way to school was a bricked-off yard with a vineyard and some oranges. They passed this place every day and every day the old woman would throw old grapes at them."

"Why?"

"Because she was mean," Eva replied. "She enjoyed throwing the dried up ones."

"Hey, are you telling the story or am I?"

"Go ahead, Fräulein Becker." Eva motioned with her hand amidst giggles from Zoe.

"Where was I?" Leila glared at Eva. "One day Eva decided—"

"Hey, I didn't decide. Your brother did."

"Don't interrupt me, Fräulein," Leila admonished. "Eva decided that she'd had enough of the pelting and was going to collect some grapes to fling back at the old woman."

"You were going to steal grapes?" Zoe asked in mock outrage.

"No, I was going to fling them back at her," Eva replied and chuckled at the memory.

"So they had a problem," Leila continued. "The wall was high, Willie was really short and lo' and behold, the only tall one was Evil over here." Eva made a face at her. "So he gets a crate and he stands on it and helps Eva over the wall."

Eva put her hands over her eyes.

"Eva jumps over and Willie doesn't hear anything so he climbs up on the crate. Next thing he hears is this growling dog." Leila laughed, along with Eva, who fell over onto Zoe.

"The dog . . ." Leila wiped the tears from his eye. "Satan . . ."

"The old lady called the dog Satan?"

"Yeah," Eva said and laughed again.

"Satan sees Eva on the ground collecting the fallen grapes." Leila tried to control her laughter. "Willie could just barely see over the wall. He tried to warn Eva but the dog went straight for her butt."

Leila stood up. "When Satan bit Eva on the butt, she jumped so high Willie thought she was going to come right over the wall. So after tangling with Satan, Eva climbed over the wall." Leila wiped her eyes.

"How big was this dog?"

Leila and Eva burst into hearty laughing again.

"A sausage dog," Leila squeaked.

"Sausage dog?" Zoe asked.

"A dachshund," Leila explained. "Eva comes over the wall and flops down next to Willie." Leila grinned at Eva and put her hand on her backside. "Eva is yelling at the top of her voice, 'Satan bit me! Satan bit me!' and hopping up and down."

Leila held her backside while limping across the parlor.

Zoe fell off the sofa, laughing.

"Oh God, that was funny," Eva said as she wiped the tears from her eyes.

"Is that why you nicknamed her Evil?"

Leila nodded. "Satan bit Eva in the garden." She laughed uproariously. "But there's more to this story."

"Oh, Leila," Eva protested, but she knew Zoe wouldn't rest until she was told. She fell back and waited for Leila to finish telling a story that had happened a lifetime ago. It felt good being able to laugh like that again.

"When they stop yelling, Eva wants Willie to see if the dog really did bite her hard. So what is a friend to do? He checked where the dog bit her ass."

Zoe collapsed onto the carpet laughing.

"So he's trying to see if Eva's butt has bite marks and then . . . it got worse."

"Satan scored a hit?" Zoe giggled.

"Yeah, he did, but while Willie was checking that, their headmaster came around the corner to find out what the howling was about."

"Oh, no," Zoe roared.

"Willie had his hand on Evil's butt when the headmaster stopped in front of them, took one look, made a face and walked away." Leila sat down, laughing. "So from that day she was known as Evil, but I promised not to tell her mama because it was our secret."

Zoe stopped laughing long enough to kiss Eva on the cheek. "That's so sweet."

"Willie did go around calling her Scarbutt for a while, but I preferred Evil." Leila chuckled.

"You are evil telling that story to Zoe," Eva said.

Leila gave her a wink and a full-blown belly laugh. "Yes, I am, but I thought you might like a bit of a laugh. You know, your room is just as you left it."

"You have your own room?" Zoe asked.

Eva gave her a sheepish look and nodded. "I was over here so much that Aunty Marlene decided I needed my own room."

"It's just the way you left it," Leila said.

"Exactly?" Eva asked.

"Exactly." Leila bumped Eva with her shoulder. "Even the diary you kept under the loose floorboard." Eva stared open mouthed at her. Leila giggled. "I didn't read it. I can't read Greek."

Eva stared at her. "Calm down. Willie told me to get it so it wouldn't get lost."

"Willie knew where you kept your diary?" Zoe asked.

Eva nodded. "Yes." She smiled at Zoe. "If you were a boy, you would be Willie."

"Wow," Zoe exclaimed. "Can I read the diary?"

Eva nodded.

"I bet it has a lot about Greta," Leila quietly said.

Eva stared at her, shocked.

"Tsk." Leila shook her head. "Do you really think I didn't know about Greta?"

"Um . . ."

"Darling, you can't hide your emotions. You have a very expressive face and you are really not that good at lying."

Zoe giggled. Eva flashed her a mock glare.

"I knew the minute I saw you at the cemetery that Zoe was more than just a friend." Leila took Eva's hand. "Who do you think told Willie?"

"That sneak," Eva exclaimed. "He told me he had figured it out."

Leila rocked back and laughed. "My brother figured it out? Are you serious? That boy couldn't find his way home if it was a straight line."

"Oh." Eva felt her cheek warm again. "That means . . ."

"Yes, darling, that does mean whatever you were thinking. I was flattered." Leila grinned. "You also had great taste."

Eva hid her face in her hands.

"Oh come on, that was funny." Leila pulled Eva's hands away from her face and tipped her head up to meet her gaze. "You know I would never embarrass you just to be mean. You are my sister."

"I know."

"I'm your older sexy sister," Leila added. "Come on, let's show Zoe your room, and I've asked Isabella to prepare Willie's room."

"Is that still—"

"Yes." Leila nodded. "Mama doesn't want to change it, so we don't."

"I want to see it again."

"Hmm, it's still the same pigsty it always was but a little bit cleaner," Leila replied with a hint of melancholy. "Let's go and see if we can get Zoe speechless again with the artwork in the rooms." She put her other arm around Zoe's shoulders.

CHAPTER 36

EVA STOOD IN front of the door and waited. Carved into the wood on the upper middle panel of the door in elegant script was the name "Eva." Her hand rested on the doorknob. She wasn't sure why she hesitated, but she didn't move.

"Evy, are you going to go in?" Zoe asked.

Eva glanced down and nodded. She turned the doorknob, and a very familiar *click* made her smile. She opened the door and stepped across the threshold. The balcony door was open and a light breeze caused the lace curtain to flutter in the wind.

She leaned against the doorjamb as a thousand memories came flooding back. "I spent more time in this house than at my grandmother's."

"Why do you always refer to it as your grandmother's house?" Zoe passed Eva into the bedroom and stood to the side. "Wow, this is a gorgeous bed." She looked at the four-poster bed. "I used to think these beds were only in the films."

"A bit high for you."

Zoe poked her tongue out and went to the bed. The mattress was high—it came to Zoe's waist. "I would need a ladder to get up on this."

Eva laughed and came forward. "I don't have a problem." Eva sat down on the bed and patted the side next to her.

Zoe gave her a long-suffering look which only made Eva smile and then settled herself down next to Eva and looked down at her feet, which dangled over the edge. "I feel like a two year old."

Eva looked around the room and was content they were alone. She turned to Zoe. "You just fulfilled a fantasy of mine."

"Really?"

"Yes. My fantasy was that the woman I loved would be in bed with me." Eva giggled.

"You were such a wild child." Zoe laughed. She took Eva's hand and kissed it. "So, are we going to talk?"

Eva gazed at Zoe, then got up from the bed and closed the door. She joined Zoe back on the bed and turned to her. "I don't know anything anymore, Zo."

"Why don't we start with what we do know?"

"My name is Eva Theresa. I'm married to you and your brother. I have an aunt Theresa Rosa. She's not dead. I have a great aunt Irene and a great uncle Johan, and I've got this inherited gift or curse or whatever it is. That's it."

"Well, that was short and sweet."

"That's about the extent of what I'm sure of at the moment."

"You know that Marlene and Leila are your family."

"Yes. They have always been my family."

"You know Tessa is your aunt." Zoe held up three fingers. "Stella is Tessa's partner."

"Irene and Johan. Those two are a mystery to me. What is their purpose?"

"I don't know."

"You are married to me and to my brother." Zoe giggled. "I'm married to your cousin."

"Something is bothering me."

"You mean this whole Tessa, Stella, Theo, Thomas, Irene and Johan family connection is not what is bothering you?"

"That's not it," Eva replied and stood up. "I didn't want to scare you when we were walking around, but someone was following us."

"Yes, I know."

"You do? How?"

"He was very bad at it and even without any gifts, I could tell he was following us."

"Describe to me what the man looked like. Why didn't you say anything?"

"You had enough to think about but I thought I saw you go all PentaSensy."

"Can you stop calling it that?" Eva grinned. "It makes me think I'm going to grow an extra head."

"What else am I going to call it?" Zoe replied with a tiny shrug. "He followed us from the house to Elena's shop."

"When did you see him?"

"I saw him at the end of the street. He looked like he was out on a stroll."

"So why did you notice him?"

"You're going to think I'm totally crazy." Zoe looped her hand through the crook of Eva's elbow. "His walk."

"You noticed a man in Berlin because of his walk?" Eva asked. "Zoe, that's just—"

"Crazy. I know." Zoe shrugged. "That's the first thing I noticed. He also reminded me of Hans Muller."

Eva let her head fall back and smiled up at the ceiling in relief. "He reminded you of Muller? Same gait, same walk."

"Yes, although I don't think that's very funny."

"That's my Uncle Wilbur," Eva said. "Uncle Wilbur is Hans' twin. That's why he reminded you of Hans. Did he have a beard?"

"Yes." Zoe nodded. "Glasses too."

"That's my uncle." Eva smiled. "Of all the Muller men, Wilbur was my favorite."

"You're accumulating relatives faster than I can keep track of them." Zoe giggled. "To be fair, you had Wilbur beforehand. So why was he following us?"

"Uncle Wilbur is shy," Eva said quietly. "He used to suffer from chronic shyness for as long as I could remember. My father didn't suffer from that affliction but Wilbur did. He really is a very smart man, a good businessman who kept AEMullerStahl operational. His brothers just didn't take much notice of him. He probably was told by Beatriz to follow me."

"I'm beginning to really dislike this woman," Zoe muttered. "I just don't understand her."

"You're not supposed to. That's her game. She wants to keep you off balance and not understand her."

"That's cold."

"Welcome to the Muller family." Eva shrugged.

"I don't understand, Evy. You have some really happy memories growing up."

"I do. Most of them involve my mother." Eva took a deep breath. "I never connected with my grandmother and now I know why."

"Why?"

"I'm not her blood." Eva had finally accepted that however much she wanted her grandmother to love her, it wasn't going to happen.

"You've accepted that."

"What else is there to do?" Eva asked.

"I wonder if Beatriz knew about your mother's abilities. She appears to be the type to want to be in control of everything."

"What are you saying?"

"I wonder if Beatriz knew that your mother was gifted," Zoe said. "She must have known the family history, right?"

"I don't know."

"Think about this for a moment." Zoe stood up and paced. "Your grandmother, correct me if I'm wrong, comes across as being a controlling woman."

"That's a nice way of putting it. Yes."

"Right." Zoe went to the window. "So, if your grandmother has this need to control what goes on in her family, why wouldn't she investigate your mother?"

"Huh?"

"Her eldest son is marrying a woman with a child. This appears to be a marriage of convenience, doesn't it?"

"Yes. My maternal grandmother Eva Mitsos was Beatriz's friend."

"Right."

"So whose convenience was it for?" Zoe faced Eva. "Who did this benefit?"

"My mother and I."

"No." Zoe shook her head. "Think about this, Evy. Use your PentaSense."

"Zoe . . ."

"Humor me and let me call it that for now."

"Fine. So what do you want me to do?"

"Think about this. Who did this benefit? Your mother married Hans, who she didn't love as the letter suggests. She was still pining for Father H and that was when you were sixteen years old. Your mother still loved Father H after all those years."

"Yes, but Beatriz didn't know that my mother was gifted." Eva shook her head. "My mother didn't even tell her own mother."

"So Eva Mitsos didn't know about the gifts?"

"She knew but—"

"From what Aunty Tessa was saying, she thought Tessa was possessed and that's why she was sent to the lunatic asylum. If she knew, why put her daughter through that?"

"My brain is going to be mushy mush by the end of this trip," Eva muttered.

"Let's assume Grandmother Eva didn't know."

"Alright, so Grandmother Beatriz found out from someone about these mysterious gifts. She had to find out from someone. Who was that someone? Irene?"

"No, it doesn't make sense, and Irene is protective of Tessa and you."

Eva stood and also paced for a short while. "Erika?"

"No. She was old when Irene was a young woman so it couldn't be her. She would have been dead long before you were born. For argument's sake, let's say Beatriz heard a story and she went looking. She was told about the gifts, the passing on to the later generations."

"She was told that all the women with the names of Theresa or E . . ." Eva froze and turned to Zoe.

"What?"

"I was the prize," Eva whispered in shock. "Zoe, I was the prize."

"What prize?"

"Beatriz heard of this. How she heard of it? I don't know, but someone must have told her that the women in my family acquired these gifts. They were named either Eva or Theresa and if there was one girl . . ."

"Oh, Sweet Jesus." Zoe put her hand over her mouth. "No, no, no, no, that's just too calculating. That is cold."

"This is a woman who wants to control everything and everyone around her."

"When did she find out?"

"More than likely when Hans fell in love with my mother and wanted to get married to her. I don't have any doubt that Hans loved my mother even if she didn't love him. She did it for me. So Hans brings her home to meet Beatriz."

"Beatriz sees an unmarried mother, probably not very impressed with Hans, but he can't have children so it's the lesser of two evils, right?" Zoe asked. Eva nodded. "Now, Beatriz sends some investigators to Larissa to find out about the family. Tessa by that stage is officially dead but the town knew all about her problems."

"Right, and you know how small towns can keep a secret."

"So someone must have said something which set them off looking and we come to Daphne, who kept her abilities a secret even from her own mother," Zoe reasoned.

"The inheritance jumps a generation and never in two girls of the same generation . . ."

"Usually but not this time, right? Tessa is dead. She was the gifted one. Daphne is just plain ol' Daphne, but she has a daughter named . . . Eva . . . You were the prize."

"Yes. I was going to be the one that Beatriz was going to nurture and I would help her. How I was going to help her is a mystery to me but that doesn't matter."

"But Hans went and spoilt her plans when he nearly beat you to death." Zoe came up to Eva and put her arm around her waist. "That's why he didn't finish the job."

"Beatriz stopped him." Eva sat down and exhaled slowly. "It's why she sent me to Aiden."

"Why?"

Eva glanced down at their interlocked hands. "It was to cure me of this deviancy but also to find out if I had any gifts."

"Er . . . what?"

"You give me drugs and my mouth runs off a mile a minute, right?"

"Yes, I can't shut you up."

"So what would happen if I knew about these gifts . . . ?"

"Your grandmother would have found out."

"Not only did she condone what they did to me but she was the one that instigated it." Eva's voice wavered as the emotional impact of her words made her anxious that she was in the same city as her grandmother. "Zoe, this woman set out to systematically see if I had these gifts."

"By torturing you?"

"I don't know, yes, maybe. She knew my mother did not have them because Tessa proved she did have them and it was the understanding that two sisters could not possess them at the same time."

"What Beatriz didn't know was that your mother did have those gifts but she kept them hidden. She hid your training by silly parlor games," Zoe continued.

"Beatriz killed my mother," Eva said, barely above a whisper. "With her gone, I would have been looked after by my grandmother."

"No, Evy, that is just too cold. I don't believe it. That is just beyond heartless, to kill a child's mother like that."

"There is someone who can tell us," Eva quietly said and got up from her seat. She went in search of Marlene, brought her back to the room, and closed the door.

"Aunty Marlene, can I ask you a question?" Eva asked.

"Of course, darling, anything," Marlene said.

"Who knew that you and Mama were going to be at your house painting?" Eva leaned forward.

"Well, the plans changed that day. I was supposed to go over there but John told me it wasn't going to be safe that night and to stay home," Marlene quietly explained as she watched Eva carefully. "Daphne told the housekeeper where she would be."

"I was told to stay home by my mother but I didn't listen."

"Why?"

"Greta came over and urged me to join her. So I went with her."

Zoe gasped.

"I was out of the way and out of harm's way."

Marlene nodded as she gazed at Eva affectionately. "Your mama would be so proud of you. That is exactly what happened."

"It is?" Zoe asked incredulous.

"Your mother saw her own death and knew what was going to happen. She wrote you that letter, knowing that her death was fast approaching. She also knew Beatriz was not aware of her abilities." She sighed deeply and wiped the tear that ran down her face. "Your mother entrusted me with this knowledge, and some days I wished she hadn't."

"Why?"

"I wanted to kill the old hag but you would never have found out."

"There's one missing puzzle piece. Why did she send Mrs. Muldoon to concoct that whole story on the ship?"

"That story is not sitting right with you, never has for some reason," Zoe said. She turned to Marlene. "Mrs. Muldoon is the wife of the owner of Muldoon & Sons, one of the largest iron-ore mining companies in Australia. She was organizing a Jewish refugee trip where the Jews that were displaced were going to return home. She hired Eva initially as an interpreter and then as a photographer. She offered me a job and other enticements. She eventually told us that she worked for Beatriz and that all Beatriz wanted was for Eva to come back."

"I'm sure she did."

"She also told this story that Beatriz saved her sister's life during Kristallnacht and that she was indebted to her," Eva said.

"Really? How did Beatriz save her sister?"

"She worked at our factory and somehow the Brownshirts had entered the factory. Beatriz stopped them with Wilbur's help."

Marlene shook her head. "That could not have happened. Beatriz had gone to Bonn to attend some Nazi function."

Eva and Zoe looked at Marlene in astonishment.

"Are you sure?" Eva asked.

"Positive," Marlene replied. "Beatriz Muller helping a Jew? There was more chance of Hitler becoming a priest than of that happening."

Eva stood up and went to the balcony door where she gazed across the rooftops to the house on the hill. A house she knew so well and one that used to be a safe haven, but now the idea of stepping into that house was horrific. It was akin to her walking back into Aiden.

"Aunty Marlene, can we call Australia from your telephone?"

Marlene glanced at Zoe, who shrugged. "Yes, darling, of course."

"Who are you calling, Evy?" Zoe asked as she came up behind Eva and took her hand.

"David and Friedrich," Eva said in a voice devoid of emotion. "It's time to deal with Beatriz Muller."

CHAPTER 37

IT WAS GOING too fast. Her life was just spinning around and around and Eva felt like those children's tops where there was no end until the toy ran out of puff. She stood at the balcony and watched the sun setting. So much had happened to her, to them, since they had docked in Athens that she just needed time to process everything in her mind. The problem was that as soon as she tried to do that, something else took its place.

Eva looked down at the street and could barely see someone outside, hidden behind the thick foliage. The smoke from his cigarette drifted upwards. She smiled.

"Uncle Wilbur, you could never be a good spy," Eva mumbled. She took a deep breath and left the balcony and walked out of the room.

"Is he still there?" Zoe asked when Eva entered the living room.

"Still there, and he probably hasn't had anything to eat all day," Eva said in passing.

She opened the front door, walked down the driveway, and stopped just inside the gate and to the right of the thick foliage.

She leaned against the brick fence. "Psst, Uncle Wilbur." She grinned when he chuckled. "You want to come inside? It's going to be easier to keep an eye on me."

"Am I going to be safe from Zoe?" he asked.

Eva leaned back against the fence and laughed. "Yes, quite safe."

"Oh good," Wilbur said as he came around from the brush and stood in front of the gate.

Eva released the gate and Wilbur approached her. Slightly taller than herself, he wore a black hat over his short grey-blond hair. Thick black-rimmed glasses framed deep-set dark blue eyes. A full black beard with flecks of white made him older than his fifty years.

Wilbur stood his ground for a moment then Eva took a couple of steps and engulfed him in a hug. He put his arms around her and closed his eyes.

"It's so good to see you again," Wilbur said.

"Come inside. We have a lot to discuss." Eva took his hand, and they walked up the driveway. Wilbur took off his hat as they entered the house.

"How long have you been courting Aunty Marlene?" Eva whispered.

Wilbur's shocked expression confirmed her suspicions. "How?

"Aunty Marlene is smoking the same cigarettes as you." Eva giggled.

"That's no way to greet your uncle," Wilbur said with a slight grin. He cupped Eva's face in his large hands and kissed her on the cheek. "I missed you."

"You're the only one I missed," Eva replied as she melted into his embrace. "I want you to meet Zoe."

"As long as she doesn't have a gun."

"Did you go and see Dieter?"

"I did. He was always such a hothead." Wilbur shook his head. "I can't believe he tried that."

"I can't believe he's still walking free."

"He's not walking anymore," Wilbur quipped. Eva slapped him gently on the arm. "Whatever hit him caused his face to cave. There goes the pretty boy looks."

"It was a poker."

"Ouch. Ah, well, he had it coming." Wilbur shrugged. "So where is she?"

The door swung open and Zoe walked through carrying a tray with a tea pot and cups. She set the tray down and adjusted her shirt before she looked up at Wilbur.

"So you are Uncle Wilbur?"

"I am. You are Zoe."

"I am."

"I heard what you did to my brother." Wilbur folded his arms across his chest and looked down at Zoe over the top of his glasses.

"No need for thanks," Zoe quipped.

Wilbur's mouth twitched as he attempted not to laugh. "You are more beautiful than your photographs."

Eva coughed to hide her chuckle. That was the uncle she remembered.

"Oh, that is not fair." Zoe wagged her finger at Wilbur but her twinkling green eyes betrayed the genuine likeability of the man.

Wilbur smiled shyly and sat down on the sofa. "So did you enjoy your walk? The city is very different from when you left."

"Where is my grandmother?"

"She had to go to Bonn and will be back tomorrow night."

"She's waiting for me to go to her?"

"Yes."

"No," Eva said quietly. "That's not going to happen."

"You will have to see her. At some point, you will."

"Why is she doing this?" Zoe asked as she leaned back on the chair and regarded Wilbur with a slight tilt of her head.

"Money," Eva responded. "It's all about money with her. My inheritance from my grandfather."

"Not just that. My father put aside a trust fund in your name and property. When you turned thirty, it became yours."

"I don't want it," Eva said quietly.

"Well, that's not smart." Wilbur tapped Eva on the knee. "I don't take you for a dumb woman."

"I'm not dumb but—"

"That money was not given to you by my mother. That is a gift from my father, your grandfather."

"He's not—"

"Hush," Wilbur replied sternly. He took off his glasses and regarded Eva. "He loved you so much. Don't cheapen that love by throwing his gift away."

"But I wasn't even his blood."

"Eva Muller, you do not disgrace that man's name or his love for you." Wilbur's voice rose a little. "You can say whatever you want to say about your grandmother, and she deserves it, but not about my father and your grandfather. He was an honest man who worked hard to build his business. You know he loved you. Don't let your heart overrule your head."

"I know," Eva said. "It's difficult."

"No." Wilbur shook his head. "No, it's not difficult. He never once gave you an excuse to doubt his love. He loved you. Now, your grandmother on the other hand . . . well, we both know what I think of my mother."

"Why shouldn't Eva be feeling like that when your entire family has betrayed her?"

Wilbur gazed at Zoe for a long moment. "I never betrayed my niece. She may not be related to me by blood, but that doesn't mean I stopped loving her."

"Uncle Wilbur, Zoe—"

"I know why Zoe said that," Wilbur replied. "I've always known that Hans was not your father. I loved you not because of whose blood was flowing in your veins but because you were the child I never had nor would have."

Zoe looked down at her hands, then looked back up. "I'm sorry."

"You have every right to question my motives, Zoe. It's perfectly understandable."

"What did Opa leave me?" Eva asked.

"He left you ten thousand Swiss francs and—"

"Ten thousand Swiss francs? Ten thousand?" Zoe asked. "Wow."

"Your father owned Aiden Spa and that is now in your name."

Eva shook her head in disbelief. "I own Aiden Spa?"

"Yes. You inherited that when your father died. You also own the Research Facility attached to the spa."

"How do you know this?" Zoe asked.

Wilbur glanced at Eva with a tiny shake. "You really do question everything. Don't you?"

"The only person I trust completely is Eva, so, yes, I question everything."

"Not that I blame you," Wilbur replied. "I'm a lawyer and I am the legal counsel for AEMullerStahl and the other companies under the control of the Muller Company."

"Oh, yes, you would know, wouldn't you?" Zoe said, looking a little sheepish.

"You will have one problem with the property and the money my father left you. It was stipulated in his will that when you turned thirty years old you would inherit it."

"I'm already thirty," Eva replied with a wry smile. "January twentieth."

"Yes, I remember, but there is also another caveat. This one your grandmother told me to include in 1938."

"She can't do that, can she?"

"She can. She is the executor of my father's estate."

"What is the caveat?"

"You need to be married to receive the inheritance." Wilbur looked at Zoe apologetically.

Eva fell back on the sofa and laughed. "Oh my, that conniving woman thought of everything."

"I don't think that's funny." Wilbur looked puzzled and he scratched his beard.

Eva held up her left hand and pointed to her ring finger. "I am married."

"To a man?"

Zoe laughed. Wilbur's face went from confusion to embarrassment. "I'm sorry, that was rude of me."

"Yes, I am married to a man. Zoe's brother, Theodore Lambros."

"Er . . ."

"I'm also married." Zoe held up her left hand and showed him her ring. "I'm married to Eva's cousin."

"You married Franz Muller? Really? How could you do that to her?" Wilbur turned to Eva, his face a mixture of disgust and sorrow.

"Oh, I love you." Eva cupped her uncle's face with her hands and kissed him on the cheek.

"I'm surprised Zoe is still talking to you after that marriage," Wilbur replied.

Zoe giggled.

"No. Zoe is married to Thomas Lambros, my cousin."

"You have a cousin named Thomas Lambros? Isn't that Zoe's last name?"

"It's a long story, but suffice to say that I am married."

Wilbur chuckled heartily. "Oh, this is going to be the wind up my mother's skirt. I can't wait to tell her."

"No, don't." Eva put her hand on Wilbur's shoulder. "Don't tell her. I want to see where she is going to go with this clause."

"Wilbur, how do you know so much about me?" Zoe asked.

Wilbur sheepishly gazed at Eva. "My mother had private investigators follow you."

"Since when?"

"She didn't know where you were until Hans showed up and was arrested."

"1947? She's been following us since then?" Zoe's voice rose in anger. She quickly glanced at Eva, who shook her head.

"Yes." Wilbur nodded. "She also had a private investigator take photos of your house."

"Our house?"

"Large house, two large trees at the front," Wilbur said quietly. "I saw the photos."

"Inside or just outside?"

Wilbur pursed his lips. "Inside and out."

Zoe got up and walked to the window. Wilbur followed her with his eyes and then glanced at Eva, who shook her head. Eva could see Zoe was trying to keep the anger at bay.

Zoe turned to Wilbur. "Which rooms did you see?"

"Um . . ."

"What color were the walls?"

"I don't know. They were black-and-white photographs."

"What was on the walls?" Zoe asked.

"Um . . . I don't think I recall seeing anything on the walls."

"I told you." Zoe wagged her finger at Eva. "I told you that couple across the road was being a little too nosey."

"We got new neighbors who rented the vacant house across the road from us just after we moved in," Eva explained to Wilbur. "Zoe didn't like the way they were always looking at us."

"I'm with Zoe," Wilbur said. "I know how you feel, Zoe. My mother has tried to keep an eye on what I do, who I see and where I go."

"Argh," Zoe muttered. "If you didn't see anything on the walls then that means they were taking photos from outside the windows."

"Um, not exactly." Wilbur gazed at Eva. "They did break in."

Zoe groaned loudly and muttered under her breath several expletives in Greek. Wilbur raised his eyebrows. "I knew it. I knew it because they moved that damn easel. I told you that someone had been in the house."

"Zoe, it's gone, it's done."

"It's our house. Our life. How dare she stick her nose where it doesn't belong." Zoe raised her voice higher and threw the pillow across the room where it struck the door.

Eva and Wilbur looked at each other.

"I'm sorry, Zoe," Wilbur said.

"Not your fault," Zoe muttered darkly.

"Are you coming to the house?"

"No. Beatriz Muller will be coming to me," Eva said.

"Here? You know she hates Marlene."

"Why does she hate Marlene?" Zoe asked.

"Marlene never liked her hero Adolf Hitler, so I doubt you will get my mother in this house."

"Not to worry," Eva said calmly. "She will come to Dahlem."

"What's in Dahlem?"

Eva glanced at Zoe before she turned to Wilbur. "Let's just say everything she has worked for, she will get her reward."

"I have a feeling I'm going to find something important to do at the office."

"Have they charged Dieter yet?"

"I don't know. I'm not his lawyer." Wilbur shrugged. "I'm not a criminal lawyer and even if I was, I wouldn't defend him."

"How is it you are the only ethical member of this family?" Eva asked as she snuggled up to her uncle.

"You're wrong. I'm not the only one." Wilbur looked down at the Eva's head resting against his shoulder. "You are a member of this family as well and as far as I can tell, you are a very ethical woman. I don't want you to deny your roots."

"Are we back there again?"

"Yes, we are. You didn't grow up in a void," Wilbur gently admonished. "Your mother, your grandfather, my Clarice, and myself were there for you."

"Clarice?" Zoe asked.

"My late wife. She passed while she was giving birth. We also lost our baby." Wilbur met Eva's eyes. "You became the daughter I never had, so don't deny the chance for me to claim you as my niece. You are my niece."

Eva wiped the tear that ran down her cheek and nodded. Without a word she kissed Wilbur's cheek and snuggled up against him.

"Did Grandmother know what was going on in Aiden?" Eva asked the one question that had haunted her for the past ten years.

Wilbur remained quiet for so long that Eva thought he would refuse to answer the question.

He finally nodded. "My mother was in charge of the Research Facility and the spa and knew exactly what Dieter and Hans were up to. She thought that their treatment would help you."

"You didn't think so?" Zoe asked.

"I took an interest in your medical care after I came to visit you. You did not look like you were being healed so I got your medical records and read them."

"Did you understand them?"

Wilbur shook his head. "Unfortunately I did not, but there was this wonderful nurse who must have felt sorry for me looking so confused. He helped me understand what the records said."

"What did that nurse look like?"

Wilbur scratched his beard. "I really can't remember but I know I found it funny that he looked like Kaiser Wilhelm II. That made me laugh."

Eva smiled. "Did you tell Grandmother about this?"

"No, I would rather she didn't know what I was doing. The last thing I needed was for her to pay attention to my activities."

"Is anyone still working at Aiden Spa?"

"Not at the moment, no. We were going to renovate it. Why?"

Eva looked at Wilbur. "I want to raze it to the ground. I don't even want the foundations to remain. Bulldoze everything on that property."

"It's a vast property. Do you want the entire thing bulldozed?"

"Every last bit of it. Do you have the records from it?"

"Yes."

"No. I mean do you personally have the records?"

"Yes, I do. I supervised the removal of all the offices and put them in storage for when the renovation would be completed . . ."

"Does anyone know the location of this storage facility?"

Wilbur glanced down with a puzzled expression. "Does that matter?"

"Uncle Wilbur, does anyone know the location?"

"My secretary does."

"Can you go to the office and remove the name of the storage facility?" Eva asked, glancing at Zoe.

"Of course I can, but why?"

"Oh, it's a little surprise I'm planning for Grandmother Beatriz," Eva said as she gazed at Wilbur.

They shared a smile.

"Whatever you want, I will do."

"Now." Eva put her arm through the crook of Wilbur's elbow and leaned in. "Tell me about you clandestine courting of Aunty Marlene?

CHAPTER 38

EVA SAT OUTSIDE on a long wooden seat which had been a fallen down tree. The seat was carved out of the bark and had a bed of multi-colored flowers on one side. The tree behind her acted as her back rest. Tessa's and Marlene's excited voices made her smile, as her aunt and her adopted aunt had met for the first time. More than a few tears had been shed when Marlene embraced Tessa.

Eva closed her eyes and leaned back as she felt the sun's rays warm her face. She took a drag of her cigarette, exhaled and, watched the smoke rise into a cloudless sky. The French doors leading from the living room were open. She turned to see Zoe walking towards her. Zoe wore long cotton shorts with an emerald green shirt. Eva sighed contentedly at the sight. Zoe spotted Eva and made her way to where she sat.

"Do you want to know what I was just thinking?" Eva said as Zoe sat down next to her.

"If it was anything like what I was thinking, we would scandalize the relatives." Zoe giggled.

"No, it wasn't that, although that would be nice out here, under the tree."

"We could neck behind the tree and no one would notice except the squirrels, but I don't think they care."

"No, no necking."

"What were you thinking, Mrs. Lambros?"

"How much I love you," Eva replied as played with Zoe's hair. She pushed a long strand behind Zoe's ear. "You are so beautiful. If we didn't have so many eyes upon us I would make love to you right here."

"Hmm, that would be nice. Just you, me, and the squirrels." Zoe grinned. She took Eva's hand and kissed it. "Can I have a drag of your cigarette?"

Eva offered her the cigarette, and Zoe took a drag and gave it back. "This isn't your favorite brand."

"I ran out and Marlene gave me one of hers." Eva glanced towards the open French doors in the living room where Marlene was talking to Tessa. She laughed lightly. "Marlene and my mother were sisters. Not by blood but just as good."

"What are you doing out here?"

"I wanted to talk to Uncle Johan. There are so many questions swirling around my head, Zo. I need to know from Johan about my mother."

"Aunty Stella said he was in the garage."

"Hmm. Do you want to come with me?" Eva asked. Zoe shook her head. "Are you sure?"

"I think you and Johan need to have this chat alone. You can tell me about it when you come back. I want you to have some rest before the banshee comes tonight."

Eva gazed at Zoe for a moment. "I want you to promise me something."

"What's that? I bent the good poker on Dieter's ugly face and I don't have a gun."

"I'm hoping you are joking." Eva grinned. She brought up Zoe's hand and kissed it. "Don't get angry tonight. She feeds off that."

"She sounds like the type of woman whose personality might be improved by a poker to the head," Zoe quipped.

Eva stifled the giggles, and doubled over laughing.

"You are priceless." She put her arms around Zoe and kissed her. "Don't ever change. Thank you, my love, I needed that laugh."

"I know," Zoe quietly said. "I missed sleeping next to you last night."

"I was nearly tempted to come into your room. We were in Marlene's home and I didn't—"

"I know. I heard you pacing. Did you know your old room has a floorboard that creaks when you walk towards Willie's room?"

Eva nodded. "It's a false floorboard. I used to hide my diary under there."

"You were very secretive even back when nothing was going on."

"I've always been like this, Zo, they didn't change me. You read some of the diary?" Eva asked.

"I did. I just wanted to come into your room and hug you, but I didn't. Marlene is family and I felt it wouldn't be the right thing to do since we were guests in her home. It's never bothered me before, but she's different."

"Marlene's opinion means a lot to me." Eva watched Zoe take a drag of her cigarette. "You never used to smoke, and look at you now."

"Yes, it's your fault. How are you feeling?" Zoe asked. "This will be over soon."

"I'm going to go stir crazy by tonight. I need to just walk around or maybe Uncle Johan's dead car might need a hammer or two at it."

"You have waited ten years for this meeting, you have rehearsed it enough in your head. Let it go now and wait for tonight," Zoe said.

Eva gazed down at her, bemused.

"I know, I'm the last person to tell you to have patience but you're rubbing off on me. Beatriz is going to expect a reaction from you."

"I know. She expects me to be upset, to be unsure, because that's what her spies have been telling her that I am."

Zoe snorted in derision. "They don't know you."

Eva turned her head and smiled. "You are just biased. I love you but you are biased. It's exactly what I was."

"You were, not you are. This trip has changed you in a good way."

"Has it?" Eva asked. She could feel the change in the way she thought about Aiden and her father, but she wasn't sure how much Zoe knew of that change or whether anyone else had seen it or cared.

Zoe rocked back a little, rested her head against the tree, and looked up into the sky. "Yes, it has. I started to notice it with Mrs. Muldoon. You sensed something was wrong and you didn't accept her word at face value. We both sensed it but you felt it more. You had some rough days in Larissa, we both did, but we managed to get through that."

"Rough?" Eva took Zoe's hand and held it tight. "That wasn't rough, Zo. That was brutal."

"It could have been worse if Stella and Tessa hadn't been there."

"That's true." Eva nodded. "I think Tommy's surprise gave me some time to think as well. It wasn't 'let's do this and get out of here.'"

"I did like his rabbit story." Zoe glanced at Eva, who was smiling. "Noticed that he deliberately left out why you were restrained."

"The restraints were there to stop me from killing the rabbits," Eva quipped. They giggled. "Whatever they gave me, they didn't give it to me again because I never saw those rabbits again."

"Experimental drugs?"

"From what Tommy said, they were," Eva replied, leaning back against the tree and crossing her ankles. "Beatriz must have thought those drugs would make something happen."

"Didn't it?"

"I don't know," Eva replied with a tiny shrug.

"When did you start seeing Irene?"

Eva cocked her head and regarded Zoe. "Right after the third electroshock and right about the time they gave me those drugs."

"So Beatriz did succeed. It was around that time that Tommy showed up, so she would have got what she wanted had Tommy not interfered."

"Wow," Eva exclaimed as she sat straight in the seat. "She was close."

"She was more than close, Evy. If Tessa and Tommy hadn't been there, you would have been hers to do what she wanted. To use you whichever way she wanted," Zoe replied quietly.

"I owe Tessa and Tommy for saving my life. That extraordinary gift my aunt possesses saved my life." Eva turned to look through the windows at Tessa, who was speaking animatedly with Marlene. As if sensing eyes were on her, Tessa turned and gazed back. She smiled at Eva and with a slight nod, then turned back to Marlene.

"So what's your plan for tonight?"

"I keep telling people that they should never underestimate you, Zoe. People do that a great deal with you."

"Huh? It's not about me."

"No, it's about me, but I'm going to do what you do."

"Whack people with a poker and shoot them? I like that idea," Zoe joked as Eva put her arm around her and leaned down for a chaste kiss on the cheek. "I think that deserved more than a kiss on the cheek."

"We have critical eyes on us," Eva quietly said.

Zoe turned to Eva with a puzzled expression. "Evy, Marlene knows we are lovers, Tessa and Stella definitely know, our husbands know . . ."

"Our husbands know we are lovers." Eva giggled. "Mrs. Lambros?"

"Yes, Mrs. Lambros?"

"Don't react at all to what I'm about to tell you, but there are two men spying on us," Eva said and smiled. She plucked a few leaves from the tree branch above her. With her other hand she touched Zoe's hand, which was clutching the seat. "Don't react."

"They were there before Muller decided to trespass and they are still here?"

"Yes. My uncle didn't do that. It was my grandmother. I can feel them."

"Taking a poker to this conniving bitch is—"

"Don't react. Smile."

"Taking a poker to this conniving bitch is going to be one of my wishes tonight," Zoe said with a big grin. "Are they still looking?"

"Yes."

"Doesn't she ever give up?"

"Would you?" Eva looked at Zoe. "Would you give up if someone told you that your granddaughter may or may not have this special gift that could benefit you in some way?"

"Didn't Aiden show her that you don't have this ability?"

"I don't know. Every time we think we know something, something else gets us asking another dozen questions. It's never ending."

"I'm getting tired of this game and you must be exhausted by it."

"I want it to end," Eva said. "Psst."

Zoe turned towards Eva and grinned. "Yes, Mrs. Lambros?"

"Run away with me?"

"Where are we going to go?"

"Back home." Eva shook her head and closed the distance between herself and Zoe. She took Zoe's hand. "I want to go home and leave all of this behind. I want us to go home and have our children. I really hope we have a daughter who looks exactly like you and has your personality."

"We are in big trouble." Zoe laughed. "My mama used to say that she wished when I finally became a mother that I would have to deal with a child just like me. I would eventually see that Mama was a saint."

Eva chortled at the idea of a miniature Zoe.

"Oh, shudder." Zoe giggled. "I don't think I can survive that."

"It's going to be fantastic." Eva put her arm around Zoe and kissed her on the cheek. We could practice tonight with that syringe after I deal with Beatriz," She whispered in her ear.

"We will have to be very quiet."

Eva giggled. "As long as you don't bolt when you see that syringe again, we will be very quiet."

"I can't believe a woman would let that kind of thing anywhere down there," Zoe exclaimed as Eva gazed at her for a moment before she fell over laughing.

Zoe grinned and buffed her nails, and Eva forgot the men that were spying on them, forgot her evil grandmother, and forgot this entire trip. Even if it was for just a few minutes.

CHAPTER 39

EVA LEFT ZOE in the garden and made her way further down the property to where she could hear a great deal of noise emanating from the garage. The noise would stop for a while and then start up again.

She stopped at the threshold of the garage and looked inside. The garage light flooded the workshop, and in the center was the old car. Johan sat on an old tire, a hammer in his hand and a piece of the fender perched on the ground.

"I'm going to assume that the house resembles a get together of the sewing circle," Johan said as he inspected the fender.

"I wouldn't let Aunt Stella hear you say that."

"No, I wouldn't want to get her on her bad side." Johan chuckled. He pushed up his glasses, and glanced up at Eva. "I was wondering when you would come down here."

"You were?"

"Aye, it seems you enjoy the quiet times yourself and getting away from the chatter."

Eva grabbed the nearest thing she could find to sit on, which was an old footstool. She brought it over to where Johan was sitting and sat down. Her dress scraped the oily floor but she didn't give it too much notice. "Do you like the quiet?"

"I do. I come out here and I hammer away. I find it comforting that the only voice I can hear is my own." Johan looked at Eva with a slight smile. "You didn't come out here to talk about why I enjoy hammering and trying to fix a dead car, did you?"

"No, although I do understand the notion of getting away and just being by yourself. I like doing that in the darkroom."

"So, what is on your mind, great niece?" Johan put his hammer and the fender aside. He leaned back against the car and waited.

"Well, Great Uncle, I've got so many questions that every time I get one answered, ten more take its place."

"Hmm. Let's see if we can answer some of them before they sprout new ones."

Eva dropped her eyes to the oil-stained floor for a moment, not quite knowing how to broach the subject that had been nagging at her since she found out about her mother's letter. She looked up and met Johan's gentle blue eyes. "When did my mother give you that letter?"

A smile tugged at the edges of Johan's mouth before it returned to a neutral expression. "What makes you think that your mother didn't give that letter to Willie?"

"Don't answer a question with another question. That's how these questions sprout out new ones. Can you please answer my question first? I don't believe my mother would give such an important letter to Willie, no matter how much she loved him."

"You are right that she didn't give it to him. She gave it to me just after she wrote it and it was imperative that she wanted it to be kept safe and out of the hands of certain people."

"I just don't understand the subterfuge. Why couldn't you just hand me the letter when you saw me? Why did you lie to Marlene that my mother gave Willie the letter? I would have thought it would have been Marlene and not Willie that was given the letter."

"Whoa!" Johan put up his hands. "Slow down, Eva. Slow down. Let's take this slowly, all right? Now to your first question, why didn't I just hand you the letter?"

"Yes. You could have said, 'Eva, this is a letter from your mother.'"

"How would I have known your mother? In what context would I have known her?"

"You were her uncle, so that's easy," Eva reasoned. "It's not that hard."

Johan shook his head. "I think a little bit of Zoe's personality has taken hold." He chuckled. "It wasn't that easy. We kept a great many things secret for her safety and yours."

"So you knew about her inherited gifts?"

Johan nodded. "I did. I had known for a long time and when she married Hans she came to me and confided in me."

"Why did you lie to Marlene and say Willie had the letter?"

"I did not lie to Marlene. She knew the truth. We just didn't tell you."

"So that makes it all right? You lied to me, you both did," Eva said as she looked away, trying not to let feelings about the deceit overshadow why she truly came to see Johan. "I hate being lied to."

"I know. I'm sorry we had to do it that way. In hindsight, or if I had Irene's gift, I would have done it differently. I apologize." Johan gently turned Eva's face towards him. "Sometimes we don't always make the right choices and in this instance it wasn't the right choice."

"I just didn't understand why my mother would give the letter to Willie. It made no sense." Eva shrugged. "Why didn't you just tell me about everything when you first met me?"

Johan closed his eyes and bowed his head. Eva watched him and wondered if he was praying.

After a moment he opened his eyes and looked at her. "When our Lord walked the earth, he selected the men who would one day be with him in heaven. Did He tell them everything when he first met them?"

"I don't think that's the same thing."

"I'm trying to explain why I chose to do it this way. So did He?"

"No." Eva sighed. She was resigned that her uncle was going to take the long route in answering her questions.

"That's right. He gave them information by piece meal. Slowly slowly, until they fully understood the ramifications of following Him. Some left, others stayed. It is the way of our God that He chooses to slowly reveal His plans for us all. Slowly slowly."

"So why did you choose to go slowly slowly?"

"You were not in the right frame of mind to be able to handle the whole truth. You had just discovered that you had an aunt who was believed to be deceased. In addition to not being dead, she was gifted. You then found out that you had a cousin. Not only that, but your cousin was the one who nursed you, in what for you was hell. So we had those two surprises," Johan patiently explained as he gazed at Eva. "Once you digested that information, you found out that you were gifted yourself. Having all of that revealed to you while you were dealing with your memories is enough to make someone run screaming the other way."

Eva tugged on her ear as Johan rattled off the big revelations for her. "A lot has happened."

"A lot has happened and it's not over yet. You then found out your mother was also gifted but she didn't tell anyone other than her friend Marlene and myself."

"Marlene knew and kept silent. My mother befriended someone who she knew she could trust."

"Yes, Marlene kept that secret and your secret since you were born. They both knew and feared what would happen. That fear came to fruition when your mother was murdered."

"She was not supposed to be at Marlene's house. She was supposed to be at the house. I was told to stay home that night."

"Yes, you were, but Greta lured you away."

"I don't understand why. What has Greta have to do with this entire thing?"

"Greta was paid off by your grandmother to stop associating with you," Johan patiently explained. "You don't seem surprised."

"I'm not. Greta didn't care about me. My grandmother knew where I would be and also knew where my mother would be. She was murdered by my grandmother," Eva said, and watched Johan to gauge his reaction. He didn't react and she shook her head. "More secrets. All these damned secrets."

"I know you are angry, but don't swear, not in my presence."

"I'm sorry," Eva replied. "This whole story within a story, secret within a secret is making me doubt my own existence."

Johan chuckled. "Now let's not get into too much hyperbole."

"I'm not joking. This morning I woke up and I wasn't even sure what day it was or what city I was in. I was sleeping in my own old bed in my old room. I could hear Isabella moving about in the corridor and for a brief moment I thought I had dreamt the last ten years."

"That would be very disconcerting."

"It wasn't until I heard Zoe trying to speak Italian to Isabella that my mind registered where I was."

"I would be very worried for you if it didn't affect you like that."

Eva shook her head. "This trip was all about settling Zoe's inheritance and coming home to Germany to pay my respects to my mother. That's all it was going to be. Now look where I am. I'm waiting for my grandmother, who I now despise with such ferocity that I don't think I can bear to look at her."

"Sometimes the hardest journeys are the ones where we find ourselves."

"Where did you find that quote?" Eva asked.

"The wisdom of Johan Faber," Johan replied with a chuckle. "Ah, Evy, no journey will be what we think it will be. It's just the way it is."

"So you knew my grandmother is a murderer?"

"She didn't kill your mother herself but she did have a hand in it."

"So why haven't you done anything to bring this to the attention of the police? Why am I sitting here waiting for her and not alerting the police?"

"What are you going to tell them? What proof do you have?"

"None." Eva threw up her hands in defeat and got up from the foot stool. "This is all just too much."

"You do have evidence of her involvement in the systematic abuse and war crimes against Jews and yourself in Aiden. I was rather pleased to meet Wilbur Muller. He is a very nice fellow."

Eva nodded. "My Uncle Wilbur has always been the best of that rotten lot."

"I did think you ringing the War Crimes agency in Australia for them to talk to the agency here was a stroke of good thinking. They do work fast. I spoke to those two War Crimes agents and they are very eager."

"Ten years too late," Eva mumbled.

"Sometimes we have to wait for justice. It doesn't just happen when we want it to happen."

"What a whole load of . . ." Eva caught sight of Johan's disapproving stare. "Rot," she said with a slight grimace. "All those poor people who didn't have my aunt Tessa, Tommy, or Irene to help them. They suffered so much at their hands. They have to pay."

"You are not the one to exact revenge for those people or for yourself. It is not your job. Do not let your judgment be clouded by the need for revenge," Johan said.

She sighed and shook her head. "I want justice to be done. I don't care who does it but I want justice."

"You will have it. Your stepfather was executed for his crimes, but you didn't do the judging or the execution. You didn't kill him. You could have but you didn't. This is the same," Johan reasoned as Eva looked away. He tapped her on the knee to get her attention. Eva turned back to him and brushed the tears from her eyes. "I know your pain, but you must let others do their job."

"I don't have a choice," Eva said, her voice breaking.

"We all have a choice, darling, it's just which way you decide to jump."

"Can I ask you another question?"

"Ask as many as you like."

"Why didn't Grandmother Eva know about these gifts? If she knew, then she put her daughter through unimaginable hell."

"Your maternal grandmother was a very sweet, gentle woman. She wasn't a monster, nor did she want her children to suffer. She just didn't believe in that inheritance. She saw what it did to her aunt Erika and how that woman lost her mind. Your grandmother was one of the kindest women I ever met. She just didn't believe."

"Why did she name her daughters Theresa and Daphne Eva?"

"Theresa is a family name and so is Eva, and it was her name as well. She didn't make that connection. Not all believe. Just because we believe doesn't mean the rest of the world will."

"So what happens when you are gifted and you don't believe?" Eva asked.

"You either go insane trying to figure out why you are hearing voices or seeing visions or can move objects with your mind or you kill yourself," Johan gently explained. "Living with the gifts and not understanding or believing where they came from is just painful."

"Isn't it cruel for God to let this happen two thousand years after Theresa Eva initially received those gifts?"

"It would appear to be cruel but that's not God's plan. When you have a child, would you want to hurt that child? Of course you wouldn't. You would want to take on that child's pain to stop it from enduring that suffering. Why would our Father not be the same? No, I don't believe he is a cruel God. These gifts have helped many and they will continue to do so."

"What happened to Erika?"

"By the end of her life, Erika had truly gone mad. It's not an easy thing to know you have a God given power. Erika's gifts were indeed great but she didn't know what to do with them. No one taught her or showed her the way."

"How old was she when she was sent to the Lunatic asylum?"

"Twenty," Johan said.

Eva, put her hand over her mouth in shock.

"She kept going in, being released, going in and so on for years. She died when she was ninety. We took her out of that place when she was sixty and looked after her. She was a very lost soul."

"It's just not natural."

"What is natural? Is it natural for you to be so tall when Zoe is shorter? You have blue eyes, others have brown or green or gray. What is normal?" Johan reasoned. "The gifts we have are not gifts from the devil, but gifts from God."

Eva gazed at Johan for a moment. "The gifts *we* have?"

Johan sighed. "Yes, the gifts we have. We are all gifted some way, we have—"

"Uncle Johan, don't lie to me again," Eva quietly but firmly said. "You were not referring to the everyday gifts everyone possesses."

Johan nodded. "No, I wasn't referring to that at all. Daphne and Theresa are sisters, and according to what Irene has uncovered, you wouldn't be able to find the gift in both women until Daphne and then Theresa were born. We don't know why it happened, but it did."

"So what does that have to do with you?"

"Patience, Eva." Johan put his hand on Eva's knee and chuckled. "When I was a young boy, I discovered something so horrifying that I locked myself away in my room for days. Irene, in her no nonsense kind of way, broke my window and came in through it."

Eva smiled at Johan's description of her aunt. "That doesn't sound like her."

"No, it doesn't, but I find myself smiling and remembering a young Irene when I see Zoe. She had the same fire, although she didn't cave anyone's face in with a poker." Johan chuckled along with Eva. "Irene was gifted and she confided in me when she first realized it. We both knew what that meant. She wanted to enter the convent when she was old enough because she had seen what happened to the others. She could hide her gifts and rightly claim they were miracles from God."

"She didn't want to get married?"

"No, that was not the life she wanted. So we were aware of the Pentecost gifts. What we didn't know was that the fork that happened with Daphne and Theresa also occurred in our family."

"You got the gift?"

"I did." Johan nodded. "It was most unexpected and frightened me."

"What is it?"

Johan took out of his pocket his cigar and lit it. He leaned over and found his jacket. He lifted the garment and put it over his knee. Eva smiled when she was offered a cigar and waited for it to be lit. "I have the gift of healing." He watched Eva's face intently.

Eva's mouth dropped open, causing the cigar to drop from her mouth and into her lap. She quickly picked it up and looked up at Johan. "You have what?"

"I have the gift of healing," Johan repeated. "It's not the full 'get up from your bed and walk' type healing, but there is a power to heal."

"What do you mean you can heal?"

"Give people a little bit more time in this life," Johan said quietly. "Those dying wish for a little bit more time, whether to say goodbye or to look at a loved one's face before they pass away."

"Wow."

"I can heal wounds and erase pain," Johan continued as he gazed at Eva. "It's not as flashy as visions or moving objects with your mind but I suspect that is for you women folk to deal with."

"Wow. How is that possible?"

"We don't know. First time it happened, as I said, I locked myself in the room. I was terrified."

"How did you find out?"

"I was a young lad of fifteen. One day I was fishing in the lake and caught some fish. I put them aside in to gut and clean. I then went for a dip in the water and had a bit of a nap on the bank. The sun was setting and I didn't want to take ungutted fish into the house so I set out to clean them. Imagine my surprise when I picked up the last one and it sprung back to life."

"A fish came back to life?" Eva asked incredulously.

"Yes, a very dead fish was alive."

"Are you sure it was dead?

"Oh, I'm pretty sure it was dead because I had sliced his head and was about to gut him. I had gutted his brothers and they were deader than dead."

"So what did you do?"

"I dropped it." Johan chuckled. "I dropped it and raced around the camp site like a headless chicken. Once I stopped running around and yelling like a fool, I picked up my now very much alive fish. Not only was it alive, but when I looked at where I had sliced its head, there wasn't a scratch on it. I'm not quite sure what frightened me most, the live fish or the cut that never was. I ran home with my fish. When I got there, I stormed into the house to tell Irene. She couldn't get anything intelligent out of me because I was speaking gibberish."

"You have the gift of languages?"

Johan grinned. "I did and I was speaking Hebrew, although I didn't find that out until much later. I dropped the now very dead fish on the counter and stormed out of the kitchen and blockaded myself in the bedroom."

"Wow."

"Indeed. So you see, it's a little difficult to explain this without sounding like a lunatic." Johan put his arm around Eva's shoulders. "I understand how you are feeling, Evy. I do. There is so much to make sense of and to try to come to terms with."

"So all those people you give the last rights to, do you give them that gift of just a few more hours?"

"Not all, because every time I do that, I become weak and find myself unable to move. It's not like what the Apostles used to do where they would cure the blind or the lame. Those miracles would last till that person passed away naturally. Nor can I raise the dead for an infinite time. Our Lord Jesus did that with Lazarus and others, but then He was our Savior."

"So a little bit of you dies when you give someone that gift," Eva asked quietly, now fully understanding what Johan was talking about. "You give your own life for theirs."

"I wouldn't say I die but there is a part of me that is given away. I give them a little bit of my life," Johan explained. "It completely drains me and I come here and hammer away at a useless car for a few hours."

"That is just extraordinary," Eva said in admiration. "You are extraordinary." she gave Johan a kiss.

"No, darling, it's not. It's just something God gave me and I use it in His service. It also comes in handy when I cut myself." Johan chuckled and looked at his hands.

"You can heal scars?"

"I can. Sometimes when we can't see a scar, we forget and what used to hurt us is no longer there." Johan smiled at Eva. "If you want, I can remove yours."

"No," Eva said and shook her head. "I don't want you to. The physical scars may be on my body but the mental ones have started to heal. They are physical reminders that Zoe calls my badge of courage, and I'm begin-ning to think they are. I survived, with a little bit of help, and I'm stronger for it. Please, save your strength for those that really need your gift. They deserve a little bit more life and they deserve peace."

Johan bowed his head and smiled. "You are indeed a beautiful soul, Eva Theresa Muller Haralambos Lambros." He laughed, took her hand, and kissed it. "Your mama would have been so proud of you. You are the woman she always wanted you to be. She was proud of you for being you."

"I wish I could talk to her and just tell her how much I love her."

"She knew how much you loved her. She knew and knows. You not only look like her but you resemble her in ways that are the most important. You have a good heart and a gentle soul." Johan hugged Eva and nodded. "Now why don't you go back to the house and pretty yourself up for your grandmother?"

Eva gently laughed and got up from her stool. She stood for a moment, then she leaned down and kissed Johan on the cheek.

"Thank you," she said and walked out of the garage. The sound of hammer on steel echoed out of the garage and followed Eva as she walked towards the house.

CHAPTER 40

EVA SAT ON the wicker chair in her room, staring at the floor. She tried to meditate but her concentration was jumbled. After coming back from her chat with Johan, she just wasn't able to focus.

Zoe entered the bedroom and shut the door. Zoe knelt in front of Eva and began to button her shirt.

"You don't have to do that."

"I'm practicing for when we have our babies," Zoe replied, making Eva smile. "I know you're scared."

"I'm not scared."

"You're not?"

"No." Eva shook her head slowly. "I'm terrified."

"Of what? She's a woman, and the last time I checked you were the one with the special powers."

"She's my grandmother."

"Yes, she is, but so what?"

"I loved her," Eva quietly responded. "She was going to use me."

"That only proves that she isn't worthy of your love or your respect."

"What do I say to her?"

Zoe gazed at Eva for a moment. "You tell her what you have been practicing for the last ten years. You tell her how you feel."

"Isn't that showing her my weakness?"

"What is your weakness?"

"That I loved her."

"When did it loving someone become a weakness?"

Eva stared at Zoe for a moment. "When it's my grandmother."

"No. She's human, she has feelings buried under her evilness. I think she has feelings."

"I don't know what to do."

Zoe gazed at Eva as they touched foreheads. "You will know what do to when the time is right."

"I hope so," Eva replied.

They turned towards the door at a gentle knock.

Moments later Tessa opened the door and waited. "Thought you might like to take a walk with me?" Tessa asked Eva.

"Now that's a great idea," Zoe replied and tapped Eva on the leg. "Go."

Eva looked at Zoe, then kissed her. She got up from her seat and walked out of the room.

AS THE SUN set, casting shadows into the living room through the open French doors, Eva sat outside reading after her walk with Tessa. When they had come back, Zoe had noticed Eva was calmer than when she had left. Tessa's influence with Eva was a welcome development as far as Zoe was concerned. Tessa had become a surrogate mother—something Zoe could not be for Eva. Zoe was her best friend, confidante, and wife.

Zoe sat on the steps leading up to the bedrooms on the top floor. She had her sketchbook on her lap and was drawing Eva reading outside in the sun. Eva's floppy hat shielded her from the sun and her face was hidden in the shadows created by the hat. Zoe had Eva in a shaft of light surrounded by shadows with just the hint of physical forms around her.

Stella came up next to Zoe and looked at the sketchpad. "Shadows. It's different."

Zoe looked up from her pad. "This whole trip has been about shadows—shadows within shadows, secrets within secrets. The only thing for certain is Eva's light."

Stella nodded her approval and sat down on the step beside Zoe. "It has been an emotional trip for the both of you."

"More for Eva than for me. I've had my moments but for Eva, this has been something out of her nightmares and also her desires."

"Tessa needs this as much as Eva does," Stella replied quietly. "She has been missing that link with her family more than she would admit, and now she has it. You don't mind?"

Zoe stopped her drawing and turned to Stella, puzzled. "Why would I mind?"

"Sometimes having family around can be burdensome."

Zoe shook her head. "We have family around us. We have our friends Earl, Elena and her husband Friedrich and now their little one, Henry, David and his wife Debbie. We used to have Father H before he left to go back to Greece. That's the family we created, but you and Tessa, Tommy and Theo are our blood. Of course we don't mind."

"As long as you or Eva don't mind. We announced, without asking, that we would descend on you. In our exuberance we forgot to ask you."

Zoe gazed at Stella affectionately. "Like in your exuberance to prove Tessa's gifts were real?"

"Yes, like that," Stella admitted with a slight grimace. "I didn't think of Eva's feelings but was worried about Tessa."

"Did you think that Eva wouldn't accept her?"

Stella looked away for a moment and nodded. She gazed at Tessa, who had joined Eva. "Yes. Had that happened, I feared what it would have done to Tessa."

"I don't think there is any need to fear that now. Tessa has a very calming influence on Eva. It's good."

"Something you don't know is that they have a connection. I don't quite understand how it works but ever since Eva was born, Tessa has been able to connect with her even if Eva wasn't aware of it."

"That's a weird thing."

"It is. It was also very hard for Tee when Eva was in Aiden. She felt everything Eva went through."

"How is that even possible?"

"I don't know, Zoe. I don't know how this gift works and sometimes I think it's a curse," Stella replied. "Tessa's gift has caused her a great deal of pain."

"Is it only Eva? Does she know when Tommy is ill?"

"Yes. She is connected to both of them in ways that should not be physically possible, but they are."

Zoe watched Eva. "Oh."

"Oh?"

"When I fell off my motorcycle, Evy said she could feel it, she knew something was wrong. I just thought she was upset."

"Hmm." Stella nodded. "It's part of her gift."

"Wow. No wonder she knew . . ." Zoe stopped. "I wonder if she will feel our babies . . ."

"From what Tessa has told me, she has the ability to do so, but Eva's gift may be different."

The doorbell rang, signaling the time had arrived for Eva's ten-year open wound to finally be closed.

Zoe glanced at Stella. "Where is Irene?"

"Upstairs."

"Alright then, I'm getting the door," Zoe said and walked away.

She took a deep breath and quietly made her way to the front door. She opened it to find an older woman, her white hair up in a tight bun, dark blue eyes peeking out from round silver collared wire-framed glasses. Her thin lips were set in a half smile that Zoe found extremely disconcerting. She wore a navy blue dress under a black-and-white coat. A gold broach peeked out from under the coat, giving the dress some color.

"Hello," Zoe said, keeping her expression neutral. A younger man stood at the woman's shoulder dressed in a dark uniform. Zoe assumed him to be a driver. The woman motioned for him to leave. Zoe watched him go back down the driveway.

"I'm here to see Eva Muller."

"Who may I ask is here to see her?" Zoe asked politely. She suppressed the urge to take the umbrella stand that was near the door and shove it into the older woman's chest.

"Her grandmother."

"Mrs. Mitsos, so nice to see you," Zoe exclaimed excitedly and stuck her hand out. The woman gave her hand a frosty stare instead. Zoe took back her hand and sighed.

"I am not Mrs. Mitsos. I am Eva's paternal grandmother, Mrs. Beatriz Muller."

"Oh, silly me. Mrs. Muller." Zoe kept her eyes lowered so Beatriz Muller wouldn't see the outright hatred in her eyes.

Beatriz brushed past Zoe and entered the house.

"You can come in," Zoe muttered as she mimicked holding a gun with her fingers and shooting Beatriz.

"Can I take your coat?" Zoe asked as she came up Beatriz, who was now standing in the middle of the living room. She admitted that Beatriz was imposing but it wasn't her height but her bearing. She had a very intimidating personality, and Zoe felt somewhat uncomfortable in her presence. Her son Hans resembled his mother, which chilled Zoe.

"Would it be too much to ask if you could let my granddaughter know I am here?"

"Of course."

"What's your name?"

Zoe looked back at Beatriz. "Zoe Lambros."

"Hmm. Did you not know who I was when you opened the door?"

"No, I did not. We were not expecting company so I'm not sure how you would think that I knew who you were," Zoe reasoned as she took Beatriz's coat. "I don't read minds." Zoe thought she saw uncertainty in Beatriz's eyes. "Maybe Eva forgot to mention that you were coming today. Did you call?"

"No, I didn't call."

"So, if you didn't call, how was I to know you were Eva's grandmother?" Zoe concentrated on translating what she wanted to say from Greek to German. For some reason, she felt she had to prove herself to this woman. "I'm actually surprised it's taken you this long to come and meet her. She has been in the country for a week now."

Beatriz narrowed her eyes and scowled. She looked away. "Tell my granddaughter I am here."

"Yes, ma'am." Zoe saluted. She threw the coat onto the sofa as she walked past it. She passed Stella and sneered.

Stella shook her head as she picked up the coat and hung it up on the coat rack.

"HELLO." STELLA CAME into the living room and smiled warmly at Beatriz.

"Who may you be?"

"I am Dr. Stella Andronikakis-Lambros," Stella said. "I see my niece has taken care of your coat. Please sit down."

"Your niece? Well, she is one very rude young woman."

"I'm sure you must have misunderstood her—her German is not that great."

"Oh, I understood her perfectly," Beatriz said. "Rude and impolite."

"What brings you here today?"

"Is this your home?"

"It's not. It belongs to Johan and Irene Faber, Eva's great aunt and uncle."

Beatriz stared at Stella for a long moment. "I wasn't aware Eva had any other relatives other than her family in Zehlendorf. I was wondering what she was doing in Dahlem."

Stella smiled. "It was so nice of Eva to contact you to let you know she was in town. Have you not seen each other for some time?"

"Yes, very nice of her," Beatriz said coldly. "It's been ten years since I last saw her."

"That is a long time."

"Can you find out where Eva is for me? I would hope that rude woman didn't wander off and forget to tell her."

"She didn't forget to tell me," Eva said as she entered the living room and stood a great deal away from her grandmother.

Stella looked on silently. She smiled at Eva and walked past her, giving her a reassuring tap on the shoulder in passing. She joined Zoe, Tessa, Tommy, and Theo at the top of the stairs that was not visible from the living room so they could listen.

"EVA, DARLING." BEATRIZ got up from the sofa and approached Eva with open arms. "You are looking very healthy." She took Eva into her embrace. "Give your grandmother a hug."

Eva forced herself to remain calm just as Tessa had urged and tried to relax her posture. She embraced her grandmother and gave her a kiss on the cheek. "You are looking good."

"Thank you, darling. Uncle Wilbur had a pressing matter that he couldn't get away from or else he would have been here."

"I saw Uncle Wilbur yesterday," Eva replied with a genuine smile. "He was following me around Berlin."

Beatriz' smile froze. "Well, we were concerned for you so I asked your uncle to keep an eye on you. Berlin is not a safe city anymore. As you saw, those horrible Americans nearly demolished this beautiful city. We won't talk about those awful Russians. What a horrible race of people, worse than the Jews." She put her arm around Eva's shoulders. "Is there anything wrong with sending Uncle Wilbur to make sure you were safe?"

"Of course not," Eva replied as they sat on the sofa. "Don't mind the rug here—there's some blood that was spilt and we're trying to get the stains out."

"Oh? That's most unseemly. I was wondering what that stain was."

"It was a rather unfortunate incident. We had Uncle Dieter mistaken for an intruder and he got himself struck by a poker to the face and then shot. Very messy," Eva said.

"Your uncle Dieter? Here?" Beatriz asked. "I was in Bonn and haven't seen Dieter for a week or so. What possessed him to do such a daft thing?"

"I don't know." Eva shrugged. "I'm assuming he came here to finish the job my father started."

"The job your father started?"

Eva stared at her grandmother for a long moment. "Father tried to kill me. We both know that. Uncle Dieter wanted to finish the job."

"Your father did not try and kill you, Eva. Your father was out of his mind with grief. He overreacted and I think you should find it in your heart to forgive him. It wasn't you that hurt Dieter, was it?"

"No." Eva shook her head and smiled. "That was Zoe. He surprised her when she went for some water."

"Not to worry. Isabella will wash it off." Eva smiled as the housekeeper came forward with a tray. "I thought you might like some coffee."

"That was thoughtful of you."

Eva sat back and smiled at Isabella, who handed her a cup of tea. She waited for her grandmother to continue.

"I don't know where to begin, Eva. It's been so long since I've seen you . . ."

"Not so long." Eva took a sip of her tea. She leaned across the coffee table and picked up the cigar she had placed on the table beforehand. It was her grandfather's favorite brand. She took the cigar and bit the end off, which she knew would totally disgust her grandmother. She smiled as she took the cut end out of her mouth. She lit the cigar and waited for a moment before she took her first drag from it.

"Do you have to smoke those horrible things?"

"I like them," Eva replied. "It relaxes me."

Beatriz made a noise to convey her disgust that sounded like a cross between a snort and someone gagging. Eva smiled. "Your grandfather was a huge smoker and look where that got him."

"He was a happy man," Eva responded. "He loved simple pleasures."

"Yes, he did, he was a rather simple man." Beatriz sniffed. "Now where was I?"

"You were saying how lovely it was to see me again and that I should forgive father for trying to kill me," Eva reminded her.

Beatriz scowled. "I do not like the tone you are taking with me. You are not showing the proper respect to your elders."

Stay focused, Eva, and don't let this woman get under your guard. Eva heard Tessa's voice in her head and she took a deep breath and resisted the urge to tell her grandmother what she really thought. "You are happy to see me?"

"Yes, I am. You are looking very healthy. How is your back?"

Eva drew on her cigar for a long moment, letting Beatriz wait. "As you would expect it to be. It won't ever get better than it is." *Eva, calm down.* Tessa's voice echoed in her head and she shook it. "The bomb blast in Paris made it worse."

"I understand you don't want to talk about it but I was only asking out of concern for you. Your grandfather had a bad back and it did make him very agitated some days," Beatriz explained. She captured Eva's attention with the mention of her grandfather. "I understand your pain."

"Do you?"

"I said I understand your pain. There is no reason for your rudeness."

"Did you visit Papa before he was executed?" Eva stared at Beatriz.

"I did," Beatriz replied without missing a beat. "It was unfortunate that he was sentenced the way he was."

"Unfortunate?"

"Yes, darling. Unfortunate. The victors always lay down the rules. That's how they did it after The Great War."

"What about what he did to me? Did the victors lay down those rules as well?"

Beatriz shook her head. "As I said, that was not your father. He was out of his mind with grief at the death of his wife. You will have to forgive him. Hans was a very damaged soul. Dieter and I were very concerned for his health and for yours as well."

"Of course," Eva said quietly as she restrained herself from bolting from the room. The conversation was making her stomach churn.

"You will have to forgive your father for the vicious way he assaulted you."

"I have forgiven him," Eva replied honestly.

"You have?"

"Yes. I loved my father even though he tried to kill me, three times," Eva said with a slight shrug.

"He was out of his mind."

"Yes. Was Uncle Dieter out of his mind as well?"

"No." Beatriz shook her head. "He was acting in your best interests."

"In my best interests?"

"It is unseemly to have deviant thoughts." Beatriz put her cup down and clutched her hands in her lap. "You are a Muller and as my granddaughter and the heir to the Muller fortune and reputation, we couldn't have deviancy like that take hold."

"You condoned what they did?"

"I felt that you needed the proper treatment. If that was the wrong thing to do, to care for my granddaughter, then yes, I am guilty of caring," Beatriz explained. "I will never say that it was wrong to look after my granddaughter. Your father beating you was wrong. He was out of his mind with grief and although I don't think he was right, you can excuse him for that."

"Do you know what they did, Omi?" Eva asked, using the affectionate term for her grandmother.

Beatriz leaned back and relaxed. "I do. Sometimes the cure is as horrible as the disease," she replied in a gentle tone. "It wasn't easy for me to know that you were suffering. Not a day did go past when I didn't feel your pain."

"You felt my pain?" Eva shook her head as she stood up outraged. "You felt the electric shocks go through my body, felt my back spasm in agony, felt my terror?"

"No, but—"

"Did you feel my fear when they gave me drugs that invaded my mind and made me so ill I didn't even know my own name? When I soiled myself like an infant? Did you feel that?" Eva's voice trembled with emotion. "Did you feel it every time they robbed me of my dignity? Every time my heart thundered in my chest because I was so terrified what they were going to do to me? Did you feel my heart exploding, Omi? Did you?"

"Eva, you must realize—"

"What do you want me to realize?" Eva's voice broke. "What? You cared so much that you let me be tortured so you could get what you wanted? Was that worth it to you?"

Eva heard a gentle thump and turned to find Zoe bounding down the steps. She blinked back the tears as Zoe come to her defense. Zoe went up to Eva and they turned away from Beatriz for a moment.

"I'm here now," Zoe whispered in Greek. "You are not alone in this."

"I never was. I knew you were here," Eva's said softly. "Together?"

"Together." Zoe smiled, and out of sight of Beatriz's line of sight, took Eva's hand and kissed it.

They turned to Beatriz.

"I am having a private conversation with my granddaughter, do you mind?"

"Your private conversation is over. I do mind. It's now my business." Zoe put a protective arm around Eva's waist and glared at Beatriz.

CHAPTER 41

BEATRIZ LEANED BACK on the sofa and regarded Zoe with a long hard stare. "You don't seem to understand, young lady, that I am having a private conversation with my granddaughter."

"I'm not deaf," Zoe countered. "I know what you are doing and I'm telling you that your private conversation has just ended."

"Who do you think you are to be talking to me that way?"

"My name is Zoe Lambros. We were introduced earlier but you may have forgotten my name," Zoe replied.

"You have a smart mouth."

"And you, Mrs. Muller, are a despicable, callous woman who gave no thought about the pain she was putting her granddaughter through."

"I'm not even sure why I'm still talking you," Beatriz replied with a shake of her head. "You wouldn't know the pain I went through. Do you even know how it feels to know your beloved granddaughter is a . . ." She took out her handkerchief from her purse and dabbed it against her eyes. "I found out my granddaughter was a deviant and you don't think that is painful?"

Zoe pulled the coffee table over and sat on the glass panel facing Beatriz.

"That was a performance worthy of an award." Zoe slow clapped Beatriz for a few moments. "*You* were in pain because Eva was a lesbian?"

"Yes."

"My papa used to say that some people were dumber than two planks of wood. I never knew what he meant until now," Zoe said with a little shake of her head.

"You are a very disrespectful and rude woman."

"But you are still sitting here," Zoe countered with a tiny smile.

"I am. I want to let Eva see the kind of woman you really are." Beatriz folded her arms.

"You want to let Eva see what kind of woman I am?" Zoe giggled. "I'm sorry, Mrs. Muller, I pre-judged you. When Eva talked about you when we first met, I took you for a woman of integrity and a kind, gentle soul."

"Eva was right."

"No." Zoe shook her head. "Eva was lying to herself and making herself believe that's what how you were, but you not.

"How old are you, young lady?"

"I'm twenty-two years old."

"Your parents, if they weren't dead, would have been very disappointed to find their daughter was a deviant."

Zoe got up from the coffee table and picked up one of the pokers by the fireplace. "Do you know what a war does to a person, Mrs. Muller? It makes them a little crazy. When someone goes crazy they do this." She lifted the poker.

Beatriz screamed and covered her head with her hands. Zoe swung and hit a vase beside Beatriz.

"My aim is really off," Zoe muttered and then chuckled.

"You are crazy."

Eva got up and sidled up to Zoe. "You are dangerous with that thing."

"I know!" Zoe giggled. "My aim is a little off. I was aiming for the other vase . . . I hope Aunt Irene didn't like that one."

"You are a lunatic!" Beatriz screamed and got up off the sofa.

Zoe tapped her ankles with the poker. Beatriz lost her balance and fell.

"I'm not really." Zoe sat back down on the coffee table. She rested the poker on the floor and leaned her weight on it. "I'm going to tell you a story."

Beatriz put her hand over her heart and took a deep breath. "You both had your fun. I understand that you are hurt by what happened to you in Aiden and you wanted some fun at my expense."

"Is that what you think this is? Some fun?" Eva asked.

"Eva, darling, I want you to think before this farce continues any further. I will press charges against this lunatic woman when all of this is over."

"What do you want me to think about?"

"Your life," Beatriz replied. "Think about what your life would have been like had you not been seduced by that wretched girl, Greta Strauss."

"She's got a point there," Zoe muttered. Beatriz gave her a surprised look. "I agree with you about that evil she-devil." Zoe smiled at her.

"You are a strange woman," she said to Zoe, then she turned back to a bemused-looking Eva. "I want you to think about this, Eva. I managed to stop the damage that Strauss girl had done on your life."

"How did you do that?" Eva asked. She sat next to Zoe on the coffee table.

Beatriz leaned back and adjusted her gloves. "I gave Greta what she wanted. I gave her what all those types of deviants want. I gave her money and property."

Zoe resisted the urge to really use the poker on Beatriz.

"That is why I'm going to offer the same deal to your friend here even though she is a completely crazy woman."

"You want to offer me money?" Zoe asked. She turned to Eva with a smile. "Now this is more like it."

"It is?" Eva asked. "How much do you want to walk away from me?"

"I know you girls are just playing with me but I'm serious, Miss Lambros. I am willing to offer you property and money. If I were a peasant from some backward little village, I would take it."

"I am a peasant girl from a backward little village." Zoe nodded. "I agree with you."

"You do?"

"Oh, I do. I come from this really small backward little village, Mrs. Muller. Really small, and it's a farming community. I don't want your money because I don't need it. Nice of you to offer it, but I don't take blood money. Do you know what happened in this small village in 1942?"

"No. What?"

"Your son came to town. Do you know what else happened in 1942?"

"No, but I'm sure you will tell me," Beatriz replied, obviously tired of the games. She turned to Eva. "You are my granddaughter and despite everything that has happened, it doesn't change the fact that you are Eva Muller."

"Was your granddaughter."

"You are a Muller, and whatever you may say or do, you remain a Muller. You were married to that wonderful Erik Hoffman for a very brief two years and I believe he was killed somewhere I can't remember."

"He died in Africa." Eva shook her head. "Did you know my real father was in Larissa?"

"Is that what the place was called? Oh yes, I know that." Beatriz waved Eva's statement away. "I knew the man lived in Larissa. I suggested to your father that if you saw the dirty backwater, you would realize that you hadn't missed out on anything."

Eva stared at her, looking aghast. "You wanted Papa to take me into a warzone? Into Larissa?"

"I wanted you to get close to your father. What he did was wrong and you needed to spend time with him. If you saw what your life would have been like had he not married your mother, then you would appreciate your life more," Beatriz reasoned and sat back on the sofa.

"You wanted to send me into a *warzone*?" Eva raised her voice. "Let me get this clear, Grandmother. You sent me into a warzone so I could get close to my father?"

"Don't raise your voice at me, young lady. Yes, that is why I sent you there."

Zoe shook her head in disbelief. "You are amazing, Mrs. Muller. I find it truly amazing that someone can live as long as you have, raised three sons, had a loving husband and yet be totally devoid of common sense."

"How dare you."

"Oh, sit down, you old windbag." Zoe poked Beatrix in the chest with the poker.

Beatriz quickly sat back down and touched the spot where the poker had touched her.

"There is something I need to thank you for."

"What's that?"

"Sending Eva to Larissa," Zoe replied. She gazed at Eva and didn't try to disguise the love she felt for her. Beatriz snorted in disgust but she ignored it. "The best thing to happen to me."

"That's disgusting. Eva, think about what you are doing. Your grandfather left you with quite an inheritance. You can't claim it if you are not married."

"Is that right?" Eva held up her left hand with her wedding band. "I am married."

"To a man?"

"Who else would I marry?" Eva chuckled. "Yes, to a man."

"You are married to a man?"

"Yes. His name is Theodore Lambros."

"I don't believe you." Beatriz shook her head. "So this crazy woman professing her love for you is wrong?"

"I am married to Theodore Lambros. I have a marriage certificate."

"How? In church?"

"No, at the Registry. Just as good."

"I'm assuming there isn't a Catholic priest alive who would want to conduct such a solemn ceremony under such false pretenses. Makes a mockery of the institution of marriage. I don't believe it."

"Ah, but that is where you are very wrong, Beatriz." Father Johan Faber came down the steps and walked to Beatriz.

"Johan, what are you doing here?"

"You know Father Johan?" Zoe asked.

"Mrs. Muller and I go back many years, don't we, Beatriz?" Johan took Beatriz's glove covered hand and smiled.

"Yes, we do. Father Johan was the hospital chaplain when my Alexander passed away," Beatriz said quietly. "I don't understand what you are doing here."

"This is my home."

"It is?"

"Indeed." Johan nodded. "Eva is my great niece."

Beatriz stared at Johan for a long moment and then at Eva, who now sat on the third to last step on the staircase. "So it's true Eva and this fellow I have never met got married?"

"I'm very sure. His name is Theodore Lambros, a very nice fellow whom she met in Larissa."

"She met him in Larissa?"

"Told you great things happened there," Zoe quipped.

Beatriz scowled at her. "She's legally married?"

"She is. So is Zoe."

"I don't care about that child." Beatriz waved her hand. "I'm only interested in my granddaughter."

"Of course you are." Johan held Beatriz's hands. "Now we have a small problem."

"I don't see it as a small problem. Eva's treatment in Aiden worked and she was healed from her deviant behavior."

"You approved of this treatment?" Johan held up his hand to silence Zoe. "Of course."

"I've been told this treatment was used on others there as well?"

"I believe so. My son was very successful in treating this mental disease," Beatriz proudly said. "I believe Eva may need more treatment. As a priest you must agree with me."

"Were the other patients at this facility there by their own choice?"

"Why so many questions, Father Johan? Of course not all of them were there out of their own choice—like our Eva they were sent there to be cured. Their families sent them there to have my son treat them. Good, upstanding families who wanted this disease eradicated."

Johan nodded. "What your son was doing was illegal."

"No." Beatriz shook her head. "It was legal and approved by the Fuhrer himself."

"It was a war crime. Germany invaded Austria in 1938 and it was against the Geneva Convention. What your son did was a war crime."

"I don't believe that is correct."

"It is. You are responsible for what occurred in Aiden during that time and therefore you will also be charged with war crimes," Johan said.

"I don't own Aiden. It is owned by Eva."

"She inherited the property when she got married four days ago," Zoe said with a smile.

"Is Zoe correct?" Johan asked Beatriz.

"Yes."

Zoe turned and watched as Abels and his partner walked down the stairs. Tessa, Stella, Thomas, and Theo followed the two agents.

Beatriz stood and picked up her handbag. "I think it would be a good time to leave."

"You haven't met the rest of the family yet." Zoe got up from her makeshift seat. "This is Eva's aunt Theresa Lambros, my aunt Stella, who you have already met, Eva's husband Theodore and my husband Thomas."

Eva came forward and stood in front of Beatriz. "Zoe forgot to mention these two gentlemen. They are War Crime investigators. I called them because what you did was a war crime."

"Eva! How could you do this? I love you."

Eva took Beatriz's hands. "How could I do this to you? You disowned and abandoned me. You encouraged and condoned what they did to me. I feel nothing but contempt for you," she whispered. "I feel your pain, I do. Just like your felt mine.

"I love you, darling, we can sort this out."

Eva shook her head and let go of Beatriz. Without a backward glance she took Zoe's hand and they left the living room. They left the War Crimes agents to do what they were sent to do.

EPILOGUE

Somewhere Out In the Ocean Heading For Sydney

Eva yawned for the second time in as many minutes. She turned to gaze at Zoe who was asleep in the next bed. Zoe was sleeping soundly, and her light snoring made Eva smile affectionately. She closed the book she was reading and turned off the bedside light.

"Are you sure?"

"Yes."

"Really?"

"Yes. Mutti is in the blackroom."

"Why is it called a blackroom?"

"Because it's black?"

"But it's red."

"Red light is on."

"That means we can go in, right?"

The two children looked at each other and then glanced back to their room. Without waiting any longer, Larissa took hold of the doorknob and entered, closely followed by her brother.

The door opened unexpectedly and Eva groaned loudly, causing the children to stop.

"Oops."

"Oops, sorry, Mutti."

Eva put down the film and turned to find two sets of eyes looking up at her through the red haze of the darkroom. She went down on her haunches and gazed at both children affectionately.

"What's the matter, my babies?" Eva said as she brushed Nicky's hair away from his eyes.

"There's monsters!" Larissa whispered.

"Yes, Mutti, there are, lots of them." Nicky followed his sister's lead.

"Who said that?"

"Uncle Wiggy told us that monsters from outer space live under our beds."

"Really?

Nicky nodded. "From outer space."

"They made the light go out too."

"There are monsters from outer space and they made the light go out?" Eva shook her head. "Where are they now?"

"Under Nicky's bed. I looked under mine and I couldn't see anything, but I think they went under Nicky's bed."

"Hmm, maybe we should go tell the monsters to leave?" Eva suggested.

"Um . . . will they listen?" Nicky asked in awe that his mutti would do that.

"Of course, I'm your mutti—they listen to me." Eva ruffled Nicky's hair and stood. She took a look at the damaged film and sighed.

Larissa took Eva's right hand and Nicky took Eva's left hand as they led her out of the darkroom and to the room that they shared. They stood just outside the room and waited for Eva to enter. Eva flipped the switch but it wouldn't turn on. "Wait here."

The children chose to follow Eva into the kitchen, where she rummaged around in a drawer and found a flashlight. She tested the light by shining it on Larissa's face, which made the young girl giggle. They returned to the room and once again the children stayed outside.

Eva went down on her knees and looked under the bed, using the flashlight to search for the monsters.

"Be careful, Mutti. They have big teeth and are invisible."

"You stay here, Nicky. I'm going with Mutti to protect her," Larissa told her brother.

"Invisible monsters with big teeth?" Eva repeated as the red-headed little girl followed her inside the room. Larissa knelt by the bed as Eva wiggled her long frame under it, with only her legs below her knees sticking out. "Monsters with big teeth, go away!" Eva yelled out so the children could hear. "I think the monsters are all gone."

"Wow!" Nicky stuck his head on the other side of the bed. "Really?"

"Want to see?" Eva asked as her fearless daughter joined her under the bed, cuddling up close to her. Larissa looked around one more time and then looked at her mother.

"Wow, you made them go away!" Without saying another word Larissa leaned in and kissed her mother on the cheek. Eva's blue eyes sparkled with love. She heard footsteps coming towards them. She grinned when Zoe bent down and looked under the bed.

"Hey, is this a new game?" Zoe chuckled.

"Mutti was telling the monsters from outer space to leave," Larissa explained to her mother.

"Oh, did they listen?"

"Of course!" Nicky exclaimed.

"Mutti, the Monster Destroyer." Eva chuckled as she wiggled herself out from under the bed. She sat cross-legged at the foot of the bed and looked at Zoe. "I made them leave."

"Mutti, it is the Invisible Monsters with big teeth destroyer," Larissa exclaimed, perched on Eva's right knee. She cupped Eva's face and kissed her on the cheek.

"Yeah!" Nicky followed his sister's lead and also sat on Eva's left knee.

Eva's eyes popped open and it took a moment for her to register what had just happened. She laughed. She sat up in bed, putting her hands over her face and couldn't stop the bubble of happiness she felt from infusing her whole body. *"Invisible monsters with big teeth,"* she said softly and started to laugh anew.

Zoe stirred. "What's funny?"

"Invisible monsters with big teeth." Eva chortled.

Zoe turned on the bedside light. "What's the matter, Evy?" She scrambled up from the bed and looked around the cabin to see what Eva was laughing at. She turned to Eva and her words died in her mouth.

"What?" Eva grinned.

"Y . . . y . . . your eyes!" Zoe raced to the main light switch. She flooded the room with light and ran to Eva's bed. She faced Eva and cupped her face in her hands. "Your eyes, Evy."

"If I think what just happened, happened, then something is going on, right?"

"They're white," Zoe whispered in amazement. "Can you see?" She held up two fingers, to which Eva nodded.

"Uh . . ."

"What happened? Why are your eyes white?"

"I had a vision."

"You had a vision?" Zoe tilted Eva's face to the light. "Oh god, your eyes. Do they hurt?"

"They . . . ah . . . feel gritty," Eva replied and got another fit of the giggles.

Zoe smiled at Eva's exuberance. "What did you see?"

"Our babies," Eva said in wonder as she blinked. Her eyes felt like sand had been thrown at them.

"Our babies? More than one?"

Eva smiled. "More than one . . . twins."

"Oh, dear."

Eva looked right into Zoe's eyes and smiled. "Remember your mama's wish that you have a daughter just like you? Well, I think she is getting her wish and mine too." Eva chortled with delight. "Red hair, green eyes and fearless."

"Oh, dear. The other one?"

"You are getting your wish." Eva grinned. "Dark hair, blue eyes."

Eva laughed as Zoe held her face to the light. "They wanted me to scare the monsters from outer space with big teeth under Nicky's bed."

"Nicky? As in Nicholas?"

"Larissa and Nicholas."

"Sweet Mary, Mother of God!" Zoe exclaimed and crossed herself. "We have two babies."

Eva couldn't stop grinning. "Um . . . how are my eyes?"

"Green." Zoe giggled. "You look great with green eyes but I prefer the blue."

"Oh god, Zo."

"Do you want me to wake Tessa?"

Eva nodded vigorously. "It was amazing. I know I wasn't asleep . . . I just finished the book and um . . ."

"Your eyes are dark blue," Zoe said. "I'm fascinated by this."

"Oh good, one of us is." Eva put her hand on her heart and took a deep breath. "Zoe, that was—"

"We are going to have very beautiful babies. Oh look, here's the sky blue I love so much," Zoe said as she kissed Eva tenderly on the lips.

"Zoe . . . this is everything I've ever wanted and more."

"It is and you deserve it."

"We deserve it," Eva amended. "That little girl of ours is you all over. Fearless. And the little boy . . . what an absolute sweetheart."

"God help us." Zoe giggled.

"Can you go get Aunt Tessa now? I'm getting a really bad headache."

"It's from all the laughing you have been doing." Zoe kissed Eva before she got out of the bed. She put on her robe and slippers and bolted out the door.

"Mutti." Eva grinned in delight as she fell back on the bed and started to laugh.

The story of Eva and Zoe, Eva's new abilities/gifts and how these will impact on their lives will continue in Gifts Of The Spirit, *Book 5 in the* Intertwined Souls Series.

Muller / Haralambos / Lambros Family Tree

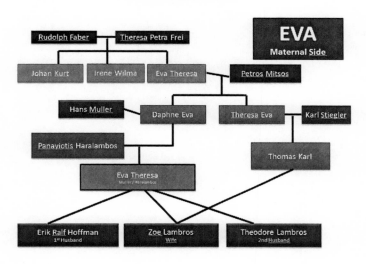

EVA
Maternal Side

Rudolph Faber — Theresa Petra Frei

Johan Kurt · Irene Wilma · Eva Theresa — Petros Mitsos

Hans Muller · Daphne Eva · Theresa Eva — Karl Stiegler

Panayiotis Haralambos

Thomas Karl

Eva Theresa
Muller / Haralambos

Erik Ralf Hoffman
1st Husband

Zoe Lambros
Wife

Theodore Lambros
2nd Husband

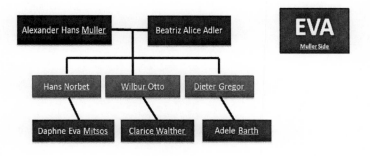

EVA
Muller Side

Alexander Hans Muller — Beatriz Alice Adler

Hans Norbet · Wilbur Otto · Dieter Gregor

Daphne Eva Mitsos · Clarice Walther · Adele Barth

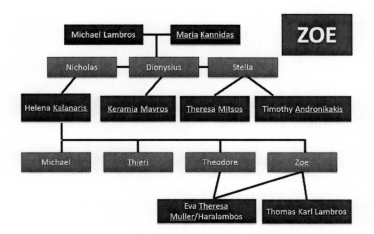

ZOE

Michael Lambros — Maria Kannidas

Nicholas · Dionysius · Stella

Helena Kalanaris · Keramia Mavros · Theresa Mitsos · Timothy Andronikakis

Michael · Thieri · Theodore · Zoe

Eva Theresa
Muller/Haralambos

Thomas Karl Lambros

About the Author

Mary D. Brooks lives in Australia and has been writing for forty years. She published short fiction stories for various Australian magazines and some nonfiction pieces before she turned her attention to the *Intertwined Souls series*. Her first novel was *In the Blood of the Greeks* which was quickly followed by *Where Shadows Linger*. She now continues the series with Awakenings. When she's not writing, she's graphic and web designer, travels when the travel bug hits and is chief editor for various multimedia sites. You can find out more on Mary's official site *The Next Chapter* http://www.nextchapter.net

CPSIA information can be obtained at www.ICGtesting.com
Printed in the USA
LVOW12s0757170214

373983LV00001B/271/P